Wolf War

Lycanthropic Book 3

Steve Morris

This novel is a work of fiction and any resemblance to actual persons living or dead, places, names or events is purely coincidental.

Steve Morris asserts the right under the Copyright, Designs and Patents Act 1988 to be identified as the author of this work.

Published by Landmark Media, a division of Landmark Internet Ltd.

Copyright © 2018 by Steve Morris.
All rights reserved.

stevemorrisbooks.com

ISBN-10: 1792090587
ISBN-13: 978-1792090585

The Lycanthropic Series

Acknowledgements

Huge thanks are due to Margarita Morris, James Pailly and Josie Morris for their valuable comments and help in proof-reading this book.

Chapter One

*Holland Gardens, Kensington, London,
waning moon*

Warg Daddy sneaked back into the house in Kensington just after dawn broke, hauling himself through an open window at the back. The night had been long, and full of killing and treachery, and the relentless storm that raged inside his skull had risen to a new peak of torment.

The ungodly headaches had plagued him ever since becoming a werewolf. He'd tried every way he could think to ease them. Aspirin, ibuprofen and even morphine. None of them had helped in the slightest. His old friend beer should have come to his aid but it seemed that alcohol had deserted him in his hour of need. These days, beer and whisky just made him sick. Popping a pill, smoking a joint or snorting coke did nothing to quench the pain. Even the sweet ice-white rocks of crystal meth had no effect on werewolves.

He couldn't say he missed his narcotics too much. Being lycanthropic gave him a permanent high. His old friend and rival, Snakebite, had described the feeling best, not long before Warg Daddy had pumped a barrel full of lead into his skull. 'Being a werewolf, man, it's life lived in ultra-high definition, the volume turned to the max, all the brightness and contrast pushed up way too high. It hurts, man. That's what I'm saying.'

You couldn't live that way too long, perhaps. Very quickly, you would simply burn out.

For a brief period in the night, as the blood of his victims flowed from his claws and teeth, and his shotgun blasted his enemies and rivals into oblivion, Warg Daddy had forgotten the migraine that stalked him. But it had returned again as he'd walked home, the pain rising with every step, until he could hardly think. All he wanted now was to rest. The half-light of early morning already irritated his eyes, and he was grateful that the house lights were all switched off. Even wearing his blackest Ray-Bans, the jab of electric lights had come to feel like a spike driven into his skull.

He was hoping to avoid Leanna, at least until after he'd snatched a few hours of sleep, but the self-styled queen of the werewolves was waiting for him as he crept quietly into the house, her cold eyes glinting like polished sapphires in the early morning gloom.

'Warg Daddy,' she said. 'Welcome back. I've been expecting you.'

When Warg Daddy had first met Leanna, she'd been one hot chick, for sure. Golden blonde hair, high cheekbones, and a nice line in hotpants that showed off her long legs to good effect. But ever since the mysterious acid attack that had burned off half her face, he could hardly bear to gaze upon her ruined looks. Even in the half light of the darkened house, the red welts and scars stood starkly on her once-beautiful skin. The prospect of having to look upon those angry red marks for the rest of his life was daunting. He felt disgust. He couldn't help it.

This morning she looked even worse than usual. Her golden hair was dirty and tangled. Her clothing was muddy and ripped, and beneath the torn fabric her slender body showed signs of scratches from long fingernails, or perhaps even claws. She stood hunched, as if her back or chest had been battered. She had obviously been in a fight. But with who, or why, he couldn't guess.

'Fuck,' he said. 'You look terrible.' He rubbed his bald head with his thumb, soothing away the relentless throbbing that filled his skull. 'What happened to you?'

But Leanna never answered questions, only asked them. 'Where are the others?' she asked. 'Adam and Snakebite. I want to congratulate them on their victory.'

Warg Daddy hesitated, his tongue temporarily tied as he pondered his reply. Last night's battle had gone well, and under his leadership, together with Adam's athletic prowess, and Snakebite's military genius for planning, the Wolf Brothers had completely destroyed the isolation hospital where hundreds of werewolves were being held. They had butchered the soldiers, stolen their weapons, and freed the captive werewolves. The operation had unfolded exactly according to plan, except for one small detail.

He felt his throat dry as he contemplated the only possible answer to Leanna's question. 'They're not coming back,' he said, keeping his voice as flat as possible. 'Adam and Snakebite are both dead.' He looked at her eyes, watching the glacial blue turn colder as the weight of that last word fell from his tongue.

'What did you say?' Her voice was tight, with icy control.

'Dead. They're both dead.'

Her fury was even worse than he had feared. A scream escaped her red lips. Her fingers curled like claws, and she bared her teeth at him. Her voice cut the air like ice, each word knife-edged. 'Tell me how.'

Warg Daddy shifted uneasily. He'd had hours to

prepare his story. And yet somehow he still didn't know how he was going to explain this. How could he possibly hide the fact that he'd engineered the downfall of his two rivals himself? If Leanna ever discovered his treachery, he would be dead meat for sure. He might be physically larger and more powerful than her, but she possessed an inner steel that terrified him.

And she could read him like a book. The best way to tell her a lie was to clothe it in as much truth as he dared. 'Adam was the first to die,' he told her. 'Snakebite killed him. He shot him in the back.'

Leanna's head shook gently, the dirty blonde hair swaying from side to side. 'Why would he do that?' She turned her questioning eyes on him again.

Warg Daddy didn't flinch from her gaze. To look away now would mean certain death. 'Snakebite said Adam was becoming too greedy for power. He said the only way to stop him was to kill him. I think he may have been right.'

She stared at him, weighing his words. Her fingers clenched and unclenched viciously at her side.

He stared back blandly. There was no reason for her to doubt him. It had happened just like he'd said. The only detail he'd left out was that he and Snakebite had planned Adam's murder together. After all, there was only room for one Leader of the Pack, and Warg Daddy couldn't tolerate an ambitious rival like Adam.

Leanna seemed to believe him. 'And Snakebite?'

He felt her cold clear eyes boring into his skull, almost like a physical pain. It did nothing to ease the pounding in his head. He rubbed his scalp harder, but to little effect. The only way to ease the pain now was killing. Hunting for prey or gunning down his rivals was the best medicine. Watching Snakebite's hot brains spill out across the freezing snow last night had helped to release some of the pressure inside his own skull. But now, under Leanna's interrogation, it had returned with a vengeance.

'I shot him myself.' Warg Daddy hefted the combat

shotgun in his hands. 'Right between the eyes. Snakebite was dangerous. What choice did I have?' Warg Daddy might not have been as smart as Snakebite, but even he had guessed Leanna's secret plan to put Snakebite in his place.

He waited while she examined him, probing for the truth with her X-ray gaze. If she guessed it, she would kill him without blinking. She was utterly ruthless. He could see the urgent hunger in her eyes. It wasn't just knowledge she lusted after, it was power. Leanna would never stop until all the power of the world was in her hands. He wondered if even that would be enough for her.

He tightened his sweaty grip on the shotgun. A sudden idea seized him. Two of his rivals had already died tonight. Why not three?

Leanna paced around him, her eyes blazing with anger. Was this the moment of discovery?

He eased his finger around the trigger. A single blast would be enough. He recalled the look of surprise on Snakebite's face as he'd aimed the weapon at him and pulled the trigger. After he'd emptied the twelve-gauge barrel at point blank range, there'd been no trace of surprise left on Snakebite's face. His old friend and companion no longer had a face.

'All right,' said Leanna at last. 'You have served me well, Warg Daddy.' Her face relaxed and he knew that he had passed her test. He was safe again. For now, at least.

'Yes,' he growled, not looking her in the eye. Still he clutched the gun tightly. The combat shotgun was his new best friend, his all-time favourite weapon. He gripped it tighter, his finger curled around the trigger. A single shot and he could be free of Leanna's control forever. The open road beckoned, and he pictured himself back on his bike, the engine throbbing hungrily as it devoured mile after mile. Adventure and freedom were his for the taking. He had only to pull that trigger and they could be his.

She came to him and pressed one small hand against

his giant chest. Perspiration beaded his skin. His jacket creaked as his muscles rippled nervously beneath its tight leather skin.

She moved closer still, pushing her body up against his, letting her thick hair brush his skin. He shivered at her touch. She pressed her lips to his neck and he felt his resolve to escape her growing weak. She reached out with her fingertips and began to touch him in that way she did. She unbuttoned his trousers. Very soon he was hard as a rock in her hand.

His resolution crumbled to nothing. Damn the woman! She had a power over him, he couldn't deny it. All thoughts of leaving her deserted him.

She continued to work him with her fingers until he gasped.

When it was over he pulled her hair and kissed her firmly on the lips, wrapping one strong arm around her slender waist. She returned his embrace with a passion that belied her cold eyes.

He pulled away from her at last. 'What next, then?' he asked. He'd happily have crashed into bed now and spent the rest of the day asleep, but Leanna barely slept. She was always too busy with her plans and her schemes.

'It's time to marshal your forces, Warg Daddy.'

The Leader of the Pack frowned. His forces were now significantly diminished. He'd lost Wombat when Leanna had ripped out his throat the night they'd first encountered her on Clapham Common. Two more of the Wolf Brothers had been lost to the fever during Stage One of the condition. Now Snakebite was dead at his own hands, and Adam gone too. He barely needed all his fingers to count his surviving followers, leaving his thumbs to spare. Marshalling the remaining Brothers would take an instant. He just had to kick them out of bed. 'You want me to assemble them now?' he queried. The poor bastards had probably only just gone to sleep after a long and bloody night.

'Not the Wolf Brothers,' said Leanna. 'Let them rest. I'm talking about the werewolves that you freed from the hospital.'

'But they all ran off,' said Warg Daddy, scratching his head. 'Dispersed. Scattered. I thought that was the plan.'

'It was. Now we bring them together again. We gather them into a fist. You and I are going to build an army, Warg Daddy. And then we're going to win a war.'

Chapter Two

Richmond upon Thames, West London, waning moon

Chris Crohn walked on through the night, his best friend Seth at his side, the girl with no name following closely behind. The winter wind whipped around them, drifting waves of snow across the road and stealing every last shred of heat from his skinny body. But he walked on regardless, heading west out of London, away from danger, step by step toward safety.

He walked in silence, too cold to speak, too shocked by his escape from the quarantine hospital to have anything worth saying. He had almost died this night, very nearly ripped to pieces by werewolves turning beneath the full moon as they fled the hospital. He had to get out of the city. Get far, far away.

Seth's eyes darted nervously about behind his heavy-rimmed glasses, his straggly brown hair plastered over his face. From time to time he flicked his head to one side, but the wet hair stayed stuck to his skin. The girl with no name stared into the distance yet seemed to see nothing. Her pale freckled face held no trace of expression or awareness. She was a ghost trailing them through the dark and empty streets.

Fires still burned in places along the roadside, but they were tame campfires compared with the blazing inferno of the hospital building he and Seth had narrowly escaped from at the beginning of the night. They smoked and smouldered and Chris walked past them, barely pausing to glance. He had seen too many fires already.

Chris had never done much walking before. Walking was a time-suck, an inefficient use of scarce resources, and he had almost completely managed to eliminate the need for it through smart lifestyle choices. At work, his computer chair was fitted with wheels, so he could slide around his office like a human cannonball, launching himself from desktop to filing cabinet to wall and back. If he needed to communicate with other people, he could message them with his phone. And since he lived on the same road as the school where he worked, he could get to his office in a matter of minutes. Efficiency was his watchword and he had honed it to a fine art.

His elimination of wasteful activities had left him extremely unfit, however. In the modern world, that hadn't seemed important. It wasn't as if he needed to hunt for bison or flee from tigers in twenty-first century London. Walking and running were outmoded skills, like using carbon paper to make copies of documents, making calls from a pay phone, or formatting a five-and-a-quarter-inch floppy disk.

But the world was changing fast. Civilization was beginning to unravel. Modernity would soon become a thing of the past, and advanced technology would be rendered obsolete. If Chris was going to survive and prosper he would need to embrace some new life hacks.

He had briefly taken up running and weight training in

an attempt to build a body fit for the post-apocalyptic era. But his fitness drive had failed after he'd been captured and secured in the isolation hospital. The only walking he had done in the past two weeks had been when he'd needed to go to the bathroom, or if he wanted to put some distance between himself and one of the other patients. Sharing a ward with a bunch of werewolves had certainly sharpened his survival instincts, but it hadn't done much for his cardiovascular system.

But how difficult could walking be? You took one step with your right foot, then another with your left. Repeat until destination reached.

It was just that he was so cold, walking through the night, with snow on the ground, and ominous clouds massing low in the sky.

His journey this night had begun at King's College Hospital in South London. His goal was to escape from the city and reach the wilderness. More precisely, he was heading for the small market town of Hereford in the west. According to his research, it was the nearest you could find to actual wilderness in modern England. The county of Herefordshire was a rural paradise of green fields, docile grass-chewing cattle, and scattered villages and farms. It also happened to be the home of his grandparents. He hadn't seen them for several years, but he was certain that he would be given a warm welcome when he turned up unannounced on their doorstep.

He would be there soon, once he had mastered the art of walking. Right foot forward, left foot forward. It really wasn't that difficult.

It was just that his legs were getting so stiff and tired.

The distance from the hospital to Hereford was 136 miles. That didn't sound far. If he could walk at an average speed of just one mile per hour for eight hours a day, he would reach his destination in two weeks at most. Maybe he could double that pace if he really tried. Then in just over a week he would be safe.

Right foot forward, left foot forward. No problem.

It was just that he was dressed only in his hospital pyjamas, dressing gown and slippers. The winter wind snapped through his gown, and his slippers were heavy with melted snow. His feet felt like blocks of ice.

He stopped. They had been walking for hours already, trying to put some distance between themselves and the burning hospital. Hundreds of werewolves had escaped from the hospital under the full moon, including that horrible headmaster Mr Canning, and they were presumably still roaming the streets nearby. He and Seth had been lucky not to get killed, especially when the soldiers guarding the hospital had opened fire with automatic weapons. But they must have walked for miles now, and it was time for a rest.

'Hey,' he said to Seth, through chattering teeth. 'Let's stop for a bit.'

'Okay,' said Seth. His friend came to a halt in the middle of the darkened road, his arms shaking from the cold, his legs quivering with cramp. He leaned against a parked car for support.

The girl who had followed them continued to walk on, as if in a daze.

Chris wondered if it would be best to let her go. They didn't need strangers slowing them down, although to be fair, the girl showed no sign of slowing. She had arrived in the middle of the night, wandering aimlessly around the streets. Chris had given her Seth's coat to wear, and she had accepted it without a word. They didn't even know her name. The only thing she'd said to them was that she had seen Chris somewhere before. She was probably just one of the girls from Manor Road School where Chris worked as tech support guy.

Had worked. It was still hard to accept that almost everything he knew was now in the past. All he had now was the road ahead, and the slim hope of survival. Perhaps that was all he had ever had, all that anyone might hope to have. Anything else was simply an illusion.

The girl with no name walked on, saying nothing, seeing nothing, her ginger hair like a beacon in the night.

'Hey,' Seth called to her. 'It's time for a rest.'

She didn't seem to hear him. She just trudged on, through the snow and the night. Not stopping. Not slowing. Around her, snow danced in whirling snow devils, but she walked straight through them, not once deviating from her path.

Chris watched her go. 'Save your energy,' he said to Seth. 'We need to rest.'

Seth leaned his weight against the car, motionless, in contrast to the girl's relentless forward movement. He stretched out across the body of the car, heedless of its icy metal and frost-covered windscreen, a picture of total exhaustion. Chris wondered if he might freeze to the car if he stayed there long enough.

His old friend had changed during these past few weeks in captivity, and not for the better. His neat goatee beard had thickened and become dishevelled. His straggly brown hair had grown so long that it fell permanently over his eyes, covering his face like a mop. He had let himself go, as if he no longer cared. Perhaps he didn't.

Chris would have to care for him instead. 'Come on,' he said to Seth. 'You can't stay there. You'll freeze to death.' As much as Chris hated the idea, they needed to keep walking if they were going to make it through the night. He prodded Seth until he reluctantly stirred.

Seth stroked his raggedy beard. 'Why don't we steal this car?' he suggested. 'We could break the window and hotwire it.'

'Yeah?' said Chris. 'Really? Do you have the slightest idea how to hotwire a car? Do you have any of the equipment needed to do that? Do you even know what equipment is necessary?'

Seth gave him a sullen look. 'Got a better idea?'

'Yeah,' said Chris, looking ahead. The nameless girl was

well ahead of them now. They would need to increase their pace if they were going to catch up with her. 'We can't let her walk off on her own.'

'Why not?' asked Seth. 'Why can't we do exactly that?' But he started walking on again, his legs stiff in the freezing night, his hair falling over his face.

Chris went after him, walking onward despite his exhaustion.

Right foot forward, left foot forward.

They were already coming to the edge of Richmond Park in the west of London. Another day of walking and they would leave the city and head out into open countryside. They would trek across England, sticking to the old roads and keeping far away from the major population centres. Eventually they would reach their destination. They would arrive in the wilderness, or paradise, or wherever it was they were heading. One mile an hour. Eight hours a day. Maybe twice that if they pushed it. They'd be in Hereford in just over a week, two weeks at the worst.

One foot forward, then another. Then the same thing again. On and on and on.

They would make it. They had to.

Chapter Three

Brookfield Road, Brixton Hill, South London, waning moon

Police Constable Liz Bailey woke early to the unmistakable smell of frying bacon. She lay in bed, uncertain what to do about it. Her stomach turned over in disgust at the smell of the meat.

Last night, beneath the light of the full moon, she had turned into a savage monster and killed two men with her bare hands. The memory of hot blood filling her mouth as she sucked greedily at their throats remained fresh and vivid, and she had to suppress an urge to gag. Yet she felt a ravenous hunger too. Transforming into a monster was hungry work, it seemed.

It was still dark and she had slept little, twisting and turning in her bed, just as her mind repeatedly turned over the night's events, listening to the soft breaths of Mihai, the ten-year-old Romanian orphan she had adopted, and the noisy snoring of her father, Kevin, sleeping like a baby in the same room. How he could sleep so well after coming so close to death she couldn't begin to fathom. It was just one of the many differences that separated her from her father. He wasn't here now, however. It must be him frying the bacon.

Mihai was slumbering soundly on the camp bed. After last night's killings, he hadn't wanted to share Liz's bed like he usually did. Instead he had slept next to Kevin. He'd insisted on spending the night with his "grandpa" and who could blame him after he'd watched her slaughter those men?

Still Liz couldn't help feeling resentful. There was no point denying that the Romanian boy had grown much closer to her father than to her, even before the events of last night. It wasn't too surprising, really. She hadn't been spending enough time with him. She'd simply been too busy. At Christmas she'd been very sick and Kevin had looked after the boy for days while she lay unconscious. Now that she had recovered, she was always out on duty. How could she be mother to an orphan boy as well as being a full-time police officer? But still, she couldn't deny feeling sore that Mihai had been unwilling to give her a bedtime kiss last night. He'd actually seemed afraid of her.

She pushed back the coverings on her side of the bed and crept into the kitchen of her apartment to see what was up. An off-tune but cheery hum greeted her, along with the sound of sizzling oil, as her father fried bacon, eggs and sausages on the gas cooker. A blue-and-white striped apron protected him from the fat spitting from the pan and the tomato sauce bubbling from a saucepan of baked beans.

The TV on the kitchen worktop showed news images of burning buildings and army soldiers standing in front of checkpoints. In one shot, the debris of a crashed helicopter lay strewn across a road, smoke still rising from the fire that had engulfed it. *Just another day in apocalypse town*, thought Liz, only dimly registering what she was seeing.

Kevin turned as she entered and gave her a broad grin. 'Morning,' he said. 'Get some of this down you. I bet you're ravenous after last night.'

Liz gave him a scowl. How her father could be so hungry and cheerful after the events of last night was beyond her. After all it was Kevin who had got them into the terrible scrape that had nearly resulted in them all being killed – her, Mihai and her police partner, Dean. She had known he was up to no good – he always was – but she had never imagined that he would be trying to buy guns and ammunition from a gang of Serbian arms dealers. Now the Serbians were all dead, along with Gary the butcher, and it was Liz herself who had killed two of them, slashing the throat of one with her bare finger nails, and killing the other with her teeth. She examined her fingers now and was dismayed to find remnants of dried blood under the nails, even though she had scrubbed them clean before coming to bed.

And yet the smell of the frying meat did seem to be awakening a fierce appetite in her too. Her stomach rumbled loudly as Kevin slapped thick butter onto doorstop-sized slices of white bread to go with the bacon and eggs.

'Eat up,' he said, offering her a plate of food. 'I don't know when we'll get our next delivery of meat, now that Gary's dead.' A cloud passed across his face, darkening the sunny grin that had been there a moment earlier. 'Shame about Gary. He was an idiot sometimes, but he never deserved what he got.'

The butcher had been Kevin's business partner, and had been shot dead by one of the Serbians.

Liz placed a hand against her father's grey-stubbled cheek. 'I'm sorry, Dad. I know you two were good friends.'

'Yeah, Gary was a good mate. A good butcher too. He made the best pork pies I ever tasted. Not such a bright spark, really, but he never meant nobody no harm.

'He didn't have no family, you know,' continued Kevin. 'I was the closest he got to anyone. So it's gonna be up to me to make the funeral arrangements.'

'Funeral?' Liz gaped at him in a kind of horrified admiration. While she had lain awake half the night thinking of nothing but the horror of the previous day's events, her father had not only enjoyed several hours of beauty sleep, but was already looking ahead and planning his next move.

'Yeah,' he went on, chewing on a hunk of buttery bread. 'We won't do nothing for the three Serbians. Better if we get rid of their bodies sharpish, like. Reckon we'll dump them in that old factory around the corner later on this morning. Dean can give me a hand with that when he's up. They don't deserve better.' He took a bite of the bacon, both meat and rind, and washed it down with a gulp of hot tea. 'But we need to make sure that Gary gets a proper send-off. I reckon he'd like a little gathering of old friends round at the butcher's shop. Nothing fancy, just some beer and sandwiches, maybe a few pork pies. I'll have a word with the vicar about it. Slip him a few bottles of whisky and I'm sure he'll ask no questions about the cause of death. Know what I mean?'

Liz stared at him, sipping the strong tea with two sugars he had made her. 'You've worked it all out, haven't you?' she said. 'You're just going to dispose of the bodies and then carry on business as usual.'

'Right,' said Kevin. 'No time to waste. I'll have to work out a new supply chain now that the Serbians are – you know – out of business. But as soon as I find someone who can supply me with cigarettes, spirits, meat and whatever else is in demand, I can be trading again in no time.' He stuck his fork into a meaty sausage. Hot fat oozed onto his plate. 'We can even use the van they left behind. They won't be needing it no more, right?'

Liz dropped her cutlery onto her plate with a clatter. Her appetite had deserted her once again. 'You haven't learned a single thing, have you?' she shouted at him. 'Not one damn thing! You nearly died last night – we all did. Me, Dean, even Mihai. Your best friend is lying dead in his own butcher's shop, along with the bodies of the men who shot him. And you're planning to just go back to doing what nearly got you killed.'

Kevin paused, the sausage halfway to his open mouth. 'What do you want me to do then?' he asked, puzzled. 'Just give up and join the ranks of the hungry, waiting for someone to help? What good will that do?'

'It will keep you alive,' she said.

'Yeah?' asked Kevin. 'Do you really think it will?'

Behind him, the news footage on the TV switched to a scene of people standing in lines outside some kind of makeshift soup kitchen. In the distance, the clock tower of Big Ben indicated that this was central London, not some earthquake zone in a far-off land.

Liz dragged her eyes away from the news and back to her father. 'You're going to do things differently from now on,' she told him. 'No more dodgy deals in back alleys. No more buying and selling cigarettes. No more supplying booze. And definitely no more guns. Got it?'

'What, nothing?' he asked, astonished.

'I'll let you buy food and other essentials,' she conceded, 'just so long as you get them from reputable traders. Someone needs to keep supplies moving, after all.'

'Well, yeah.'

'And I want you to promise me one more thing,' she said.

'What's that?'

'You'll get rid of the guns you got from the Serbians.'

He stared at her, sizing up how much she meant it. 'Okay,' he agreed reluctantly.

'I want them gone by day's end. And the bullets too. You can hand them in at the police station, no questions asked. You promise?'

'I promise.'

'Good.' That was one thing less to worry about, but she still had bigger matters to concern her. Her father might have diplomatically avoided mentioning the fact that she'd slaughtered two men with her hands and teeth, but dozens of other people must have witnessed last night's murders. She had no idea what she was going to do about that.

She tucked in to the sausages. Now that she had begun to eat, her appetite had come on with a vengeance.

Kevin watched her as she devoured the sausages. 'You like those?'

'Yeah,' she said, chewing hungrily at the richly-flavoured meat.

'They can be an acquired taste,' said Kevin appreciatively. 'Not everyone enjoys blood sausages.'

Chapter Four

*Number Ten, Downing Street, Whitehall,
Central London, waning moon*

Doctor Helen Eastgate looked at the face of the Prime Minister in alarm. 'You surely don't mean to resign?' she asked. It was just hours since the PM had stood up in the House of Commons to announce the failure of her government's strategy to contain the lycanthropy outbreak. The thought that the Prime Minister had lost confidence in her ability to lead the country shocked Helen to the core.

They were sitting in the Prime Minister's private office upstairs in Downing Street. Neither of them had slept. The PM's skin looked grey and thickly lined in the early morning light streaming in through the Georgian windows. She seemed to have aged years in the brief time that Helen had known her. She turned her face to gaze at the heavy clouds that filled the low sky outside. 'I have not yet decided,' she said.

The PM did not normally shy away from making decisions. Helen had been a privileged observer of the Prime Minister as the crisis that had engulfed the world had steadily deepened, these past days and weeks. As scientific adviser to the government's emergency COBRA committee, she had watched the PM wrestle with difficult situations that had required her to act ruthlessly at times. She didn't jump to snap conclusions, nor did she procrastinate. Helen had watched many times as she weighed the available evidence carefully, then made her choice.

Like Helen, the Prime Minister was fond of facts. Her brain seemed capable of amassing almost limitless quantities of data and statistics. *Seek truth from facts*, was one of her favourite mottoes. It had been a saying of the Chinese leader Mao Zedong. The Prime Minister seemed to find amusement in reusing the Communist revolutionary's words.

But unlike Helen, the PM did not allow a scarcity of facts to prevent her from making decisions when speed was of the essence. She possessed a ruthless determination that awed and sometimes frightened Helen. To see a look of profound uncertainty on the older woman's face was unexpected and disturbing.

'I watched you on television earlier,' said Helen. 'You announced a state of war. I don't really know what that means.'

The Prime Minister turned back to study Helen's face. 'It is the single greatest responsibility that a country's leader may face,' she said. 'One that requires the strongest kind of leadership. Few are truly up to the task, and those who are not have a duty to acknowledge the fact and step aside for the sake of their country. Winston Churchill was one of those fit to wear the mantle. When he later wrote his memoirs of World War II, he called the first volume, *The Gathering Storm*. It's a fitting title for the challenge we now face. Churchill was victorious and was able to write his own history. It is highly unlikely that I will enjoy that luxury.'

'Why do you say that?' demanded Helen. 'You are not usually so pessimistic.'

The PM turned her mouth downward. 'I am neither pessimistic nor optimistic. It is simply a statement of fact. A balance of probabilities, if you prefer.'

'No,' insisted Helen. 'You are as strong as any leader.'

'You are kind to say so, but not everyone agrees. The leader of the Opposition has tabled a motion of no confidence in my leadership.'

'Surely he won't win the vote?' said Helen uncertainly. But what did she know about the workings of the parliamentary machine? She didn't even know for certain what would happen if the Prime Minister lost the vote.

'No,' acknowledged the PM. 'My parliamentary majority will ensure that the motion is defeated. Nevertheless, he makes a good point. If I do not have confidence in my own ability to defeat the threat that faces us, why should others place their trust in me?' She bowed her head and stared at her hands, which were moving restlessly in her lap.

Helen shook her head, dismayed by the Prime Minister's self-doubt. The only time she had previously heard the PM express an unwillingness to continue in her role was in the aftermath of the Trafalgar Square Massacre, when the army had opened fire with live rounds on civilian demonstrators, killing hundreds. But then the Prime Minister had been animated by a palpable sense of anger, not this current hopelessness.

'I have confidence in you,' said Helen.

The PM looked up. 'Do you? Why?'

'Why?' repeated Helen. 'Call it a hunch.'

The Prime Minister stared intently at her. Then a look of amusement spread across her face. She began to chuckle. 'A hunch. Doctor Eastgate, is that part of your scientific method, to have hunches?'

'Absolutely,' said Helen earnestly. 'In science we call them hypotheses. We test them, and if the evidence supports them, they become theories. Prime Minister, I have seen plenty of evidence that you are the right woman for the job. In fact, I can say with some confidence that this is not merely a hunch, nor a hypothesis, but an established theory.'

'Hmm,' said the Prime Minister. 'So that's how science works, is it? Are you aware that I appointed you as scientific adviser to the COBRA committee against the advice of certain of my colleagues?'

'Yes,' said Helen, shifting uncomfortably in her seat. She was well aware that General Sir Roland Ney, Chief of the Defence Staff, had opposed her appointment to the committee. But even the General had begun to show her some grudging respect, eagerly adopting her term *lycanthrope* to describe victims of the disease in preference to the word used by most of the news media – *werewolf*. The initial hostility of the General had also been diffused by Helen's endorsement of his containment strategy, despite her misgivings about the General's record on human rights.

'In reality you have proved to be an excellent adviser in many respects beyond your scientific expertise,' remarked the Prime Minister.

'Really?' asked Helen. She hadn't been aware of that. 'I know nothing about politics, Prime Minister.'

'That is why I find you so refreshing. I enjoy your candidness and your disdain for the machinations of government. Your *idealism*, you might call it. In many ways you remind me of myself at your age. In fact, if it is not too presumptuous of me,' continued the older woman, 'I would like to say that I have come to think of you as a friend.'

Helen swallowed. She had no idea how to respond.

'I think I will continue, after all,' said the PM. 'In fact, I have made my decision. The alternative would be to leave the fate of this country in the hands of a man.' She winked at Helen mischievously. 'I don't think I could possibly stomach that. A time of such peril calls for a woman's strength and determination. What do you think, Helen?'

'I agree entirely,' said Helen, doing her best to keep a straight face.

'Besides,' continued the PM more gloomily, 'if I resign now, my government may fall, and I fear that the country would follow. Too much is at stake for an old woman to behave self-indulgently at this time.'

'Good,' said Helen, relieved. 'Although I don't think you are an old woman at all.'

'It is kind of you to say so. And what about you?' asked the PM. 'What are your plans? I'm sorry about the ban I placed on international flights. I hope you weren't planning to visit your relatives back in Australia.'

'No problem,' said Helen. She had often longed to fly back to the hot climate in the land she called home, but Australia had closed its borders at the beginning of the global werewolf crisis. Her family would have to wait for her to visit them again. A little longer, at least.

There was something else on her mind, but she wasn't quite sure how to raise it. To buy herself a little thinking time she reached across the table for a glass of water. Her fingers closed around it clumsily, knocking it rolling.

The Prime Minister caught it deftly in her own hands.

'Oops,' said Helen. 'Sorry.'

The older woman frowned. 'Helen, I hope you don't me saying anything, but I have noticed a certain ... awkwardness in your actions. Are you quite all right?'

Helen swallowed. She knew what was coming. She had been able to conceal her illness from her work colleagues easily enough. Her tendency to knock things over was carelessness, that was all. That tremor in her hand was nothing more than a craving for her next cappuccino. The stumbling on the stairs merely a sign of impatience.

But it was not so easy to fool the PM.

There was no point lying. Helen cleared her throat. 'No,' she said. 'I'm not all right in fact. My behaviour is not awkwardness. It's not clumsiness. It's the early sign of Huntington's disease.'

The PM reached her hand across the table and laid it on hers.

'It's a genetic condition,' she continued. 'The symptoms usually start to become apparent from the age of thirty.' She had passed her thirtieth birthday a year back. 'I can pass it off as clumsiness at this stage, but the disease is progressive and irreversible. Soon the jerkiness in my movements will become obvious to everyone. Ten years from now my speech will begin to slur. My mental abilities will decline. Early onset dementia leading to premature death is to be expected soon after. I might live to the age of fifty if I'm lucky. At present the disease is completely incurable.'

'Oh, Helen, I am so sorry.'

Helen brushed aside a tear. 'No need to be. I've known about this for a long time. It's one of the reasons I decided to study genetics. Such a fascinating subject. In fact, I need to ask for your help.'

She hadn't spoken to anyone about her idea before. It had only gradually been taking shape in her own mind and wasn't yet fully formed. But seeing the Prime Minister acknowledge and then face down her own uncertainties had boosted her confidence too. Now was the time to put her thoughts out into the open. 'I have an idea for a cure,' she said. 'Or possibly a vaccine. Not for Huntington's, but for lycanthropy. I don't yet know if it would work, but I'd like to see what I can do.'

The PM seemed excited at the prospect. 'What do you need to develop one?'

'I'm not exactly sure,' admitted Helen. 'It's a long shot.' That was an understatement. The difficulty of developing a vaccine would be immense, even under normal conditions, let alone in time of war. Yet she was buoyed by the fact that the PM hadn't questioned whether her idea would work. She had only asked what she needed.

'You shall have whatever you require,' said the PM. 'I will give your request the highest priority.'

'Thank you.'

The PM smiled. 'I wish you luck, Helen, and I will miss having you around.'

'Miss me?' asked Helen. 'I don't understand.'

'If you are going to be working on such an important project, you will not have time to sit in interminable meetings with a bunch of politicians. I will have to manage without your wise words to guide me.'

'Oh,' said Helen, surprised. She had grown used to sitting in on the government's COBRA meetings. Often she'd resented having to endure the endless discussions and arguments. But it had been a privilege to witness the Prime Minister's careful decision-making process at first hand, and sometimes provide input to the debate. The PM was right though – she couldn't possibly do two jobs at once. 'I'll miss you too,' she told her friend. 'But maybe we can fix this problem together, just you and me. *Sisters doin' it for themselves,*' she added with a wicked grin. 'I'll be Annie Lennox and you can be Aretha Franklin.'

The Prime Minister grinned back, and for an instant her tired and lined face became that of a young woman again. 'I hope so. If we can't, I don't know who will. Call me if you need anything.'

Chapter Five

*Upper Terrace, Richmond upon Thames,
West London*

James Beaumont knelt before the wooden cross that hung on the wall of his room, two feet to the left of his bed. Like a monk's cell, the room was almost bare of furnishings. James needed none. He needed only to hear the word of God again.

He had prostrated himself here for hours, ever since returning in the early hours of the morning, half-carried up the staircase by Ben and Melanie, half-dead from hunger and exhaustion. Yet he did not seek food or sleep. Instead he prayed to God for forgiveness and understanding. Over and over he prayed, but God did not reply.

He raised his eyes again to the cross on the wall, seeking meaning in the grainy swirls and lines of its wooden arms. The letters INRI carved into the cross spelled out a message – *Iesus Nazarenus, Rex Iudaeorum*, Jesus the Nazarene, King of the Jews – the inscription that

Pontius Pilate had caused to be nailed above the head of Jesus as he endured the last stage of his Passion. James could barely imagine the suffering that Christ must have felt at that moment. And yet it somehow seemed to reflect his own wretched misery.

'My God, My God, why have you forsaken me?' he prayed, echoing the words of Jesus himself, but still no answer came.

The cross was the one constant at the eye of the storm that had engulfed James. He couldn't begin to understand why God had decided to test him in such an extreme way. He had always tried his best to be good and to obey God's laws. Yet for some reason, God had heaped a torrent of plagues upon him, as if he were a modern-day Job.

His trials had begun on Halloween night, when a man possessed with a devilish disease had tried to kill him and the children he was taking for trick or treat. The man had bitten him, turning James into a devil just like him. He had briefly discovered happiness in the arms of Samuel, but then Samuel had been taken from him by a police marksman's bullet.

And now his parents were both dead too, at Leanna's hands. He wept for them freely. It was unbearable knowing that he was the cause of their deaths. Leanna had killed them simply in order to make him suffer. Why did they have to die? He would willingly give himself in their place, if only he could.

'My God, take me instead,' he prayed, but even as the words left his mouth he knew that God did not make bargains with sinners.

James' sins were piled up in heaps, and it was no use begging for forgiveness. The priest, Father Mulcahy, had offered him a chance to repent, and instead James had killed him and devoured his flesh. He bowed his head to the floor in shame at the memory. To kill a priest – was any sin worse than that? Yet it had marked just the beginning of his descent into butchery.

He had slaughtered innocent commuters at a railway station under the light of the moon. He'd savaged a young woman at the fireworks display on New Year's Eve. He'd infected a boy his own age and left him for dead in the street. And even when he had tried to do the right thing and had rescued Melanie from a madman, he had ripped open her captor in an orgy of violence. He had very nearly savaged her too.

He was a killer. He had killed once, twice, three times. He had killed so many times that he had lost count. He couldn't stop the killing.

Tears fell from his cheeks and splashed on the floor before the cross. 'My God, tell me what I should do,' he prayed, over and over again, but still the voice of God remained silent.

He was a sinner. Sin piled on ever more grievous sin. With every day, the teetering weight of guilt that he carried on his back grew greater.

He had vowed never to kill again, yet the corpses kept piling up. Last night two more innocent people, Richard and Jane Hallibury, who he hadn't even known, had died because of him. He had tried to save them from harm, had placed his own body between them and danger, offering himself as a sacrifice, but still Leanna had slaughtered them in his name. Nothing he did seemed to make any difference.

'My God, you did not even give me a choice.'

A roar escaped from his throat. He had no more words to say. He grabbed at the wooden desk by his bed and shook it with both hands, tipping books, writing paper and pencils onto the floor. He ripped the paper into pieces, snapping the pencils one by one and tossing them against the wall. The books he tore apart, scattering pages across the sparsely-furnished room. He lifted the desk high over his head and brought it crashing down. It splintered and broke into pieces.

His rage grew stronger.

He grabbed at the narrow bed where he slept and up-ended it, spilling the mattress and sheets onto the floor. He pounced on them, rending and tearing the white cotton with his teeth. With a cry he flung them at the cross that watched silently over him.

When it was done he lifted his eyes to the wall once more.

The plain wooden cross was the one point of stillness in the room. He paced toward it, sweat running from his brow, anger leaking from his pores. The cross seemed to taunt him, mocking him as he raged, watching with indifference as he suffered. Jesus had died on the cross, and God had done nothing to help him either. He reached out a hand to grasp it, but the door behind him burst open.

Sarah rushed into the room. 'James, what are you doing? What's wrong?'

His hand curled around the cross, fingers grasping at polished wood. He wanted nothing more than to rip it from the wall and hurl it to the floor. What use was a God who would not reach out to him in his darkest hour?

Sarah crossed the room, stepping over the wreckage of the furniture. She came to him and stood shyly by. Then slowly, she wrapped her arms around his shoulders and hugged him to her.

His rage seemed slowly to drain away. He let Sarah hold him, felt the warm and tender arms that embraced him and held him close. He knew how difficult it was for her to show affection. He knew how hard it was for her simply to be in the presence of another person. Yet here she was, reaching out to him. Suddenly his anger turned to shame.

He was still alive.

He should be grateful, not resentful. While he had killed, others had been killed. Countless people had died since the sickness of lycanthropy had begun to spread across the world. Yet he lived on. Either God was saving him for some purpose, or else there was no God and he must find a purpose of his own.

Sarah's own words came back to him then. *Can you still be certain that God really exists?* she had asked him once.

He has to, James had replied. *Otherwise there's no meaning to anything.*

It doesn't have to be like that, Sarah had told him. *We can find our own meaning.*

That was the challenge then, to find his own meaning in life, now that God was gone. Now that Samuel was gone. Now that his old life and everything he held dear had gone.

The answer lay before him, in the ripped bedding and smashed wooden furniture he had scattered around the room. *Violence. Destruction.* It was the one thing a werewolf was good for.

He would harness his rage, guide his strength toward protecting his loved ones. Sarah, Melanie, Ben and Grandpa. They were his family now. He would defend them, with his own life if necessary.

God had not come to him, but Sarah had. He hugged her closer. 'I'm sorry,' he said. 'I lost my temper.'

She hugged him back, cradling him in her arms. 'It's all right, James. You don't need to apologize. You've suffered so much. And after everything you've done to keep us safe, you are the last person who needs to say sorry.'

Yes, that was his role now. James the protector. They depended on him, for food and safety. He would use his strength for good. He would turn his back on fear, weakness and his own selfish desires. And he would never let his new family down, whatever the cost.

Chapter Six

Richmond upon Thames, West London, waning moon

Chris and Seth trudged along the deserted road, one frozen foot after another, steadily leaving the horrors of the night behind them. Every step put more distance between them and the escaped werewolves and brought them closer to their final destination.

Dawn had broken, the weak sun rising behind them as they headed west, turning the dark clouds a light grey, and there had been no further snowfall. But the coming of the day did nothing to raise the temperature. They had been walking all night and were frozen and exhausted. They needed to stop and rest soon. But there was nowhere to shelter.

The girl with no name led the way, walking as if in a trance, looking neither to the left nor the right. They came to an iron gate marking the entrance to Richmond Park, but the girl took a sharp turn away from the park and headed down a side street. Chris had no idea what guided her in her choice of route, if anything did at all.

He didn't really mind. He was too exhausted to think, and since they had no map, one road was as good as another. As long as they continued to head roughly west they would leave London within a day or so and break out into the safety of the surrounding countryside. Once there, they would follow the setting sun, leading them ever onward to the promised land.

They might have stopped earlier to rest in a shop doorway or beneath a tarpaulin on a construction site if they had only thought of it at the time. He had lost count of the number of shops, houses, apartment blocks and building sites they had passed during the hours of darkness. Now as they walked through Richmond, bricks and mortar gave way to bare trees and glimpses of open parkland behind walls and fences. There was nowhere to find shelter here.

Large houses lined one side of the road, but the gates that led to them were all locked. Or, if they were open, the houses that stood back from the road stared down at them like fortresses, hard and unwelcoming. Chris had no doubt that if they knocked on one of those doors, they would be turned away.

The girl walked on, and Chris and Seth followed.

Each step was harder though. He had long since lost all feeling in his feet. He stumbled as he walked, his legs cramping, his arms shaking, his vision clouded. Tiredness had given way to fatigue and then to exhaustion. What came after exhaustion, Chris couldn't say, but whatever it was, he had reached it about a mile back. Now he was entering a state of delirium. 'Can't go on,' he muttered. 'Too tired to walk. Must rest.' If they didn't find a place to shelter soon, he would probably just drop to his knees in the middle of the road and fall asleep right there.

The idea began to grow in appeal the more he thought about it. Just stop walking. Lie down. Curl into a ball and sleep. It was a plan, probably the best one available right now. He would count to sixty and if he didn't come up with a better idea, he would do it.

He had reached forty when the girl with no name stopped suddenly.

'Wassat?' said Seth, as if startled from a dream. 'Wassapening?'

The girl pointed. They had reached an old grey church, its square stone tower jutting high above the surrounding trees and houses.

Chris looked up. The tower seemed to reach all the way to Heaven. It was a bell tower, wooden slats covering the arched windows where the bells were housed. Carved stone saints gazed down at them beneficently, conveying a blessing. At ground level a stone porch beckoned, protected from the elements by a triangular slate roof. Deep shadows filled the porch, but Chris felt no fear. There was no room in his mind for anything but exhaustion.

The girl opened the gate leading to the church tower and he and Seth followed.

The hollow of the porch was dry, and deep enough to shield them from the wind. The tiled floor was cold and hard, but all three sank onto it as if it were a feather bed.

'Thank the Lord,' thought Chris, and then he was asleep.

A scream woke him some hours later.

He opened one eye and saw daylight glinting on stone tiles. For a moment he couldn't remember where he was. His body had stiffened on the cold floor and he could hardly move. A second scream came from nearby. He opened his other eye and tried to identify the source of the sound.

He didn't have far to look. The girl was sitting up, her back pressed against the stone porch, her eyes closed and her mouth wide open. A third scream issued from it.

Seth was scrabbling around next to him, looking

confused. 'What's that noise?' he said.

'It's the girl,' said Chris. 'I think she's having a nightmare.'

The girl remained in a seated position, her eyes still closed. Only her mouth moved as she continued to scream.

'Is she asleep?' asked Seth.

'I think so.'

'What should we do?'

'Wake her up,' said Chris. He reached out to shake the girl's arm.

'No!' said Seth, grabbing at him. 'If you wake her, she might die.'

'Nonsense,' said Chris. 'That's just a stupid myth. You can't harm someone by waking them up.' He shook the girl's arm gently.

The girl stopped screaming and opened her eyes. They were vividly green in the early light. Her chest lifted and fell and her gaze switched from Chris to Seth and back.

'You were having a nightmare,' said Chris. 'Are you okay?'

The girl shook her head. She said nothing in reply.

'It's all right now,' said Chris soothingly. 'You're safe here. We can rest, then find food. In a day or two we'll be out of London and it'll be much safer.'

The girl still said nothing, just looked at them, frightened.

'I think she's suffering from trauma,' said Chris. 'We have to be patient with her.'

A growl came suddenly from the street beside the church. Chris looked up. A huge dog stood watching them, its lips drawn back. A pink tongue dripping with saliva flashed between white teeth. The dog darted forward aggressively through the open gate, barking loudly.

'Who left the gate open?' asked Chris. Then he remembered. It had been him.

Seth struggled to his feet. 'What is it?' he cried. 'A

werewolf?'

'No,' said Chris. 'It's just a dog.' It was a big dog though. He had never liked dogs of any kind, big or small. They didn't usually like him either. He looked around the porch for a weapon, but there was nothing around. If the dog attacked, he would have to wrestle it to the ground with his bare hands.

'Keep away from it,' said Seth. 'It looks dangerous.'

'You don't need to tell me that,' said Chris. The dog opened its jaws, revealing sharp canine teeth. Grappling with the dog probably wouldn't be a smart move. Putting Seth between him and the dog was a better idea. He began to shuffle to the back of the porch, hoping to disappear into the shadows.

The dog barked again and bounded forward. It stopped at the entrance to the porch, barking loudly. Its body looked half-starved. The bones of its ribcage jutted clearly beneath its skin. Drool slipped from its hungry jaws.

'I think it wants to eat us,' said Seth, taking a step backward. He tripped over and fell to the floor, sprawling over the tiles.

The dog went for him. It powered forward, jumping up and lunging at him with its slavering jaws, trying to bite his face. Seth rolled aside, but the dog was on him again, teeth clamping around his arm. Seth screamed. The dog's tail flapped wildly from side to side.

Chris watched, too scared to do a thing.

Seth struggled to pull his arm free, but the dog tugged at it viciously. It began pulling him from the porch out into the open. Seth was on the ground, unable to defend himself as he was dragged toward the road.

Suddenly the girl moved. She rushed to the dog's side, kneeling down, wrapping her thin arms around it. Chris could hardly bare to watch, yet he couldn't drag his eyes away either. The girl held the dog tight, but she wasn't wrestling with it. Instead she seemed to be hugging it. She whispered in the dog's ear.

To Chris' amazement the dog broke off its attack and lowered its nose. The girl continued to talk to the dog, and it dropped its front paws to the ground, putting its snout down too. It looked up at her with frightened eyes.

The girl stroked the dog's body with her pale hands. 'There, there, girl,' she said. 'It's all right now. The bad man won't hurt you.'

'Bad man?' said Seth indignantly. 'That monster nearly ripped my arm off.'

'Ssh,' said Chris. 'Don't frighten the dog.'

'Frighten the *dog*?' echoed Seth. 'I'm the one who nearly got torn to pieces.' But he allowed the girl to carry on calming the creature.

She seemed to be casting some kind of magic over the dog. The animal became docile as the girl rubbed its nose with her fingers and laid her head against its body. In half a minute she had turned it from a rampaging beast into a calm, friendly pet.

'You were just frightened, weren't you?' said the girl to the dog. 'Hungry, cold and frightened, like us.'

She was right about that. They needed warmth, and they needed food. Carefully, Chris rose to his feet, half-expecting the dog to attack, but the animal seemed contented now. He looked outside but there was no one around. The only movement was a small dark figure in the distance, slowly coming toward them through the white snow. Steadily the figure drew closer. It was an old man wearing what appeared to be a black cloak. Chris blinked and rubbed his eyes. Was the hunger and fatigue causing him to hallucinate now? Would angels begin to descend from the bell tower next?

He waited patiently for the man in the black cloak to arrive. Eventually he stopped at the gate leading into the church grounds. The man wore a cassock. He was a vicar. His black robe was buttoned tightly all the way down the front, and around his neck was a clerical collar. 'Hello?' he enquired, regarding Chris, Seth, the girl and the dog without a trace of surprise. 'May I help you?'

'I hope so,' said Chris. 'If you can't, then no one can.'

'I see,' said the vicar. 'You'd better come inside the church. Your dog can come too.'

Chapter Seven

High Street, Brixton Hill, South London, waning moon

Liz stood with Kevin outside the butcher's shop, glancing nervously around the empty street. After last night's massacre none of the residents dared leave the safety of their house, but that didn't mean they were too scared to watch. Net curtains twitched in the windows opposite, and inquisitive eyes peered from behind the wooden blinds of the house next door.

All eyes were on Liz and Kevin.

A heavy bunch of keys rattled in Kevin's cold fingers as he struggled to find the one that would unlock the door.

'Come on, Dad,' said Liz. 'Get a move on.'

'Yeah, yeah,' he muttered, 'Just give me a minute.' He tried another key. 'My fingers are numb. It's minus bloody freezing out here.'

The street was silent and white this morning. The snow had stopped but a thin film of white still covered the rooftops and windowsills of the houses and shops. The cars parked outside them were coated with frost. Even the pavement and road surface were painted white. Against the milky backdrop, the bright splashes of blood where men had died were hard to miss. That one just outside the butcher's shop showed the spot where the Serbian gang had ruthlessly shot Gary. The red trail stretching from farther down the street marked where Dean and Kevin had dragged the dead body of the Serbian ringleader, Zoran. And close behind the delivery van, the two crimson pools in the chalk-white snow must have belonged to Zoran's bodyguards who Liz had killed with her own bare hands.

And teeth.

Don't forget the teeth, Liz. Don't ever forget what you did with your own teeth.

Last night the street had been lit by bright moonlight, its cold beams sparkling on the snow and ice, giving the scene an otherworldly quality. It may have looked like a winter wonderland, but a nightmare had unfolded here. After one of the Serbians had shot her in the arm, Liz had become the moon's creature under its cold light, killing senselessly in its name.

She shuddered at the memory. It was hazy, like the waking memory of a dream. Her mind had contrived to hide certain details from her, for her own protection, and she only partially recalled the sequence of events. But she knew it was not a nightmare. It had really happened. The blood in the snow was proof of that.

And the memory of hot blood filling my mouth.

She rubbed briskly at her arm where she'd been shot. It still itched where the skin had sewn itself back together under the healing caresses of the moonbeams. There was no sign of the torn flesh that should have been there. Miraculously the wound had completely healed.

She could not yet fully grasp the change that had come over her. Twice now she had transformed under the moon. Yet she had not changed into one of the werewolves she had seen on television, with thick coats of fur and wolf bodies. They even had the tails, muzzles and ears of wolves. She had none of those features. Yet she was not fully human any more. Of that she had no doubt.

Dean, Kevin and the others had not properly discussed what had happened. They had tiptoed around the incident, speaking only of how the Serbians had cheated Kevin, and how terrible it was that Gary had been killed. They skirted over the fact that the three Serbian men were now dead, not stopping to discuss the violent manner of their deaths, or who was responsible.

Everyone was too polite – or too scared – to mention the fact that Liz had transformed into a monster last night, however briefly. She would be happy if no one ever did.

But it wasn't just her own extended family that had witnessed events. Frightened eyes continued to watch them from behind half-drawn curtains as Kevin fumbled with the lock. Liz could stand it no more. 'Oh, for goodness' sake, give them to me.' She grabbed the keys from him. The key ring held an astonishing number of keys. She began to try them one at a time.

It was a miracle that no one had yet reported last night's incident to the police. Two men had been gunned down in a residential street, and two more ripped to pieces. Perhaps because she and Dean had been wearing police uniform, the residents had assumed that they were witnessing a legitimate police operation, not just two rogue officers taking the law into their own hands. But if they were going to keep people believing that, then they would have to go door to door as soon as possible, speaking to the residents and reassuring them that all was in hand.

It seemed incredible that she was thinking this way. The right solution – perhaps a better one – would be to go and confess everything to her superiors. She, Dean and Kevin were all murderers. They ought to be locked behind bars. And yet, what would happen to Mihai then? What about Samantha and Lily?

She knew she wasn't going to confess. She had broken all the rules already, and to protect Mihai and the others she had no choice but to keep on breaking them. She would break every rule in the book to make sure no harm came to her loved ones.

The key twisted in the lock at last and she pushed the door open. Kevin followed her inside and shut the door behind them.

Walking inside the butcher's shop was like re-entering the nightmare world of the previous night. The bodies of the three dead Serbians lay on the floor just where Kevin and Dean had dumped them. In the gloom of the shop it was easy to imagine that she had dreamed it all, that the men were not dead, just sleeping. That they might rise up before her.

Kevin switched on the light and the reality of the situation became all too clear. Zoran, the ringleader, had a bullet wound in the middle of his back where Kevin had shot him as he tried to escape. Next to him was the thin man who had tried to kill Mihai. A gash of congealed blood around his neck marked where Liz had slashed his throat with her fingernails. On the other side was the second bodyguard. Liz blanched as she saw the wound where she had opened the man's jugular and drained his blood.

The body of Gary the butcher was stretched out next to the three Serbs. He'd been her father's business partner and perhaps the closest he'd had to a friend. He was a victim of Kevin's stupidity as much as the brutality of the Serbs.

Kevin kicked at Zoran's stiff corpse. 'Bastard,' he said. 'Gary might have been a berk, but he never deserved this.'

'No,' agreed Liz. Gary had been a cheerful, easy-going man. He would probably never have got into any kind of trouble if it hadn't been for Kevin.

The dead Serbs were a different matter. Who knew

how many victims they had committed crimes against over the years? She couldn't completely regret their deaths. If anyone else ever threatened to kill Mihai, she wouldn't hesitate to do the same again.

There was a suggestion of a tear in Kevin's eye. 'I feel like I should take some of the blame for Gary getting shot,' he said. 'Like it was partly my fault.' He sniffed.

Liz glared at him. 'Partly your fault?' she said. 'This was entirely your fault.' The butcher was laid out like a side of beef in his own butcher's shop thanks to Kevin. 'You nearly got us all killed last night,' she added.

He seemed shocked by her accusation. 'I was just doing some business,' he protested. 'If it wasn't for these double-crossing bastards, everything would have been all right.'

'It was just a matter of time. You can't get mixed up with gangsters like that and not expect trouble.'

'Yeah, well,' said Kevin. 'It's in the past now. We need to decide what to do next. Here's my thinking. First we need to get rid of these three bodies. If we load them into the van, we can bury them in shallow graves round at the old factory.'

Liz winced at the suggestion, but he was probably right. They had little choice now.

'Gary deserves a proper burial,' he continued. 'He was a popular man round here. I'll make the arrangements.'

'What about his family?' asked Liz.

'He didn't have anyone. No wife, no kids. His old folk were dead. So the next question is the reading of his will.'

'I suppose so,' said Liz. 'Do you know where it is?'

'As a matter of fact, I do,' said Kevin. 'And I know what it says too.'

'What?'

'That in the eventuality of Gary's untimely demise, everything comes to me.'

Liz gawped at him, her mouth wide open. 'Why you?'

'I was his business partner,' said Kevin. 'So we had an arrangement, like. If anything happened to Gary, all his estate passed to me.'

'Wow,' said Liz. She narrowed her eyes suspiciously. 'And what if something happened to you?'

'Then all my stuff would have gone to Gary. It was only fair.'

'Fair?' Liz couldn't believe it. 'After all I've done for you, there's nothing in your will for me? Your only daughter gets nothing?'

'Well, I can change that now,' he said Kevin. 'But the point is, all this is mine now.' He waved his arms around the room. 'The butcher's shop, all Gary's savings, the van, the stock, the lot.'

'What are you going to do with a butcher's shop?' she asked.

'Well, if it was up to me, I'd carry on trading,' said Kevin. 'It's a golden opportunity. Daft to waste it.'

She glared at him.

'But I know you won't let me do that,' he continued. 'So what I'm thinking is, your apartment is very nice and all that, but it's getting a bit cramped, what with all of us in it.'

Liz couldn't deny it. The apartment had seemed expansive when she was living there alone, but after she'd brought Mihai home to live with her, it had no longer felt too big. When Kevin had moved in, it had become small, and now that Dean, Samantha and Lily were living there too, there was hardly a spare inch. When Samantha's baby arrived, she couldn't imagine how they could all live there. Gary's place was enormous by comparison and the shop took up only the ground floor of the building. Above it were two whole floors of living space. It would easily accommodate the six of them – seven when the baby came.

'Okay,' she agreed. 'We'll move in. But first, let's get rid of these bodies.'

Chapter Eight

Holland Gardens, Kensington, London, waning moon

In the privacy of her own room, Leanna carefully removed her halter-neck top and cast it to the floor, wincing with pain. Her torso was badly bruised, and five red stripes marked the pale skin beneath. The stripes showed where James had scratched her with his talons.

A bandage bound her waist where a knife had nicked her skin during last night's fight with James and his friends. She unwound it slowly, unwrapping herself one loop at a time. The wound beneath still wept blood. She cleaned it with hydrogen peroxide and bound it again, wrapping a fresh bandage around her middle until the bleeding stopped.

She had been careful not to reveal the full extent of her injuries to Warg Daddy. She could not conceal the acid burns to her face, but she would not permit him to see these new wounds. She would not allow him to discover the extent of her failure.

She had hoped to dispose of the traitor James last night, to take her time over it, and savour his look of horror as she first butchered his friends and then killed him. Instead, they had somehow beaten her off. She had killed two of his friends, but two others, a man and a woman, still lived.

She examined the purple bruising on her chest where the woman had struck her with a metal bar. Melanie, James had called her.

Well, pretty Melanie, with your long dark tresses and your lovely skin, you will die next time we meet. And I will make James watch every exquisite moment of it.

They had said the man's name was Ben Harvey. He was the one who had stuck the knife into her side.

I'll see you dead too, Ben Harvey. But not before you suffer.

Next she touched the scars on her face where the acid burns still remained. The full moon had the power to heal fresh injuries, but these old wounds would never heal. The acid had peeled her beauty away, ruining one half of her face, leaving only a raw underlayer of tissue to cover the muscle and bone. The memory of the pain flooded back as she relived the moment the acid had struck her, thrown by her former mentor, Doctor Helen Eastgate.

I haven't forgotten you, Doctor Eastgate, nor have I forgiven you for doing this to me. I never will.

The burns no longer hurt quite so badly, but the scarred skin seemed to turn Warg Daddy's stomach whenever he saw it. He tried to hide his reaction, but the horror in his eyes couldn't be mistaken.

James, Melanie, Ben, Helen. You will all die at my hands. You will wish you had never been born.

But there was no hurry. Revenge was best served cold. Right now, she had more urgent things to think about.

Warg Daddy was a fool if he thought he could deceive her with his ridiculous story. His explanation of how Adam and Snakebite had died was obviously a lie. She had guessed the truth as if the blood still dripped from his hands. Warg Daddy had always been a jealous man, and jealousy made men weak.

I should have anticipated his treachery.

Warg Daddy was physically big, but his ego was even larger, and his fragile pride could tolerate no rival.

He had made no secret of hating Adam right from the start, and had grown increasingly afraid of Snakebite's growing intelligence. He had obviously been terrified by the idea that one of them might replace him in Leanna's chain of command.

He was right to fear that.

Leanna had considered making Snakebite her right-hand man in place of Warg Daddy. Snakebite had possessed all the qualities she needed – intelligence, loyalty and utter brutality. Warg Daddy was brutal to be sure, but he wasn't intelligent, and his loyalty was highly questionable. He was hardly fit to be a leader of Leanna's new super-race. Still, he had demonstrated a surprisingly ruthless cunning in eliminating his two rivals. Perhaps there was hope for him yet.

She would not waste time mourning the loss of Adam and Snakebite. They had served as useful tools for a while. But when a tool was broken, you replaced it.

For now, Warg Daddy was the best tool available to her. She needed him to manage the Wolf Brothers. The biker gang formed an effective fighting unit when working as a team, but as individuals they were stupid, and none of them had half of Warg Daddy's leadership ability. Without him as Leader of the Pack, the Brothers would quickly disintegrate into an orgy of violence.

At least her sexual bond with him had the desired effect of keeping him in tow. However much he might dream of freedom, he would always keep coming back to her. Just as long as she wanted.

For better or worse, Warg Daddy was bound to her, and she to him. For the moment, at least. But he would not serve her forever.

Under her instructions, he was already beginning to gather an army, a new Wolf Army. Soon they would come, one by one at first, then two by two, more and more each day. Not even Warg Daddy guessed the true number of werewolves who had already reached Stage Three of the condition. No doubt he imagined that just a couple of hundred werewolves were at large in London.

The true number was far, far greater.

Since returning to England from Romania almost a year ago she had set about spreading the disease far and wide. Working together with Adam and Samuel she had sent her servants to all four corners of the globe. Each one of them had a simple task. To spread lycanthropy, and to infect as many as possible. To seed the foot soldiers of the apocalypse.

An army worthy of Leanna's ambition now roamed the streets of England's capital. At present the wolf soldiers were scattered, undisciplined, living alone or in small groups, fearing for their safety. They hid during the day, coming out to hunt at night. They did not even know they were an army. They lacked a leader and were without purpose. But under her command, Warg Daddy would gather them and turn them into a formidable fighting force.

Mostly they would be foot soldiers, cannon fodder, ready to die if she commanded it. But among them would be generals, military strategists and commanders. She would watch them closely, pick out the best. One among them would be the one she sought. A leader, brave and resourceful, intelligent and cunning, and above all loyal. Once she had found him, she would have no further use for Warg Daddy. And when that day came, Warg Daddy would discover for himself the bitter taste of betrayal.

She turned and touched the disfiguring marks on her face and body again. Those marks might sting, but they served a valuable purpose. They had taught her two

essential lessons.
Never trust anyone. And never forgive treachery.

Chapter Nine

*Richmond upon Thames, West London,
waning moon*

Chris crammed the bread into his mouth, trying not to seem too rude in his eagerness to eat more. The bread was freshly baked and smeared with butter and honey. He had never tasted anything so heavenly. The others were eating bread and honey too, and even the dog had been given food out of a tin.

The vicar smiled at them indulgently. 'Some say that it is wrong to eat in church,' he remarked. '"If anyone is hungry, let him eat at home." *1 Corinthians 11:34.*'

Chris stopped mid-bite, a guilty cascade of crumbs trickling down the front of his pyjamas.

'That's all very well for people who have homes to go to, and food there,' continued the vicar. 'But not everyone is so fortunate.'

Chris resumed chewing his meal. 'Thank you for feeding us,' he said through his stuffed mouth.

'More?' enquired the vicar when they had finished.

'I think we're full now,' said Chris. He glanced down at the dog, which was licking its paws. 'Although maybe the dog would like another bowl.'

'The poor creature does look emaciated,' said the vicar, opening another tin and tipping it into the dog's bowl. 'But she is very well behaved. What is her name?'

They all turned to look at the dog, which had already begun to devour the second tin of meat.

'She doesn't really have one,' said Chris. 'At least we don't know what it is. We kind of found her. Or rather, she found us.' It seemed strange to think of the dog as a *her*. Chris had always regarded animals as things.

The vicar examined the dog while it ate, but it wore no collar or name tag. 'I wonder who her owner is?' he said.

The girl, who was sitting on the floor cross-legged next to the dog, hugged the animal tightly to her. 'No owner who loved her would ever allow her to become so hungry.' It was the first time the girl had spoken, except to comfort the dog.

'You may be right,' said the vicar. 'I don't think she's eaten properly in days. She needs someone to take better care of her.'

The girl's green eyes shone fiercely. 'I'll look after her.' Her tone defied anyone to contradict her.

Chris looked at Seth, who shrugged in resignation. 'Well, she does seem to have calmed down now,' Chris said to the girl. 'But you'll have to make sure she doesn't turn on us again. And you'll have to find food for her too.'

She nodded.

'So what are your plans?' asked the vicar. 'Where are you travelling?'

'West,' replied Chris. 'We're leaving London and heading into the wilderness, where it's safe.'

'The wilderness?' echoed the vicar, raising his white eyebrows. 'Well, I hope you find safety there. When Jesus went into the wilderness, he was tested by the Devil.

Matthew 4:1-11. I hope that doesn't happen to you. You'll need to be careful leaving London. The army is blocking all the main routes out of the city. In fact I hear that they are massing their forces at Heathrow Airport. There's speculation that they mean to mount an attack to recapture all of the escaped werewolves.'

'Recapture them?' Chris snorted. 'Kill them, more like. Good luck with that. We were there last night when they escaped. At the hospital, I mean. Hundreds of werewolves got loose. The soldiers won't be able to find them. They'll all have turned back into human form now.'

'No doubt,' said the vicar. 'But there may be ways of identifying these monstrous creatures. As *Hebrews 4:13* remarks, "And no creature is hidden from his sight, but all are naked and exposed to the eyes of him to whom we must give account."'

'I guess so,' said Chris. 'Anyway, we should be leaving now. If the army is setting up roadblocks, we'll need to get out of the city as soon as we can.'

'Just bear in mind what I said about Heathrow Airport,' cautioned the vicar. 'You might want to think about travelling north to avoid it. In fact, you may find you have no choice.'

Chris shook his head. 'We can't go north. That will add miles to our journey. We can't risk the delay. We have to keep heading west.'

'Whatever you say,' said the vicar.

'It isn't safe to stay in the city,' continued Chris. 'This is where the werewolves are most concentrated. And it's where all the fighting will take place once the army starts to ramp up its operations. You should leave too. You should tell all your parishioners to leave.'

The vicar seemed unperturbed by Chris' appeal. 'My place is here with my church, and my parishioners will make up their own mind. I will bear in mind what you say, but there is safety in numbers too.'

'No,' said Chris. 'That's where the greatest danger lies.'

The vicar smiled politely. 'I wish you God's speed,' he said.

'Thanks for the food,' said Seth.

'No problem,' said the vicar. 'I'll wrap the rest of the bread for you, and I can give you some coats and shoes to wear too. I keep some old ones in the vestry just in case. I wish you the best of luck. But if you're going to be adopting this dog, I think you should give her a name.'

'Yeah,' said Chris. 'I suppose so. What's a good name for a dog?'

'Biter,' muttered Seth, rubbing his arm where the dog had bitten him. It hadn't actually broken his skin. In fact, Chris thought it had probably only torn his sleeve. Now that the girl had calmed the dog down, it didn't seem remotely dangerous.

The vicar chuckled. 'Greyhounds aren't usually known for being aggressive. In fact, they make very affectionate and loyal companions.'

'It's a greyhound?' said Chris. He hadn't really studied the dog properly before. All dogs looked the same to him. This one was quite large, but very thin, almost hollowed-out in places, with bones very clearly visible beneath its skin. Its head was small, with a long muzzle and small, folded ears. Its eyes looked intelligent and were now quite placid. The dog had short, smooth fur the colour of fudge or light caramel, with a white neck and underbelly.

'I will call her Nutmeg,' said the girl.

'A lovely name,' said the vicar approvingly.

'Talking of names,' said Chris to the girl, 'you still haven't told us yours. We don't really know who you are.'

The girl turned her penetrating green eyes on him, holding his gaze for a moment before he looked away. 'Rose,' she said. 'My name is Rose Hallibury and my family are all dead. Is there anything else you want to know?'

Chapter Ten

West Field Terrace, South London, waning moon

Vijay Singh stood in the middle of the street, staring at the black void that seemed to swallow all hope and happiness. Tears streamed freely down his hot cheeks. The space that Rose Hallibury's house had occupied the day before was now a burned-out shell. Its brick facade was blackened. The chimney stack and half of the roof had caved in. No glass remained in the windows, and the green-painted door that he had knocked on just a few short hours before was completely gone. The front room where he had kneeled before Rose and told her that he loved her had been reduced to empty blackness.

All life was gone.

Rose was dead. Her kid brother, Oscar, was dead. Vijay had risked everything to steal life-saving medicine for the boy, and it had been for nought. Now the twisted wreckage of Oscar's wheelchair stood silently in the front garden.

Vijay's heroic act had not saved Oscar, nor had it swayed Rose when he'd confessed his love to her. She had rejected him. But that didn't change the way he felt about her. He would never stop loving her, even if she didn't love him back.

He choked on his tears. A dead person could never love him back, could never love anyone again.

It wasn't possible that Rose's bright hair and beautiful face were gone. It simply wasn't.

A neighbour had told him what happened. The fire had started not long after he had left last night. Rose herself had set the house ablaze according to eye witnesses, though why she would have done such a thing Vijay couldn't imagine. Had his declaration of love somehow caused her to act in that mad way? If so, he was responsible for her death. The fire service had been called, but they had been too busy attending major fires across the capital city, including the blaze that had engulfed the nearby hospital. By the time they finally arrived, in the early hours of the morning, the house was already destroyed, all hope gone.

Grey ash spilled out of the ruined building and blew around the deserted street, drifting like the snow that had fallen during the night. Somehow the ash was the worst thing. To think that a family's home and accumulated belongings could be reduced to this lifeless residue. Furniture, photographs, clothes, books, all turned to a colourless dust.

His face paled. The ash was more than just mere possessions. It was the stuff of life itself. Skin, bones, hair. The bodies of Rose and Oscar had been cremated inside their own home, their flesh consumed by the raging fire.

The thought of crimson flames licking at Rose's red hair was too much for him to take. He would not accept it as truth. The firefighters had pulled no survivors from the blaze, only Oscar's charred body, but they might easily have missed something. In some small corner, Rose might have found a hiding place. She could have crawled into that space and be there now, still alive, buried under rubble, desperate for help, her faint cries unheeded. She had to be. She couldn't be dead.

He let out a strangled cry and began to stumble forward.

The property had been sealed off with yellow tape and warning signs, but that couldn't stop him from entering the burned remains of the building. His foot slipped on the rubble and he fell to his hands and knees. But a moment later he was back on his feet and scrabbling forward. He would pick his way through the wreckage with his bare hands if he had to. He would lift every brick, shift each blackened timber beam, sift through every ember and heap of smouldering ash if there was just the smallest chance of finding her –

A hand grabbed him from behind and held him fast.

'Let me go!' he shouted angrily, his arms flailing for balance. He spun round to see who was keeping him from entering the building.

The hand belonged to Drake Cooper.

Drake and Vijay had been implacable enemies once, but now Drake was Vijay's best friend, his only true friend. Drake had run with him when they'd escaped from the killer headmaster at school. They'd fought together on the night of New Year's Eve, facing racist thugs and then werewolves. And Drake had been his partner in crime when they'd broken into the butcher's shop to steal the medicines for Oscar. But now he was trying to stop Vijay from searching for Rose.

Vijay lashed out at him. 'You can't stop me!' he shouted. 'I'm going to look for Rose. She must be in there somewhere. She might still be alive!' He shook himself free of Drake's grip, turned, and began to scrabble back toward the house.

Drake hauled him back again, holding on to him with

two hands this time. 'You can't go inside. It ain't safe. Just feel the heat coming off it.'

Vijay could feel it. Despite the freezing weather, the blackened bricks of the house still radiated heat. Inside the ruined building, it must be even hotter. Among the ashes, bright embers glowed like coals in a dying fire.

'No one could be in there,' said Drake. 'She's gone. You know she is.'

'No,' wailed Vijay, but he knew that Drake was right. The fierce determination that had animated him just a moment before drained from him like water sinking through sand. He crumpled and leaned against Drake, clutching his friend weakly for support.

'No one could have survived that fire,' said Drake. 'And if you go looking inside, you're likely to end up dead too.'

His friend spoke the truth. Vijay began to sob again, a fresh wave of tears rolling down his cheeks. If only he could have been here last night when the fire started. He would have cried enough to douse the flames. He would have done anything to save Rose and Oscar.

'Why didn't they put out the fire quicker?' he asked. 'Why did Rose and Oscar have to die?'

'Ain't no reason, mate,' said Drake, gripping him by the shoulders. 'These things just happen.'

Vijay shook his head. 'It didn't just happen,' he said angrily. 'They said that Rose did it, that she started the fire herself. But how can that be true? Why would she have done that?'

Drake shrugged. 'Dunno. Did you give her the drugs for Oscar?'

'Yeah. Of course.'

'Then something must have happened afterwards.'

Vijay nodded. He knew what that was. Guilt flooded him, washing away his anger. He had handed over the stolen medication not to save Oscar, but as a way of impressing Rose. He had gone to her and told her that he loved her, as if her love was somehow his reward for doing good. But Rose didn't love him back. How could he have imagined that she would? She had turned him away instead.

So had the fire been his fault? Had he upset her so much that she'd decided to end her own life, and Oscar's too? He couldn't accept it. There must be some other explanation.

'You know that their parents are dead too?' asked Drake.

'Yes,' said Vijay, more tears running from his eyes.

'They say that Mr Harvey killed them. They say he's a werewolf.'

'That's a lie!' yelled Vijay, pushing himself away from Drake. His former Biology teacher was no werewolf. He was one of the kindest, bravest men Vijay knew. 'Mr Harvey would never have hurt Rose's parents!'

Drake shrugged again. 'I'm just telling you what people are saying. I don't know nothing.'

'It's a lie,' repeated Vijay. But what did he know about anything? His entire world had been shaken by its foundations and upended. There was nothing left now, just embers and ashes.

'Come on,' said Drake, leading him away from the burned-out house. 'Ain't nothing more to see here.'

Vijay nodded mutely. Drake was right. There was nothing more for him to do. Nothing he did now could possibly make any difference. It was all too late. Far too late. He allowed Drake to lead him down the street, away from the home that had once been Rose's.

The wind lifted the dust and whirled it around the street. Soon it would all blow away, and all traces of Rose would be gone completely. There was no one to remember her, only Vijay. But Vijay would never forget. He would carry Rose in his heart for ever.

Chapter Eleven

Cabinet Office Briefing Room A, Whitehall, Central London

The motion of no confidence was defeated, but it was a close call, much closer than the Prime Minister had anticipated. Some of her own side had backed the Leader of the Opposition in his demand for her to be removed. It would seem that not everyone shared her views on the need for decisive military action. They did not see the enemy in the way that she did. But at the final count the numbers fell in her favour and in politics that was all that mattered.

Her first act after defeating the motion was to dissolve Parliament. She could not risk another near-defeat or worse. From now on she would govern directly through a War Cabinet, invoking royal prerogative to silence opposition and remove obstacles to her leadership.

The Leader of the Opposition had warned her explicitly against such actions, quoting Friedrich Nietzsche during his speech this morning. 'Whoever fights monsters should see to it that in the process he does not become a monster,' he had told the House. 'Or in this case, that *she* does not become a monster.'

She did not want to become a dictator, but she would not hesitate to act like one if that's what it took to defend her country and its people. She would have much preferred to lead a cooperative government of national unity. During the Second World War, Churchill had created a cross-party War Cabinet to run the country. But the Leader of the Opposition himself had made that an impossibility.

She travelled to the first meeting of her War Cabinet straight from Parliament, fighting exhaustion. A brief half-hour of rest had been snatched between sessions in the House of Commons but she had not slept properly for over twenty-four hours. She didn't know when she would be able to sleep again.

When she arrived, her advisers were already waiting for her. She took her place at the head of the huge mahogany table in the Cabinet Office in Whitehall and stared grimly at the few dozen men and women seated around it. Each one was hand-picked and loyal. Ministers of State, Secretaries of State, the Chief of the Defence Staff, the Metropolitan Police Commissioner, the Director-General of MI5, together with their advisers and personal assistants. She would have to rely on these men and women to stop her becoming an autocrat. To stop her becoming a monster. She hoped they were strong enough to do that.

The one person missing was her scientific adviser, Doctor Helen Eastgate. The PM would need to continue without her most trusted friend and ally.

She studied the faces ranged around the conference table. The Home Secretary was a grey man, always choosing the safest course. But he was hard-working, diligent and efficient. The Foreign Secretary and the

Chancellor of the Exchequer were two of her closest allies, unswervingly loyal and calm in a crisis. The Director-General of MI5 was a heavyweight and had already proved himself useful in bringing Doctor Helen Eastgate to the Prime Minister's attention. The Metropolitan Police Commissioner was another dependable ally. To her dismay the Mayor of London had sided with the Opposition and was no longer present in the room. But the man she would depend on most over the coming days and weeks was the Chief of the Defence Staff, General Sir Roland Ney.

General Ney rose to his feet now to deliver the first of the morning's briefings. As far as the PM knew, the General had slept no more than she had, but seemed indefatigable and as indomitable as ever with his bull-like stance. His short hair had taken on a cold steel glint beneath his peaked cap. His thick silver monobrow ran parallel to his square shoulders. The only colour the General wore was a wall of bright medals across his broad chest.

'Prime Minister, I wish that I could offer you reassurance that all is well,' he began, 'but unfortunately that is not the case. The lycanthropes inflicted a significant defeat on our forces last night when they attacked the quarantine hospital. Their victory was as decisive as it was unexpected, and I will be the first to admit that we were inadequately prepared. Although some of the fleeing lycanthropes were shot and killed, we estimate that some three hundred may have escaped from the hospital. Some of them are now armed. They are openly attacking civilians, and people are being bitten and infected at unprecedented rates. The quarantine hospital was destroyed in the attack and we now have no capabilities for confining patients infected with the disease.'

Three hundred escaped. It was worse than she had feared.

'What do you suggest we do with the infected, then, General?' asked the Foreign Secretary.

The General did not hesitate to reply. 'I suggest we

shoot them on sight. We have no other option.'

The PM winced at the General's words, but she remained silent, waiting for him to continue. There was no room now for anything other than the absolute truth, no matter how unpalatable it may be. *Seek truth from facts*, she reminded herself.

'The attack on the hospital was not the only defeat we suffered last night,' continued the General. 'Army checkpoints were attacked by wolves, and soldiers were killed. Again, weapons were taken from the fallen men. Many buildings were set on fire, leading to significant loss of life. Criminal gangs engaged in violent acts under cover of the chaos, leading to police casualties, not to mention the murder of civilians. All told, it was a bad night for the forces of order. We were perhaps too complacent.'

The old general paused, stony-faced, as if considering how best to handle his next piece of news. When it came, he delivered it like a punch to the PM's stomach. 'The reason for our failure was quite simply that we seriously under-estimated the size and capability of our enemy. The number of lycanthropes active in London is not a few hundred as we had believed. Based on the reports of the enemy's activity last night, our experts now think that as many as five thousand lycanthropes may be operating in the capital.'

'Five *thousand*?' repeated the PM. 'How could there be so many?'

The General stood tall, his hands clasped behind his back. 'Our intelligence was inadequate. The disease is spreading faster than first thought, and the lycanthropes have succeeded in avoiding our attention. It is clear now that they have certain skills that enable them to move with stealth. They are intelligent and resourceful, and above all organized. We had not suspected such a high degree of discipline and cooperation. It has cost us dearly.'

The Director-General of MI5 shuffled his briefing papers awkwardly. 'Prime Minister, in fairness the situation is the same in other countries too. European and American cities are all reporting far greater werewolf activity during last night's full moon than anyone had expected. It's as if our enemy was waiting in the shadows, deliberately giving a false impression of its numbers. No one could have anticipated the true magnitude of the threat.'

The PM cast him a stern look. 'Is that so, Director-General? I thought that MI5's role was to anticipate threats. Well, there is no point in beginning an inquiry into the matter now. We do not have the time. Instead we must look to the future.'

General Ney spoke again. 'Prime Minister, I agree. And on that note I have more positive news to report. Certain actions have already been undertaken. This morning the Royal Family was moved from Buckingham Palace to Balmoral Castle in Scotland for safety.'

The Prime Minister nodded. The news felt more ominous than positive, but it was standard procedure in an emergency. In the event of her own death or incapacity, only the reigning monarch held the power to appoint a new prime minister.

The General continued. 'As you are aware, our forces currently stationed in London consist of almost eight thousand troops from the Parachute Regiment and associated forces forming 16 Air Assault Brigade. These units are highly capable and fast to react, but we need now to bolster these forces with additional soldiers. I had, in fact, already anticipated this need, despite the counsel of others.' He glared at the Director-General of MI5, who looked away, saying nothing.

'To that end,' continued the General, 'I have assembled reinforcements consisting of three armoured infantry brigades, plus a force of infantry battalions drawn from several regiments. Specialized logistical brigades are standing by to support them. In total, a large fighting corps numbering some tens of thousands of men and women is now ready and at our disposal.'

This was certainly news to the Prime Minister. 'And where are these forces now, General?'

'To the immediate west of London, awaiting my command. With your permission, Prime Minister, I will give the order for them to enter the city today.'

A positive murmuring greeted the General's announcement and the mood around the table seemed to noticeably lift. 'What about the police?' enquired the Police Commissioner. 'Can they be of assistance?'

The General answered his question. 'I anticipate that they will have a key role supporting the army within the city, and also in the continued enforcement of law and order. We will need all the help we can muster. I would add that the Royal Air Force is available to supply close air support to our ground forces. Number 11 Fighter Squadron based at RAF Coningsby in Lincolnshire is in a state of high readiness. Typhoon Eurofighter jets can be scrambled and in the air over London in six minutes. They are equipped with Paveway laser-guided bombs, Storm Shadow cruise missiles and Brimstone anti-tank missiles. In addition we have fifth-generation F-35Bs with stealth capabilities that can operate alongside the Typhoons.' The General returned to his seat.

'I hardly imagine that we will need stealth aircraft and cruise missiles to engage with werewolves,' remarked the Home Secretary. 'Unless they are driving tanks now.'

The General was back on his feet in an instant. 'We should learn from our previous mistakes,' he said sternly. 'To underestimate our enemy for a second time would be an unforgivable dereliction of duty.'

The Prime Minister weighed the General's words carefully. His reputation as a military hard man was known to all, and he had already acted brutally in the few short weeks that the army had been operational in London. She feared what he might do in her name. The array of weaponry he had just listed was chilling. And yet she could not deny the gravity of the situation. The threat facing the country, and indeed the world, was existential.

Churchill had faced the threat of invasion by a foreign enemy, but this war was different. The enemy soldiers were already here, walking alongside ordinary people, invisible and deadly. And their numbers were growing, day by day. As far as she could tell, their enemy did not seek simply to invade and occupy. Its aim was to subdue and to kill, perhaps even to exterminate. It must be resisted with every means available. When this struggle for survival was over – if it ever was – she knew that a long list of regrets would haunt her. She did not want her biggest regret to be that the war had been lost because of her inaction.

'Do it,' she said. 'I authorize the immediate movement of land forces into the city. We must minimize civilian casualties, and to do that we must act decisively and deliberately. Keep air support on standby, and make sure that I am briefed of any new developments.' The time for half-measures was over. If she was going to become a dictator, she might as well embrace the role to the best of her abilities.

The General had not quite finished. 'There is one further matter, Prime Minister. The so-called People's Uprising is gaining momentum. We must stamp out this rebellion, else it will consume our energies just as we struggle to defeat the lycanthropes.'

The People's Uprising comprised a mixed bag of civil rights protesters and would-be revolutionaries. There had been enough trouble already with rioters, vigilantes and criminal gangs. Now this new group talked openly of overthrowing the government. The idea that she was their target filled the PM with dismay. In previous times, she might have had some sympathy with their anti-authoritarian stance. She had long campaigned for open government and the rolling back of the powers of the state. But the emergency situation was fuelling a lurch toward extremism and violent confrontation. The leaders of that movement were spreading their subversive messages across social media like wildfire. And now the Leader of the Opposition had expressed support for those messages. He had as good as declared himself to be her enemy.

'What do you suggest, General?'

'The Leader of the Opposition and the Mayor of London are both openly supporting the forces of disorder. They must be arrested immediately.'

The PM winced. 'Is there no other way, General?'

The General said nothing. They both knew the answer to her question.

'Arrest them, then.' Her orders were coming thick and fast now, and she liked the sound of none of them. She was following a seamless progression from popular leader to authoritarian oppressor, seemingly without choice. If she was not careful, a line would soon be crossed. Perhaps it already had been.

Did she already wear the garb of the monster the Leader of the Opposition had warned her about? She wondered what the other men and women in this room saw when they looked at her face. What frightened her most was that she could no longer tell.

Chapter Twelve

High Street, Brixton Hill, South London, waning moon

Liz and Dean spent the morning going door to door, speaking to all the residents, interviewing those who had witnessed the killings of the night before, finding out what they knew, and seeking to reassure them. Most people seemed happy that the police were taking charge and that the perpetrators were dead. A few expressed reservations about what they had seen. One or two gave Liz fearful looks. They had seen too much, it seemed. But no one accused her openly of being a monster.

Dean did most of the talking, doing his best to calm people's nerves. 'These are not normal times,' he told them, as if that could justify what they had witnessed. 'But don't worry. You're safe now.'

But still some people could not look Liz in the eye.

'Do you think they'll talk?' she asked when she and

Dean had left the last house.

'They might gossip. But I don't think any of them will go to the authorities. And even if they did, who would believe their version of events? I can hardly believe what I saw myself. You were like a wild thing, all teeth and nails. And so fast. You were just a blur.'

Liz put out an arm to stop him. 'It scared me, Dean. I might have killed you last night. If the moon hadn't gone behind a cloud when it did, I don't know if I could have stopped.'

'Yeah. That thought crossed my mind too. But so far you've only ever attacked the bad guys, right?'

'I can't take the risk,' she told him. 'Next full moon I must stay indoors. I would have done this time if it hadn't been for Kevin's stupidity.'

'Yeah, sure,' he agreed. 'That sounds like a good plan. We'll all stay in and drink cocoa next time.'

'I'm serious.'

'Me too. I like cocoa.'

Next they took the bodies of the three dead Serbians to the derelict factory nearby. They used the Serbians' own white van to transport the corpses. They had been here before, to dispose of two men Dean had shot and killed when they'd attacked Samantha in her home. By the end of the morning, three more shallow graves had been dug and filled. Disposing of dead bodies was becoming a habit. Liz hoped and prayed they wouldn't have to go back there a third time.

'I'm exhausted,' she said, leaning on her spade when they'd finished. 'Let's go home.'

Home was now above the butcher's shop. When they returned they found Samantha busily making up the beds and putting out towels. Kevin and Mihai were helping, moving furniture around and doing whatever Samantha commanded. They had scrubbed the tiled floor where the dead men had lain overnight and opened some upstairs windows to allow cold, clean air to remove the smells of mustiness and neglect – not to mention the stink of meat and blood from the butcher's shop downstairs. Samantha and Lily had placed sachets of dried lavender in the bedrooms to freshen them up.

'It's a big house,' said Samantha, smiling. 'There's plenty of room for all of us here. And with a little work it could be quite cheerful. Dean and Kevin can give the walls a fresh coat of paint, and I'll find some new curtains and cushions. It just needs a woman's touch,' she added, giving Liz a wink.

'This is your room, love,' said Kevin. 'What do you think?'

'Nice,' said Liz. In truth she would have been happy with anything. Interior design had never been her thing, and soft furnishings were far from being her top priority right now. She was much more interested in Mihai. The boy still hadn't spoken a word to her since the previous night. In fact he seemed to be taking pains to avoid her. He shuffled out of the room now, Kevin following him. 'All right, Mihai?' she called after him, but he vanished without looking back.

'Is something wrong with Mihai?' she asked Samantha.

'He does seem a bit quiet. Hardly surprising after what happened.'

'Sure,' said Liz. She followed the boy downstairs and into the store room at the back of the shop. He and Kevin were rummaging inside some cardboard boxes. 'Hi,' she said. 'Everything okay?'

Mihai looked up sharply and hid behind Kevin.

'Hey, what's wrong with you?' Kevin asked him. 'It's only Liz.'

The Romanian boy shook his head and said nothing. His eyes were filled with fear.

The boy had shown no fear last night when he'd jumped at one of the Serbian gangsters to stop him firing his gun. She wondered if he was still shaken up after seeing her kill two men. But Kevin had also shot and killed a man, and he seemed perfectly okay with that. 'What is it, Mihai?' she asked softly.

He shook his head.

'Come on,' she insisted. 'Something's wrong. I can tell.'

'Is *pricolici*,' he said, pointing at her.

'Is that a Romanian word? I don't know what it means.'

The boy was evidently struggling to express himself. '*Pricolici*,' he repeated. Then, '*Nosferatu*.'

Baffled, Liz looked at Kevin, who shrugged.

'*Vampir*,' said Mihai at last.

'What? A vampire?'

'*Vampir*, yes.' The boy nodded vigorously. 'You drink blood,' he accused. 'When you kill man last night, you drink his blood. I see it.'

She stared at him incredulously. The boy was completely serious. 'I did swallow a mouthful of blood,' she admitted. 'But I didn't mean to. I didn't want to. It was just that …' her voice trailed off. She had gulped the men's blood down in great mouthfuls. A kind of bloodlust had taken hold of her. But it was gone now. 'Vampires aren't real, Mihai,' she said gently.

He reached out cautiously and touched her arm. 'Is real.'

'But Liz ain't no vampire,' said Kevin, chuckling.

Mihai wasn't laughing. 'Is not funny. Is many vampires in Romania. Is very bad monster.'

Liz shook her head. 'Mihai, vampires are a myth. A legend. They're simply folk tales.'

'No, is real,' he insisted. 'Is just like werewolf.'

Liz frowned. She could hardly deny that werewolves were real. And she had been infected with the disease that turned some people into wolves. But she hadn't become a wolf, so what was she, exactly?

'I've seen vampires on the telly,' said Kevin. 'Not real ones, like. Just in stories. Now I'm no expert, but I know that to become a vampire you have to die and then rise from the dead, right?' He seemed pleased to have skewered Mihai's argument.

But Mihai nodded vigorously. 'Just like Liz. She rise from dead. I see it. She get sick. Then die. Then come back again. At first I thought all was good. But was bad. Was very, very bad.'

Liz stood open-mouthed, wondering what on earth he meant. Was he talking about when she'd been scratched by that maniac up on Clapham Common? That was when she'd first become infected with the disease, whatever it was. *Lycanthropy*, the experts were calling it. Her memories of that time were pretty hazy. She had been sick with flu symptoms for a week before collapsing on Christmas Eve. Her father had tended to her for several days while she lay in bed with a fever.

'But I didn't die,' she protested. 'I was just ill for a few days.' She looked at her father. 'Tell him what happened. Tell him I didn't die!'

'Yeah, well,' said Kevin awkwardly. 'You was pretty much out of it for a while, love. You was unconscious for a few days. Out of it completely. Dead to the world, like. At one point I almost thought ...' He trailed off.

'Thought what?' shouted Liz.

'I thought that you really had died.'

'What?'

'Yeah, well, I didn't mention it, cos I didn't want to worry you or nothing, but you kind of stopped breathing for a bit. Not long. A minute, maybe a couple. Five minutes, tops. I tried to find a pulse, but I couldn't find nothing. Mihai looked too. Couldn't find one. You even started to turn a bit blue around the edges. I was gonna call the doctor, but then you started up again, right as rain. I didn't think you was really dead, though,' he added sheepishly. 'I mean, not *really*.'

'You didn't *think* I was dead? You weren't completely sure?'

'Yeah, well, I'm no doctor, am I? I was just doing my best. You're okay now, ain't you?'

She glared at him. 'Let me tell you this, Dad, I am one hundred percent *not* okay. I am so far from being okay that I don't know where to begin. You saw for yourself what happens to me under the light of the full moon. And now you're telling me that I might have died while you were looking after me?'

Mihai was hiding behind Kevin again and she realized just how angry she had become. She breathed deeply to calm herself back down. The last thing she needed now was to get mad with Kevin. She might end up losing more than just her temper. She might scare Mihai away for good.

Kevin was shuffling his feet and fiddling with his hands. 'Yeah, well, you ain't dead now, are you?' he said. He turned to Mihai. 'She ain't no vampire either, kid, so don't go saying that.'

Mihai didn't look at all reassured. 'Is *nosferatu*,' he said again. 'Is *vampir*.' He made the sign of the cross with his right hand.

Liz stared at him in dismay. The boy really believed it. He was petrified. And maybe he was right to be scared of her. She was definitely *some* kind of monster. And if not a werewolf, then a vampire made as much or as little sense as anything.

'Just hang on a minute,' said Kevin. 'I've got an idea. A test, like. There's some garlic in the kitchen. Let me grab a handful of that.' He disappeared and was back a moment later with a string of white garlic bulbs. He waved them in Liz's face.

'Hey!' she cried, fending him off.

Kevin and Mihai looked dismayed.

'Try it again,' she said. 'But don't whack me round the head with them this time.'

Kevin lifted the garlic again, and this time Liz stood still and let him drape the string around her neck. She wondered if the garlic would do something terrible to her, but nothing happened. 'I'll even eat some,' she said. She snapped a clove off one of the garlic bulbs and took a cautious nibble. The garlic burned her tongue and its papery skin stuck to her lips, but she munched it until it was gone, forcing herself to swallow every last bit. Its juice burned her throat like bleach. When she was finished she forced something akin to a smile, or perhaps a grimace, onto her face. 'Convinced?' she asked Mihai. 'Or do you still want to hammer a stake through my heart?'

The boy said nothing. Instead, he pulled at the fine silver chain that he wore around his neck. A silver cross dangled from it. He solemnly lifted the chain over his head and held the cross in front of Liz's face.

She braced herself in case the holy symbol made her flee in fear, but it had no effect. She did her best to smile.

The boy came closer and pressed the silver cross against her forehead.

Liz held her breath and felt its cool touch kiss her skin.

He pulled it away and examined the place that it had touched.

'See,' said Kevin with a look of relief. 'It ain't left no mark. It didn't burn her or nothing. Liz ain't no vampire.'

Mihai put the chain back over his head. He said nothing, but still didn't look convinced.

Liz breathed out. She wasn't entirely convinced either.

Chapter Thirteen

Upper Terrace, Richmond upon Thames, West London, waning moon

By the time Melanie Margolis began to stir from sleep, the day was almost done. There was nothing unusual or surprising about that. She was a night owl, acting out the waking fantasy of her life while respectable people slept at home in bed, only dreaming of the kinds of things that Melanie got up to. *Before sunrise* was early enough for a girl like her to return home, especially if the champagne was flowing freely and the company was sweet. The only reason for her to venture out during daylight hours was if one of her clients wanted to meet for lunch. She would always make an exception to her routine for black-truffle risotto at Stefano's or an *hors d'oeuvres* of Norfolk crab at the Ritz.

She rolled over lazily in her soft, wide bed, wrapped in nothing but silk sheets and the loosening threads of sleep that clung to her still.

Her sister always chided her of course, warning her that the pursuit of pleasure and fleeting gratification would inevitably lead to tears.

There must be some grain of truth in that, Melanie supposed, especially since Sarah had read it in a book. There had certainly been tears from time to time. But nothing that a fresh application of mascara couldn't hide. And so far the gratification outweighed the tears by a long way.

In any case, a life consisting of late-night encounters in expensive restaurants and trendy bars followed by parties in exclusive clubs and luxurious homes certainly beat a daily commute and the smothering dullness of a job in an office.

Or did it? Perhaps as Sarah annoyingly insisted, Melanie's glamorous lifestyle might be nothing more than a thin veil designed to conceal a tormented soul with emptiness at its heart. Those words had surely also been found in a book.

Melanie stirred, her eyes fluttering open as the late afternoon light began slowly to fade. Whatever truth Sarah's pseudo-psychobabble might contain, that way of thinking was never going to pay the bills. Someone needed to be the breadwinner in this house, and that role had always fallen to Melanie. Whatever Sarah said, Melanie had always succeeded in bringing home the money the two sisters needed to survive.

She yawned and rolled over again. The bedding on the other half of the bed was disarrayed where Ben had slept.

Ben Harvey.

She sat up, suddenly fully awake. How could she have forgotten about Ben? She had slept so soundly she had completely forgotten the drama of rescuing him and bringing him home with her last night.

I saved him from a werewolf.

The thought was absurd. But true.

Ben loves me.

That thought was equally unbelievable. But also true.

One long night had changed her life forever. Her single-girl nights of partying were over. Her bad-girl days of living off the stolen riches of wealthy men were also gone.

I will never leave Ben again.

Another truth, as ridiculous and yet as real as the others.

But where was he? She was alone in her room. She swept the sheets aside and slid out of bed. A slight bruising on her side was the only physical reminder of a night spent battling werewolves and rescuing Ben from his captors. She threw on some clothes and headed downstairs.

It was hard to believe that after years of thinking only for herself, she had risked her life to save another. It was a good feeling though. She would take the risk again, without question.

And she had saved James too, repaying the debt she owed him for saving her own life.

I promised James I would change. That I would become a better person.

It seemed like she was already beginning to do that.

She hurried on down the stairs and found Ben, James and Sarah in the living room, engaged in some heated conversation. All three looked grim. They broke off as she made her entrance.

Ben stood tall and broad, his face clean-shaven again, his hair combed neatly. The rugged, battered looks of recent days had gone, and he looked well-rested and in good health. But his face was stern, and he stood apart from the others.

James would almost have matched Ben for height if his shoulders hadn't been hunched in a stoop. He looked like a sick animal, his fair hair and sandy beard grown long, thick and straggly. His cheeks and neck bore raw red scratches where Leanna had mauled him. Bite marks on his throat, and the ill-fitting clothes that hung loose from his emaciated frame completed his wasted looks.

Sarah stood behind him, wearing a worried, frightened frown.

'Hi,' said Melanie. 'Good morning, or whatever it is.'

Ben turned as she entered and a smile cracked the granite facade of his face. 'You call this morning?' he said. 'It's just after four o'clock in the afternoon. But I'm glad to see you.'

She let him wrap his strong arms around her, and gave him a quick kiss in return. 'What's up?' she asked.

'James needs food badly,' replied her sister. 'He hasn't eaten for a whole month. He's literally starving to death.'

Melanie stared at the skinny boy. James had been thin for as long as she'd known him. How long had that been? One month exactly, from full moon to full moon. Sarah was right. She couldn't remember James eating a mouthful of food the whole time he'd been living with them. His body was dangerously thin.

A pang of guilt thrust its way up inside her throat. The problem had been plain to see all along. She had known from the outset that James was unable to eat normal food. Yet she had done nothing about it, had barely even given it a thought. 'So what are we going to do about it?' she asked.

Sarah replied. 'Ben thinks we should give him some meat.'

'Okay,' said Melanie. 'Why is that a problem?'

'Because we don't have any. We have very little food left in the house at all.'

'Sarah tells me that James has been going out to find food for you,' said Ben.

'That's right,' said Melanie. More guilt stabbed at her like a spear. She and Sarah had come to depend on James for even this most basic requirement. How would they have coped without him to help them? And what had they given him in return?

'So where have you been going to get food?' Ben asked

James.

The boy spoke for the first time and his voice sounded strangely weak. 'Most shops are closed. They're boarded up, burned out or shut down. The nearest food shop I found was the one where you were working.'

Ben frowned. 'Kowalski's supermarket? In Brixton?'

'We can't go back there, Ben,' said Melanie quickly. 'If you show your face around Brixton, those jerks from the Neighbourhood Watch will find you. We broke you out once, we're not going to let them get you again.'

'I know,' said Ben.

'We'll just have to find somewhere else,' said Melanie. 'Ben, you come with me. We'll go looking.'

'What now?'

She glanced at James again. He had lowered himself into a chair and looked desperately weak. 'Yes. Come on. You can wear some of Grandpa's old clothes.'

Ben had come to the house with nothing but the outfit he was wearing, and that didn't include a winter coat. Grandpa's old things might have long since fallen out of fashion but they were made to withstand the British winter weather. 'Here,' said Melanie, picking out some items from one of the old wardrobes in a room off the hallway. 'Try these for size.'

She grabbed a coat and some money for herself while he dressed. Ben followed her out into the cold, swathed in an old black coat and a thick fedora hat. A long scarf wrapped his neck and trailed almost to the ground. 'I feel like a *film noir* extra,' he joked.

'You look very glamorous.' She slid one arm through his as they walked down the road in the direction of Twickenham, away from Brixton. 'I still can't believe that we're living together now,' she said. 'That you're sharing my bed.'

He chuckled. 'A guy needs to take the best deal available. Salma Ali locked me in her dungeon. Your offer seemed more appealing.'

She punched him gently in pretend outrage. 'I still don't fully understand this Neighbourhood Watch business, or who Salma Ali is. Why did they imprison you? They said you were a werewolf.'

His face grew serious again. 'That was a false accusation, obviously. I tried to topple Salma Ali from power. She's the self-appointed leader of the Watch in Brixton. The Watch is basically a front for her to take control of the district. People are scared stupid because of the looting and rioting, not to mention the werewolves. She promised to protect them. Foolishly, I helped her. When I eventually woke up to the truth, it was too late for me to stop her.'

'There's nothing like that happening around here,' said Melanie. 'Just a kind of anarchy. The police seem powerless to stop it. Patrol cars rush past, but normal law and order has come to a halt. It's every man and woman for themselves now.'

'The world is falling apart faster than I could have imagined,' said Ben. 'I hope that the army will take control soon. The police certainly can't cope.'

'I don't really understand how it all happened,' said Melanie. 'One day the news was reporting a string of murders, and just a month or so later, we're in a war zone.'

'It's happened quickly,' agreed Ben. 'We've become like one of those war-torn countries we used to see on the news. It was an illusion to think that we were different, that our country could never become like that. We should have taken more notice, I suppose. Civilization only works if the majority of people are committed to the rule of law. Once people become too hungry and frightened, they start to not care about ideas like law and justice. They're too busy just trying to survive.'

They walked along the road, passing burned-out and barricaded shops and offices. A few people passed them by, but nobody spoke. They kept their eyes to the ground, or regarded them warily. Once a police patrol car zoomed past, lights flashing, siren blaring.

'What about James?' asked Ben. 'What's going to happen to him now?'

'What do you mean?' asked Melanie. 'He'll stay with us.'

'Will he? He's a werewolf. Can we really just feed him scraps of meat and hope he doesn't become dangerous? Werewolves eat people. Did you know that he completely trashed his room today? His strength is incredible, even in human form, even after not eating for a month. He turned his furniture into firewood. I don't know how far we can trust him.'

Melanie spun angrily to face Ben. '*I* trust him absolutely. James isn't like other werewolves. He's not a monster.'

'Has he ever killed anyone?'

'He killed once to save my life,' she admitted. 'But he hasn't killed since then.'

'As far as you know,' said Ben. 'I don't know how you can trust him so easily.'

'You're only here thanks to him,' said Melanie. 'James saved your life. Don't ever forget that. And don't make me choose between you and him.' She threw the words at him, challenging him to respond.

At last Ben nodded. 'I'm sorry,' he said. 'I shouldn't have doubted you.'

'No. You shouldn't.'

They carried on together, no longer arm in arm. The last pale light of evening was fading as they walked. Eventually they found a small shop whose doors were open. It was small, really just a convenience store, the kind of place Melanie once might have gone to buy a pint of milk or a newspaper. A couple of wide-shouldered bouncers guarded the entrance, warming their hands over a fiery brazier. A long line of people waited outside, wrapped up warm and carrying bags.

Melanie and Ben joined them. They waited nearly an

hour, talking little. Melanie shivered in the cold. Her coat was stylish, but too thin – unlike the warm trench coat Ben was wearing. She really ought to learn to dress more sensibly. Ben offered her his scarf, but she shook her head, still mad at him.

Eventually it was their turn. The shopkeeper agreed to give them a basket of food in return for all their money.

'All of it?' protested Ben. 'Are you serious? That's more than five hundred pounds.'

The shopkeeper shrugged. 'Money isn't worth so much these days. You are lucky I still accept it.'

'Here, take it,' said Melanie, handing him the wad of banknotes. 'We need fresh meat. What do you have? Beef, pork, chicken? It doesn't matter as long as it's raw.'

The shopkeeper shook his head. 'Who wants raw meat? Cooked is better.' He pointed them toward a chilled area at the back. The shelves were mostly empty but a few packets of processed meat remained. 'Sausages, ham and pork slices, corned beef, chicken drumsticks. Take your pick.'

They took some of each. They had no other choice.

Chapter Fourteen

Brixton Village, South London, waning moon

Salma Ali descended the steep steps that led down to the cellar beneath her house. It was noticeably colder below ground than upstairs, and a lingering smell of damp greeted her as she reached the basement level. Until the nineteenth century this part of London had been marshland, and the foundations of the house seemed to reach back in time to that more primitive age. Down here, below street level, she could sense the bulked mass of London clay tightly pressing against the other side of the retaining wall, always seeking to reclaim this patch of ground for nature. She placed her palm against the wall, pushing back against the weight of the earth. The wall felt cool. One day the marshes might return. But not today. Today she was master of this domain.

Mr Kowalski, the Polish shopkeeper, was at her side before she could open the cellar door. 'Ms Ali, let me go in first,' he said. 'May be dangerous inside.'

Salma smiled graciously at him. The prisoner locked inside her cellar was no more dangerous than a pet poodle. All his energy and rage had long since been expended. She had sat upstairs listening to him banging on the door, screaming and shouting for release for much of last night and all through the morning. He had ceased his tantrum just after lunchtime. It was now the early evening, and she had not heard a sound from the cellar in hours.

Not that she had ever feared him. She feared no man.

She had no need of Kowalski's assistance, but she wanted him to feel important and valued. 'Thank you, Mr Kowalski,' she said. 'I am so glad I have you here to help me.' She gave him the key.

The shopkeeper twisted the key in the brass padlock fixed to the cellar door and removed the heavy chain that threaded through it. He grasped the steel bolt of the door and slid it back with a satisfying clunk. The door showed signs of being thoroughly battered, but it had held up, thanks to the heavy wooden struts that reinforced it. Ironically, it was the man who had fixed those wooden struts to the door who had ended up being locked inside.

Kowalski grunted and turned the handle with his meaty hand. The door to the cellar swung open and the Polish man stepped inside.

The cellar was a guest room, furnished with a double bed, wardrobe and a pair of comfortable armchairs upholstered in gingham fabric. Salma had selected them carefully and chosen bedding and curtains to match. She was disappointed but not surprised to see that the chairs had been upturned and used as battering rams in a futile attempt to burst open the door. The curtains had been torn down, presumably in a fit of petulance. She pursed her lips. Her prisoner was a destructive imbecile, little more than a brute. But his mistreatment of her soft furnishings was the least of his offences.

Jack Stewart.

She had set him a simple task, to lock that meddling fool Ben Harvey in the cellar, along with Richard and Jane Hallibury, and to keep watch over them. Somehow he had failed to do even that. Now the Halliburys were dead, Ben Harvey had vanished, and Stewart had ended up getting himself locked inside the cellar he was supposed to be guarding.

He was about to learn the true price of his failure.

Her prisoner was curled up on the bed. He sat up when the door opened, pulling the gingham duvet over him. Bizarrely, he appeared to be naked underneath.

Mr Kowalski's forehead creased up when he saw him. 'Jack Stewart,' he said in astonishment. 'What are you doing here?' He turned to Salma in confusion. 'I thought Ben Harvey was in here. Where has he gone?'

'It would appear that our prisoner has miraculously escaped,' said Salma. 'And that Mr Stewart here – who was supposed to be guarding him – has mysteriously swapped places with him. Somehow his clothes have vanished too. I do hope that Mr Stewart has a good explanation for what happened.'

Jack Stewart stood up, wrapping the bedding around him. 'I have been locked in here all day,' he told her angrily. 'Why didn't you let me out sooner? Didn't you hear me shouting and banging?'

'No,' said Salma raising her eyebrows in feigned surprise. 'I didn't hear a thing.' She stared at him with ill-concealed distaste. Even now he thought he was superior to her. How stupid could a man be?

She despised people like Jack Stewart. He was white and he was a man, and he took those twin privileges for granted, not even aware that he was privileged at all. He had very little to show for all the advantages of his birth. Jack Stewart deserved to be treated like an animal. It was time for the privileges he assumed so easily to be removed, and she would see to it that they were. It was payback time for the Jack Stewarts of this world, and all the men like him.

Salma Ali enjoyed no such advantages of birth. She had grown up painfully aware that she was the wrong gender, had the wrong skin colour, and practised the wrong religion too. Her parents had come to Britain from Bangladesh and had settled in the East End of London. Her mother had barely learned a word of English her whole life. Her father had resented the fact that Salma was not a boy, and had not been shy about letting her know. So she had defied her parents, firstly by refusing to cover her hair, and then by not only rejecting the man they had chosen for her to marry, but by dismissing the notion of marriage outright. She had left home at eighteen and never looked back, steadily raising herself up from her lowly origins, struggling against resistance at every step. She put herself through university and then bar school, fighting against deep-seated prejudice to become one of the few female Muslim barristers. Now the tables were turned and the world that had treated her with contempt would begin to learn how that felt.

A new power was rising and soon the government would fall. The weight of opposition forces ranged against it was simply too great – the werewolves, the vigilantes, the People's Uprising, not to mention organized gangs and petty criminals. Together they would sweep the established social structure aside, replacing order with anarchy. And when civilization collapsed, power would be seized by those with the strength and will to take it.

When that moment came, Salma did not plan to watch from the sidelines. She intended to ride that wave as far as it would carry her.

But first she had to set her own house in order. She forced her mouth into the semblance of a smile. 'Have you been locked in here since last night?' she asked Stewart in a sympathetic tone. 'You must be very hungry and thirsty now.'

The man said nothing in response. Even he seemed to

Lycanthropic

sense the sarcasm in her voice.

'And what has happened to your clothes, Mr Stewart?' she enquired. 'You seem to have mislaid them.'

He had nothing to say to that either.

'I still don't understand,' said Mr Kowalski. 'How did the prisoners escape?'

'I'm sure we can get to the bottom of this,' said Salma. 'But first, would you be kind enough to fetch a bowl with some water from the kitchen, Mr Kowalski?'

Kowalski frowned at the request, but did as she asked.

'So, are you going to let me out now?' asked Jack Stewart.

'Soon,' said Salma. 'But you'd better give me an explanation first. I can't imagine how you allowed a school teacher and a married couple to escape from a locked cellar with you guarding it.'

He shrugged his broad shoulders. He was a strongly muscular man with a hairy chest. He would have been good-looking if it wasn't for the perpetual scowl he wore on his face. As it was, he reminded her of little more than a gorilla. 'I was tricked,' he said.

'So I see,' she said. 'You weren't hard to trick, were you?'

Mr Kowalski returned, the bowl of water in his hands. 'Here you are,' he said to Salma. 'What do you want the water for?'

'I'm sure that Mr Stewart here is thirsty after his ordeal.' To Stewart, she asked, 'Are you?'

'Yes.'

'Then give him the water to drink, please, Mr Kowalski.'

The Polish man offered the bowl to the other man.

'Not like that,' said Salma sharply. 'Put it on the floor for him to drink from.'

Kowalski turned back to her. 'What?'

'You heard me. Mr Stewart needs to learn his place in the world. Put the bowl on the floor.'

The steel edge to her voice made the big Polish man obey. He lowered the bowl to the floor and backed away from it.

'Now get on your knees and drink,' said Salma to Jack Stewart.

Stewart eyed the bowl defiantly. 'You must be joking.'

Salma stared at him hard. 'If you think I am, then you have learned nothing and are going to spend a very long time locked in this cellar. By the time I decide to release you, you'll be begging to drink water from a bowl. Now if you want to get out of here today, you'll drink from that bowl. On all fours, like a dog.'

Jack Stewart shot a look of contempt at Kowalski. 'Are you just going to stand there and let her do this?'

The Polish man narrowed his eyes and flexed his arms. 'Whatever Ms Ali says. If she says drink like a dog, then drink like a dog.'

Stewart scowled briefly at the shopkeeper, then shrugged as if the words meant nothing to him. He got down on his knees next to the bowl, the bedding wrapped around his legs. 'Sure,' he said. 'Play your sick little game if you want.' He reached out to lift the bowl to his lips.

'Not like that!' shouted Salma, her voice sharp as a blade. 'Lap it with your tongue.'

Jack Stewart gave her a look of hate. Even Kowalski looked uncertain.

'Do it!' she shrieked.

Slowly, the man did as she commanded. He placed his palms on the floor and lowered his face to the bowl. She watched with satisfaction as he poked his tongue out and stuck it in the water. Soon his chin was in the bowl and he was gulping down water, mouthful after mouthful.

When he had finished he wiped his chin with the gingham duvet and looked at her again. He was only half the man he had been when she had first entered the room.

'Good,' she said. 'Very good, Mr Stewart. You are a dog now, nothing more than a dog, and you will behave like a dog and do exactly as I tell you. Do you understand?'

He nodded and bowed his head, unable to meet her gaze.

'And never forget that a bad dog gets punished, but a good dog – well – a good little doggie can expect to earn treats and be rewarded.' She smiled at him then, and had to resist a sudden urge to pat him on the head.

Chapter Fifteen

Upper Terrace, Richmond upon Thames,
West London, waning moon

A military convoy began to enter the city from the west under cover of darkness. Sarah and Grandpa watched the television as live news footage showed lines of Challenger 2 heavy tanks, Scimitar armoured reconnaissance vehicles and AS-90 artillery units with their distinctively long 155mm-calibre barrels lowered for transit. The news reporter claimed that each AS-90 could fire six rounds per minute with a range of up to eighteen miles – enough to hit almost any target in the city if the artillery unit was located centrally. With the armoured units came truck after truck carrying troops, ammunition and other supplies, and they were escorted by Wildcat attack helicopters sweeping low over the convoy, their lights flashing brilliantly in the darkening sky.

'It's war,' said Grandpa. 'Quick, go and tell Barbara. We have to go down to a bomb shelter. Somebody fetch the gas masks.'

Sarah laid a soothing hand on his arm. 'It's all right, Grandpa. We don't need to go anywhere right now. Let's wait and see what the government tells us to do, shall we?'

The old man looked up at her, confusion written on his face. 'Barbara?' he asked, hesitantly.

'I'm Sarah,' she said. 'Barbara isn't here anymore.' Barbara had been dead for twenty years, but that was just one of the many facts that Grandpa could no longer recall.

'Not here,' he said uncertainly. 'Are you sure you're not Barbara? You look just like her.'

'No, I'm Sarah,' she assured him. 'Your granddaughter. Now let's watch the news and find out what's happening.'

The military convoy wasn't travelling far this evening. Its destination was Heathrow Airport on the western edge of the city. According to a government-issued statement, this was to be the army's frontline base for the immediate future. The airport had been closed to civilian activity following the Prime Minister's announcement of the suspension of all international flights.

'These reinforcements of soldiers, vehicles and heavy weapons will strengthen the existing troop deployments in London considerably,' said the TV reporter. 'The stated objective of the army's operation is to secure the capital from further attacks by lycanthropes and by the loose coalition of forces supporting the so-called People's Uprising. The government has declared the People's Uprising to be a banned organization and has placed prominent members of the group under arrest – including the Leader of the Opposition and the Mayor of London. In addition to providing security, the military operation is intended to restrict movement of people in order to contain the spread of lycanthropy, and then – in the words of the government – to neutralize the lycanthropic threat as rapidly as possible.'

The news footage switched to show the runways and perimeter of the airport being fortified by Rapier surface-to-air missile installations.

'The Parachute Regiment – known as the Paras – is leading the operation,' continued the reporter on the ground, 'with extensive reinforcements from infantry brigades drawn from several army regiments, including the first Battalions of the Welsh, Scots and Grenadier Guards. Special forces troops including the SAS are believed to be engaged in a number of covert missions, although we do not have any information about that, for obvious reasons.'

The news changed to an interview with a defence expert who claimed that hundreds more tanks, artillery units and 'copters were available to the British Army, although on questioning he admitted that some of these were currently deployed overseas or in storage.

'And do you think that the government's objective of neutralizing the lycanthropic threat is realistic?' asked the reporter.

'Yes. But only with severe collateral damage.'

'You mean civilian casualties?'

'It isn't possible to fight an enemy of this kind without substantial civilian casualties,' said the expert. 'A quick, decisive campaign might prove to be highly destructive in the short term, but a failure to eradicate the werewolves rapidly might result in far more casualties in the long term. The number of werewolves is increasing every day. The public must understand that we are faced with an existential threat to human survival.'

The studio discussion continued with questions about the capabilities of the Royal Air Force and the Royal Navy and even whether a British government might ever sanction the use of its submarine-based nuclear warheads against its own cities *in extremis*, but as was becoming increasingly the case, no one knew anything for certain.

'I saw a boy,' announced Grandpa when the programme had finished. 'A nice boy with blonde hair and a beard.'

'Oh yes?' said Sarah, who was quite used to the way the

old man's mind veered from subject to subject, apparently without connection. For all she knew, the boy Grandpa was referring to might have been dead for half a century. She pressed the *mute* button on the TV remote.

'He sat here, by my bed, just where you're sitting now,' he continued. 'He asked me how I was. I told him … I can't really remember what I told him.'

'James?' enquired Sarah. 'Do you mean James?'

'Is that his name?,' asked Grandpa. 'Does he live here?'

'Yes, James lives with us now. His parents are dead and he has nowhere else to go.'

'I used to have a friend called James,' said Grandpa. 'In the army. We called him Jim. Don't ask me why. He was killed by a bomb.'

'I'm sorry,' said Sarah.

'He was a polite boy, that boy who came to see me, very polite. Not like most young people today, wearing their hair long and riding motorbikes. I remember what I told him now. I said that I was feeling very well, thank you, although something was missing.'

'What was missing, Grandpa?'

'A part of me, I think. I don't know what it is or where it's gone, but part of me has definitely disappeared. At least that's how it feels. That's what I told him, anyway. He said he was very sorry to hear it. Such a nice boy. Are you sure we shouldn't go to a bomb shelter now? I don't want to end up like my friend Jim.'

'No,' said Sarah. 'The government will tell us if we need to do that.'

'I had a motorbike once,' whispered Grandpa conspiratorially.

'You did?'

'Yes. I took Barbara to see a film on it. Gary Cooper and Ingrid Bergman. We sat together in the back row of the cinema. We didn't get to see a lot of that film, I can tell you,' he added wickedly.

'Grandpa!' said Sarah, pretending to be shocked. 'You

old dog.'

The old man's face turned suddenly melancholy again. 'She's gone now, you say? Barbara? She was my wife, you know. I wonder what happened to her. That boy, James. Tell him to come and visit me again soon. I get lonely sometimes. Such a nice boy. I wish more young people were like him.'

Chapter Sixteen

James crept out of the house just after evening turned to dusk. It was the witching hour, the time of twilight, when the night was still fresh and young, and anything was possible. This had been Samuel's favourite time of day, and he had taught James to love it too. They had gone hunting together at this time, when James had first changed into wolf form. He'd been so eager to experience the change, he'd insisted on going out as soon as the moon rose. He had killed for the first time in wolf form that night. He and Samuel had killed together.

He hadn't told Melanie and the others he was going out tonight. It was better that way. They might try to stop him. They would ask awkward questions, or at least Ben would, and he didn't want to answer any of Ben's questions.

The others meant well, but the cold, dead meat they had brought back from the shop was no use to him. He had eaten cooked meat when he'd first turned lycanthropic, but it had made him sick. He had tried raw meat and fish, and that had been all right at first, but once he had changed under the full moon into a fully-developed werewolf, he had only been able to consume freshly-killed prey. If he was going to stop himself from starving, he would have to become a killer again.

He slid out quietly using the back door and dashed across the lawn behind the house. The property had a large garden, much bigger than his parents' house on the edge of Clapham Common. In leafy Richmond, the houses had been built on a grand scale, some of them more like country homes than town houses. The garden here stretched for almost half an acre. It was a good place to begin hunting.

He slipped into the mixed border at the back of the lawn, in the lee of the old brick wall that encompassed the property, and waited. His wolf senses were keen, and his eyes adjusted to the darkness almost immediately. This must have been a fine garden once. Perhaps a full-time gardener had worked here. A large lawn rolled across much of the area, edged with deep borders, densely planted with trees, shrubs and perennials. Thick tendrils of ivy clambered up old oak trees. Dark green box hedges retained a distant memory of the clipped shapes they had once held. The spiky husks of last season's flowering poked like spears between tight evergreen bushes. There were lots of weeds though. More weeds than anything. Slowly they were strangling the other plants. It didn't look like Melanie and Sarah were such keen gardeners.

The light of the sun had slipped away, but the moon had yet to appear. Yet James had no trouble seeing in the dark. His other senses were strong too. After a few minutes, he began to hear the sounds of night creatures re-emerging from the undergrowth that he had disturbed.

A bird flew out of a nearby tree, wings beating quickly in the still air. James watched it go. Catching birds was no way to begin his hunt. He was weakened by lack of food, and needed easy prey. The house backed almost onto Richmond Park itself. Larger creatures must surely come out at night. Ones that were easier to catch.

He waited silently, his face hidden by the leaves of a yew tree.

After a while he heard a rustling above him, to his left. He tilted his head to see. A squirrel darted along a bare branch, highlighted by the dim light of the city sky. It stopped, paused, sniffed the air, then bounded on, its body undulating like waves as it ran from branch to branch, moving through the canopy as easily as on a flat surface.

James sat motionless, utterly soundless as the squirrel descended the trunk. It stopped once, vertically downward, its paws fixed to the bark of the tree as if glued. It sniffed, then continued to the ground, jumping clear of the tree and heading toward the grass.

It didn't make it. James' hand flashed forward, striking the squirrel's back, snapping it like a twig. His fingers closed quickly, scooping up grey fur and lifting his kill to his mouth. With careful incisions, he pulled the meat from the squirrel's body with his teeth and chewed.

It was his first meal in weeks but not the best he had ever enjoyed. The squirrel was lean and tough, hardly enough to satisfy his hunger. In fact, his hunger now felt boundless. The hot flesh of the squirrel was no more than an appetizer, enough to remind him how desperately he craved meat and sustenance.

He looked around the garden, feeling a sense approaching despair. He could not hope to live off such meagre fare. Yet what other options did he have?

A movement in the dark shifted his focus back to the hunt. A black shape moved between the shadows, slinking silently through the undergrowth.

A hunter, just like him.

A cat this time. Black.

Unlucky, but not for James.

He watched and waited as it came closer. It moved

more confidently than the squirrel, assured of its own safety. That was a mistake.

The cat padded easily forward, its movements fluid and undulating, graceful and deadly.

It stopped, one paw raised, suspended between steps. Its green eyes turned in surprise to stare at James.

He leaped, powering forward with all his speed and strength.

The cat ducked back, twisting to flee. It was fast, but not as fast as the squirrel had been.

And not as fast as James.

His hands closed around its middle. The cat tried to bite, but James bit first, severing the artery at the cat's neck, almost taking its head off. The cat was dead before it could even cry out.

James sat contentedly on the damp grass, devouring his new meal.

The cat was more satisfying than the squirrel. He chewed the meat, drank its blood, cracked open bones and sucked the sweet marrow from inside.

On balance, cats tasted better than squirrels. They weren't as fast either. Catching squirrels seemed hardly worth the effort.

When he finished, he felt stronger than he had done since he had lost Samuel. This meal he had eaten tonight was the first real food he'd tasted in more than a month. His self-imposed abstinence had almost starved him. He'd been willing to accept death, if it meant that he never had to kill again. But what use had that been? People had died anyway, despite his refusal to kill. People he should have protected.

We can find our own meaning.

Cats and squirrels were a start, but he would never recover his full strength by hunting for animals alone. A werewolf was meant to eat human meat. He had tried to deny it. He had tried to do what he thought was the right thing. But he had made the wrong choice.

His sins had blinded him with guilt, but now he saw clearly again. It was better to kill the wicked than to allow the innocent to die.

Sarah, Melanie, Ben and Grandpa. He would kill for them gladly and lay down his life for them if necessary.

And he would do more than just protect his loved ones. He would use his strength to defend the weak and the needy everywhere. This city was filled with people who needed his help. He would go out at night, patrolling the streets where criminals wandered freely under cover of darkness. Looters, muggers, murderers, and gangs. James would find them. He would hunt them down like vermin. And he would bring the justice that God had failed to deliver.

Chapter Seventeen

Whitechapel, East London, waning moon

Warg Daddy crouched low beside a rusty ironwork gatepost, veiled in the dark, his black leather jacket blending with the deep shadows of the overhanging buildings. Slasher and Meathook waited behind him, hands on knives, listening, watching.

This corner of London was old, and the darkness felt thicker here, wrapping him like a cloak. Jack the Ripper had stalked these crooked streets and lanes once, and some claimed that the ghosts of his victims haunted them still.

He rubbed at his head with his hand, pressing his thumb down hard where the pain was greatest, vainly trying to soothe it away. His skull was squeezing mercilessly tonight, pressing inward like an iron cage fixed to his crown, as if screws were drilled into the very plates of bone. Every day those metal screws seemed to twist tighter, ratcheting up the pressure, crushing his brain one quarter-turn at a time. At times like this he feared his skull would shatter, and liquid brains would burst out through his eardrums, his eyes popping from their sockets like jelly in a glorious surge of relief. He almost wished that day would come soon.

But not tonight. Tonight he had work to do.

He tilted his head back and sniffed, wrinkling his nose in concentration, taking a deep drag of the pungent urban smells. He drew them in through his flaring nostrils, enjoying the rich and fragrant bouquet the city breeze brought his way.

It was an unexpected gift, this heightened sense of smell that he had acquired as a werewolf, though it was poor compensation for the murderous headaches. He had expected to become strong and fast and agile when he turned into a wolf, and he had. He'd known that the condition would turn him into a cannibal with a lust for human flesh, and he accepted that without regret. He had known too about the yellow eyes, the teeth and claws, the coat of black fur that the moon would gift to him once every month. But he had never suspected that he would gain the super-senses that lycanthropy had blessed him with.

All of the Wolf Brothers had gained new sensory powers, but none like Warg Daddy. His senses were amplified a hundredfold. He could smell a thousand different smells, and identify the source of each one. His taste buds were as refined as those of the most experienced gourmet or connoisseur, and he had learned to enjoy the unique flavour of every one of his victims, just as a wine taster savoured the characteristics of each grape variety. He could see by night, the stars burning in the sky and illuminating the streets far below, making them clear as day. He could hear the rustle of leaves a block away, or the patter of a mouse creeping beneath the floor at midnight. Once when he was alone, and the night was still, he had stood transfixed, listening to the faintest creaking and scratching sounds of a spider spinning its web.

Now, with his finely developed sense of smell, he sampled the scents that floated along with the night wind.

Dominant, like a heavy, oaky undertone, was a cocktail of diesel particulates and exhaust fumes, much diminished since the troubles had begun, but now growing again as dirty army vehicles lumbered through streets barely wide enough to accommodate them.

The stink of the Victorian-era sewers, crisscrossing the city like a buried labyrinth, added a pungent piquancy to the mix.

Burned and charred ash from the columns of smoke that punctuated the city skyline lent an acerbic aftertaste.

On top of that he smelled cigarette smoke; food, both fresh and decaying; the trails of cats, dogs, foxes and rats. Everywhere in London was the underlying and all-pervasive aroma of people – their meat, their sweat, their stink.

And there, almost hidden by the more commonplace odours, faint but distinct, the smell he was seeking, brought to him on the icy wind that gusted hard between tall buildings. The smell of she-wolf. It came from the darkened street ahead.

He adjusted his Ray-Bans. 'Follow me,' he said to his companions.

The three crept silently through the night, slipping from shadow to shadow, searching for the slightest movement that would reveal the location of their prize. She was here somewhere, not far away. The Brothers fanned out across the street, tip-toeing, stopping, listening, then continuing on. Wolves hunting a wolf. The Leader of the Pack sniffed again. The scent was stronger now. He raised his arm and Slasher and Meathook stopped beside him.

This area of London was half derelict. The houses on this street had stood for a century, home to countless families. They had survived the fall of German bombs during the wartime Blitz, and the onslaught of wrecking balls and bulldozers during the regeneration booms of the 1980s and just before the financial crisis of 2008. Now they were barricaded up, scheduled for demolition.

Some of the abandoned buildings had fallen foul of arsonists. Their windows were boarded, their bricks blackened. Graffiti scrawled across the wooden hoardings that barred access to the houses read *Welcome 2 Hell. Please make yourself at home.* Warg Daddy stopped at the barrier. The rich resinous fragrance of the wooden panel masked the smell of wolf, but Warg Daddy was pretty certain that his quarry was hiding on the other side of the hoarding. He motioned to the others to climb over. Meathook went first, then Slasher linked his hands, forming a step for Warg Daddy to climb up. He scaled the wooden barrier quickly, hauling Slasher over too. They dropped to the other side like cats.

The row of terraced houses stretched out to left and right. Warg Daddy pointed left and they crept soundlessly over the nearest garden wall. The house here was a burned-out shell, the garden a patch of brown weeds, the doors and windows of the building boarded with thin plywood. One corner covering a ground floor window flapped loose. Warg Daddy motioned for the Brothers to enter the building.

Slasher went first, creeping cautiously through the tangle of dead plants that filled the front garden of the house. He lifted the wooden covering on the window and slipped inside, Meathook at his heels.

Warg Daddy waited and heard a screech from inside. He punched a hole in the wooden ply and hauled himself through the empty window.

A stench of death greeted him as he landed on the other side. A corpse lay on the rotting wooden floor of the room. The freshly-killed man was in the process of being dismembered. A teenage girl crouched behind his body, her eyes wild, her hair unwashed, her clothes filthy and ragged. Her hands were soaked in blood up to the wrists.

She wore blood on her lips too. She flicked her eyes toward Warg Daddy, watching him with wary curiosity.

The dead man looked to be twice the girl's weight. She must somehow have lured him back to this filthy hovel before killing him, or else killed him elsewhere and carried his body here. An impressive feat either way.

Meathook and Slasher stepped in front of the girl, advancing cautiously toward her with their knives still drawn. She leaped backward as they came, pressing herself against the far wall of the room.

'Hey,' said Meathook in a gruff voice. 'Don't be frightened.'

'We're friends,' said Slasher. The way he said it suggested the exact opposite.

The girl didn't look frightened. Meathook and Slasher were the ones who seemed more nervous. The girl slowly drew her lips back, revealing sharp pearly teeth.

Warg Daddy watched to see what she would do next.

He wasn't surprised by her reaction. She sprang forward, leaping at Meathook, her fingers clawed, a war cry issuing from her mouth. She landed on him and sank her teeth into his forearm.

Meathook shrieked and tried to shake her off. 'Fucknhell!' he shouted as her teeth bit deeper into his flesh. 'Gerrorff!'

The girl clung on tightly a moment longer, before releasing him and springing toward Warg Daddy. But despite her formidable speed, she wasn't quite quick enough. The barrel of the combat shotgun was already pointing in her face.

The girl immediately crouched down low like an animal, her yellow eyes glittering with anger, assessing her options, preparing to leap again. She had good reactions. Warg Daddy was impressed.

Slasher seized her from behind and forced her onto her knees.

She was all skin and bone, despite the evidence of her

recent feasting. Perhaps she'd been among the ones held prisoner in the quarantine hospital, starved almost to death by the so-called doctors there. Bastards. If Warg Daddy ever got his hands on any of those doctors, he'd teach them a hard lesson about hunger and mistreatment. The girl didn't protest as Slasher held her down. The fight seemed to have gone out of her, just as quickly as it had flared up.

But Warg Daddy wasn't deceived by that. He remembered how Wombat had underestimated Leanna that night on the Common when they'd first encountered her. Wombat had paid for that mistake with his life, and Warg Daddy didn't intend to underestimate this girl either.

Meathook was back on his feet, blood streaming from the wound where she had bitten him. 'Bitch!' he said. He lifted the butt of his rifle to strike her, but Warg Daddy held him back.

'This girl is our friend,' he reminded him. 'Slasher, let her go.'

The two Brothers looked doubtful, but they did as he said. He was Leader of the Pack, after all.

The girl stared at him suspiciously. 'You are no friends of mine,' she hissed. 'I'll kill you all. I'll kill you and eat you.' She rose to her feet again, crouching low, ready to strike. The fact that she was facing three armed men didn't seem to daunt her in the least.

Warg Daddy admired her fighting spirit. He could use a girl like this. 'I don't think you will kill us,' he told her. 'We're not going to let that happen. Besides, werewolves don't kill other werewolves.' That wasn't strictly true, he had to admit, remembering how Snakebite had looked after the combat shotgun had done its work on his face. But his words seemed to have the desired effect on the girl.

'Werewolves?' she said, uncertainly. She sniffed at the air, a surprisingly delicate action for such a vicious girl. She was skinny, but beneath the dirt she was pretty, with big doll eyes.

'Werewolves,' agreed Warg Daddy. 'And there are more like us. You've suffered a lot on your own.' He gestured to indicate the hovel she was living in. 'But you don't need to stay here alone any longer. You can be one of us.'

The girl still seemed unsure. 'And who are you exactly?' she asked.

'We're the Wolf Brothers,' said Warg Daddy.

'What do you want from me?' asked the girl, narrowing her eyes.

She really was the mistrustful kind. But then, who knew what she had suffered, to end up living alone in this filthy squalor? Warg Daddy spoke kindly to her. 'We're building an army,' he explained. 'We're gathering our forces for the final battle. We're going to take revenge on the people who made you suffer. And you can be a part of that,' he added, 'if you're willing to fight.'

The girl considered his offer. 'I'm not afraid of fighting,' she said at last.

'Good,' said Warg Daddy. He grabbed her arm before she could change her mind. 'Slasher, the knife?'

The girl spat at him and twisted violently in his grip, but Warg Daddy was too strong for her, even with one hand still holding the shotgun.

Slasher came with the knife. The steel blade flashed quickly. He sliced her thumb, and then cut each of the Brother's too. Droplets of fresh blood welled up where the blade had kissed them. Warg Daddy pressed his thumb against the girl's, blending their lifeforce into a single flow. She gasped.

'Welcome, sister,' he said. 'My name is Warg Daddy.'

Slasher and Meathook pressed their thumbs to hers too and told her their names.

Her eyes were wide in the dark. 'My name is Victoria,' she said.

Warg Daddy nodded. 'From now on, your name will be Vixen. You're a very special girl, Vixen. You are the first of

Lycanthropic

the Wolf Sisters.'

Chapter Eighteen

*Bath Road, Hounslow, West London,
waning moon*

The dream came to Rose again that night. It came to her every night now, relentless in its torment. No matter how hard she tried to shut it out, she couldn't escape. She knew how it would begin. It started the same way every time.

First came the dogs out of their kennels. They trooped past her, a procession of dead dogs – animals that she should have protected. 'I'm sorry,' she said to the first dog, an Irish Setter. It opened its jaws and snarled at her, showing teeth like fangs, saliva drooling from its long pink tongue. The second dog came, a Labrador. 'I'm so sorry,' she said to it. A deep growl issued from its throat. 'I'm sorry,' she said to the third dog, but she knew it was hopeless. She had allowed wicked men to kill the dogs, and being sorry about it was no good.

The men came next – the Wolf Brothers, they had

called themselves – all dressed in black leather, white wolves emblazoned on their backs. They carried baseball bats and knives, iron bars and sharpened wooden stakes. 'Kill the dogs,' ordered their leader. He stood watching her as the men set about their work, slaughtering the dogs. Then the man turned into a wolf, black hair as thick as fur, his yellow eyes glowing like lanterns, before running into the forest of twisted black trees that had appeared.

Rose walked through the dark forest in the other direction, following criss-crossing paths, through tangled undergrowth, deeper and deeper into the thickening trees, until she came to a clearing. Her own house stood in the middle of the clearing, looking like a gingerbread cottage. The cottage was ablaze. Oscar was inside the burning building, slumped in his wheelchair, already dead. His unseeing eyes followed her as she approached.

She had started the fire herself, she remembered. She had burned the house so that Vijay would not come looking for her. Such a sweet boy, Vijay. He loved her and perhaps she loved him too. But everyone Rose loved had died. She had run away to save him from that fate.

A twig snapped behind her in the clearing and Rose turned cold, as if a freezing black liquid had begun to fill her veins, pinning her in place.

'So you burned the house down,' said a familiar sneering voice. 'Did you think that would save you?'

Rose turned slowly to face him.

The headmaster, Mr Canning, stood gloating over her, one eye covered with a patch, his voice like the twist of a knife in her stomach.

'You lied to me,' she told him. 'You said I would never see you again. But you come to me every night in my dreams.'

He laughed at her words. 'You can't get away from me, Rose.' His smile was like the rictus grimace of a corpse. 'I haven't finished with you yet. I have so much more to show you.'

'No!' she screamed. She turned from him, away from the flames that engulfed her house and her brother, and tried to run. The freezing blood in her veins turned her limbs into lead weights. Creeping roots clutched at her feet as she tried to lift her legs. But still she ran from the headmaster, following a twisting path ever deeper into the forest. The canopy of trees closed tighter as she went, sealing her into a dark tunnel between their grasping branches.

She came to another clearing, but Mr Canning was already waiting for her, pushing Oscar's body along in his burned and blackened wheelchair. 'The truth is that by killing your brother I saved you from having to care for him,' said the headmaster. 'He was a burden to you. A weight around your neck. I killed him so that you wouldn't have to worry about him anymore.'

'No!' screamed Rose. It was a lie. She had loved her brother like life itself.

Mr Canning grinned. 'You don't have to admit it,' he continued. 'Not to me, not to yourself. Not even here, where no one can hear you say it. But it's the truth.'

'No!' she screamed again. She turned and ran down another path, twisting and turning to escape her accuser, but he was waiting for her again behind the trunk of a tree. She doubled back and took another turn, but the headmaster was there too, his one good eye glittering with malice.

'You can't escape me,' he said. 'So stop trying. I've shown you the past. Now I'm going to show you the future.'

'No,' she gasped. But she knew she couldn't get away.

'See?' he said. 'This is how it happens.'

A group of soldiers appeared among the trees, marching toward her. They were heavily armed, carrying rifles and machine guns. Bound prisoners walked before them, their hands tied behind their backs with ropes. Men, women and children. Rose herself was among them, and

Chris and Seth too. They had been beaten, she saw. 'This is far enough,' said one of the soldiers, an officer. The soldiers pushed their prisoners roughly to the ground. 'No one will see us here,' said the officer. 'Open fire!'

Rose woke screaming. She realised she had been screaming for some time.

She was sitting bolt upright, her back pushed back against a wall. Someone was shaking her arm, firmly but gently.

A warm wetness pressed against her face. It was Nutmeg, licking her with a long tongue. She grasped the dog and hugged her close.

The person shaking her arm was Chris. 'Are you okay?' he asked.

She shook her head.

'What was it?' asked Seth. 'Another nightmare?'

She nodded.

Nutmeg laid her head on her lap. Rose stroked the dog gently.

'Tell us about the nightmare,' said Chris.

She shook her head again. There was no need to tell them. They would find out for themselves soon enough. The dreams foretold the future. Soon they would all be dead.

'Well, come on, then' said Chris. 'Let's get some breakfast.'

They'd slept in a homeless shelter this time. The vicar from the church had given them directions to find it. A couple of dozen other people had also slept here. By the look of them, Rose guessed they were regulars.

Some young volunteers were running the place, handing out sleeping bags to those who needed them, making soup and cups of hot tea. They had slept on mattresses, and it was warm inside, and safer than sleeping on the streets. They had even given Nutmeg some food.

She got up and followed Chris and Seth to join the people getting breakfast. Bread rolls, butter, cheese and coffee. It was simple, but filling.

Some of the other people sleeping in the shelter looked rough. Rose was glad she had Nutmeg with her. The dog would protect her from danger.

They left the shelter when daylight came. The weather had turned milder overnight and all the snow had melted. But dark clouds on the horizon promised rain.

Chris was studying the road signs. 'I asked one of the organizers the quickest way out of London and he said to keep following the Bath Road. That's the road we're on now. It will take us west, straight past Heathrow Airport. If we keep up a good pace, we could be out of the city the day after tomorrow.'

'But where will we sleep then?' asked Seth anxiously.

'We'll easily find somewhere,' said Chris. 'We won't be out in the wilderness yet. We can just stop in the nearest town. It will be safer once we've left the capital behind.'

'No,' said Rose. The image of the soldiers firing their rifles was as vivid now as it had been in her dream.

'No, what?' asked Chris.

'Not Heathrow Airport.'

'Why not?'

'It's where the soldiers are.'

Chris frowned. 'We don't need to be afraid of soldiers,'

'Really?' said Seth. 'The last time we encountered some soldiers, they locked us up and put us in a hospital ward with a bunch of werewolves.'

'But I don't want to go all the way around the airport,' said Chris. 'That would mean heading north instead of west, and that could add days to our journey.'

'We go north,' said Rose. 'It's safer.'

'No, we stick to the plan,' insisted Chris. 'We go west. Come on.' He started walking. Seth followed.

Nutmeg lifted her hazel eyes to look at Rose. 'They don't know, girl,' Rose told the dog. 'They haven't seen the dream.'

But it was just a dream. Perhaps it wouldn't come true.

Perhaps Mr Canning had lied. But he hadn't lied to her about what he intended to do to Oscar. He had kept his promise to the letter, throttling her little brother right before her eyes.

Nutmeg barked, looking uncertainly from Rose to Chris and Seth, then back to Rose.

Reluctantly, she began to walk after the two men. The dog followed at her heels.

Chapter Nineteen

High Street, Brixton Hill, South London

The morning was bright and Liz felt a stab of pain in her eyes as soon as she stepped out into the sunlight. She pulled her sunglasses on for protection.

'Nice cheery day,' remarked Dean. 'Enjoy it while it lasts.'

At least the daylight doesn't turn me into dust, she thought darkly. *That would be awkward. And I ought to be glad I don't have to sleep in a coffin either. Especially since I don't happen to own a coffin.*

She climbed into her car and peered at herself in the rear-view mirror. Her skin looked a little too pale, her lips rather too red, but she had no pointed fangs in her mouth. If she really was a vampire, it wasn't obvious from the way she looked. She didn't feel like a vampire either. And that was the kind of thing you'd know, surely?

Dean clambered into the passenger seat beside her.

'You're looking peaky,' he said. 'Are you all right?'

'Too many late nights.'

There was truth in that. Late nights and long shifts were becoming normal now. The police were stretched to breaking point and were dealing with emergencies only. But everything seemed to be an emergency. The 999 number was almost overwhelmed. Liz didn't know where things could go from here. At this rate the system would simply fall apart.

When they arrived at the police station they noticed a military Land Rover parked outside, together with an armoured car painted in desert camouflage. The armoured car resembled a monster truck, twice the size of the Land Rover and maybe three times its weight. It occupied four spaces of reserved parking, but Liz reckoned that nobody would be in a hurry to complain to its driver.

'Handy for getting about in rush hour,' said Dean admiringly. 'I wonder what's up.'

They didn't have to wait long to find out. An army officer wearing a peaked cap was standing inside their Superintendent's office, talking earnestly. A dozen soldiers slouched in seats outside the nearby conference room. They were dressed in green camouflage uniforms with dark green berets and brown boots. One wore a single V-shaped chevron as insignia and sat apart from the others.

The men looked bored. They leaned in to snigger among themselves when they saw Liz, sharing some private joke. She was glad she couldn't hear it.

The Superintendent pushed open the door to his office and beckoned Liz and Dean over.

'Things are looking up,' whispered Dean. 'Perhaps we'll get a chance for some real action now.'

Liz hoped not, but she feared Dean might be right. The streets were becoming more and more dangerous by the day. Law and order had broken down and the new infantry regiments brought in to support the troops from 16 Air Assault Brigade were here to make the city safe again. *Real action* might be precisely what awaited them now.

'Ah, good morning, Constable Bailey, Constable Arnold,' said the Superintendent briskly, stopping them just outside the door to his office. At least this meeting looked like it was going to be a quick one. That was something to be thankful for. 'This is Corporal Jones from the 1st Battalion, Welsh Guards. As you know, the army are taking over responsibility for frontline security operations in this area. We'll be assisting them in any way we can. I've assigned the pair of you to work with the corporal's section. For the duration of this operation you two will accompany them wherever they go, liaising with the public, providing police expertise, and so on. In day-to-day matters you will report directly to the corporal. Questions?'

So many, thought Liz, but she shook her head. She had none that the Superintendent might know the answer to.

Corporal Jones stepped forward and grasped Liz's hand. The man was a small mountain, not especially tall, but broad-chested and thickset. His eyes were a pale blue, almost grey, and his hair, cropped very short, was fine and light blonde, giving him a boyish look. She guessed he was about the same age as her, perhaps in his late twenties.

'Pleased to meet you,' he said in a deep voice with a strong Welsh accent. She was immediately reminded of a Welsh male voice choir she had heard perform at the Albert Hall. The men from the mountains had produced a sound like a force of nature. Corporal Jones held her hand with an iron grip and shook it firmly. She returned his handshake as best she could but was relieved when he finally released her and offered his hand to Dean instead.

'You're from the Welsh Guards?' inquired Dean.

'That's right,' confirmed the corporal. 'Infantry boys, we are. We're here to finish the job the Paras couldn't manage. Isn't that right, boys?'

The other soldiers were mere kids, barely out of their teens. They jeered loudly in agreement.

Pure bravado, thought Liz. She wondered if any of them had seen active service. She thought not. Their combat gear and machismo posturing hid a jumpiness that was all too obvious. If she yelled "boo" at them, they'd probably leap out of their chairs in fright. The prospect of going out on patrol with them, each one armed with a rifle, was having less appeal by the minute.

The corporal introduced them to her. Seven men were under his command – six privates, who he addressed as guardsmen, and one lance corporal, who wore the chevron on his arm. Corporal Jones himself wore two chevrons.

The lance corporal was a trained dog handler and appeared to be newly assigned to the team. His name was Hughes, but he was known to the others as the Dogman. They seemed to treat him as a joke and howled whenever his nickname was used. That would get irritating pretty quickly, Liz thought. The Dogman didn't seem amused by his nickname either and wore a permanent scowl.

Corporal Jones continued breezily. 'I don't need to tell you the other boys' names, because they're sewn on to their uniforms. That's so they don't forget who they are,' he joked. 'If any of them give you any cheek, let me know about it.'

She looked at the soldiers' name labels. The names were all Welsh – Edwards, Evans, Griffiths, Jenkins, Lewis and Rees – and she was glad she wouldn't have to learn them all by heart.

'So what's the brief?' asked Dean. 'What do you want us to do?'

The corporal smirked. 'Apparently you're here to protect us. Our last combat mission was in Afghanistan, so you'd think we'd be able to take care of ourselves here in London. Then again, we've never seen the rough end of Brixton before.' The other soldiers laughed noisily at his joke.

Perhaps they had seen some real action then, thought Liz. So much the better. She suspected they were probably a decent bunch once you got past the initial show of swagger. But they needed to know that she and Dean were a match for them. 'I can show you the rough end of Brixton, all right,' she said. 'The rough end is where I live.'

Corporal Jones laughed. 'Really?' He sounded sceptical.

'Really. It's a lot more dangerous around here than in your green valleys,' she said. 'And that was before the werewolves arrived.'

In response the corporal just smiled.

'So are you really all Welsh?' asked Dean.

The men rolled their eyes at each other. 'Mostly,' said the corporal. 'Is that a problem, then?'

'Not at all,' said Liz quickly. 'We were just curious.'

The corporal seemed amused. 'Other regiments sometimes call us the foreign legion,' he joked. 'We're not all Welsh, but most of us are. The Dogman here is half-English, but we don't hold that against him.'

The men began their howling again. The Dogman threw a pen at one of them, who caught it and threw it back. Liz shot him a withering look and the howling and pen-throwing quietened down pretty fast.

Liz's ideas about Wales were sketchy at best. It had always struck her as something of an afterthought, tagged on to the western edge of England for no good reason. A land of lush sheep-filled valleys where the sound of harps and songs drifted across the hillsides. She knew that the Welsh language dated back to the country's Celtic past, and was full of poetry recounting its rich tales of myth and legend – tales of Merlin, of Avalon, of Morgan le Fay and the Lady of the Lake. The male voice choir she had admired had sung many of their songs in Welsh, and she had enjoyed the sound even though she hadn't understood a word.

The English and the Welsh hadn't always been on friendly terms though. She had read once that Wales was the country that had the most castles per square mile in the world, some of them built by the Welsh to keep out the

English, the rest built by the English to oppress the Welsh. But all that had been centuries ago. The flame-haired warrior Celts were a thing of the past, surely? Looking at some of these men, she wondered. Several had red hair and freckled skin. Were they descendants of warriors who had battled against her own ancestors?

'I can show you proof that I'm Welsh,' continued Corporal Jones. He rolled up one sleeve to reveal the tattoo of a fire-breathing dragon, the symbol of Wales. 'But my accent probably already gave it away.' He gave Liz a wink.

His voice was naturally musical and seemed to flow up and down like the mountains and valleys of his homeland. It was an easy voice to listen to, and Liz became suddenly conscious of the flat vowels of her own London accent.

'And is it true that Welshmen prefer sheep to women?' asked Dean.

'Ho ho ho,' said the corporal drily. 'Have we heard that one before, boys? A few times, yes,' he said, answering his own question. An iron edge entered his voice, and he spoke slowly and deliberately to Dean. 'Let's put a few things straight in your mind, Constable Arnold. We wouldn't want to start with any misunderstandings, would we?'

'No,' said Dean, looking abashed.

'First of all. The only one of us who loves animals more than people is the Dogman here, and as I told you he's not even properly Welsh. Secondly, we don't all belong to choirs, although we do enjoy a good sing-song after a few pints. Thirdly, it doesn't rain every single day in Wales, only on most of them. And to answer your question directly, none of us has ever had an intimate encounter with a sheep. Say it once, it's funny. Say it twice, and I'll leave you bleeding on the floor.'

'Is that right?' said Dean, squaring up to the belligerent Welshman. He stood a couple of inches taller than Jones, but the thickset corporal didn't look the least bit intimidated. They were both spoiling for a fight.

Liz stepped between them. 'Hey, cut it out, boys. We have to work together as a team, so let's make sure we get off on the right foot, shall we?'

The two men faced each other silently for a few more seconds before the Welshman relented. 'Sure,' he said. He offered Dean his hand. 'Only joking, like. No offence.'

Dean glowered at the hand, then took it reluctantly. 'No offence taken,' he muttered.

The corporal turned back to Liz as if nothing had happened. 'Constable Bailey, may I ask you something?'

'Please, call me Liz,' she said. 'Everyone does. And my colleague's name is Dean.'

'Okay then, Liz. Tell me, do you know how to use a gun?'

The question took her off guard. 'I'm not licensed to use a firearm,' she answered.

'That wasn't my question though.'

She looked around to make sure no one was listening. 'I know how to use a Glock,' she whispered.

The corporal seemed amused by that. 'We mostly use Heckler & Koch.'

'She can handle a G36 too, if she needs to,' said Dean.

The corporal's grin widened. 'I like a chick who knows how to use an assault rifle. It's kind of sexy.'

'Is that right?' said Liz. 'Well, while we're getting things straight between us, let's make something else perfectly clear. I'm no chick. And if you call me that again, I might just show you how well I can handle myself, with or without a gun.'

A few of the boys whistled. The corporal laughed out loud. He raised his hands in a gesture of submission. 'Okay, Liz, message received loud and clear. You can call me Llewelyn, by the way. If we're going to be friends, we'd better be on first name terms.' He pronounced the first syllable of his name with a strange sound in his throat as if he had a thick cold.

'Now I know why you don't use first names,' Liz said. She tried saying the name back to him, but she couldn't make the same sound.

He looked a little disappointed but unsurprised. 'All English people say it like that.'

He wrote the name down for her. 'In Welsh, w and y are vowels – w is pronounced like "oo" and y is like "i". The double l at the start doesn't really have an equivalent in English, but try saying "Clue-Ellin" and you won't be too far wrong.'

She tried it again like he'd said. 'Llewelyn.'

'Not quite,' he said. 'But I'm sure you'll get the hang of it eventually. I have a feeling that we'll be sticking together for a while.'

Dean tried it too. The way he said it sounded nothing like the real name, even to Liz's ear.

The corporal laughed again. 'I've heard worse. Say it however you like. I'm used to it.' He gestured at his men. 'But be sure to call this lot by their surnames. I don't want them getting ideas above their station. And call the Dogman by his nickname. He likes it better that way.'

Jones grinned broadly, and he was a boy again. The other, the Dogman, still looked surly. They were a tricky bunch, these Welshmen, but Liz was beginning to get a handle on them.

Something they had said earlier had bothered her however. 'You have a dog?' she asked the lance corporal.

'That's why they call me the Dogman, yeah. Why? Don't you like dogs?'

'What do you use them for?' she asked.

'Hunting werewolves. That's our mission. Did nobody tell you?'

Liz stared at him. 'Hunting?'

'Not hunting so much. Jones and the rest of the team are the hunters. Rock's job is to identify them.'

'Rock is the name of your dog?'

'That's right. Some dogs are specially trained to detect

arms and explosives, but Rock hasn't been trained for that. He's a protection dog. His usual job is to keep the base secure. But all dogs are able to sniff out werewolves pretty easily. When they get the scent they go a bit berserk, barking and growling. Even Rock, who's been specially trained, can't help responding instinctively when he picks up the scent of a werewolf.'

A cold feeling was spreading slowly down Liz's spine. 'So where's Rock now?' she asked him.

'Being looked after in the kennels,' he said. 'I'll pick him up on the way.'

'On our way where?'

Corporal Jones answered. 'The rough end of Brixton. Show us the way, Liz. Let's find out how rough it really is, and let's see how many werewolves we can find living there.'

Chapter Twenty

Cabinet Office Briefing Room A, Whitehall, Central London

The job of a Prime Minister often seemed to consist of little more than chairing meetings. It had always been this way, she reflected, but now every gathering was a crisis meeting, or an emergency debate, or simply a series of demands for her to put ever-more authoritarian policies into effect. What had happened to the normal business of government? It had fallen by the wayside. Schools were closed, the ticking pension timebomb had been forgotten, and pledges to combat climate change thrown aside. The economy was in freefall. All that mattered now was public order, defence, and humanitarian aid. The United Kingdom had become a failed state, and the PM seemed powerless to reverse the situation.

This morning's crisis meeting was focussed on domestic issues, and mercifully General Ney had found other matters to attend to. The Director-General of MI5 had also made his excuses. Instead, the Chancellor of the Exchequer had stepped in to deliver an apparently endless catalogue of the dire problems that her emergency powers were creating for the British economy.

The Prime Minister listened miserably. She quickly lost count of the number of times the Chancellor used the words *catastrophic*, *collapse* and *disastrous*. After ten minutes of his lecturing, she brought him to a halt. 'Please, Chancellor, we cannot deal with all of these matters at once. We must focus only on the most urgent needs. That means food, transport, energy, water. How are these basic resources being affected by the crisis?'

'Badly. As I have already explained, the United Kingdom is a trading nation. The collapse of the world's financial markets and the catastrophic failure of the banking sector are having a disastrous effect. It completely eclipses the global financial crisis of 2008 and the Great Depression of 1929. A developed country like ours is perhaps more vulnerable than most, and the closure of our external borders is pushing both the service sector and manufacturing toward a cliff edge.'

The Foreign Secretary butted in angrily. 'Chancellor, you have already told us all this. You must realize that the closure of our borders is central to our strategy to defeat the werewolf threat. We are fortunate that as an island nation we have been able to pull up the drawbridge so easily. Mainland Europe is becoming overrun with refugees from the Middle East and Russia. In China, they are gunning down migrants by the thousand. Would you like to see that happen here?'

'Gentlemen, please,' interrupted the Prime Minister. 'The closure of the borders to goods and people was a necessary security measure. It is done. Let us consider how to move forward.'

'It goes without saying,' continued the Chancellor, 'that most of the goods and services that form the backbone of the economy are simply becoming irrelevant as the crisis progresses. Many people have already stopped going to work. We'll see vast parts of the economy shutting down in the coming days and weeks.'

'Is there any way to avoid that?' asked the PM. But she already knew the answer.

'I don't think so. The damage is likely to be irreversible already.'

'What about key workers? Police, doctors, workers in essential industries?'

'They have been issued with identity cards so they can pass through the army checkpoints.'

'What about the people who are no longer working? Can they be redeployed to critical jobs?'

'Not easily. Retraining would take time. Time we do not have.'

'What about raw materials?' asked the PM. 'How critically dependent are we on imports?'

'Our key imports are – or rather, were – oil, gas, plastics and metals. The loss of these imports will have a significant impact in the medium to long term. As for food, the UK relies on imports for around half of its supply. However, the situation isn't as bleak as that headline suggests. We export significant quantities too, so our net production is around three quarters of the total required. We are self-sufficient in many categories, with an excess in certain areas.'

'In which categories do we have excess production?' asked the Home Secretary.

'Mainly whisky and Scottish salmon.'

'I think,' said the Foreign Secretary, 'that as long as we have enough whisky, we can get along just fine. Well, at least I can,' he added.

The PM glared at him angrily.

'There's some good news on energy,' continued the Chancellor. 'Thanks to the government's policy on climate change, the UK is consuming less energy than it has done for decades, and a record amount is coming from renewables like wind and solar. However, we are still significantly dependent on imported oil and natural gas. We will have to regulate electricity supplies and ration sales of fuel. In fact I recommend that we stop all supplies of fuel for domestic use immediately and restrict petroleum to commercial vehicles supplying essential goods. That will have the added bonus of preventing large-scale movement of the population.'

The PM nodded as she considered the implications. A ban on sales of fuel for domestic use. In other words, a world without cars. And that was just one of many knock-on effects. Very quickly, the country would slide back a century or more.

But the Chancellor was by no means finished. He was ready to deliver perhaps his bleakest announcement. 'As for natural gas, we import half of our supplies. Our gas reserves amount to a few days at most. Our choice is stark. Either we shut down the domestic network that people use to heat their homes, or we cease electricity production. Our choice is either a cold winter, or else a dark one.'

The meeting erupted in uproar.

'We can't turn off people's heating in the winter,' protested the Foreign Secretary. 'That would be a catastrophe.'

'But we can't shut down the electricity supply either,' said the Home Secretary. 'That would also be life threatening. Think of the effects on hospitals, on food storage, on communications, on basic morale. There would be riots. The government would fall within days. Without electricity, there would barely be a country left to govern!'

'Is there no way of securing gas supplies from overseas?' asked the Prime Minister.

The Chancellor shook his head. 'Russia has already turned off its pipelines. European countries are following. By the end of tomorrow, we'll have to rely on our own limited production.'

'What do you suggest?' asked the Prime Minister. 'We cannot turn off people's heating, nor their electricity. There must be a middle way.'

'We're looking at rationing supplies of both,' said the Chancellor. 'That means regular electricity brownouts, especially at peak times. Maybe even total blackouts if the situation worsens. Natural gas supplies for heating will be greatly restricted. People will just have to get used to wearing more layers.'

The Prime Minister remembered the days of her own childhood. Her grandparents had lived in a house heated only by a coal fire in the living room. The insides of the windows had often been covered by a layer of ice during cold snaps. Woolly sweaters, vests and thick stockings had been the order of the day. Her grandparents had never seemed to mind. But a population raised with central heating and air conditioning would struggle to cope.

The Chancellor was still speaking, in response to a question from the Home Secretary. 'During the last war, millions of workers were deployed to work in essential industries like arms factories and on the land. But these days, agriculture and most industrial processes are almost totally automated. Unskilled workers would simply be a liability.'

The last war. He was talking about World War II, a war in which both of the Prime Minister's grandfathers had fought. She found her gaze drawn once again to the portrait of Winston Churchill that hung on the wall of the meeting room. The ghost of Churchill was a constant brooding presence at the seat of government now. What would he have made of a world that had become so critically dependent on machines, facing an enemy that wasn't even human? Had humans themselves become obsolete? If she failed in the challenges that lay before her now, they might well become extinct.

As a young woman studying politics, she had learned

the key speeches of the great leader by heart. His words seemed very appropriate now. Back in 1940, as Britain stood alone against the overwhelming threat of invasion, he had delivered one of his most stark and uncompromising warnings to the nation. 'The battle of Britain is about to begin,' he had told them. 'Upon this battle depends the survival of civilization. The whole fury and might of the enemy must very soon be turned on us.'

He had continued in a similarly uncompromising fashion. 'You ask, what is our policy? I will say: It is to wage war, by sea, land and air, with all our might and with all the strength that God can give us; to wage war against a monstrous tyranny, never surpassed in the dark and lamentable catalogue of human crime. That is our policy. You ask, what is our aim? I can answer in one word: Victory. Victory at all costs—Victory in spite of all terror—Victory, however long and hard the road may be, for without victory there is no survival.'

The words were not meant to reassure. Quite the opposite. Churchill had used the speech to galvanize the nation at a time when all seemed lost. It had taken a leader of his magnitude to turn the war around. She did not believe for a moment that she could match his formidable example. But if she did not try, the war was as already as good as lost.

'There is no further time for discussion,' she said, cutting off another fruitless debate between the Home Secretary and the Chancellor. 'We will deal with the most urgent problems, and we will implement solutions. On electricity, we will begin a policy of restricting power during peak times. Home Secretary, put the necessary measures in place, and issue a press release informing the public what is happening.'

'Yes, Prime Minister.'

'On gas, we must prioritize supplies for heating homes and public buildings. On fuel, the priority should be to keep commercial vehicles on the road. We must maintain supplies of essential goods. Implement a ban on sales of fuel for private cars immediately. Explain why we are taking this measure. If necessary, use the police and the army to enforce the restrictions.'

'Yes, Prime Minister.'

'Regarding food, the critical problem as I see it is not so much in production, but in distribution of supplies. Is that correct?'

'Exactly, Prime Minister,' agreed the Chancellor. 'We simply can't get enough food into the towns and cities where it is needed. The big supermarkets and wholesalers can't cope any more. Their staff aren't turning up for work. Their supply chains are broken. Road and rail links are blocked. And nobody can pay for anything. Hyperinflation is making the money in people's pockets worthless.'

'What is the Bank of England doing to solve that?'

'Printing money around the clock, but that just feeds the problem. The core issue is that confidence in the financial system has evaporated.'

The PM nodded. 'We have to stop thinking in terms of employment, taxation and spending,' she told them. 'From now on, it must be about people and how we meet their basic needs. The most critical of all needs is food. How can we deliver it to the people who need it most? Forget about money. This is a humanitarian crisis. How do we get the food into our cities?'

A row of blank, silent faces looked back at her.

'What about an airlift?' she suggested. 'Our airports are closed to civilian flights. We could use military transport planes to bring in supplies. Is that feasible?'

The Home Secretary scratched his head. 'It might be. London City Airport is the closest to the capital. It's a relatively small airport with a short runway but we could switch it from passenger flights to freight. The planes would probably need to take off and land at steep angles.'

The Foreign Secretary nodded eagerly. 'City Airport

would be ideal. The runway is long enough for the Airbus A318, so it could certainly handle military transport aircraft. We could bring in supplies using Hercules, Atlas and Globemaster planes, and use Chinook helicopters to distribute them across London. In normal times noise restrictions would be a problem, but I think we can dispense with such considerations. If we operate 24/7 we could handle up to a thousand flights a day.'

For once, the Chancellor raised no objections.

The Prime Minister cracked a smile for the first time today. 'Gentlemen,' she said. 'Why are you all still sitting here? Let's do this thing already.'

Chapter Twenty-One

Brixton Hill Police Station, South London

Liz's morning was beginning to turn into one long crash course in military jargon.

'We split into two fireteams now,' announced Corporal Jones when they reached the military vehicles parked behind the police station. 'I'll be leading Charlie Fireteam. That's Edwards, Evans and Rees. The Dogman's in charge of Delta Fireteam, with Griffiths, Jenkins and Lewis. They'll be going in the Land Rover, so that they can take Rock with them. That leaves the Foxhound to us.'

The Foxhound was the armoured car that Liz and Dean had seen earlier. She eyed the monster vehicle with trepidation. 'Is that thing road legal?' she asked.

The corporal gave a mighty laugh. 'If it's not, who's going to stop us?' he asked.

'I'll go and fetch Rock from the kennels,' announced the Dogman. He wandered over to the police kennels that were situated on the other side of the secure parking area.

Liz watched him go. She wondered if Rock would go berserk when he smelled her scent. She couldn't imagine what might happen if he did.

'So what's the plan?' asked Dean. 'The Dogman talked about hunting werewolves.'

'That's right,' agreed the corporal. He noticed Liz's wary look. 'But don't worry,' he added, 'we're not just going to cruise around Brixton hoping to meet some. This is an intelligence-led operation. Our intel says we're looking for one John Hadfield, resident of Herne Hill, husband to Janet Hadfield, father of two teenage children. And a werewolf to round it off. He's one of the patients who escaped from the quarantine hospital. We have a tip-off that he's hiding out at the family home.'

'All right,' said Dean. 'So we search the house, and if we find him, we arrest him?'

'We're not planning to take any prisoners, Dean,' said the corporal. 'After the fiasco at the hospital, our instructions are to deal with werewolves as and when we find them.'

'You're going to shoot him?' asked Liz in astonishment.

'He's not human, Liz. That's what you've got to bear in mind. Creatures like that, they eat humans.'

'He has a wife and family,' she protested.

'So did many of the militants we shot dead in Afghanistan. So did some of the men we lost out there,' said Jones. 'This is war, Constable Bailey. If you haven't got the stomach for it, I suggest you stay behind. Tell your Superintendent you were surplus to requirements. We can do the job ourselves.'

He stood eyeballing her, seeing how she'd react. She wasn't going to give him the satisfaction of seeing her bottle out. 'We're in, Corporal Jones. It sounds like someone needs to keep an eye on you. And if we can safely make an arrest, then we will.'

Jones seemed satisfied by her response. 'All right. Good. Dean, you can go with the Dogman in the Land

Rover. Liz, why don't you join my team in the Foxhound?'

'Why don't Liz and I go together?' asked Dean.

'Because there isn't room. Anyway, the whole point is for one of you to accompany each team.'

Dean nodded but didn't look happy. 'You'll be okay, Liz?'

'Sure. I can look after myself.'

The Dogman was returning from the kennels with Rock, a large German shepherd dog. He held the dog on a tight lead, but it jumped up constantly, wagging its tail and pulling him along energetically. 'Good boy,' said the Dogman. 'Easy, easy.'

Liz didn't plan on hanging round, waiting for the dog to reach her. 'Come on, then, Clue-Ellin,' she said. 'Let's go.' She clambered up into the Foxhound and slammed the door.

Jones climbed in round the other side, and Dean, the Dogman and Rock joined the other fireteam in the Land Rover. The corporal slapped his hand against the metal door. 'Let's be off!'

They drove through the empty streets of South London past houses whose doors stayed shut but whose windows filled with curious faces as they passed. The Foxhound produced a huge roar wherever it went.

'Bit of a beast, isn't it?' said Jones. 'Seven tons of steel. It's even bigger than the Humvee's the Americans use. But it saved our arses from an IED when we were out in Helmand Province. We drove right over the bastard, and the Foxhound took the blast, no problem. Even a werewolf can't touch us inside one of these.'

He was trying to reassure her, Liz guessed. She must look just as apprehensive as she felt. What was she doing here? On her way to kill a father of two in cold blood? His only crime was to have been bitten or scratched by someone just like him.

Like her.

She should have bailed out of this operation when she

had the chance. Llewelyn had given her an invitation to leave. Stupidly she had turned it down. What had she been thinking? One sniff from that dog, and she'd be up against the wall along with this man, John Hadfield. Would they shoot her too? Would Dean let them? She didn't hold out much hope that he'd be able to stop them.

The Foxhound pulled up at the end of a residential road, lined with terraced houses.

'This is the street,' said Jones. He spoke into the personal radio headset that allowed the members of the infantry section to stay in contact with each other. 'Dogman, this is it. You take the Land Rover to cover the rear exit. We'll wait two minutes, then go in from the front. We'll follow the usual protocol.'

He turned to Liz. 'You can stay put if you want, Liz. You'll be safe in here.'

She thought about it for a second then shook her head. 'I was assigned a job,' she told him. 'I'm damn well going to do it.'

Chapter Twenty-Two

Herne Hill, South London

The soldiers jumped from the armoured car before Liz, clutching their weapons. Jones and Evans carried assault rifles. Rees had a sharpshooter rifle. Edwards held a machine gun with an underslung grenade launcher. All four of them had gas masks pulled on over their faces. Jones had offered her one, but she'd refused. It was surely too late for her to worry about catching any disease.

Jesus. She didn't know what frightened her most. The weaponry, the gas masks, the dog or the prospect of meeting a live werewolf. One thing was for sure – she wasn't staying alone in the armoured car while the soldiers went about their business. She jumped down after the men and followed them to the house.

'Want to do your police thing now, Liz?' asked the corporal. His voice sounded muffled through the gas mask and she could no longer see the expression on his face. It was hard to tell how much sarcasm he intended. She decided to take his invitation at face value.

The downstairs curtains of the house were tightly shut. She went to the door and rang the bell. No one answered.

Jones looked pointedly at his watch. 'Two minutes, Liz,' he reminded her. 'Then we go in.'

She rang the doorbell again, then banged loudly on the door. 'Police! Open up!'

The door stayed closed, but across the street an elderly man emerged from his own home, carrying a walking stick. 'What on earth is going on?' he asked.

Liz crossed the street to block his path. 'Please return to your home, sir. This is a combined police and military operation. Stay inside and lock your door.'

'What's going on? Is there going to be trouble?'

'Please go back inside, sir,' she said urgently. 'It's not safe for you here.'

The man turned to go.

Behind her, a small explosion went off.

Edwards had launched a grenade at the door of the house. Smoke billowed across the street and stung her eyes. Liz stared at the scene in anger. The bastards had said they'd wait two minutes. They'd lied.

'Bloody hell,' said the old man to Liz. 'You weren't joking.' He scurried back inside the safety of his home.

The soldiers were already piling into the house. In the distance a second explosion went off. Delta Fireteam presumably, going in the back way. A dog barked excitedly. It was too late to stop them now.

The smoke from the grenade filled her nostrils. Now she understood why the soldiers were wearing gas masks. Cursing her stupidity she covered her nose and joined the melee inside the house.

The house wasn't a large one and it seemed to contain far too many people. Soldiers' boots hammered loudly up the wooden stairs in the entrance hall. Jones' bulk filled the doorway to the front room. Shouts came from beyond, followed by a woman's scream. Rock's barking echoed in the kitchen at the back, and more shouts rang from upstairs. The smoke drifted into the hallway from outside making Liz's eyes sting, and she plunged on, almost blind, following the sound of the screaming.

The woman, Mrs Hadfield presumably, was in the front room, up against the wall, terrified out of her wits. She clutched her teenage son and daughter close. Edwards had his rifle in their faces and Jones was interrogating them.

'Where is he?' asked Jones. 'Where are you hiding him?'

The woman shook her head.

'Your husband,' repeated Jones. 'John Hadfield.'

The woman found her voice at last. 'I don't know what you're talking about. Leave my family alone.'

More barking came from the hallway behind Liz, and she heard the clacking of Rock's claws as the dog hurried across the wooden floor and headed upstairs. Heavy feet pounded in the room above.

Liz stepped between the soldiers and the family. 'Stop it!' she said. 'This is no way to treat innocent people.'

Three terrified faces stared back at her.

'Let me do it my way,' she said to the soldiers.

Jones nodded his consent but Edwards kept his gun raised.

Liz pleaded with the woman. 'We're looking for your husband, Mr John Hadfield. Is he here somewhere?'

The woman shook her head again.

'Do you know where he is? Can you tell us if you know anything about his whereabouts?'

Another shake of the head.

'When did you last see him?' persisted Liz.

The daughter raised her eyes to the ceiling.

'Is he upstairs?' asked Liz. 'Is there an attic in this house?'

The woman grabbed her daughter and shook her. 'There's no attic here,' she said. 'I don't know what you're talking about. I haven't seen my husband in weeks.'

A shout from upstairs rang out. 'Sir, I think we've found him! There's a hatch in the ceiling. Rock's going wild.'

'Okay,' said Jones to Edwards. 'Keep these three down here. I'm going up to see.'

'Open the hatch,' cried a voice from the room above. The loud thump of men's boots followed from directly overhead.

The corporal was starting to leave the room when the first shot went off. A wild, inhuman bellow issued down the stairs, like the roaring of a hurricane. A burst of gunfire followed. Jones dashed through the doorway and rushed up the stairs two at a time.

Edwards kept his gun trained on the woman and her children. 'Don't move,' he said. His forehead was slick with sweat.

'Just stay still,' Liz begged them. 'I promise that you'll be safe if you stay here and keep still.'

Upstairs a maelstrom had been unleashed. The ceiling shuddered as boots pounded and heavy objects flew. Bursts of automatic fire were punctuated with men's shouts, the barking of the dog, and the unbridled howling of the beast that had once been a man. The teenage girl burst into tears and Liz took hold of her hand.

A bloodcurdling scream issued from above, followed by a roar. Liz heard the corporal shout a command, and another burst of heavy gunfire rang out.

Eventually, silence returned to the house. Footsteps came down the stairs, followed by the padding of Rock's paws.

Liz breathed a sigh of relief as Dean's huge form reappeared in the doorway. His face was grim. 'He was hiding in the attic. The bastard jumped down and killed Rees. But he's dead now.'

The woman's face turned white. 'He's dead?' she hissed. 'My husband?' Hysteria edged her voice. A black rage bubbled behind her eyes. 'You killed him?'

Edwards raised his rifle toward her. 'Good riddance to him,' he said. 'The bastard killed my friend.'

A piercing shriek whistled from the woman's lips. She advanced toward Edwards, her fingers curling and uncurling.

'Stay where you are,' ordered Edwards, but the woman took another step toward him. He dropped back, panic in his eyes. 'I'm not shitting you,' he said, his voice rising. 'I'll fucking shoot.'

The woman paused, turning her face to the open doorway. The tapping of claws against the wooden floor announced the return of Rock. The dog came into the room, unleashed, its hackles raised. A soft growl came from its throat. It sniffed the air. The Dogman followed the animal inside, looking puzzled. Two more soldiers, Lewis and Jenkins, joined him.

Suddenly the room felt full to bursting. Liz backed away toward the window. If only there were more space. She had to put as much distance between herself and that dog before it found her.

The dog's eyes were wild. It turned its head one way and the next, sniffing furiously at the people filling the room. Left and right its nose swept, its nostrils flaring, its tail wagging madly.

Liz pressed herself into the furthest corner of the room.

Suddenly the dog went into a frenzy.

Liz closed her eyes.

The dog went berserk, barking loudly. 'Rock, go find!' called the Dogman. The dog rushed forward, barking madly. But it didn't come for Liz.

She jerked her eyes open. The dog was dancing around the woman, Janet Hadfield, leaping up as high as her face, snapping its jaws.

The soldiers looked on in confusion.

'It's her!' shouted the Dogman. 'She's a werewolf too!'

The woman lunged at Edwards, grabbing the rifle and

twitching it from his grasp. He cried out as she fixed her jaws to his neck. Sharp teeth tore through skin, ripping muscles and glands, slicing open veins and arteries.

Edwards shrieked. Blood erupted from the wound. The woman threw her weight on him and he went down.

'Holy fucking Saint David,' said Jenkins and opened up with the machine gun. A fountain of bullets ripped through bodies and furniture, shattering glass and ornaments. Above the fireplace, a row of china ducks exploded into smithereens.

Meanwhile the two children had leapt onto the other men, clawing and biting.

'They're all fucking werewolves!' shrieked the Dogman.

The boy wrapped his arms around the Dogman's neck, struggling to sink his teeth into the man's flesh.

The girl jumped at Dean. Only half his bodyweight and a foot shorter, she quickly had him in a stranglehold and wrestled him to the floor. He fought back, holding her off as she whirled sharp fingernails before his face.

The dog was no use, just barking wildly and adding to the chaos.

Liz went for the girl first. She grabbed her thin arms and tried to pull her away from Dean, but to little effect. The girl seemed possessed by some demonic force.

Dean rolled, trying to pin her down with his weight. The tactic seemed to work, and the girl struggled to move. Liz grabbed one wrist, stopping the deadly nails from doing their work.

The Dogman threw the boy off him, but in an instant the kid was back on his feet. He leapt onto a table then dived onto Jenkins' back. Blood sprayed across the room as the boy's teeth tore at the man's neck. Jenkins cried out, but a vicious bite to his throat brought his scream to a sudden end.

The gunfire resumed as another soldier entered the fray. Whether that would save lives or bring them to an end, Liz had no idea. Cries, shrieks, shouts and bellows added to the din.

The girl rolled suddenly free from under Dean, yanking her wrist out of Liz's grasp. Dean smashed into a table leg as she rose to her feet. The girl turned to flee, but Corporal Jones stood in her path.

'Watch out!' shouted Liz.

A single gunshot drowned her words. The girl fell to the floor, a bullet hole in her forehead, her wild eyes now calm.

Quiet descended at last.

Liz crawled across the floor to Dean. 'Are you all right?' Did she scratch you?'

'I'm fine,' said Dean. 'Don't worry about me. Not a mark.'

The same could not be said for Edwards or Jenkins, or for the other members of the Hadfield family. All lay dead, sprawled on the floor or slumped across chairs. Half of Janet Hadfield's head had been blown away by point blank automatic fire. The carpet that cradled her remains had turned dark red.

'What a fucking shitstorm,' said Jones. 'The whole family were werewolves. Mother, father, son and daughter. Every single God-damn one.'

Liz stared in disbelief at the carnage that surrounded her. Seven people dead in less than seven minutes. Was there something she could have done to prevent this massacre? If there was, she was too shocked to see it right now. But at least she and Dean were safe. And Jones too. Llewelyn. Even though she'd known him barely a few hours and still wasn't sure if she liked him, for some strange reason she felt a surge of relief that he had not been harmed. She even managed to smile at him when he looked her way.

A whining noise at her shoulder made her whirl around.

In all the fighting, she had forgotten the dog. It lay beside her, its front paws outstretched in her direction, its muzzle pressed to the floor, its tail subdued. A curious keening sound emanated from its throat almost like it was in pain.

'Rock?' The Dogman was at its side quickly, his hands over its body.

'Is it hurt?' asked Liz.

The Dogman shook his head. 'Not hurt, no. He seems puzzled. I've never seen him act this way before.' He glanced up at Liz and their eyes met. Understanding slowly began to dawn on the Dogman's face. 'He doesn't know what you are,' he said.

She returned his gaze and let the dog continue its whining.

'Never mind that,' said the corporal. 'We just lost Edwards, Rees and Jenkins. Let's get the clean-up crew in to sort this mess. They'll get rid of the werewolves and take our boys back to base. The dead must be honoured. And then I'm going to give the intel boys a real bollocking.' He came over to Liz and offered her a hand up. 'You did well there, Liz. Nice work. I'm sorry this went down so badly. Better luck next time?'

'Next time.' There would have to be a next time, she supposed. That was the way of things. However much life threw your way, you just had to catch it and keep going forward. Forward was the only choice she had.

Chapter Twenty-Three

Number Ten, Downing Street, Whitehall, Central London

Colonel Michael Griffin waited patiently outside the Prime Minister's office at Number Ten, Downing Street. It was late in the evening, but activity in the heart of government showed no sign of slowing. A chair had been provided for his use in a busy corridor of the house. The chair was an antique, no doubt, in keeping with the grandeur of the seventeenth century building, and was particularly uncomfortable to sit on for any length of time.

Stern faces glared down at him from the gloomy, darkened portraits that lined the walls along the narrow corridor. He shifted his position on the seat, but comfort continued to elude him. The reason for him being summoned here tonight was clear enough. The lateness of the hour, the discomfort of the chair and the disapproval of those painted faces spoke all too clearly. He was in disgrace.

He had been offered tea and coffee but had politely declined. He did not deserve to be treated with such courtesies. So far he had waited for over an hour while civil servants and politicians bustled up and down, their arms filled with briefing papers and other documents, eyeing him with irritation as they squeezed past him. His seat had not grown any more comfortable with time. Yet he would happily wait any number of hours here. Anything to postpone his meeting with the PM.

He had waited outside the Prime Minister's office once before. His chair had been more comfortable that time, and he had been allowed to wait in a room rather than a corridor. He had gladly accepted coffee and a chocolate biscuit while he waited. On that occasion the PM had personally assigned him the role of Medical Director at King's College Hospital. His brief for that post had been simple – to keep the infected patients securely within the quarantined hospital wards, and to safeguard the doctors, nurses and other hospital staff who worked there.

His failure to fulfil that mission could hardly have been more complete. The hospital had been attacked and reduced to smoking rubble, hundreds of the infected had turned to wolves and escaped, and many medical staff and soldiers had lost their lives. In addition he had allowed the enemy to capture the weapons of fallen soldiers.

A court martial was to be expected, and in time of war the penalties for such failings could be severe. He had already been rebuked and stripped of his command by an enraged General Ney in the immediate aftermath of the attack. Now the Prime Minister herself had requested to see him. He was surprised that she was able to spare the time. She obviously felt that he had let her down personally.

The colonel was stoical however. He would answer for his part in the failed operation, take full responsibility for his shortcomings, and accept the judgement of his superiors without question. After shouldering the heavy burden of command for so long, it would be a relief for someone else to make the decisions at last.

The door to the Prime Minister's office opened and a middle-aged woman wearing a pin-striped navy suit emerged. She approached his chair and Griffin rose to his feet. 'The Prime Minister will see you now,' said the woman.

The colonel entered the Prime Minister's office and closed the door behind him. The PM was sitting behind a vast desk, her half-moon glasses perched on the end of her nose. Just like the previous time he had met her, he was startled by how small she was in real life. But this time she seemed much older, and more troubled. He was alarmed to see the deep furrows that creased her forehead and the grey lines of tiredness framing her eyes.

Despite her evident exhaustion, she was ploughing her way through a heap of reports piled on the desk before her. 'Ah, Colonel Griffin,' she said, glancing up. 'Please sit.'

The colonel took the seat offered as she returned her attention to one of the opened documents. She turned a page in silence, scanning the text quickly before turning another page. The colonel peered at the document, trying to read it upside-down. He realized with a start that it was his own report of the attack on the hospital. He had submitted a blow-by-blow account of the failure of the operation, taking care to assign the bulk of the blame to himself. Accompanying the report was his letter of resignation.

The Prime Minister continued to read. The colonel looked at the other papers spread across the desk. Among them he recognized his own personnel file. Photographs taken during his deployment in Afghanistan were clearly recognizable. The colonel sighed. Looking back now, he realized that his command of a field hospital in Helmand Province during that period had marked the pinnacle of his career. He'd been decorated with a Military Cross and had returned to England a hero. Now he was a disgrace to himself and to his country. He lowered his head as the Prime Minister turned another page.

Eventually she gathered the papers together and replaced them in their folder. She picked a single sheet of paper from the top of the file. It was his letter of resignation. The PM read it through, laid it on the desk in front of her and began to speak.

'When I was young and naive I used to have faith in the democratic process,' she said. 'I believed in the institutions that supported our system of government and subjected it to scrutiny. I assumed that if Parliament passed the right laws, and had open and fair procedures, all would be well.'

The PM removed her glasses and folded them onto the desk. 'Over the years, I've changed my mind. I've learned to trust people, not rules and systems. It's not institutions I put my faith in now, but those few exceptional individuals who make them work. So when I find someone I can rely on, I keep that person close to me. When someone of ability fails, I give them a second chance. Those who fail persistently, I remove from office.'

Griffin nodded. It was hard for him to imagine the Prime Minister as a naive young woman. She had surely always possessed a steel edge and a commanding demeanour.

'I have read your report,' continued the PM, 'and I do not accept your resignation. You are a good man, a capable soldier, a qualified doctor, and you are uniquely knowledgeable about the disease of lycanthropy. I need men like you around me now. One battle was lost. We must not lose the war.'

She screwed his resignation letter into a ball and dropped it into her waste basket.

'Prime Minister, I –'

'I have not finished,' she said, cutting him off. 'Colonel Griffin, my initial assessment of you, based on your service record, was that you were a soldier of exceptional ability.

When I first met you, I was impressed by your confidence and obvious expertise. I haven't lost faith in you. I hope you haven't either. Have you?'

Had he? He thought back to the event again, allowing the horror to flood over him once more. The roar of explosions, flames climbing into the darkened sky, wolves running free. And bodies. The bodies of dead soldiers, doctors and civilians strewn everywhere. It had been utter carnage. 'General Ney has suspended me from my command,' he said.

'That was not my question. Have you lost faith in your own ability to command?'

'No,' he whispered.

What might he have done differently? Nothing. The hospital had been overwhelmed by surprise. Nobody had suspected that the werewolves would carry out a coordinated attack in human form, using explosives and other weapons. He had kept his head and preserved the lives of as many of the soldiers, doctors and medical staff under his care as had been possible. He had done his best, remaining calm under extreme pressure. If presented with the same situation and the same limited knowledge, he would do the same again.

'No,' he repeated, more confidently this second time. 'I have not lost faith.'

The Prime Minister swept the files to one side. 'Good. Then let us move forward. I have a new assignment for you, Colonel. Please don't refuse it. Believe me when I say that I desperately need people like you on my side. And there are few people quite like you.'

'What kind of assignment?'

She smiled for the first time since he had entered the room. 'A very important one. I do hope that you'll consider it an interesting challenge.'

Chapter Twenty-Four

West Field Gardens, South London

Vijay spent the hours and days after returning from Rose's house alone in his room with the curtains closed against the light, curled up in bed with the covers drawn over him. When he'd been younger he'd always run here whenever his big sister Aasha had teased or bullied him, pulling the bedding up to his chin, like armour.

Poor little Vijay, sulking in his room.

It was his sanctuary, his fortress, the place in the world where he felt safest. Perhaps the only place he felt safe. He was not sulking.

What was he doing here then?

Hiding. Vijay is a coward. A chicken. A scaredy-cat. A namby-pamby baby.

'No,' he cried aloud. He wasn't afraid of anything anymore. He had proved it beyond doubt. He had stolen medicine to help Oscar and nobody could say that he was a coward now, not even the cruel, mocking voice in his head. It was grief that he was feeling, not fear. Rose was gone, and it was right to shed tears over her.

It's your fault she's dead. You killed her, Vijay. You're so stupid. A stupid little baby.

'No!' He pummelled the mattress with both hands. It wasn't his fault. He'd done nothing wrong. He'd tried his best to help.

Then why is she dead? asked the voice in his head.

He didn't have an answer to that. Nothing made sense to him. All he knew was that Rose was gone and wasn't coming back. His life would always be empty without her.

The negative voice that would never shut up had nothing to add to that. On this matter, he and the voice were in perfect agreement. His life was as good as over.

He could hear sounds coming through the wall from Aasha's room. His sister's voice, and Drake's, probably arguing as usual. He couldn't make out their words, and he didn't want to. He grasped the soft pillow of the bed and pulled it around his ears, blocking out the raised voices.

Drake and Aasha argued all the time. And yet, at least they had each other. They were a couple. His mum and dad had each other too. He had no one. He never would.

He wondered if Drake and Aasha would get married one day and have children. His best friend – *your only friend, Vijay* – married to his big sister. It was hard to picture it, but it was what couples did. He'd hoped that he might marry Rose one day. Once the idea had entered his head, it had been impossible to imagine that he wouldn't marry her. If Drake could be with Aasha, Vijay could be with Rose. They would live together happily and start a family.

Now that could never happen. Rose was gone. And without Rose he had no one. He would never marry, and never have kids. He would grow old and lonely and no one would care. The Singh family line would end with him.

The Singh family tree was framed proudly for everyone to see on the wall above the fireplace downstairs. At the top of the tree sat a photograph of his grandmother, her aged face lined with wisdom. Next to her was his grandfather, a man whose sepia-coloured features he knew as well as his own, and who he had often heard stories about, but had never known. Directly opposite them, on a different branch of the tree were his father's parents, both dead, and largely unknown to Vijay. The female line had always been dominant in his family.

His own mother and father occupied the middle of the branching tree, with Aunty Gurinder from Hackney out on a limb, and Vijay and Aasha and their various cousins at the base of the tree, like acorns from which the great trunk had sprouted. But that was an illusion. The tree was upside down. It was really his grandmother who was the strong root of the family, anchoring it firmly in the past, and he was nothing more than a spindly twig that would blow away if the wind ever grew too strong.

The wind was blowing hard now, and the twig was ready to snap.

And where was Rose in this tree metaphor he had imagined for himself? A leaf, fluttering past as the wind gusted. A beautiful, bright red leaf, blown away and lost forever. Fresh tears ran down his cheeks and soaked into the pillow.

Take a look at yourself, Vijay. Imagine if Rose could see you now.

The voice was cruel, but sometimes spoke hard truth. The one thing Rose had always wanted was for him to step up and show some backbone.

He dragged himself out of bed and wiped his eyes, blowing his nose loudly into his soggy handkerchief. He could not stay in this darkened room any longer. Instead, he went downstairs in search of his grandmother, seeking comfort and inspiration in her eternal, unbending presence.

She was in the living room as usual, sitting in her favourite armchair opposite the fireplace where the family tree hung, her busy, gnarled fingers knitting furiously. She was a tiny, wizened old woman, reaching barely five foot when standing. Even Vijay felt like a giant in her presence. But her heart was as strong as an oak tree. She was full of kindness too, and always had time for him.

Now, suddenly in her presence, he felt an urge to flee from her and be alone again. What could he possibly say to her? She would see that he had been crying, and he would have no choice but to tell her everything. He turned again to go.

Her voice stopped him from leaving.

'Come and sit with me, Vijay.' It was a command, not an invitation. She put aside her knitting. 'Come,' she repeated. 'I *wish* to speak with my favourite grandson.'

He couldn't escape. When his grandmother *wished* for something, she could not be refused. He pulled up a chair and sat opposite her in front of the fireplace, his head bowed, his hands fidgeting in his lap.

'Look at me, Vijay,' she said in her quietly assertive voice.

He looked up and tried to fix a smile to his face.

The old woman was not fooled by his attempt. She sighed loudly. 'Vijay, it pains me to see you this way. You have been like this for days. Hiding in your room. Skulking about. Looking as miserable as a wet dog. Do you think I do not know it? What is the matter with you?'

'Nothing,' said Vijay. 'Nothing's wrong. Really.'

'Nonsense. It is not nothing. It is very much something.' His grandmother studied him closely over the reading glasses perched on the end of her nose. 'Tell me.'

He shook his head.

her brow furrowed in concentration as she sought to divine his problem. At last her expression cleared. 'It is a girl,' she pronounced. 'I can tell.'

'No,' protested Vijay. 'It's not a girl.'

But there was no point trying to conceal anything from her. 'What is the girl's name?' she persisted. 'I *wish* to know her name.'

It was hopeless. 'Rose,' said Vijay mournfully. 'But it's not what you think.'

'No? When girls are involved, it is very usually what I think. I think that you are in love with this girl. Yes?'

'Yes,' he said, and a loud sob escaped from him. He couldn't contain his grief any longer. 'But she didn't love me,' he wailed. 'And now she's dead.' He went to his grandmother and knelt beside her, lowering his head to her level, crying properly now, unable to keep the pain inside.

His grandmother's hand touched his. Her touch was firm, even though her fingers were so aged. Her voice was soft. 'Dead? Oh Vijay, I am so sorry. How did you know her? Did you meet her at the Gurdwara?'

The Gurdwara was the Sikh place of worship. 'No,' said Vijay. 'Rose wasn't a Sikh. She was a girl in my class at school.'

'How long have you known her?'

'Only a few months,' he sobbed. 'She joined our school at the start of the school year. She lived just around the corner.'

'And how did she die?'

'In a fire. Her brother and her parents were killed too.'

His grandmother hugged him tight with her bony arms. 'It is a tragedy. My poor, poor, Vijay.'

She let him cry without restraint, not trying to calm him, just holding him until he had quietened. He cried until his eyes ran dry.

When he had finished, he found that anger had filled the hole that grief had carved inside him. 'How can it have happened?' he asked. 'Why would God take her like that? Rose was a caring person, kind and generous. Her brother was just a little kid. Her parents were good people. None of them deserved to die.'

'You ask why God did this?' said his grandmother. 'I have asked myself that same question often enough. Why does God make us endure these tragedies? Now sit up, and

Lycanthropic

listen carefully, I have a story to tell you.'

He sat and listened as his grandmother spoke.

'When I first came to this country with your grandfather many years ago, I thought that our future would be filled with joy. And at first all was well. I thanked God for his blessings. We found a beautiful house to live in, and your grandfather quickly found work. We were blessed with two children too – your mother and your aunt. But your grandfather didn't live to see them grow up. God took him from us when your mother was still a little girl. I cannot say why. He had done nothing wrong. And not a day passes when I do not miss him terribly.'

'How did he die?' asked Vijay.

'An accident at work. A horrible accident that I do not wish to talk about. God blessed him with a job, and then that job killed him. It was too cruel to make sense. For a long time I was angry, just as you are angry now.'

'But why does God take good people?' asked Vijay. 'And if good people die, what is the point in being good?'

'We should not question why, Vijay, because we can never know. It is a test, perhaps. A test of faith, of courage, or of something else that we do not understand. Questioning will not help us. Instead, our response must be to renew our vows, our faith, and to resolve to do more good in the world. Being good is its own reward. It is the way that we work together to make the world a better place. When tragedy happens, it reminds us of why we need to be good. That way, tragedy can become a tool to make us stronger. It made me stronger. It will make you stronger too, if you let it. Do you understand?'

'I was trying to be strong,' he wailed. 'Rose was helping me. And then this happened. Now I don't know what to do.'

'You must find your purpose,' said the old woman. 'Do you know what it is?'

'Mr Harvey, my teacher from school, told me that my purpose in life was to help people. He said I was doing a great job for the Watch, delivering food to the old people, and that they all looked forward to my visits.'

'Then do it. Do it and remember Rose. Never forget her. But do not stop helping people. Remember that to live a life with true purpose and to help others is a great privilege. And that is all that we can ask.'

Chapter Twenty-Five

Hillingdon, West London

Three days. It was already three days since Chris Crohn had escaped from the isolation hospital. Three whole days and he was still in London. He was walking though, and that was key. You'd get nowhere without walking. Even an idiot like Seth could understand that.

He was walking despite the blisters on his feet, despite the relentless cold rain that drenched and froze him, despite the various diversions and obstacles that had been thrown in his path.

Walking. Always walking.

Three days so far. The plan said they needed to walk eight miles a day. Chris had no way of knowing if they were doing that or not. Without GPS or a map how could anyone answer such a question? They could not. He would just have to press forward and hope.

Hope alone wouldn't be enough though. He needed

determination, resilience and stamina too.

He had those things. He could do this.

Three days since the last full moon. That meant today must be 31st January. That was right, wasn't it? Surely it was. And yet without a smartphone or even a basic date-tracking device like a watch, he couldn't be a hundred percent certain. Ninety-nine percent, but not totally sure. As the days and weeks progressed, his confidence in his ability to know anything for certain would steadily diminish. Eventually, he would know almost nothing.

This was how it would be. The future would be a place of ignorance, the kind of world that someone like Seth must already inhabit. A place in which he might eventually know little more than Seth himself. Nightmare.

The Greek philosopher Aristotle had railed against the invention of writing because he believed it would ruin people's ability to remember. What an idiot. Without writing we were doomed to forget nearly everything we knew. Without books, computers, smartphones, the internet, humans were little better than savages. You only had to look at history to know that, and you could only know history if you wrote it down.

Einstein had understood the world more clearly. He'd once said, 'My pencil is cleverer than I,' meaning that with a pencil he could achieve much more than with his brain alone. Now that was smart thinking. He was a smart guy, Einstein. So much smarter than Aristotle.

When Chris had worked at Manor Road School, the children there had kept a goldfish called Einstein. They'd also had a rabbit called Aristotle. What had happened to the fish and the rabbit now? Was someone taking care of the school animals, or had they been abandoned, left to starve in their little tank and cage? Gross. Surely that hadn't happened. Chris was pretty confident it wouldn't have. Ninety percent confident, at any rate.

Three days. 31st January. Eight miles every day. 136 miles to Hereford. Expected journey time three weeks.

That meant they'd reach their destination in eighteen days from today. He had nowhere to write these facts down, however. He was Einstein without his pencil. He'd have to remember them somehow. How? By constant repetition.

Three days. Eight miles a day. 136 miles to Hereford.

At least Seth wasn't bothering him with stupid questions or comments. He was just trudging along, resigned to his fate. Good. Chris liked his friend best that way. The girl, Rose, had said almost nothing either, apart from waking in the night and freaking them out with her insane ranting and screaming. Apart from that, nothing to say. Good. The dog was docile too, just trotting along, minding its own doggy business. The journey, so far, was going well.

Eight miles a day. 136 miles to Hereford.

They might even do it quicker if they could maintain a good pace.

Up ahead there was a sign of activity. Chris squinted into the distance. Some kind of vehicle occupied the road. A large vehicle, maybe a truck. It might be an army checkpoint. They had passed through two already. The soldiers were sniffing for werewolves and seeking to prevent mass migration of civilians. That was good. Those were sensible precautions. If Chris had been in charge, he would be doing the same. He just hoped the soldiers wouldn't turn them back.

He walked on. Gradually the blockage in the road took on more shape. It wasn't a truck, or a checkpoint. It was a tank. It was advancing toward them.

He stopped.

'It's a tank,' said Seth, stroking his bushy beard.

'I know what it is,' said Chris. 'Let me think what to do about it.'

'It's like the vicar said,' continued Seth. 'The army is taking over Heathrow Airport. He said we wouldn't be able to get past.'

'Yes, I know what he said,' snapped Chris. 'Stop telling me what I already know.'

'We'll have to go another way.'

'No,' said Chris. 'If we go around, we'll have to doubleback and then head north instead of west. That will take us miles out of our way. It'll add days to our journey time. I already explained that to you.'

Eight miles a day. 136 miles to Hereford. Expected journey time three weeks.

'What then?' asked Seth.

'We carry on,' said Chris. 'I'm sure they'll let us past.' He took a step forward in the direction of the tank.

'They won't,' said Rose. 'If we carry on, they'll kill us.'

'What?' said Chris. 'Of course they won't kill us.'

'I saw it in my dream. The tank. The soldiers. Dead bodies, piled in heaps. You, and Seth.'

'It was just a dream,' protested Chris. 'Dreams can't predict the future.' He took another step toward the tank.

'We will all die,' said Rose.

The dog barked anxiously.

'No,' said Chris. 'The soldiers are here to protect us.' But how certain could he really be about that? Eighty percent? Ninety? Was that enough?

'This isn't a game,' said Seth. 'We can't just restart this level if it goes wrong.'

'I know that!' cried Chris. 'I need to think!'

They watched him thinking. Rose, Seth, Nutmeg the dog.

He turned away from them and stared at the tank. It continued to advance slowly along the road, soldiers marching alongside. Other people were walking away from the tank, or perhaps they were running. They were fleeing from the soldiers.

But the soldiers were here to protect them. Weren't they?

He squinted. The soldiers carried rifles and they wore … gas masks. Gas masks? Really? He peered into the distance, trying to see more clearly. He didn't think they could really be wearing gas masks. He was eighty percent confident they weren't.

Seventy-five percent at the outside.

He spun around to face the others. 'Okay, we'll go around. Just in case.'

They started walking, back the way they had come. Chris glanced nervously over his shoulder. The tank was still following them. It was gaining on them. 'Come on,' he shouted, gripping Seth by the collar and dragging him along. They quickened their pace, back the way they had come.

Eight miles every day. 136 miles to Hereford. Expected journey time three weeks.

Except that now they were taking a different route. Back instead of forward. North instead of west. It would take them longer. How much longer he didn't know. He didn't even know the route they would need to follow. His numbers were all useless now. His facts, his figures, his plans. He may as well forget them. He may as well forget everything.

So this was how it was. The future had arrived faster than he could possibly have predicted. A world of ignorance, in which he knew nothing more than Seth. How long had it taken? Three days. Nightmare.

Chapter Twenty-Six

Finsbury Park, North London

There had once been a time when Warg Daddy had seriously considered joining the army. Admittedly, he had been seven years old and his idea of an army career had revolved around single-handedly storming the enemy's base, a dagger between his teeth and a rocket launcher strapped to his back, slaughtering his foe by the hundreds and emerging from the battle completely unharmed, or better still with a small scar which would seal his reputation for being a badass.

He had quickly lost interest once he'd seen real soldiers being made to march up and down parade grounds and obey orders like dogs. That wasn't how Warg Daddy wanted to live his life.

But now he found himself as commander-in-chief of his own private army. The Wolf Army, no less. It was an unexpected turn of events, but he was rather enjoying himself. His army was small but effective, and growing rapidly. And each successful operation made him more confident about his aptitude for the role. In fact, now he thought about it, he realized that he was perfect for the job. Taking orders might be for dogs, but giving them required some serious swagger. Warg Daddy had it. He was Charles Bronson. He was Samuel L Jackson. He was Al Fucking Pacino.

Before leaving the house tonight he had spent some time posing in front of the mirror wearing his black leather jacket and shades, the combat shotgun gripped with both hands. It was a good look, he couldn't deny it.

The white wolf that prowled across the back of his jacket reminded him that he was Leader of the Pack. With Adam and Snakebite safely disposed of, nobody could ever take that away from him, not even Leanna, however much she talked about being god-damn queen of the werewolves. She could play at being queen. Commander of the Wolf Army was where the real power lay.

Badass, he thought. *I am a total badass.*

Even the electric pains that raged agonisingly inside his skull seemed to recede a little when he was focussed on his military manoeuvres. His latest operation was about to bear fruit, and he clung to the shadows at the roadside, watching and alert, totally absorbed in the moment, his senses finely tuned to the slightest hint of trouble. The mission was in progress, and he waited in anticipation of sweet success.

The Wolf Army was massively outnumbered by the enemy, so he had no choice but to mount a guerrilla war for the time being. *Asymmetric warfare*, the military planners liked to call it. Assholes. *Dirty war* was Warg Daddy's choice of phrase. And no one knew how to fight dirtier than him.

Tonight he'd chosen Vixen as his secret weapon and his first line of attack. It was time for the girl to be blooded. And if the operation went as planned, there would be no shortage of blood.

The girl walked forward down the middle of the road, limping on her left leg. Her hair hung around her shoulders in a bedraggled state. Her clothes were soiled and torn and hanging half off her. She staggered toward the army checkpoint that closed the road ahead, a look of wild desperation in her eyes.

Warg Daddy glanced across the street. Slasher and Meathook were in place, just as planned, assault rifles in hand. Crouching low, they were hidden from the soldiers at their command post. They signalled back to him to show that they were ready.

Vixen walked on through the night, ever closer to the troops behind their barricades. The beam of a xenon searchlight cast a golden halo around her head.

A challenge rang out in the night through an amplified speaker. 'Halt!'

The girl took no notice, limping forward. 'Help,' she cried weakly, as she drew closer to the checkpoint. 'Please, help me!'

She was good, Warg Daddy had to admit it. The distressed waif look seemed to come naturally to her. He was almost convinced himself by her act. Having a girl on side was opening up entirely new opportunities for attack.

The two soldiers manning the barrier exchanged nervous glances. Warg Daddy smelled raw fear drifting on the breeze. The girl returned their gaze, a picture of helpless vulnerability. 'Help me,' she pleaded, in a voice that almost made Warg Daddy sob.

A junior ranking officer came to join them. The three men stared hard at the girl, looking for threats. 'Is she armed?' asked the officer. 'Any indication of hidden explosives?'

The soldiers shook their heads. Vixen's ragged clothing wasn't nearly big enough to conceal a bomb. It wasn't bombs they needed to be afraid of, though.

The soldiers didn't see what Warg Daddy saw. They didn't know what he knew.

Vixen reached the checkpoint and stopped in the road, swaying weakly on her feet. She was so convincing, Warg Daddy almost worried she might faint.

She was wearing no shoes, he noticed. Her feet had turned almost blue in the freezing conditions. *Nice touch*, he thought. *Authentic.* He wished he'd come up with that idea himself.

'Please, help me,' she said to the soldiers. As she reached the barrier she tottered and fell forward.

Warg Daddy made a hand signal to the Brothers across the street. *Wait. Ready.* The signal wasn't really necessary. The Brothers knew the plan inside out. But Warg Daddy still liked to remind them that he was in charge.

This was the critical moment. Two of the soldiers came forward to help the girl where she had fallen. She lay still on the ground, her chest rising and falling gently as the men fussed around her. The dark shapes of more soldiers stood back behind the road barrier, watching.

Now, gestured Warg Daddy.

Automatic gunfire opened up as the Brothers stepped out of their hiding places. The officer and one of the soldiers went down under a hail of bullets.

Vixen clawed at the third man kneeling at her side. She drew him down with a grip of iron until his face was level with hers. He screamed as she bit into his neck and a fountain of blood gushed from the wound. Blood splattered her face in thick globs and ran over her chin. When it was over she licked her lips.

The surviving soldiers were retreating now. They ducked back out of sight.

Tricky.

Warg Daddy gave another signal. Slasher and Meathook held their fire.

But now the girl was on her feet, the soldier's rifle in her small hands. The gun jerked like a wild animal as she held the trigger down, releasing a hailstorm of death at the soldiers hiding behind the barrier.

Wolf War

Sweet mother of fuck, thought Warg Daddy as he surveyed the scene of carnage. Vixen was a one-woman killing machine. She hardly needed the Brothers' help at all.

Slasher and Meathook were advancing up the street toward the checkpoint now, but they were too late for any action. The night was quiet once more. Troops lay dead at Vixen's feet. The entire section of eight men had died in seconds.

'Collect their weapons,' ordered Warg Daddy. 'Strip the bodies. Take everything.' The soldiers were armed with the usual assorted delights of assault rifles, machine guns, sharpshooter rifles and grenade launchers. They also had a Mastiff armoured vehicle. Warg Daddy eyed the twenty-ton monster truck greedily. The Mastiff was one of the British Army's largest blast-proof patrol vehicles. They were usually fitted with a heavy machine gun or a grenade launcher. 'Take it,' he said.

Vixen waited shyly next to the bloody corpses. 'Did I do okay?' she asked Warg Daddy.

He wrapped an arm around her waist and drew her close enough to kiss. 'More than okay,' he said. 'You were badass.' He didn't often give out that kind of praise, but the girl deserved it. He let her go again and watched her climb into the Mastiff, her slim body lithe and quick.

He waited until Meathook got the engine started before he climbed aboard. 'Let's go,' he said, slamming the metal door shut with a clang. He cast a last regretful glance over the bodies of the fallen soldiers. Young men, cut down in their prime. A tragic waste. But there was no time to eat them now. In any case, he enjoyed his prey best when it was still alive.

Chapter Twenty-Seven

Department of Genetics, Imperial College, Kensington, London

It was late at night, but Doctor Helen Eastgate wasn't the least bit sleepy. When an idea came to her, it was like a drug.

At college, her fellow students had sometimes taken synthetic stimulants before going out to a party. *Uppers,* they'd called them. Helen had never taken uppers. Or downers. Or any other kind of drug. She hadn't been big on student parties either. She had got her kicks in the library or in the lab. For her, no kind of high could compare with the thrill of scientific discovery.

A *hunch*, the Prime Minister had called it. Helen had a hunch now, and it was keeping her wide awake.

She was taking a risk returning to her office at the university after her close encounter with Leanna, when she had almost been killed here. She shuddered as she remembered the vial of acid she had thrown in self-defence, burning into Leanna's face. But she didn't think Leanna would dare come back. In any case, the security desk in the reception area downstairs was manned and the Prime Minister had placed an armed guard to provide additional protection. Helen felt as safe here as anywhere.

Professor Norman Wiseman's notes, journal entries and papers were spread out on the desk in front of her. Journals were all published online these days. "Papers" weren't really papers anymore. Her Head of Department always encouraged staff to go paperless in a bid to reduce the university's carbon footprint. But when Helen's creative juices began to flow and a *hunch* took hold of her imagination, she liked to feel crisp sheets of paper in her hand. She liked to spread them all over her desk. Sometimes across the carpet too.

Her Head of Department would have been furious if he could have seen Helen's office right now. A mound of papers, charts, graphs and books spilled over her desk. More papers littered the floor, and piles of books teetered like towers on chairs and other flat surfaces. Chaos was the fuel Helen used to kickstart her creative process.

The computer screen before her displayed an image rather like an alien spaceship floating in a sky of psychedelic colours. It was a virus. The virus responsible for transmitting lycanthropy. The spheroidal object on screen rotated slowly about its axis, displaying a bewilderingly complicated structure for an object measuring a mere 150 nanometres in diameter. Larger than most viruses, but still many times smaller than a human red blood cell, the object's surface was covered with tentacle-like forms, each one coated with hundreds of protein spikes. It was this intricate outer layer that enabled the virus to penetrate its host cells so rapidly, enabling it to deliver the RNA payload contained within.

The virus was not new to nature. It was sometimes found in wolves and certain domestic dog species, where it appeared to be harmless and inert. It had never before crossed over to humans. At least that had always been the standard scientific belief. Professor Wiseman's research had proved otherwise.

The virus that spread lycanthropy from one human host to another was a mutation of the standard lupine form of the virus. It was a retrovirus, a member of a broad group of viruses that caused disease in humans and other mammals. It had some similarities with the HIV virus and also with the hepatitis B virus. Its complexity would make it tremendously difficult to counter with drugs.

The good news was that Helen had already managed to acquire blood samples of patients infected with lycanthropy and had succeeded in isolating the virus itself. The bad news was that each patient was infected with a different mutated form of the virus. Every single case was unique. It was almost enough to make her despair.

The HIV virus was capable of rapid mutation, but this virus mutated even more rapidly. It had taken over a decade of intensive research and clinical trials for scientists to develop effective anti-retroviral agents to suppress HIV. It would be impossible to repeat that kind of work for the virus that caused lycanthropy on any timescale that could help with the current crisis.

And yet there was always hope.

Buried deep in Professor Wiseman's notes she had seen a reference to a story she had at first sight dismissed as irrelevant. Now she had a *hunch* there might be more to it. It was here somewhere.

Wiseman's notes were copious and detailed. When he had submitted his paper to the journal that had ultimately rejected it, he had also sent his entire research records spanning a period of several years. She had managed to obtain a copy of the papers from the journal editors by pulling strings and calling in favours. Among the professor's notes were field reports, diary entries, photographs, hand-written footnotes and commentaries. She had read through all of them but hadn't yet had time to index them properly. She'd never before seen such a mass of supporting evidence accompanying the submission of a scientific paper. It was as if the professor was pleading with his peer reviewers to take him seriously. They hadn't though. They'd rejected his discovery at face value.

At last she found what she was searching for. In the early days after his arrival in Romania, Wiseman had spent considerable time interviewing villagers and townspeople in the area of the Carpathian Mountains where he had been based. Understandably they had at first been unwilling to talk to an eccentric foreigner asking questions about werewolves. But through persistence, charm and some considerable time spent buying drinks in taverns, he had eventually coaxed some of them into confiding with him.

One old man had related what seemed at first glance to be a tall tale. He had lived all eighty-nine of his years in Northern Transylvania, he had told Wiseman, after the encouragement of a glass or two of *tuica*, the traditional Romanian plum brandy which was 60% alcohol. He had been just a child when World War II had begun and the Nazis had handed his homeland over to Hungarian rule, and still only eighteen when the Russians had invaded the country from the east. He had once fired a shot at a retreating German soldier, he told Wiseman proudly, but had never left the Carpathian Mountains. In the decades that followed the war he had watched politicians, empires and entire political systems come and go, but still he lived on in the village in which he had been born, marrying the girl who lived across the square.

Winters were harsh in the mountains and the people did not have much to eat in the dark times that followed the war. Too many village men had died in the conflict, and the peasants' lands were seized from them during the Communist-era collectivization. They had needed to go into the forest to find food. One day when the forest floor was covered in a blanket of white, he and a friend had gone out trapping rabbits. He had been a strong young man in those days, he had told Wiseman, and could walk for miles. And he had needed to. He and his friend had travelled far setting snares. All day they walked, setting and checking traps, but did not see a single animal. Then, as dusk crept across the land, they got lucky. They came upon a rabbit warren in the side of a bank of earth and set fresh snares. Just before the light failed them completely, a group of rabbits emerged from a burrow. They caught four before night closed in fully. They gathered them up and were carrying them home when they realized their mistake. A howl of a wolf came to them through the darkened forest. It was the night of the full moon. They would never have entered the forest if hunger had not made them so desperate.

'Why was that?' Wiseman asked the man.

'*Vârcolac*,' the old man muttered, reverting to the Romanian language to express his horror. The half-human, half-demon creature that could take the form of a wolf.

The creature attacked suddenly, leaping at them out of nowhere. They lunged at it with heavy sticks and managed to beat it off, but not before the man's friend was bitten savagely on the arm. The old man's face had paled in terror as he remembered. Everyone knew that the bite from one of the creatures would turn its victim into a *vârcolac* just like it. He would be doomed to roam the forest himself, hunting for human flesh, drinking human blood. Yet, although the man's friend fell to the ground and wailed like a beast after being bitten, he did not turn into a demon. The old man cautiously went to him and helped him to his feet. He dragged him home to his house where his wife bandaged him and tended to the wound.

The village priest prayed for the man, and a miracle must have been granted, because he slowly recovered and did not turn into a werewolf. The *vârcolac* was kept at bay. He lived on, got married himself and raised a family before passing away quietly at the age of sixty.

It was just an old man's tale. A few months ago, Helen would have dismissed the whole story as superstitious nonsense. Now, even knowing that lycanthropy was real, how could she be certain that the old man's friend had really survived a werewolf attack and not turned? It was just a hastily scrawled anecdote buried among Wiseman's copious notes. Wiseman himself had not paid any particular attention to it, although he had added the footnote, 'A credible witness. I believe there may be some truth in the story.'

If it were true, it changed everything. If one person could be bitten by a lycanthrope and not acquire the disease themselves, then others might also possess a natural immunity. And if Helen could find one of these people and use their white blood cells to synthesize a vaccine, she might yet be able to find a way to block the spread of the disease, or even to immunize the entire population. Perhaps even to find a cure.

There was nothing more in Wiseman's notes that suggested natural immunity or the possibility of a cure, not even a hint. Wiseman had been interested primarily in convincing a sceptical scientific community of the existence of the disease, not finding out how to cure it.

Synthesizing a vaccine would not be easy, assuming if it was possible at all. But the alternative was unthinkable.

Helen grabbed a blank sheet of paper, sending other papers flying from her desk and began to scribble down her ideas before she lost them. She would need extensive lab facilities, state of the art equipment and a team of researchers. The university here could provide all that, if she could convince her Head of Department to allocate the resources to her. She could rope in her colleagues, her post-graduate students, even undergraduates to do the donkey work. She would need volunteers too. A whole lot of volunteers.

And last, but not least, she would need the bodies of

some of the werewolves that had been killed escaping from the hospital. As many dead werewolves as she could lay her hands on. To make that happen, she would need the help that the Prime Minister had promised her.

Chapter Twenty-Eight

West Field Gardens, South London

'You stupid girl,' shouted Vijay's mum. 'You stupid, selfish girl!' She raised her palm and slapped Aasha's face hard.

Aasha cried out, more in shock than in pain.

Vijay cringed. His mum had just found out that Aasha had been making Drake steal clothes and jewellery for her. It hadn't been Vijay who had told her about it. She had found out herself while cleaning Aasha's room. The bags containing brand-new designer goods piled high in Aasha's wardrobe had told their own story well enough.

'You stupid, stupid girl,' she raged. 'And you,' she continued, turning her wrath on Drake, 'you did exactly as she asked you. Where were your brains? You are just as stupid as her!'

Drake cowered back, raising his hands protectively, but she didn't try to strike him. 'I'm sorry, Mrs Singh,' he said, lowering his arms and hanging his head shame-faced.

'Sorry? Do you have any idea what you've done? Apart from the stupid risk you took, do you understand that while others were working selflessly to provide food and medicine to the community, you were stealing these trinkets for yourselves?' She held a silver necklace aloft and swept her angry glare from Drake to Aasha and back. 'While you did that, Vijay has been going door-to-door helping the old people, taking them food and sitting with them to talk and keep them company.'

Vijay felt his neck grow hot. He didn't want to get pulled into this argument. His mother knew only half the truth. He had also blackmailed Drake into stealing. They had gone out together on the night of the full moon, breaking into the butcher's shop to take the medicines for Rose's little brother Oscar. That was wrong, and Vijay knew it. If his mum found out, she would murder him. He tried to catch Drake's eye to plead with his friend not to tell.

But he needn't have worried. Drake kept his secret. 'Tell me what I should do to make it up to you, Mrs Singh,' he said bashfully.

'She can't make you do anything,' protested Aasha. 'You're not one of us.'

Drake looked hurt by her comment. 'But I want to be one of you,' he said. 'I want to be part of your family.'

Vijay's mum seemed satisfied by his contrition. 'It is not me you need to make amends to,' she said. 'It is the poor shopkeepers you stole from. You must return everything to them, and ask for their forgiveness.'

Drake swallowed. 'Everything?'

'Every last piece of jewellery and item of clothing. And you will do whatever they require to make amends. It is the only way you will learn your lesson. I hope that you have also learned a valuable lesson about my daughter,' she added.

Drake nodded, abashed. Aasha glared at him with fiery eyes.

'Try to make your own decisions in future and not just do what she says,' Vijay's mum told him. 'Otherwise she will twist you round her little finger, even more than she already has.'

'Yeah,' said Drake, glumly. 'I know.'

She rounded on her daughter again. 'And you. What do you have to say for yourself?'

Aasha remained as defiant as ever. 'You call me stupid?' she protested. 'The whole world is falling apart. Most of the shops are already closed. And you want us to take this stuff back to them? How stupid is that?'

Her mother gasped. 'Did I raise you to be a barbarian? We are civilized people in this house, and if you cannot behave in a civilized fashion, I will throw you onto the street.'

'Really?' said Aasha. 'You'd throw your own daughter out of the house? In the middle of a war?'

'You are no longer a daughter of mine!' declared Vijay's mum.

Aasha opened her mouth to respond but a quiet, firm voice cut across the argument from the corner of the room. Vijay's grandmother had been sitting in her chair, watching the dispute unfold. Now she intervened. 'Stop it! Both of you. We are a family. We do not fight each other. We need each other, and we must stick together. If any fighting is to be done, it should be to defend ourselves from our enemies.'

'Keep out of this, Mum,' said Vijay's mother. 'Aasha is my daughter.'

'And you are so like her.'

'I am not! That is a ridiculous thing to say. She is wilful, disobedient, and pig-headed.'

The old woman nodded. 'Yes, and argumentative too, just like you.' She winked at Vijay. 'You see what I have to put up with? I sometimes think that I did not have a daughter. Instead I gave birth to a mule. It was certainly a struggle to birth your mother, I can tell you that.'

Vijay's mum stood with her hands on her hips, looking murderous.

His grandmother had not finished yet. 'Aasha is exactly like you were as a teenager. Stubborn, argumentative, and always causing problems. I often thought of disowning you. And I'm sure you have thought the same about your own daughter. But these qualities that sometimes make Aasha so difficult are also her strengths. She will never give in, never bend to the will of another. She will achieve greatness one day, I am sure of it.'

Aasha stopped scowling at her mother just long enough to beam at her grandmother.

'You are different, Vijay,' his grandmother continued. 'You are quiet, obedient and good. Where Aasha is like the wind and the fire, always dashing from one place to another and stirring up trouble, you are like the earth and the water. You are dependable, and adaptable, and you flow with quiet persistence past obstacles, unnoticed. You are just like your own father and grandfather.' She smiled. 'Both types of people are needed to make this world, you know. Both the patient and the impatient, the loud and the quiet. We cannot make do with just one type.'

Aasha and Vijay looked at each other and burst out laughing.

Their grandmother was beckoning to them. 'Come to me, Vijay, Aasha. I *wish* to give my grandchildren a hug.' They approached their grandmother and were embraced fiercely in the old woman's arms. 'You too, Drake, come and have a hug. You poor boy, you are trapped in the middle and that is no safe place to be.'

Tentatively, Drake approached and was also drawn into a hug. He laughed nervously, trying to hide his embarrassment.

Vijay's mother was far from placated by her own mother's intervention, however. 'You make things worse by pandering to Aasha's whims,' she accused. 'How will the girl ever learn to take responsibility for her actions?'

'The same way you did. Through her own experience of life. Nothing I said to you ever made the slightest difference, and nothing you say to her has any effect either. She must find her path by making mistakes.'

'Well she is certainly making plenty of them,' retorted Vijay's mum. She gave Aasha a sharp look. 'I'll be watching you closely from now on,' she said. 'And I will expect higher standards of behaviour.' She turned back to Drake. 'And I expect you to return all of those stolen goods, as you promised.'

'Yes, Mrs Singh,' said Drake sheepishly. He couldn't look Aasha in the eye.

Aasha tossed her hair back angrily. 'All right, then. That's what we'll do. Drake will take back all my stuff like a good little puppy dog and say he's sorry.' She spun on her heels and stormed from the room.

Vijay's mum left too and Vijay breathed a sigh of relief. 'Thank you,' he said to his grandmother.

'It is no problem,' she said. 'We are all one family now, including Drake here. We must all help each other, not fight amongst ourselves. There is already too much fighting in this world.' She bustled out of the room, leaving Vijay and Drake alone together.

Drake hung around, fidgeting nervously. Vijay was reminded of the time that he and Drake had waited outside the Headmaster's office together, as Mr Canning killed and ate their classmate, Ash.

'Aren't you going up to Aasha's room?' Vijay asked him.

'Dunno,' said Drake. 'I don't think she wants to see me right now. I'm not sure I want to see her either.'

Vijay was glad. He hardly saw anything of his friend these days. Drake was always with Aasha, and now that Rose was dead, Vijay was left alone by himself.

'Thanks for not telling Mum what I did,' he said. 'About stealing the medicine, I mean.'

Drake shrugged. 'No point in you getting into trouble

too.'

'Thanks, anyway,' said Vijay. 'None of this was your fault. Not really, I mean. I know that you did all the stealing, but Aasha made you do it.'

'Yeah, thanks for pointing that out, mate,' said Drake. 'That doesn't help. It just makes me feel even more stupid.'

'Sorry.'

'Do you think Aasha meant what she said about me not belonging?' asked Drake. 'That I'm not one of you?'

'I don't know. I don't think she meant it that way.'

'Maybe she did though. Maybe she really thinks that. All I really want is to belong.'

Vijay shrugged. 'You do belong, Drake. Even my grandmother said so.'

'Yeah.'

'So what are you going to do now?' asked Vijay. 'Are you really going to go round all the shops taking the stuff back and apologizing?'

'Dunno,' said Drake. 'I guess. If they're still open, that is.'

'And what about Aasha? Will she go with you?'

'What do you think?' asked Drake. 'She can be pretty stubborn.' He frowned. 'But your mum's unstoppable when she gets mad. I don't think I have any choice.'

'Yeah,' agreed Vijay. 'It's the unstoppable force and the immovable object. Best just to avoid getting stuck in the middle if you can.'

Chapter Twenty-Nine

*Upper Terrace, Richmond upon Thames,
West London, quarter moon*

James slid the sash window of his bedroom wide open and slipped down the drainpipe to the lawns at the back of the house. Moonlight was falling in silvery shafts and he felt its power against his skin. The latent strength within his bones quivered as the moonbeams brushed his face. But the waning moon lacked the strength to change him. No matter. He would hunt in human form.

He had to be careful. Ben was always watching him, as if he suspected something. James liked Ben, and the man was polite enough in his presence, but James could tell the man didn't really trust him. If Ben found out what James was doing, he would try to stop him.

Melanie and Sarah were different. They understood. He was sure they did.

He didn't want to keep his nightly excursions a secret from the two sisters, but he couldn't risk telling them in case Ben found out. It was safer to play along, accepting the slices of bacon and salami they gave him, pretending to be the tame, domestic werewolf Ben wanted him to be.

He had used the meat as bait to catch his prey. A couple of hungry foxes had been lured into the garden by the smell of bacon. He'd even caught a crow that way. *Caw*, it had cried in indignation as he pounced. Not the greatest last words ever recorded. But the bird had made a tasty snack.

Now James was done with crows and foxes. They had helped to rebuild his health, but werewolves weren't made to feed off creatures like that.

He glanced back at the house. No one had seen him go. He crept lightly along the side of the building and sprang over the black iron gate that led onto the main road.

A light rain brushed his face as he walked, heading east away from Richmond. He didn't mind rain. He didn't feel the cold either. It was his prey who could feel the wet and the cold. His prey needed to be scared, not him.

The last time he'd walked this road, he'd been close to death, half-dragged along by Ben and Melanie. Now his strength was returning and he was ready to hunt properly. He strode purposefully along the road, his eyes looking out for prey. He would not choose who to kill. He did not have the right to choose. He would simply wait to see who came his way, and take those who sought out death. They would reveal themselves to him by their actions.

The moon ducked behind a cloud and the road grew perfectly dark, at least to human vision. All the streetlights were turned off to save power. But good people had no need to fear the dark. Law-abiding citizens stayed indoors at night, respecting the curfew. It was the others who ventured out. They were the ones who ought to feel fear. And James meant to show them why.

He hadn't prayed for days, not since the time he'd grown mad at God's implacable silence and hurled the furniture around his room. What was the point of prayer? God had made his attitude toward James abundantly clear. *Do whatever you want, James. See if I care. My ears are deaf to your pleas. My eyes see your suffering, yet I shall not lift a finger to help.*

God didn't care one jot about James, and he didn't give a damn about anyone else either. If he did, how could he possibly have allowed this terrible catastrophe to engulf the world? How could he stand back and watch as murderers, rapists and thieves rampaged around the city?

James had been a fool to believe otherwise. He had swallowed the lies of the priests, despite the incontrovertible evidence of God's true nature. You had only to turn on the TV news channels or open a history book to see how much God truly cared. God had always been this way, doing nothing as earthquakes, plagues and wars ravaged his people.

But James refused to stand back and do nothing. He would fight back. Wicked people needed to watch out. He was coming to find them. He was coming to get them.

He was coming for them now.

Ahead, he glimpsed movement on the dark street.

A group of young men swaggered along the road in front of him, their arms over each other's shoulders. They swayed down the middle of the road, parked cars to either side. Their voices were raised in shouts. With his keen senses, James could smell the alcohol on their breath even at a distance.

He stepped off the pavement and into the street to intercept them.

They came to a halt in front of him. Four young men, lean and fit, their bodies pumping with blood. James licked his lips. He wasn't yet at full strength and wouldn't be able to take them all at once, but he was confident he could handle them one at a time. But it was up to them. He wouldn't make the first move. He would only kill them if they chose to die.

The men fanned out, surrounding him. He stared at

their faces, looking each of them in the eye, one by one.

'Hey,' said one. 'Get out of our way.'

James stepped up to him, staring defiantly back.

'Did you hear me?' said the man. 'You're in the way.'

James pushed him lightly on the chest. 'No. You're in my way,' he said.

The one who had spoken looked to his friends for support. One gave James a firm shove. He was tall, with long, shaggy hair and wore a leather jacket and ripped jeans. 'What's your problem?' he demanded. 'Are you looking for a fight?'

James turned to face him full on. 'Why? Are you?'

The man narrowed his eyes, his forehead creasing in consternation. Then he spread his hands wide. 'Hey, we're only having some fun. You need to chill, man.'

James nodded. He flicked his gaze around the others. Their stances were defensive, not aggressive. They didn't want to cause trouble. These were not bad people, just young guys enjoying a night out. He stepped to one side to let them pass. 'I'm sorry I disturbed you,' he told them. 'You should hurry home before the curfew begins.'

The men walked on, muttering among themselves, casting wary glances back in his direction. He watched them until they had gone, then continued on his way.

The road wound its way east, from Richmond to Putney Heath, past Wandsworth Common and on to Clapham Common. He was unconsciously retracing his steps back toward his old home, he realized. But there was nothing there for him to return to. His parents were dead, butchered at Leanna's hands.

The memory stoked his quiet anger, reminding him of the evil that lurked all around. Wherever humans walked, evil went with them. This city was like Sodom and Gomorrah, like Nineveh and Hormah, and wicked Babylon. Those cities were brought to ruin by their sins. Now it was up to James to sweep wickedness from the streets of London.

He had just reached the edge of Brixton when a young couple came into view. The man was bull-necked and muscular with fair hair cropped short. He wore a lightweight zip-up top paired with dark trousers and black boots. His girlfriend trailed a few feet behind him, a skinny teenage girl with long blonde hair pulled back from her forehead in a tight bun and wearing a clingy low-cut top. Her face was pink in the cold air, her eyes ringed with red. She seemed to be crying quietly.

James quickened his pace, his senses heightened in anticipation.

As he drew nearer, the man turned back to the girl and grabbed hold of her thin arm. 'Shut up, I told you. Shut up your whining.'

'Shut up yourself,' said the girl.

The man drew back his hand and cuffed the side of her head.

James began to run.

The man heard his approach and spun round to face him. He held the girl by one arm, pinching her tightly. She cried out in protest.

'I said shut it,' the man growled to her. His attention was on James now. 'What you looking at?' he said angrily. The girl squirmed in his grip but couldn't break free.

'Leave her alone,' said James. 'Stop hurting her.'

'I'll hurt her all I want to,' said the man. 'She's mine. You want some hurt too? I got plenty more to give.' He grabbed the girl by the hair and threw her roughly down onto the hard pavement. She stumbled and fell to her knees, crying harder, her jeans soaking up cold water from the gutter.

'Get away from here,' James said to the girl. She looked at him uncertainly, then got up slowly, clutching a broken heel from her shoe. 'Go on, now,' said James urgently.

She retreated to a safe distance. The man ignored her, his eyes all on James.

'What you gonna do to him?' the girl called to James.

'He's my boyfriend.'

'Stupid cow,' muttered the man. He came toward James, looking him over, assessing how much of a threat he posed. He didn't seem impressed by what he saw. 'You gonna regret this,' he promised James.

James stood his ground, waiting for him to move. 'Well, are you going to do anything then?' he asked.

A scowl appeared on the man's thick features and he threw a fist at James' face.

James ducked aside. 'I thought you were going to hurt me,' he said. 'That didn't hurt at all.'

The man growled angrily. He rushed at James for a second time, his right fist swinging.

Again James dodged the blow. 'You don't have to fight me,' he said. 'You could apologize instead. You could apologize to your girlfriend.'

His comment seemed to tip the man over the edge. Furious, he swung his leg up, aiming his boot at James' groin.

James caught the foot and yanked it hard. The man crashed to the ground with a roar of frustration and fury. He tried to break free from James' grip, but James held on tight, holding him down.

The man shouted foul abuse into the night air. He was growing angrier by the second.

James twisted the man's leg hard and felt it break. A howl of pain erupted from him. The leg went limp in James' hands and he let it drop.

The man lay prone on the ground, his leg at an odd angle.

The girl began to scream.

'Go!' James shouted at her. 'Run, and don't come back!'

She stared uncertainly, then turned, hobbling slowly away down the road with her broken shoe. She stopped some way off, waiting to see what would happen.

The man was scrabbling on the ground, trying to raise

himself up, but his leg was shattered at the knee. Shards of bone poked out of his trouser leg. He wailed in agony as he crawled toward the nearest wall.

James placed a foot on the man's bloody leg and pressed it to the ground, stopping him in his tracks and making him shriek wildly.

James spoke to him. 'Now the earth was corrupt in the sight of God, and the earth was filled with violence. God looked on the earth, and behold, it was corrupt.' The words were from the Book of Genesis. James looked on the corruption of the earth a while longer, then dropped onto the man, pinning him down to stop his struggling.

The man's shrieking subsided into self-pitying sobs and he began to plead. 'Help me. You gotta call an ambulance. Look what you've done to me. Tell the girl to call for help. Tell her.'

The girl was watching from a safe distance. She could have phoned for an ambulance, or for the police if she'd wanted to, but she hadn't. Not that it would have done much good. The emergency number was rarely answered these days.

'No,' said James. 'You could have saved yourself. If you'd been kind to her, if you weren't so full of hate, none of this would have happened.'

'I'll be nice to her,' said the man. 'Just let me go and I swear I'll treat her right.'

'It's too late for that,' James told him. 'You already made your choice. You should have read your Bible, then you'd know that God gathers the wheat and burns the chaff. But God isn't here right now. I came instead.'

'You're a headcase. You're fucking nuts.'

'No,' said James. 'I am the fire that burns clean.' They were the words Samuel had spoken to him once. They were good words, and true. He tore away the man's clothing to expose his chest and arms. He could smell the blood beneath the skin, could almost hear the murmuring of its lifegiving force. Saliva dripped from his open lips.

Lycanthropic

The man's chest rose and fell rapidly as he drew in precious air to his lungs. James opened his mouth wide and clamped his jaws around the man's throat. Saliva mixed with blood as he broke through the thin skin. The man began to scream, but James ripped through the soft cartilage that covered his gorge, twisting the head and breaking the spinal column. He did not mean his prey to suffer more than necessary. This man had sinned, but so had all men. So had James.

He knelt while eating, devouring the fresh, warm meat, chewing, swallowing, gulping it down. It had been many weeks since he'd tasted anything so good. The girl was no longer watching. She had fled at some point. James continued to feast. The man had been a bad boyfriend, but he made a good meal. His youthful body was well-toned. If he had cared for his soul as well as he had treated his body, he would still be alive.

There was no one around to watch James feed, and he took his time. As he ate he felt the life force enter him. His heart pumped louder, stronger. Blood pulsed through his veins. Energy filled his limbs.

And as he ate, the words of Christ rang loudly in his ears. 'He who eats my flesh and drinks my blood has eternal life, and I will raise him up on the last day. For my flesh is true food, and my blood is true drink.'

His teeth tore gladly into that meaty flesh. Blood slipped smoothly down his throat like ruby wine. When he had finally finished he sat up, then rose to his feet. He looked around to see if anyone was watching, but he was quite alone. Not that he felt shame about what he had done. A werewolf should feel no shame for hunting.

Instead he felt good. One less sinner walked this city of sin tonight, and this was just the beginning. He would sweep these streets clean, one sinner at a time.

Jesus had held out a promise of eternal life, that on the last day the dead would be resurrected. James yearned for that day with all his heart. It was not the last day yet, nor even the day before the last. But the last day was coming.

In the meantime, he was making a difference, down here on earth among the suffering and the misery. He raised his eyes to the cold, starry night that stretched toward infinity. Was God up there, watching him now?

James knew that he was.

'I made a difference,' he shouted into the blackness. 'You would have allowed that thug to beat his girlfriend, maybe even kill her. You'd have watched her suffering and done nothing to help her. You never do.'

There was no response from on high. No bright star appeared in the sky. No angels trumpeted. No voice spoke to him. God never did a thing.

But I did. I did something good.

Chapter Thirty

Cabinet Office Briefing Room A, Whitehall, Central London

'Gentlemen, ladies,' said the Prime Minister wearily, 'let us begin.'

Another day, another meeting of the War Cabinet. The PM spent her life in a state of perpetual emergency now. It was draining. Running the country during a crisis was an exercise in personal stamina as much as anything. She was not sleeping enough. She was eating the wrong kind of food at the wrong times. She was not making time to exercise. Sooner or later she would crash, but she hoped and prayed that she could keep going long enough.

The usual faces were gathered around the table this morning. The Home Secretary, the Foreign Secretary, the Chancellor of the Exchequer, the Director-General of MI5, the Metropolitan Police Commissioner and, like the ghost at the feast, the Chief of the Defence Staff, General

Sir Roland Ney. The General was itching to brief her on the latest security situation, but the PM had little appetite to kick off the meeting listening to the old General's grim pronouncements.

'Home Secretary,' she said, hoping for some good news. 'The airlift? How is it proceeding?'

For the first few days after her government had announced a ban on all international and domestic flights, the skies over central London had been strangely quiet. Now military transport planes were landing and taking off from the City Airport at all hours of the day and night, bringing food and other essentials. Even at midnight low-altitude turboprops droned noisily overhead. In peacetime, environmental campaigners would have been up in arms over the noise. Now the sound meant food was on its way, and no one was complaining about that.

'The operation is going according to plan,' said the Home Secretary. 'London City Airport is now under full military control and we are using Hercules and Atlas aircraft based at RAF Brize Norton in Oxfordshire to transport supplies. The airport is operating around the clock and we are meeting our initial targets. The next phase will be to bring in Globemaster transport planes to increase capacity. That should be in place by the end of the week.'

'Good. Excellent. What about distribution of food across London?'

'That is proving to be more difficult, Prime Minister. Movement within the capital is greatly restricted, as you know. Bridges and major roads are closed to traffic, and that is presenting problems for the distribution of humanitarian aid.' He shot an angry glance across the table at General Ney, but the Chief of the Defence Staff did not respond to the challenge. The Home Secretary continued. 'We are planning to start using Chinook helicopters to deliver food to designated centres around the city. That should enable us to streamline distribution. But there has been violence at distribution centres. The police are having to divert significant resources into suppressing rioters and looters. We still can't be certain that all the food is reaching the people who most need it.'

Problems. Problems. They were everywhere she turned. She longed to throw open her doors and welcome some new guests to her meeting. Young people perhaps, bringing fresh voices and original ideas. Perhaps that would help her to find a path through this quagmire. Doctor Helen Eastgate had been a welcome and refreshing change. In the short time she had spent as the Prime Minister's adviser, she had opened up the debate in ways that had been quite unexpected. She had helped to steady the Prime Minister's nerves when she had been at her most uncertain and vulnerable. The PM craved to hear from more young people like Helen, not the same old voices rehearsing the same old arguments.

But it was out of the question. One of the first casualties of war was trust. It had been shot down in flames the day that members of her own party had sided with the Leader of the Opposition to support his motion of no confidence. She must face the current emergency in the company of the few trusted men and women gathered with her today.

'We are working on the problem of security at the distribution centres, Prime Minister,' the Police Commissioner assured her.

'Make it your top priority,' she told him. 'I want daily reports on progress.'

'Yes, Prime Minister.'

The Foreign Secretary was next to brief her. 'The international security situation is deteriorating rapidly. China has shut down the internet and closed all news channels. Chinese troops have entered disputed territories in Nepal, Bhutan, Malaysia, Indonesia, Taiwan and Vietnam. Our representative at the UN's Security Council has protested in the strongest possible terms, but this is unlikely to result in any positive action. Meanwhile Russian forces have occupied Belarus, supposedly at the invitation of the Belarusian government, and are massing along the borders with Ukraine and Poland. Again our diplomatic efforts are likely to have little effect.'

'What is the latest news from the United States?' the PM asked him.

'California is seeking to secede from the union, despite constitutional objections. The state has appealed to the Supreme Court, but the court is refusing to hear the case. Now there is sabre-rattling on both sides. Other states may also try to break away. The view of our ambassador is that civil war is likely.'

'And in Europe?'

'Civil unrest is growing. There have been further violent protests against the tide of immigrants fleeing the Middle East. Heavy-handed police suppression of these protests has fuelled further violence. Nationalist and separatist voices are growing louder, on a wave of populist support. Meanwhile, werewolf activity is steadily increasing in every country, despite the tightened security measures.'

'Thank you, Foreign Secretary.'

The dire international situation served as a warning of the fine line she walked. Too lenient, and there would be a surge in werewolf activity. Too hardline, and civil unrest would grow. She could afford for neither to happen. She had been wrong to keep the General waiting. However bad his news might be, she needed to hear it now, and she needed to act.

'General, your report?'

As usual, the General stood to speak. 'Prime Minister. Our deployment of reinforcements is now complete, and a secure forward base has been established at Heathrow Airport. A network of road checkpoints has been established throughout the city and all river crossings have been sealed off. Our goal, as you know, is to deny the lycanthropes the ability to move.'

'Good.'

'We are now moving from passive control of the city to active engagement of our enemy. A series of intelligence-led operations including house-to-house searches is underway to find and eliminate known lycanthropes. This tactic is proving to be successful, although limited in scope. However, the operation has resulted in some casualties, and our patrols and checkpoints are coming under continuous attack. To counter this, I would like your permission to scale up the campaign against both lycanthropes and opposition forces. Immediately.'

'In what way?'

'I would like a free hand to deploy and use the full range of military capabilities at our disposal – tanks to reinforce checkpoints, helicopter gunships and drone strikes to take out suspected insurgents, rockets and artillery units against the strongholds of enemy forces, and a concerted campaign to eliminate known members of the so-called People's Uprising.'

The catalogue of heavy weapons and the prospect of allowing the General a free hand with them made the PM shudder. 'I cannot allow that, General,' she said. However dangerous the situation was, she had to keep him under tight control. And she knew very well what he meant by the word *eliminate*. 'I thought that the leaders of the People's Uprising were all behind bars?' she queried.

'They are, Prime Minister,' said the Police Commissioner. 'However, despite that, the movement continues to gain momentum. A People's March is currently being organized on social media. The plan is for a mass march to be held in London by students and activists, with similar marches in other major cities. Our intelligence indicates that as many as two hundred and fifty thousand people may try to participate.'

General Ney was still on his feet. 'Ban it,' he growled. 'This march is a direct challenge to your authority and must not be allowed to proceed. Let my men deal with anyone who defies the ban.'

The PM glared at him. 'General, it is not your decision. Police Commissioner, what is your recommendation?'

The Police Commissioner seemed unsure. 'It would be a huge drain on police resources, Prime Minister. We are already stretched. I am tempted to agree with the General, at least as far as placing a ban on the march.'

She steepled her fingers and leaned back in her chair. It did not take her long to make up her mind. 'This is not Russia or China. Free speech is one of the foundation stones on which this country is built. And free speech has meaning only if we permit our opponents to speak out. Besides, by allowing this march to take place we will diffuse the potential for more violent opposition.'

'But the People's Uprising is a banned organization,' interrupted the Home Secretary.

'A terrorist organization,' added the Police Commissioner. 'There are voices on social media calling for the marchers to storm Parliament and overthrow the government.'

'Parliament is already closed,' she told them. 'And the leaders of the movement are behind bars. The people taking part in this march are ordinary citizens with legitimate concerns. I will meet them and speak to them directly.'

'This is folly,' said the General. 'You must at least allow the army to take charge of security.'

The PM remembered the last time the General had been allowed to manage security at a public protest. Hundreds of civilians had been shot dead. 'Policing must remain the job of the police,' she replied. 'Police Commissioner, will you be able to cope with the arrangements?'

'Of course. This is a law and order matter. But as I say, we will need to assign very significant resources.'

'Good, then it is decided.'

Chapter Thirty-One

Brixton Hill, South London, crescent moon

The winter sun hung low and bright and Liz was hiding behind dark glasses again, cursing the dazzling light. No one else seemed to find the sunshine a problem, but she'd already resigned herself to being different to everyone else. She'd even slapped some UV protection on her face beneath her riot helmet. She knew that without it, her skin risked burning in the February sun. Ridiculous, but she had too many other problems to worry about that now.

A quarter of a million people were converging on central London. Liz and Dean marched alongside them, kitted out in full riot gear. The marchers were calling it the People's March. A March for Freedom. A March for Peace. Every single uniformed officer in the Metropolitan Police Service had been deployed to watch over them, and they were prepared for violence.

So far there had been none, at least on Liz's patch.

'What's wrong with these people?' moaned Dean. 'This is the very last thing we need right now. We ought to be out helping people, not nannying these prats.'

'People have a legal right to march peacefully,' said Liz. But as soon as she said it, she knew how Dean would respond.

'No, they don't. The People's Uprising is a banned terrorist organization. We could arrest these people right now just for turning up to march.'

'Don't even think about it,' she said. The police were outnumbered a hundred to one.

'Of course not. I just hope they don't start any trouble.'

Liz hoped so too, but she wouldn't stake any money on it. The People's Uprising was a mixed bag of students, anti-war demonstrators, opposition supporters and anarchists. Their leaders had been imprisoned, but that had only fuelled their anger. She remembered the time they had marched in Trafalgar Square. That had ended with the mob attacking and killing police officers and the army opening fire in response.

At least the army was staying well out of the way this time. Bringing soldiers onto the street today would be unbelievably provocative, and someone in government obviously had the good sense to keep them confined to their barracks. Even the usual army roadblocks were unmanned. Liz wondered briefly what Jones and the others were up to. She was still coming to terms with the botched operation that had left seven people dead, and she wished she could have done something differently.

There were no soldiers here today, but some of the police were armed. Dean carried his assault rifle on open display, its barrel pointed to the ground. Liz knew it was loaded and that he was authorized to use it. She carried her Glock out of sight beneath her stab-proof vest. She was not officially allowed to carry a firearm, but Dean insisted that she bring it. She had absolutely no intention of using it.

The crowd began to shout and chant as they marched. Their slogans were familiar. *Police and troops out now. Open the borders. End the curfew. Impeach the Prime Minister.*

There was fat chance that the government would give in to any of those demands. But perhaps that wasn't the purpose of the marchers. Perhaps their real aim was direct action. Their destination was Number Ten, Downing Street. What they intended to do when they arrived there wasn't clear. But in any case they would never get there. A ring of steel had been thrown up around Whitehall, and the roads that surrounded the centre of government were all closed. In fact every main thoroughfare into central London had been shut for the day. The roadblocks were manned by armed police and they had strict instructions not to let anyone through. Liz and Dean had been briefed on how to manage the crowds as they reached the barricades that would divert them away from the centre. The key strategy was to keep them moving. If they came to a halt and started to mass, all hell might break loose.

'Police out now!' shouted a man close to Liz. He was shouting at her, punching the air with an angry fist. 'Pigs out!'

Dean walked up to him, his fingers on the pistol grip of his Heckler & Koch.

The protester glared back defiantly but he didn't shout again.

Up ahead, the road was narrowing and the marchers began to slow as the crowd filled up the street.

'Please slow down and wait,' shouted Liz. 'Do not attempt to push forward.' She had witnessed crowd behaviour in football matches and other demonstrations. She'd seen how easily people could be crushed if the crowd began to surge.

A few people were already starting to push forward in frustration.

'Come on,' she said to Dean. 'Let's go and have a word in their ears.'

She moved close to the edge of the crowd, her attention fixed on the troublemakers. 'Sir, please stop pushing. You are putting others at risk of being crushed. Please wait for the crowd to move forward.'

Dean came and stood next to her, his carbine conspicuously on display. 'Oi! Did you hear what she said?'

Angry faces turned on him. 'Pig!' shouted a man whose mouth and nose were covered by a black scarf.

Liz rested her hand on Dean's shoulder. 'Ignore him.'

'Fascist!' called the man.

'He's just trying to provoke you,' said Liz.

'He's doing a damn good job.'

'Leave him,' she said. 'He's stopped pushing now.'

They stood back from the crowd, which had begun to move forward again. The man with the face scarf turned his attention back to marching and shouting his slogans.

So far, so good.

Liz's radio crackled with a report from further along the route. 'Officer Amber Lima 793 reporting possible security breach at junction with Normandy Road.'

'Hey,' said Dean. 'That's not far from here. Shall we check it out?'

'They haven't called for assistance. Let's wait and see.'

In the distance, she heard the low pulsing sound of a police helicopter approaching. The helicopter appeared overhead, its rotors clack-clacking as it flew. The crowd raised their fists and voices to it as it flew past.

'Something's happening,' said Liz. 'I don't like it. Let's go see.'

They quickened their pace, walking past the marchers in the direction of the helicopter. It was hovering a short distance ahead, above a road junction.

The voice from the radio spoke again. 'Amber Lima 793 requesting immediate backup. Junction with Normandy Road and Brixton Road. Urgent.'

The road junction wasn't far. When they reached it, a number of other officers had already gathered, and the helicopter was circling low overhead.

'Shit,' said Dean.

From out of the side road a second group of marchers was approaching. A rival group. Instead of anti-war protest banners the new marchers held Union Jack flags and waved the red cross of England. They were here to protest against the People's March.

'Vigilantes,' said Dean. 'This is going to get nasty.'

Chapter Thirty-Two

Trafalgar Square, Westminster, Central London, crescent moon

'There is still time to change your mind, Prime Minister. You do not have to do this,' the voice of the Metropolitan Police Commissioner boomed in her ear.

'On the contrary,' protested the PM. 'This country may be at war, but we are not at war with our own people. They need to see me and hear me speak. Besides, I refuse to hide away in fear.'

She waited for the door of her car to be opened, then stepped out into the glaring sunshine of Trafalgar Square. The square was strangely empty. It had been cleared since protesters had turned violent here a month previously, killing police officers. Troops had moved into the square then, firing on the marchers. The place had become a kind of shrine for the dead, who had taken on the status of martyrs. She would not permit any more symbolism to take root. She would confront her naysayers head-on and in person this time.

Above her, the stone figure of Admiral Horatio Nelson glared sternly down from atop his column. Another war hero. You could hardly move in Whitehall without the country's illustrious history reaching out a finger to touch the present. She knew that the Admiral's famous words, 'England expects that every man will do his duty,' were inscribed in bas-relief at the foot of the granite column.

And every woman too, do doubt, Admiral? Don't worry. I fully intend to.

The Police Commissioner appeared at her side again. 'I understand your desire for visibility, Prime Minister. But please, do not take any unnecessary risks today.'

'I do not intend to take any.' She began to cross the square in the direction of Admiralty Arch, the Commissioner and his officers fanning out in a group around her.

How great could the risk be? She had never seen so many police uniforms on the streets of London before. Her personal protection officers from SO1 were with her too, of course. The officers wore bulletproof vests and carried Glock pistols and MP5 submachine guns. They clustered around her so tightly she could barely see where she was going. Each one stood at least a foot taller than her.

They had wanted her to wear a bulletproof vest too. Preposterous. What kind of message would that have sent?

In addition to her protection officers, more than a thousand SO15 officers from Counter Terrorism Command had taken over control of Whitehall from Trafalgar Square in the north to the Houses of Parliament at its southern end. The entire area was sealed off to both vehicles and pedestrians. Downing Street, the Cabinet Office and the Ministry of Defence buildings were all out of bounds to the public. And on top of all that, police marksmen had been deployed to watch over her. She couldn't see them, but she knew that armed snipers were positioned on top of key buildings throughout the area. It seemed an excessive measure, given the fact that the marchers' stated objective was to stop the war and bring an end to violence.

'This is still a democracy,' she told the Police Commissioner. 'I govern with the consent of the people. The greatest risk is that I won't be able to get close enough for them to even see me.'

'I would be very glad if you did not, Prime Minister.'

'Huh,' she said. 'That is because you are not a politician.'

The closest the crowds were being allowed to march was the Mall, the ceremonial road west of Whitehall. She strode through the archway that led out to the Mall and caught her first glimpse of the people who had marched to confront her. The People's March they had named it, in an attempt to step around the inconvenient fact that the People's Uprising had been declared an illegal organization. They were massing now, filling the broad thoroughfare that led to Buckingham Palace.

She had to stifle a gasp when she saw them.

She had seen this wide road packed with crowds before. More than a million well-wishers had turned out to attend royal weddings and for the Queen's Jubilee. There were no well-wishers today, not a single one. But she had never before seen so many people in one place. The number must be far greater than the quarter of a million that her advisers had predicted. The sunny weather might be partly to blame for that, but it couldn't in itself account for the huge turnout.

The crowds thronged the Mall along its entire half-mile length. She had never imagined there could be so many. A surging wave of humanity, dedicated to a single aim. To topple her government and see her personally brought low.

At royal weddings, the crowds had waved flags. Now

they unfurled paint-daubed banners. Each one was a rejection of her policies.

A thick skin was a necessary requirement for any politician, and the PM was better able than most to handle criticism. Yet still, the sheer size of the crowd and its overwhelming hostility shocked her. She was suddenly glad of the armed police who surrounded her, and the snipers stationed on rooftops. Their shadowy forms were clearly visible now on top of the Carlton House Terrace buildings overlooking the Mall.

A podium had been constructed in front of Admiralty Arch, the landmark building that marked the entrance to the Mall from Trafalgar Square. She climbed up to the podium, her limbs unexpectedly heavy with dread, using the rail that flanked the steps to hide the fact that her hand was shaking.

From the stage of the podium, the crowd seemed even larger.

For a moment she wavered, wondering if she had made a mistake coming here today. How could she possibly hope to convince these people that their opposition was misguided? They stood resolute, like an implacable force, chanting their slogans and their demands. She scanned the faces at the front of the crowd. They seemed possessed by a fervour, almost like zealots. These were the ones most hostile to her rule. Her words would be wasted on them.

A surge of anger flooded her then. How could they not see the peril the country faced? If she did not take the decisive action necessary to stop the werewolf threat, then every man, woman and child here today risked becoming prey to a wolf. The threat was global and without precedent. It must be stopped at all costs. She must make them see the truth of the matter.

But anger would not serve her.

I am a public servant, she reminded herself. *My duty is to all the people, whether they voted for me or not.*

She approached the microphone at the front of the

podium and stood before them.

Chapter Thirty-Three

Brixton Hill, South London, crescent moon

Liz and Dean rushed to intercept the crowds of vigilantes as they pushed down the narrow street. Their route would bring them into direct conflict with the People's March. The mob was moving at high speed, waving patriotic flags and punching the air with their fists. As they drew near to the marchers, they began to shout abuse.

A wedge of uniformed police officers swept forward to keep the rival groups apart. Liz found herself in the front line, with muscular young men towering over her. The crowd jostled up against her, but she pushed back, holding firm.

'Hey, let us through,' said one of the vigilantes, a huge man with close-cropped hair and a green jacket. He had words tattooed on his neck. Liz peered at them. *White power*, they read. 'We're on your side,' he told Liz. 'Let us get at those bastards.'

'We are not here to take sides,' she told him firmly. 'Now please step back or you will be arrested for breaching the peace.'

Another man, wearing tracksuit bottoms and a tight T-shirt that showed off huge biceps, leaned toward her. 'Step aside, darling, unless you wanna get hurt.' His fair hair was shaved with a swastika. 'We're only here to get the ones spreading the disease. You know – the immigrants, and their friends.'

Liz treated him to a flinty stare, not holding back any of her distaste for these thugs. 'I'm warning you. Threatening a police officer is a criminal offence.'

The tattooed guy leaned in. 'The immigrants should never have been allowed to come here in the first place,' he said, warming to his theme. 'England is for the English, right? And we're here to take it back.' Liz saw now that the man was carrying a baseball bat studded with nails.

The police helicopter swept overhead, momentarily drowning out the voices of the crowd. Liz glanced around to search for Dean, but he was busy in an altercation with another bunch of young thugs. More armed police were arriving and police vehicles with flashing lights and sirens were blocking the road junction behind her. She just had to be patient and hold the line and reinforcements would be with her soon.

In front of her, *white power* man grimaced menacingly and hefted his baseball bat. She remembered the men just like him who had attacked the centre for asylum seekers. She pictured the petrol bombs, and the fire that had nearly ended Mihai's young life. Blood boiled in her veins at the recollection.

The Glock concealed beneath her vest pressed against her skin. She had sworn to herself that she would not use it under any circumstances. But it was sorely tempting to draw it out.

'It's the Romanians we're after,' continued *white power* man. 'Not you. But we'll take you down if you try to stop us.'

Liz's hand shot out and grabbed his thick bull neck. The man's eyes bulged in surprise. With unnatural strength she drew him down toward her until his face was inches from hers. She flipped the visor of her helmet up. The man's expression was a mix of confusion and outrage. 'Oi!' he said. 'Police brutality!'

She sniffed at him. Beneath the stale smell of tobacco and the rank stink of his sweat, he smelled of nothing more than the bacon and sausages she had devoured for breakfast. 'You're meat,' she muttered under her breath. 'Just flesh and blood to be devoured.' She didn't know if the man had heard her words, or else if something of her thoughts were reflected in her features. Either way, he turned pale and his expression switched abruptly from hate-fuelled anger to dread fear.

The taste of blood filled her mouth and she showed him her teeth. They were normal teeth, nothing to be afraid of, but the man's eyes popped wide open and he stared at them as if they were daggers, already coated with his own blood. 'Let me go,' he muttered, struggling to get away from her. She held him firm and he began to shriek in terror. Then she shoved him and he staggered back, knocking his fellow protesters out of his way. 'She's mad,' he said. 'What's wrong with her? She's a total fucking maniac.'

The man with the swastika was staring at Liz like he'd seen a ghost. He backed away too, flailing his arms in his desperation to leave. The men around him fell back in disarray.

Dean appeared at her side, his carbine raised. The vigilantes retreated to a safe distance. 'Are you all right?' he asked her. 'What on earth did you do to those guys?'

'I'm not sure,' said Liz. Whatever she'd done, it hadn't been deliberate. Something inside her had just snapped. Somehow she'd put the fear of God into those men, and she didn't know how.

'You look pale,' said Dean. 'Even paler than before. Like, white as a sheet. Your lips are all red.'

'I feel fine.' Yet that was a lie. She felt far from fine. Her skin was pulsating as if charged with electricity, and it was cold too. Icy cold. But that wasn't the worst thing by a long way. She knew that for a brief moment, as the scent of the man's flesh had filled her nostrils, she had wanted to eat him. She'd wanted to sink her teeth into his neck, just where the artery pulsed beneath the skin, and begin to suck out his ...

'There's blood on your lips,' said Dean. 'Did you bite your tongue?'

'I don't know,' said Liz. She licked the salty, iron-rich blood from her lips. It was her own blood, but it wasn't from her tongue. It was her gums that were bleeding. She probed them with the tip of her tongue. The blood came from two small holes, one in the upper left of her mouth, and one from the upper right. It was almost as if two new teeth had forced their way through. Sharp teeth, thirsty for blood.

But that was an absurd notion. New teeth didn't suddenly appear like that. And they certainly didn't vanish again a minute later. And yet the holes in her gums were real enough. Something had made them.

The helicopter flew over once again, and more police rushed past in a baton charge. The vigilantes fought back, fighting with knives and bats, and hurling bricks and petrol bombs. Police cars burst into flames and officers were hurt.

But the tide of police swept onward with batons raised. Protesters were beaten. Arrests were made. Hands were cuffed. Soon the situation was back under control.

But for Liz the day was as good as over. She wanted only to curl up in a darkened room and go to sleep. It was three o'clock in the afternoon.

Chapter Thirty-Four

The Mall, Westminster, Central London, crescent moon

The Prime Minister stood before the vast crowd, the microphone open and ready to amplify her words. But her mouth was dry, the words stuck in her throat. What could she say to these people? They already knew the facts. They must all have witnessed the news reports of werewolf attacks for themselves. Every TV and mobile phone in the country had shown countless photos and videos of yellow-eyed beasts prowling the streets of London. The endless reports of deaths, of vicious murders of innocent civilians, of brutal mutilations of bodies had been heard by everyone, over and over again. How could they not understand the need for decisive action?

She opened her mouth to speak, but the crowd was already shouting back at her. Boos, catcalls, shouts of 'Resign,' and worse. A vast chorus of abuse, all directed at her.

'I stand before you today…' she began.

The crowd grew louder. No one was listening to her. It didn't matter what she said. No one here would be persuaded by her carefully-prepared arguments. And there were so many demonstrators, all of them united in common purpose – to defy her authority and bring down her government.

She spoke into the microphone a second time. 'Please, hear what I have to say…' Once again she fell silent, cowed by the wave of hatred coming from the crowd. Their angry voices washed over her like a rising flood.

She wondered if she had misjudged the extent of popular opposition to her leadership. She had cut herself off from her people and surrounded herself with yes-men like the Foreign Secretary, and hardliners like the General. She had permitted the arrest and detention of all those who spoke out against her, and in her windowless War Cabinet office she had shut herself off from anyone who might have offered alternative points of view.

She'd convinced herself that she could be a giant of history, like Churchill or Nelson. But standing here before the people, the truth must be startlingly obvious to everyone. She was no giant, but a tiny, diminutive woman. She had narrowly survived a motion of no confidence, and only the blind party loyalty of her fellow members of parliament had saved her from humiliating defeat.

Perhaps it would be better if she stepped down and allowed the Leader of the Opposition to take over. She could resign right now, in front of the whole nation, and order the release of her political opponents. The People's Uprising could take control, and she would see how well they handled the situation. Disastrously, she suspected. But the burden would no longer be hers to bear. Others would take the blame for whatever happened.

The roar of the crowd grew more insistent, baying for her blood, and she was powerless to respond.

She remembered then what Doctor Helen Eastgate had

said to her. *I have confidence in you.* The memory was like a small candle glowing in the dark. The glow slowly kindled a fire in her heart. Helen's words had strengthened her resolve during her darkest hour, and they were working their magic once again. Helen had spoken to her of a "hunch." That hunch might be nothing more than a thin straw, but a drowning woman needed to grasp hold of whatever was available. In politics, a hunch was often all you had. You looked at the facts arrayed before you, and you made a judgement call. The PM had already made hers. She had chosen to fight.

Behind her stood the SO1 protection officers and the Police Commissioner in his full-dress uniform. She commanded the full authority of her government. She had nothing to fear from a noisy mob.

I will not give in. I will not bow to this pressure. Someone must do the right thing, and it is my fate to be that person.

She opened her mouth once more, confidently this time, but the sound of a loud thud behind her stopped her from speaking. A shout followed.

She turned round in surprise. The SO1 officers on the stage were in motion, ushering the Police Commissioner and her ministers away, and more officers were dashing up onto the stage. Hands seized her from the side and began to pull her toward the back of the podium. She struggled briefly in confusion before realizing that two of her own protection officers were pulling her to safety.

An instant later a second noise came, this time the unmistakable sound of a bullet embedding itself in flesh. Voices in the crowd screamed. The officer standing closest to her began to fall.

More thuds sounded as bullets hit home. She had no idea where they were coming from. She allowed herself to be dragged toward the back of the stage. As she reached the top of the steps she turned and caught sight of the fallen SO1 officer. He was sprawled across the stage where she had stood a moment earlier. Thick blood covered one half of his face. The top of his skull was missing.

More bullets struck the podium in rapid succession, gouging holes in its wooden structure. She quickly descended the steps at the rear of the stage, men crowding around her as she went. She did not ask them what was happening. She simply let them do their job.

The air buzzed with voices as police officers reported into their radios.

'Control, PM's status is under attack from unidentified shooter. Repeat under attack.'

'Officer X-Ray Bravo Four down. Request urgent emergency response.'

She heard a second officer cry out and go down right behind her.

'Office Foxtrot Golf Seven down. Request urgent emergency response.'

'Shooter sighted in third-floor window of Carlton Terrace. Range three five zero metres.'

Bullets continued to thud into the back of the stage. Her blue jacket was splashed with bright red blood. She realized then that the second officer to fall had interposed his own body as a human shield to save her.

Strong hands pulled her into a waiting BMW X5 from Protection Command. The red-painted vehicle pulled away as soon as she was seated and strapped in. Her personal protection officer sat in the front passenger seat, speaking into his radio. 'Control, PM is safe and in response vehicle. Unharmed, repeat unharmed. Vehicle is mobile.'

Unharmed. She touched the blood that had splashed her suit. It was wet and still warm. *Officer down.* Two men had given their lives to save her just now. At least two.

My God, what have I done?

The car sped from the scene, tyres screeching, the seatbelt tugging at her, the driver accelerating across Trafalgar Square and back through Whitehall. In stark contrast to the Mall, the roads here were empty apart from lines of police vehicles parked bumper to bumper along its edge. The car sped along its length, with support vehicles following closely behind. Traffic lights changed from green to red, but the car didn't once slow. Waiting officers waved it through.

The radio was quiet now and so was her mind. She began to compose her thoughts. She was resolved. The way forward was clear. If the aim of the People's March had been to change her mind, it had failed utterly. She would not allow the rule of law to be usurped. Whatever it took, she would win this war, and she would tolerate no further dissent.

As she returned to the safety of Downing Street, the police radio crackled into life once again. 'Shooter down. Repeat shooter down.'

Chapter Thirty-Five

*Streatham Hill Sewer, South London,
crescent moon*

A spider scampered lightly across Mr Canning's face, rousing him from his slumber. The headmaster opened his one remaining eye and watched the spider scuttling away along the sleeve of his jacket, hoping to make its escape. It didn't get far before his fingers closed around its fat little body, trapping it, then squeezing it slowly until it burst open like a blister.

Mr Canning hated the spiders. The ugly pocket-sized monsters watched him from the darkness with their many eyes. 'And I have just one eye to return your evil gaze,' he told the squashed spider. 'A naughty girl poked out the other one with a ball point pen.' He brushed the dead thing from his fingers and washed his hand clean in the water that flowed past the end of his feet. Not very clean though. The muddy water was filthy. The spider floated away downstream and Mr Canning was glad to see it go.

Lycanthropic

You couldn't hold a conversation with spiders. They had no sense of humour.

You couldn't eat them either. Their bloated bodies were filled with slime and their spindly legs stuck in your throat.

'Nasty, disgusting creatures,' pronounced the headmaster. The spiders were not his friends.

Water dribbled down the cold brick wall behind him and he pushed himself to his feet. The sewer wouldn't have been his first choice of sanctuary, but he'd needed to find a safe bolt hole when the soldiers began their manhunt, and it had turned out to be not as bad as he'd expected.

London's sewer network was the Rolls-Royce of wastewater systems, harking back to a more elegant age when craftsmanship had been valued. Thousands of miles of tunnels crisscrossed the capital, and the Victorian engineers and labourers who had built the system had made it to last. It wasn't like those modern plastic pipes that would probably spring a leak within a few years. The men who had constructed this cathedral of sewerage had made it a work of art. Before the creation of the underground network, the whole of London had been one open sewer, conveying cholera to the masses. The introduction of the sewer system had been heralded as one of the greatest public health advances in history.

Now Mr Canning made his home in its cold, wet tunnels. 'Oh look at me!' he cried. 'I slid into the gutter, then slithered down a sewer!' He laughed raucously, and a chorus of cackling voices echoed back to him off the low ceiling of his new abode.

The smell down here wasn't too good, it had to be said. Mr Canning's werewolf nose wrinkled in permanent disgust at the reeking smell of shit. He'd hoped he would have grown used to it by now, but it seemed that he never would. But at least it was London's shit. 'I am bathing in the glorious effluent of the world's finest city!' he shouted gleefully, raising his arms to the curved tunnel roof.

Brown water trickled down his sleeves from the crumbling bricks overhead. His brand new three-piece suit was a shitty, sodden mess. He was probably overdressed for the situation, he was the first to admit it. Nobody else wore a suit down here, certainly not a waistcoat and tie. At least, he had not met anyone wearing one. He hadn't met anyone at all.

'Someone has to set the standards down here,' he announced.

There was no reply, save the dripping of the water and the echo of his own voice. That echo would drive you insane if you let it. But he wouldn't.

'No, not me,' giggled the headmaster. 'Not as long as I still have my children to talk to.'

Ah yes, his children. He'd been a school headmaster before, when he'd lived in the world up top, the world of day and night, of sun and rain. Manor Road Secondary School, that had been his domain. It felt like such a long time ago. 'I've always been very fond of children,' he said aloud.

It had been a delight to discover that the sewers were full of children.

One of them was coming now. He could hear it scrabbling along the brick wall, making quick splashing sounds as its feet dipped in and out of the muddy water. A faint light from the storm overflow above was enough for him to see it. He held himself motionless, waiting for it to come closer.

Splish-splash, splish-splash. Closer and closer it came.

He shot out a hand to grab it as it tried to run past.

'Ah, hello there,' said Mr Canning to the rat. 'Have we met before? I don't think I've had the pleasure.'

The rat struggled in his grasp and tried to nip him with its sharp little teeth.

Mr Canning stroked its furry back and tugged at its coarse whiskers. 'Naughty ratty,' he scolded. 'I insist that you stop that at once!'

Mr Canning liked the rats. They were really quite tasty, at least compared with the spiders. He liked the way they squeaked when he held them up by their stiff tails, their beady eyes rolling in panic, their bodies bending and twisting as they struggled to break free.

'You are my children now,' he whispered to the rat. 'And I love to eat my children.'

The rat thrashed in his grip and he held it tighter with both hands. First he nibbled at its tiny pink toes, then he bit off its feet, one by one. The rat squealed.

'Does that tickle?' he asked. The rat made no reply. They were not such great conversationalists, rats. Not much better than the spiders really. Mr Canning bit off its tail and spat it out. You couldn't eat rats' tails, no matter how hungry you were. In fact there was very little meat on a rat at all.

The rodent struggled desperately in his grip. 'I can't let you go now,' said Mr Canning softly. 'You wouldn't get very far with no feet.' He giggled. 'I'm not a cruel person, you know.' He bit into its soft flanks, enjoying the spurt of blood at the back of his throat. The rat's heart beat furiously, pumping the life-giving liquid into the headmaster's open mouth. He chewed at the raw meat, using his tongue to sort the edible parts from the fur and the bones. He spat out the parts that didn't taste good.

The rat lay still now. Mr Canning tossed it aside.

His hunger had hardly been abated. Nor his boredom. If he wanted a filling meal and a more satisfying conversation he would have to head above ground. The previous evening he'd eaten a hedgehog for his supper. He hoped for something more substantial this time. Something less prickly.

The dim light that shone through the metal grating overhead had faded to a dark grey, tinged with the yellow glow of a streetlamp. It was time to begin his evening stroll.

The headmaster flicked on his flashlight. The curved brick wall of the sewer arced away from him. He swept the beam upstream and down, following it with his one eye. The light reflected off the muddy water that trickled down the middle of the tunnel. 'Farewell, my children,' he called to any rats that may have been listening. 'Fear not, I shall return.'

The beam of light picked out the rusty iron rungs of a ladder, fixed to the tunnel wall. Mr Canning sloshed over to it and placed the flashlight between his teeth. In his pocket was the iron hook he used to open and close the manhole covers. That and the flashlight were all he needed to live down here.

And of course he had his children too. He would never be quite alone, just as long as he had them to talk to.

Chapter Thirty-Six

St Thomas' Hospital, Central London, crescent moon

Chanita Allen was attending to a patient – a teenage girl with fourth-degree burns – when she heard a colleague calling her name. 'Chanita, a man is here to see you.'

'Just a moment,' she called back. Her hands moved deftly and gently as she unwrapped the patient's dressings. The girl had been pulled from a house fire with burns that had stripped the skin, fat and muscle from her hands and feet, reducing them to blackened stumps. Her extremities had been impossible to save and had been amputated on arrival. The girl was unconscious now, under heavy sedation, and that was a blessing.

Chanita's job as a nurse brought her closer to disease and death than most people could comprehend. She lived on the frontline of the war against human suffering and didn't fool herself that this war could ever be won. Yet her work filled her with hope and enthusiasm, not pessimism and despair, for although she knew that sickness and misery would follow closely wherever humans walked, so too would kindness and compassion.

Since leaving her post at King's College Hospital, her skills had been in high demand. She had transferred to the Emergency Department at St Thomas' Hospital, and then into Intensive Care. The work was demanding and exhausting, but it made a welcome change from treating the bite patients on the quarantine wards. Although she had gained significant expertise in treating patients with lycanthropy, she had come to dislike them, and in doing so she had begun to dislike herself. For if she couldn't feel compassion for her patients, she did not feel entirely human.

There was no shortage of need for emergency and intensive care right now. Chanita had long since forgotten about weekends, going home in the evening, or even taking lunch breaks. She worked round the clock, sleeping on a bench near the ward, grabbing meals or snacks whenever she could.

And still the number of patients kept growing. The burns patients were some of the worst. And the girl lying before her wasn't the most badly burned she had seen this week.

'Take your time,' said a man's voice from close behind. 'I didn't mean to interrupt your work.'

She turned in surprise to see her visitor, looking up at the handsome features of the man whose life had so recently but so briefly intersected with hers. 'Colonel Griffin,' she said. She had not expected to see him again.

His bright blue eyes fixed her with that startling intensity she had come to know so well, and she swallowed hard. She had forgotten just how overwhelming the feeling of standing so close to him could be. Her hands stopped moving as she took in the strong line of his jaw, the faint creases around his eyes and mouth, and the strangely silvered hair that crowned his youthful face.

He gave her a sad smile. 'I can see you're much needed here.'

She nodded and resumed work on the patient. 'The ICU is running at Black Alert,' she said. 'All the beds are full, but we've brought in more staff to deal with the overflow. Somehow we're managing to run at double our official capacity. But the demand for intensive care keeps rising. I don't think we can continue to cope.'

He moved aside to allow a second nurse to hurry past and attend to another patient. 'You look exhausted,' he said. 'When did you last sleep?'

'Yesterday. Or the day before. I snatch a few hours when I can.' She discarded the soiled dressings and began to clean the exposed tissue beneath.

He nodded. 'I came here to ask you to do something for me, but I see now that I made a mistake. The work you're doing here is much more important than what I had in mind.'

'I do my best,' said Chanita. 'It might look hopeless to some people, but I never give up hope.'

'I can see that,' he said. 'That was why I came to see you.'

'What is it you wanted to ask me?'

The Colonel watched her as she worked. 'The Prime Minister has assigned me a new task. Apparently I didn't screw up enough last time for her to completely lose faith in me.' He laughed mirthlessly.

Chanita didn't laugh. She had nearly lost her life the night that werewolves overran the quarantine hospital. Colonel Griffin had saved her. She had never lost faith in him, not even for an instant.

'People are beginning to leave London,' he continued. 'Official government policy is to prevent them going, to stop the spread of the disease, but hundreds are already leaving each day. That number might soon become thousands. Some have relatives or friends to stay with, but others have nowhere to go. The Prime Minister has given me the job of establishing emergency camps outside the city. We'll be setting up tents and soup kitchens mainly, but there are bound to be medical requirements too. It'll be routine stuff – treating minor injuries, diagnosing infections, dispensing medications, and so on. Nothing like what you're doing here.'

'When do you start?' she asked.

'Today. There's no time for delay. The trucks are already loading up with equipment and supplies. We'll be setting up three camps initially – one to the north, one west and one south of the city. It's a military-led operation, but we'll be working in tandem with the emergency aid sector. We're used to deployment in war zones, and the aid groups have worked in Africa, Asia and South America. It's strange to think we'll be setting up camp in leafy England.'

'Do you have doctors and nurses available?' she asked.

'Yes,' he replied. 'Not enough, but we'll just have to cope. I'm hoping that we can get the resources we need over time. But I wanted to ask …'

'Yes?'

'I know that your work here is important. And I know that last time you worked with me, you were almost killed. I couldn't bear for anything like that to happen to you again.'

'Go on.'

'I'd like you to accompany me. I need as many doctors and nurses as I can find. You're a good nurse, Chanita, perhaps the best I've ever known. But you're more than that. You're –' He trailed off, embarrassed. 'I've said too much. It was wrong to ask you. I should never have come here.'

She finished the dressing and looked up again at his blue eyes. It was impossible to refuse eyes that held such yearning and compassion. 'Of course I'll come,' she said. 'Wait for me downstairs. I'll go and fetch my things.'

Chapter Thirty-Seven

Brixton Village, South London, crescent moon

Salma Ali smelled the man before she saw him. As soon as she opened the front door of her house, a stink of blocked drains, or worse, washed inside. She raised her hand protectively to shield her nose.

The man's appearance was no better than his smell. His long and greying hair stuck to the side of his head, almost concealing the black patch that hid one eye. A grey beard clotted with filth covered his face and neck. He wore a suit that might once have been smart, but now hung dripping from his shoulders like an ill-fitting and soiled cloak. The tie around his neck was stained brown. In one hand he clutched an evil-looking iron hook.

But it was the smell that overwhelmed her. That dreadful stink. The stink of –

'Good evening,' said the man pleasantly. 'Ms Ali, isn't it? Perhaps you would be so kind as to spare me a moment of your time?'

She backed away instinctively, trying to shut the door on him, but his foot shot across the threshold and prevented her from closing it. He forced the door wide open again, a look of amusement playing on his thin lips.

'How do you know my name?' she asked, horrified.

'Don't be alarmed. I mean you no harm. I have nothing to sell to you, nor do I wish to engage you in a discussion about your religious beliefs. I have something more vital to talk about.'

'What?' she asked, folding her arms across her chest and positioning herself to make it clear that this would be a doorstep conversation.

'My name is Mr Canning.' He slipped his horrible iron hook into his pocket and offered her his hand, but she didn't take it. The man was truly repulsive. He looked like he'd been living in a drain. But it wasn't just his smell, or his bedraggled appearance that appalled her. Something in his demeanour was truly abhorrent. He dropped his hands back to his side, opening and closing them like a strangler.

He didn't seem offended by her rejection of his handshake. 'I used to be headmaster of a local school,' he continued. 'Unfortunately my school was shut down after a number of children mysteriously went missing.' He patted his pot belly with a satisfied smile. 'I fear they may have been eaten.'

Now she knew him.

Mr Canning. The story about the missing children and the killer headmaster had been all over the local news. It had even made the national headlines. The children had been murdered and the headmaster arrested. It was the school where Ben Harvey had taught. In fact Ben Harvey had been the one who'd grappled with the headmaster and brought his reign of terror to an end. But if this man was really who he claimed to be, that meant –

'I'm a werewolf,' he remarked conversationally. 'Is that a problem?'

Salma backed away from him. 'Get away from here now, or I will scream for help.'

'Perhaps from your pet hooligan, Jack Stewart?' suggested Mr Canning, 'or your Polish bully-boy, Mr Kowalski? They don't frighten me. I'd break them into pieces.'

It was too late to close the door on him. He already had one foot inside the house. In any case, she doubted whether a locked door would keep him out. 'What do you want from me?' she demanded.

'I was waiting for you to ask.' Mr Canning smiled. 'It's not so much what I want from you, but what I can do for you. I have a proposal. It concerns a mutual acquaintance, Ben Harvey.'

'I don't know why you think I know anyone by that name, Mr Canning –'

'I don't think it,' interrupted the headmaster. 'I know it. I know a lot of things. Surprising for a man with only one eye, don't you think, to see so much? But nevertheless, I know everything that goes on around here. No one sees me, but I see them.'

'So you know Ben Harvey,' she said. 'I don't understand why you think that –'

The headmaster leaned in close to her and she had to pull back from the stench. 'I don't think that the local residents would be so keen to have you in charge if they knew the truth about Mr Harvey,' he said.

'What truth is that?'

'That you falsely accused him of being a werewolf, and then framed him for the death of poor Mr and Mrs Hallibury, who you had locked in your cellar. They may decide that you're a most unsuitable person to be running the Watch.'

'I see,' she said. It seemed as if she had little choice in the matter. The headmaster had her checkmated, at least for the moment.

'Don't worry,' he said, tapping his nose. 'I can keep a

secret. And I believe that I could be useful to you in other ways too. I have ways of finding things out, you see. For instance, I happen to know where I can lay my hands on some guns. That might be useful for your empire building? And I'm always happy to help out with troublesome residents. I can be rather persuasive, in fact.'

'So it would seem, Mr Canning.' A deal with the Devil always came with an upside, she supposed. She just hoped he wouldn't demand too high a price in return. 'Perhaps you'd better come inside,' she suggested. She regretted it almost immediately.

The reek that accompanied him inside the house was appalling. 'I must apologize for my smell, and for my appearance,' he said. 'I've been living below ground for a while now. It's not very sanitary in a sewer, but quite fascinating. I'd recommend a visit if you have time.'

'Thanks,' said Salma. 'Perhaps another day.'

Mr Canning nodded. 'Very wise. To tell the truth, I was growing tired of living underground. Your home really is very beautiful, you know. A change of scenery would be nice.'

She looked down at the wet and soiled footprints he had left on her carpet. 'Perhaps a change of clothing too?' she suggested. 'And a hot bath?'

The headmaster beamed at her. 'My dear, you read my mind. I do believe we're going to get along famously.'

'Are all werewolves quite as charming as you, Mr Canning?' she asked, as she led him upstairs to the bathroom.

'I fear not. In my experience, some of them can be quite uncouth.'

'I can imagine,' she said. 'Is there anything else I can get you?'

'Oh, I don't require much,' replied the headmaster. 'A hot bath and some fresh clothes would be a good start. A safe place to sleep would be even better. I don't need feeding. I can take care of myself in that regard. But do you know what I've missed most? Some good conversation. I made a few friends down in the sewers, but I would so much prefer the company of an intelligent young woman.'

Chapter Thirty-Eight

*Cabinet Office Briefing Room A, Whitehall,
Central London, crescent moon*

Hours had passed since the shooting, but the Prime Minister was still shaken. She could not stop her hands from trembling.

How close did I come?

Too close.

'The would-be assassin is dead, Prime Minister,' the Police Commissioner reported. 'Four accomplices are also dead and an additional sixteen members of the terrorist cell are under arrest. We are conducting ongoing searches at a number of addresses and are confident of making further arrests soon.'

She nodded but said nothing. The event had left her too dazed.

'The march has now been broken up and the protesters dispersed. A number of violent incidents took place along the route of the march and there have been battles between rival groups of protesters.'

She was shaken, but angry too. Angry with the people who had done this. Angry with herself for allowing it to happen.

'The total number of casualties is not yet confirmed,' continued the Commissioner. His voice trailed off. Perhaps he saw the effect his words were having on her.

Shame. That was the emotion that gripped her most fiercely.

Men had died before her eyes. Good men. Long-serving and loyal officers. They had given their lives to protect her. And for a brief moment she had stood at that lectern and considered giving in to her critics.

Shame. Her cheeks burned with it.

'I should like to meet the families of the SO1 officers who were killed,' she said.

'Of course, Prime Minister.'

'Is the city secure now?' she asked.

'As secure as we have been able to make it. As I said, the demonstrators have been dispersed. The rival groups have been separated. But rioting goes on and fires still burn unchecked in some areas. The police and fire service are dealing with these now. The emergency departments in all London hospitals are in a state of black alert. We are transferring casualties to other parts of the country where possible.'

'Good.' She lapsed into silence again.

I almost gave up. I will never do so again.

'General?'

'Yes, Prime Minister?'

'What is your assessment of the situation? Is the city secure?'

'No. Far from it.'

I should have listened to him before. I should not have been so arrogant.

'What must be done?'

The General rose to his feet, as was his habit. 'Security

of the city cannot be guaranteed. As long as opposition to your rule is permitted, there will always be a threat.'

'We are arresting the leaders of the conspiracy, Prime Minister,' the Police Commissioner interjected.

'That is just a start,' countered the General. 'The time for tolerance and half measures is over. We cannot deal with two enemies at once. Therefore, all dissent must be crushed. First of all, social media was instrumental in organizing the People's March and so all social media platforms must be blocked. Under the war powers available to us, we do not need to liaise with the companies responsible or seek legal authority for this. With your authorization, our cyber warfare agents at GCHQ can bring this into immediate effect. Secondly, all future demonstrations and marches must be declared illegal. Thirdly, all criminal elements must be dealt with harshly and quickly. The police should be given the power to arrest and detain suspected militants and lawbreakers indefinitely and without trial. Only then will we begin to have a hope of defeating the true enemy – the lycanthropes.'

'Yes. What else?'

'The strategy of containment must be amplified. Despite the roadblocks, the city remains porous. Lycanthropes, rebels and criminals continue to move unchecked. London is too large to be controlled at street level by any military force.'

'What do you suggest?'

'Immediate closure of the underground transport network and all railway stations and other forms of public transport within the capital. Civilian cars must be banned. This will have the added advantage of stemming the flow of refugees. The curfew should be extended to cover all hours from dusk to dawn.'

The Home Secretary objected angrily. 'We cannot simply deny our citizens the right to move within their own city.'

'But we must deny movement to our enemies,' insisted the General.

'Do it,' said the Prime Minister. 'What else do you need, General?'

'Prime Minister, our forces are beginning to come under increasingly heavy attack from lycanthropes. The enemy is now armed and we are taking significant casualties. But my hands are tied. We cannot fight back effectively against guerrilla warfare in a densely crowded city unless we are willing to take difficult decisions.'

'What decisions?'

'We must intensify our military operations significantly. At a previous meeting I requested a free hand to use the full range of capabilities at our disposal – tanks, rockets, artillery, and close air support – but was denied.'

The PM remembered denying his request perfectly well. She had not changed her mind on that. 'I will not authorize a strategy that leads to civilian casualties.'

The General continued undaunted. 'Prime Minister, we must build on our strategy of rooting out and destroying our enemy at source. It is no longer sufficient to carry out house-to-house searches for individual lycanthropes.'

He nodded to the Director-General of MI5, who picked up the discussion. 'Our intelligence indicates that the lycanthropes are organizing into cells based in specific areas of the city. We do not know their exact whereabouts, but we can identify certain zones where their activities appear to be most heavily concentrated.'

The Director-General brought up a map of London on the overhead projector. Hundreds of colour-coded locations appeared on the map, spread all across the city.

'What are we looking at, Director-General?' she asked.

'Sites of recent lycanthrope attacks and sightings, Prime Minister. As you can see, certain patterns are emerging. We cannot yet pin down precisely where the creatures are hiding out, but a number of potential targets suggest themselves.'

The General took up the thread. 'With your permission, Prime Minister, I would like to begin aerial bombing of these known zones of enemy activity. We will of course allow civilians to evacuate the affected areas prior to the commencement of operations. Our sniffer dogs will enable us to screen those to be evacuated. This strategy will enable us to take the fight to our enemy, while minimizing the number of casualties. I believe that it will enable us to bring about a quick victory.'

'Impossible,' protested the Home Secretary. 'You are talking about blowing up large parts of our own capital city. This is an outrage.'

The Prime Minister stared coldly at the General. He had gone too far with his demands. 'You expect me to sanction the partial destruction of London?'

The General spread his hands. 'The alternative, if we do nothing, may be to permit its destruction entirely.'

She shook her head. However bad things were, she would not allow the General to unleash total war in London. 'The answer is still no. Find another way, General.'

Chapter Thirty-Nine

Barking, East London

Leanna walked in front of Warg Daddy, striding confidently across the space of the huge warehouse building. She was clad from head to toe in black leather. Her golden hair flared each time a shaft of sun from the high windows reached down and touched her. Her boots rang out on the hard floor like a hammer striking an anvil. Warg Daddy followed in her wake, moving from alternating darkness to light, puffing out his chest and watching with pride as she inspected his troops.

Build an army, she had commanded him, and he had done it. He had gathered some of them here in this empty warehouse to show her. They stood in disciplined ranks, row upon row, column after column. The sight of them awed even him.

'How many are here?' Leanna asked him.

'Five hundred. More in other locations.'

'How many in total?'

But Warg Daddy didn't know for sure. His troops numbered thousands. Too many for this one building to hold. He had organized them into cells throughout the city. And who was counting? Not Warg Daddy. He was a fighter, not a counter. In any case his forces were too numerous to count, and were growing every day. They would continue to come as the infection spread. The tide was flowing and had become unstoppable.

His army had weapons too. The foot soldiers carried automatic pistols, assault rifles, sniper rifles, sharpshooter rifles and combat shotguns, just like the one Warg Daddy took everywhere. They wore uniforms taken from dead soldiers, and carried their equipment too. Mortars. Machine guns. Grenade launchers. The weapons were arrayed before Leanna, all armed and ready to fire.

Against the brick walls of the old warehouse stood vehicles. Land Rovers, armoured cars and combat vehicles. They had even captured a fully operational battle tank. The enormous beast towered over the troops in a corner of the building, measuring nearly fifty feet in length. The barrel of its main gun was big enough to swallow his huge fist, and it had secondary weapons too – a heavy machine gun and something called a chain gun which Slasher was itching to put to use. If they could work out how to fire the motherfucker they would be invincible.

Leana paced relentlessly up and down the ranks, seeming determined to personally inspect each soldier and every piece of equipment. Warg Daddy was beginning to grow bored. One soldier looked very like another. Each piece of body armour was the same. Every pair of black boots shone equally. What was Leanna looking for? She'd told him to build an army, and here it was. A ferocious fighting force of men and women, fully equipped and ready to go. Not exactly trained as such. But keen.

Keen and itching to fight, just like Warg Daddy himself.

Leanna stopped in front of the Wolf Sisters.

They were formidable, the Sisters. Smaller in stature then the Brothers, and at first sight weaker. But that was pure illusion. Lycanthropy had re-made these women into Amazons, just as strong as any man. Brutal too. When they got to work, there was no holding them back. Vixen was one of the most savage, parting men from their limbs like a threshing machine separating wheat from chaff. He had put her in charge of the other Sisters and they seemed to adore her. Despite her youthfulness, she had a gift for command. She was quick to praise, and never aloof like Leanna. She had the common touch.

She stood to attention as Leanna inspected her.

Leanna studied the girl closely as if hoping to see inside her very soul. 'What is your name?' she asked the girl.

'Vixen. First of the Wolf Sisters.'

Leanna fixed her with an ice-blue stare. 'And who do you serve?'

'Leanna. Queen of the werewolves.' The girl raised her right arm in salute.

Leanna's cold eyes did not blink. 'Serve me well, Vixen,' she said. 'I shall be watching.'

Vixen stared back, expressionless.

Leanna moved on to inspect the other Wolf Sisters. They stood like statues, looking almost identical in their multi-terrain uniforms and body armour, differentiated only by their black, green or maroon berets or camouflage helmets. These women were fit and just as eager to fight as the men, and carried an array of deadly weaponry from Glocks to tripod-mounted machine guns. They were equipped to the exacting standards of the British Army itself. And they were deadly fighters with hands and teeth too.

Eventually Leanna seemed satisfied. 'Come with me, Warg Daddy.'

He dismissed the troops and followed her to a private office in the corner of the warehouse building.

'Close the door.'

He latched it behind him and stood waiting.

'Who is this girl, Vixen?' asked Leanna. 'I do not trust her.'

She was predictable, Leanna. She never trusted anyone. But Warg Daddy didn't think it would be helpful to point that out. 'Vixen has ability,' he answered. 'A talent for destruction. And she has a way with others. The Wolf Sisters look up to her.'

That had been the wrong thing to say.

Leanna stepped nearer, pushing her half-burned face dangerously close to his. The frigid blue orbs of her eyes bored into his skull.

He watched her ruby lips, wondering if they would open to speak or to bite. The heft of the shotgun was in his hand, and he cautiously eased his finger around the trigger.

When Leanna spoke, her words were glacial. 'She may be like a sister to you, but I shall always be your mate. Do not forget that, Warg Daddy.'

He felt anger bubbling up. There was no need for her to treat him this way. He had done exactly what she asked. Gathered together a formidable army. Equipped it with weapons. Readied it for battle. She owed him gratitude.

'Leanna, are you threatening me?'

She smiled a viper's smile. 'Have threats become necessary?' she replied. 'I do hope not.'

Had they? Was fear the only reason he served her now? His fingers curled around the trigger of the gun. If fear was the reason, he could rid himself of it once and for all.

Her red lips parted again and kissed his neck. She touched him with her fingers, unzipping his leather jacket and pushing it onto the floor.

'Leanna ...' he began, but her fingers were on him again and he felt the way he always did when she touched him like that. His hand relaxed on the shotgun as she kneeled before him. Fear wasn't the only hold she had over him. Desire was so much more potent.

The office windows held no privacy but Warg Daddy was powerless to resist her touch. Soon her fingers and lips and tongue were melting him into sweet oblivion. Vixen watched through the glass window but Warg Daddy no longer cared. Only Leanna's touch mattered and his world grew smaller and smaller before exploding into cosmic infinity.

She uses me like a toy, he thought briefly. *I am nothing to her.* But he didn't care.

When she was done with him, she got back to her feet.

'What now?' he asked breathlessly, pulling his clothing back on.

'We attack. We strike at the heart of our enemy, and we hit them hard.'

He nodded his agreement. That was good to hear. They had spent too long talking of battle. 'By next full moon we will be strong and ready.'

'Yes. But that's exactly what the army will be expecting.'

'So what then?'

'We strike now, and take them by surprise.'

'Now?' he asked.

'In three days' time, during daylight. You already know the plan.'

He nodded. Leanna's war planning was detailed and carefully researched as always. She had briefed him on targets, tactics and troop movements. But this sudden change to a daytime attack was a new twist. So far they had always operated by night, attacking beneath a cloak of darkness. Midnight was the natural hunting hour of the werewolf. But of course, a daytime attack would give them total surprise over their enemy.

Reluctantly he grunted his agreement. As usual, Leanna's idea was cleverer than his own. He wished he had thought of it instead. Now that she had said it, it seemed entirely obvious. 'Maybe the army will be expecting us to surprise them,' he suggested begrudgingly.

She waved his objection away. 'Just do as I say, Warg Daddy. Don't try to be too clever. It will make your head hurt.'

He fought the urge to rub his bald head. He'd forgotten about the pain for a few brief moments, but it was back again, working away at his skull like a jackhammer.

Leanna treated him like dirt now. She didn't even pretend otherwise. She was openly contemptuous. Only her fingers treated him kindly, and they were treacherous, binding him to her will, making him do whatever she wanted.

But he could still walk away from here if he chose. Walk away, and never look back. He was Leader of the Pack, whatever Leanna said.

Her voice cut through his thoughts. 'So, are you ready to fight?'

He nodded. He was always ready to fight. Fighting was the one thing he still knew how to do well.

Chapter Forty

Electric Avenue, Brixton, South London

Drake stood outside the burned-out clothing store, staring in dismay at its boarded-up shopfront. It had been one of the best shops for picking up designer gear, and he had filched a couple of dresses, a handbag and a pair of jeans from here to give to Aasha. He had brought the stolen goods in a bag, all ready to return to the owner. His words of apology were ready on the tip of his tongue. He had meant to do it, he really had, just as he'd promised Aasha's mum.

Aasha still refused to apologize to anyone. Drake couldn't say he had expected anything else from her. He could clearly see now what a fool he'd been. He'd let Aasha twist him around her little finger. He was nothing more than a puppet to her. He was determined to do what Mrs Singh had demanded. Return the stolen goods. Make an apology.

But the shop was gone. How could he make amends

now? How could he fix the mess he'd made? He leaned in close, pressing his face up to the one remaining shop window, but inside all he could see was a dark emptiness.

A voice called to him. 'Hey! What are you doing there?'

A man approached. Drake had seen him before, hanging out with Mr Kowalski, the shopkeeper, and Mr Harvey, his old teacher. What was his name? Mr Stewart. He was one of the Watch. They were everywhere now. He probably thought Drake was a looter. Well, he was.

Drake dropped the bag of gear and legged it, turning down a back alleyway off the main shopping street.

Mr Stewart followed. 'Hey! You little runt! Stop!'

Drake ran as fast as he could.

The alleyway ended in a high brick wall. He leapt at it, catching the top with his fingers. His feet scrabbled against the bricks for purchase and he began to haul himself up with all his strength.

He was almost clear when a hand grabbed at his right leg.

He kicked out and was rewarded with an angry shout. But then the hand was back, a pair of hands this time, strong hands, pulling him down. He clung desperately to the wall, but Mr Stewart was too strong. A tug brought him crashing to the ground. He lay on his back panting for a few seconds, wondering how many of his bones had shattered. Then Mr Stewart hauled him roughly to his feet and pushed him up against the hard surface of the wall. He twisted his collar and sleeve, forcing his face against the bricks. 'Thief!'

'I'm not!' said Drake. 'I wasn't stealing nothing.'

'Don't lie. I saw the bag. What was in it?'

'Clothes,' said Drake. 'I was returning them. I came to apologize for taking them.'

'What?' Mr Stewart began to laugh. He released his grip. 'You came to apologize?'

'Yeah.'

'What for?'

'For doing wrong. Stealing's wrong, yeah?'

'If you say so,' said Mr Stewart. 'Not much of a thief, are you? Are you any good for anything else?'

'Like what?'

The man threw a punch at him.

'Hey!' Drake dodged aside just in time.

Another hook came from his right.

He danced away from that too. 'Stop it!'

Mr Stewart stood back, nodding appreciatively. 'Fast, aren't you?' he said. 'What else can you do?'

'What kind of thing?' asked Drake.

'I dunno. Climb walls?'

'If you let me,' said Drake, rubbing his hands where he'd hit the ground.

'Open locks? Break into buildings?'

'Maybe. Yeah.'

'Handle a knife?'

Drake gave Mr Stewart an uneasy look. 'Only losers carry knives. They get you killed, yeah? I don't carry no knife.'

The man reached inside his jacket. 'Try this one.' He handed the weapon to Drake.

Drake took it nervously. The blade was as long as his hand. He gripped it in his sweaty palm.

'Show me how to use it,' said Mr Stewart. He drew out a second knife.

Drake stood dumbstruck. 'You want me to fight you?' he asked.

'It's your choice,' said Mr Stewart. 'Fight me, or just stand there like a muppet.' He lunged at Drake, his arm outstretched.

Drake ducked aside and the knife swept past his left ear. He spun around to see Mr Stewart coming for him again. 'This is mental!' cried Drake. 'Are you trying to kill me?' He dodged away again, looking for a way to escape, but Mr Stewart blocked his exit down the alleyway.

'I've never fought with a knife before,' said Drake.

'No?' said Mr Stewart. 'Let's hope you're a quick learner then. Let me show you a few tricks.'

He wasted no time. As soon as his words were out, his right arm lunged forward, the knife aimed at Drake's chest.

Drake threw himself backward just in time. He staggered and nearly tripped over his own feet, but the wall saved him from falling. Instead it slammed into his back, almost winding him.

Mr Stewart gave a thin smile, revealing uneven and yellowed teeth. 'Basic warrior stance, kid. Keep your vital areas turned away from your opponent. Turn sideways unless you want to find a blade in your lungs or your heart.'

Drake followed the advice, mirroring his opponent's stance, turning to expose less of his body area to attack. He swung the knife in a broad arc, aiming for Mr Stewart's head.

The man reacted quickly, blocking the strike with his left hand, and lunging forward with the right.

Drake dodged his head aside just in time to avoid the blade.

Mr Stewart laughed at him. 'Knife fighting 101. Move the knife in straight lines. Keep the blade within a shoulder-width. Wide, sweeping attacks are easy to block.' He danced forward, closing to attack again.

In a sudden move, he thrust his knife hand high, bringing it down in a vicious slashing movement across Drake's left forearm. The blade cut through Drake's thin cotton jacket and the shirt beneath, drawing blood from his skin.

Drake jumped back in pain. 'You fucking cut me!' he screamed at Mr Stewart. 'You're fighting for real!'

'Don't be a baby,' said the man. 'I'm teaching you a lesson here. You should be grateful. If I really wanted to kill you, you'd be dead already.'

Black anger welled up in Drake's mind. He'd done nothing to deserve this treatment. His only crime was nicking some stupid clothes, and he'd come here intent on apologizing for the theft. With an angry roar he lunged again at Mr Stewart, pushing the blade forward, like he'd been told, throwing his entire body weight behind it.

The knife impacted the man's shoulder, but he drew back just in time to avoid injury, grabbing hold of Drake's knife arm with his free hand. He twisted Drake's wrist in a violent jerk, sending a wave of agony up his knife arm.

'Ow!' cried Drake, and dropped the knife.

The man kicked it out of his reach. 'Too slow, kid. I made it easy for you, gave you chances. But you didn't put up much of a fight.' He slid his knife back inside his jacket and bent down to retrieve the weapon Drake had dropped.

With one last wave of fury, Drake launched himself into the air. He kicked out at the back of Mr Stewart's knee, dropping his full weight on the vulnerable joint. The man crumpled to the ground.

Drake grabbed the dropped knife and sat astride his fallen opponent, pinning his arms to the ground with his knees. He pressed the edge of the blade to the man's throat.

Mr Stewart's chest heaved beneath him. The man was totally out of breath. He lay on the ground, recovering.

'I win,' said Drake. He didn't dare move the knife in case the man seized it once more. Eventually the man said, 'What's your name, kid?'

'Drake. Drake Cooper.'

'You remind me of myself at your age, Drake Cooper,' said Mr Stewart. 'Hanging out on the street. Nicking stuff from shops. No good at school. Father long gone. Mum didn't care. Any of that sound familiar?'

It did. Uncannily familiar. It was virtually his life story.

But Drake had a family to belong to now. Vijay and Aasha and their nice, old grandmother, and Mr and Mrs Singh too. They were the family he had never had.

Except that Aasha's words still stung him. *You're not one of us.* Had she really meant that? Was he simply kidding himself that he really belonged to the Singh family? He wondered what he would have to do to prove himself to her, to make her want him again.

'I have a job for you,' continued Mr Stewart. 'It pays well. Food. Drinks. What else do you like? Designer gear for your girlfriend? You can have that too.'

'What do I have to do?'

'Work for the Watch. I could use a kid like you.'

Drake hesitated. He'd been tricked before. Tricked by kids at school. Tricked by Aasha. Tricked by the system. 'What kind of things do you want me to do? Steal stuff? Hurt people?'

'Whatever Ms Ali tells us to do.'

From the questions Mr Stewart had asked earlier, Drake had a pretty good idea what kind of things those would be. There was little doubt that working for the Watch would mean doing bad stuff. But what was the alternative? Men like Mr Stewart ran the show now. If you weren't with them, you were against them. And that was no place to be.

He lifted the knife from the man's throat and laid it aside.

Mr Stewart smiled broadly. 'Smart move, Drake. Welcome to the Watch.'

Chapter Forty-One

High Street, Brixton Hill, South London

The day of Gary's funeral had come and Liz was trying to make herself useful.

Kevin was working like a trooper. He'd talked to the vicar, made arrangements with the funeral director, sent out invitations and even chosen the hymns.

It wasn't an easy time to arrange a funeral. The sheer number of recent deaths was threatening to overload the system. Bodies weren't quite piling up in the streets yet, but they were being stockpiled somewhere as they waited their turn for burial or cremation.

Somehow Kevin had managed to pull the right strings so that Gary could jump the queue. Promises had been made. Cigarettes and whisky had changed hands. It didn't seem very dignified to Liz, but she didn't want to interfere. Kevin and Gary had been close, and this was no business of hers.

The three dead Serbians hadn't needed to wait for a

funeral, of course. Their bodies had been tipped into unmarked graves the day after they'd been killed. The blood stains on the pine floor of the butcher's shop had been scrubbed clean, and no one had questioned Liz about the missing men. It was as if they had never existed.

She wondered how much Kevin was motivated by loyalty to his old friend, and how much it was guilt that was driving him. Either way, he had done a fine job. She couldn't deny it. Today was a day people round here would remember for a long time.

The morning of the funeral was glorious. Bright sun broke through the clouds as the mourners began to arrive at the church. Gary had no surviving family, but no shortage of friends and acquaintances, judging from the crowds. Hundreds had come to sing hymns and remember the life of a local character. He'd been a relatively young man and evidently well-known and liked in the local community. Either that, or the last chance to sample his famous meat pies at the funeral wake had brought out the locals in droves.

Liz had never got the chance to know Gary well, but listening to the words of praise offered by his former customers and associates it was clear the butcher had been a good, honest man. He hadn't deserved to die. The root of his misfortune had been getting entangled with Kevin and his dodgy get-rich-quick schemes. Liz felt a pang of guilt by association. She couldn't be responsible for her father's actions, but perhaps she ought to have kept a closer eye on him. In future, she would.

Her father had never been one to show his emotions, but at the graveside, as Gary's coffin was lowered into the frozen ground, Kevin began to sob. He hadn't cried like that even at Liz's mum's funeral. Perhaps his tears were partly for his dead wife now, and not just for his friend the butcher. Perhaps he was crying for all his past mistakes and losses, and the perceived injustices that life had inflicted on him.

Liz's eyes stayed dry. A shiver travelled down her spine as the cold earth welcomed the coffin into its cold embrace. If she really was a vampire she ought to be living in a coffin. Yet it was Gary in the wooden box, not her. She reached for Mihai's hand, but he shoved his fists into his pockets and refused to meet her gaze.

As clods of hard earth began to fall onto the lid of the coffin, the party turned away from the grave and made its way back to the butcher's shop for the wake. Kevin insisted that everyone come. Not that they needed much encouragement. The promise of free food and beer proved irresistible. Liz did her best to help, but for once in his life, Kevin didn't seem to need her. He stood at the door of the shop, solemnly shaking everyone's hand, while Mihai and Samantha carried round plates of sandwiches and handed out pints of beer.

Liz recognized some of the guests but she didn't know many of them well. A few she'd met when she and Dean had gone door to door seeking to reassure residents that they were safe. Those people were generally avoiding her. But most of the mourners she had never seen before.

Kevin seemed to be on first name terms with everyone, even though he'd only been living in the area a matter of weeks. She had no idea how he'd managed to become a pillar of the community in such a short time. Presumably his illicit trading in cigarettes and alcohol had something to do with it.

Mihai was still ignoring her, busying himself instead by distributing meat pies and sausages to the funeral guests, and pinching more than a few for himself.

Liz stood to one side of the crowds, watching. She turned her head and caught her reflection in a mirror. Vampires were supposed to have no reflection, yet there it was, her own pale face staring back at her through bloodshot eyes. Her lips were painted ruby red, even though she didn't wear lipstick. She looked ghastly. It wasn't surprising Mihai was so scared of her.

A vampire.

It was just superstitious nonsense. Romanian folk tales based on – what? Was it possible there was a nugget of truth behind them, just like the legend of the werewolf which had proved to be cold fact?

The man who had scratched her arm and given her this *infection* had been eating a human heart when she and Dean had discovered him. He'd seemed more animal than human, barefoot on Clapham Common on a winter's night, crouching down, yellow eyes shining like beacons. The fingernails that had raked bloody trails down her arm had been long and twisted, and the sounds that had fallen from his mouth had been the roars of a beast, not human language. When Dean had chased him, he'd leaped over a ten-foot wall before vanishing into the night.

Call him a vampire. Call him a monster. Whatever word you used, he was no longer fully human and neither was Liz.

She sniffed at the air, suddenly noticing a peculiar scent. It floated over the other smells that flooded the room; of sweat and grease, of meat pies and sausage rolls, of perfume, shampoo and the myriad other scents that hovered over a gathering of so many people in a small space. She couldn't quite place it.

Her attention was drawn by a man who had just entered the shop. He stood at the back of the mourning revellers. He was taller than most of the others here, with thick silvery hair combed back from a high forehead. He wore a formal suit and black mourning tie. A black patch covered his left eye.

That would have been attention-grabbing in itself, but there was something more about the man that drew her eye. He held an air of command, as if he were used to giving orders. He stood alone and aloof, staring back at her. She didn't think she'd met him before, and she was sure she would have remembered a man wearing an eye patch, yet something about him seemed familiar.

He saw her looking and pushed his way through the crowd toward her. 'Please accept my sincere condolences for your loss,' he said. He offered her his hand, and his slender fingers wrapped around hers as she shook it.

'Thanks,' said Liz. 'I don't think we've met before.'

'I'm Salma Ali's personal assistant,' said the man. 'If the Watch can be of any help, please just say the word.'

Liz nodded. She'd heard plenty about this Neighbourhood Watch and its leader, Salma Ali, not much of it to her liking. She'd shaken hands with Salma in the church but hadn't seen the woman since. 'I didn't catch your name,' she said to the man.

'No,' he said. 'Not many people do. I like to keep a low profile.'

Liz frowned. The nagging familiarity of the man was driving her mad. If she hadn't met him before, perhaps she had seen his photograph. She paused, sniffing the air. That scent she'd noticed before smelled much stronger now. It belonged to the man.

His one eye watched her like a hawk. 'Do you smell something?' he enquired. 'I noticed it too.'

There was no mistaking that strange odour. She'd smelled it before. It was the scent of wolf.

And now she recognized him. She remembered the newspaper articles and the TV reports that had filled the airwaves for a few days back in December. Mr Canning, the former Headmaster of Manor Road Secondary School. Here was the man who had eaten children in his school office. She had almost caught him herself. If she'd trusted her own instincts and put more faith in the story that Vijay and Drake had told her, she'd have put him behind bars before he'd been able to attack Rose and her friend. As it was, he'd been stabbed in the eye by Rose.

She'd assumed he was dead. How could he be here, strutting about as if nothing had happened? 'It's you,' she said. 'I know who you are.'

His thin lips twisted into an amused smile and he

bowed his head slightly in deference to her. 'A wolf will always recognize one of its own kind,' he said quietly. 'We're family now, you and me.'

Liz drew back a step. This man revolted her. He was no family of hers. 'I'm not like you,' she said. 'I am nothing like you.'

Puzzlement spread slowly across the man's face. 'No? There *is* something different about you.' He wrinkled his nose and leaned toward her, sniffing like an animal. 'How intriguing. I love a good mystery. Don't fool yourself though, my dear. Whatever you are, you're a cold-blooded killer, just like me.' He leered at her. 'I do hope we'll see more of each other.'

'Don't count on it,' said Liz.

'Oh, don't be like that,' he chided. 'We outsiders need to stick together. It can be lonely out in the cold. I'll make a point of looking out for you. In the meantime I have other people to speak to.'

She watched him vanish into the swirling crowd, her skin hot, her blood cold. She had a sudden longing to be with her father, to be a little girl again, curled up in his strong arms. She looked for him, but he was nowhere to be seen.

Chapter Forty-Two

Department of Genetics, Imperial College, Kensington, London

Doctor Helen Eastgate opened the stainless-steel door of the commercial refrigeration unit and peered inside. The cold dead eyes of a werewolf met her gaze.

The refrigerator was one of many that had been hastily installed in the basement of the Biomedical Institute. Each contained the carcass of a beast just like this one. Her request to the Prime Minister had yielded quick results. She now had all the werewolves she might ever want. More than she wanted.

She shivered, and not just because of the breath of cold air that emerged from the refrigerator. The dead creature was so perfectly preserved in cold storage that it was easy to imagine it might stand up and start walking at any moment. Every hair on its flanks, each pearly white tooth between its jaws, every claw on its paws looked too real for words. They *are* real, she reminded herself. Unbelievably, this monster from the pits of hell was real flesh and blood.

Without the reassuring presence of her two strong lab assistants, she might have slammed the fridge door against the unnerving gaze of those cold eyes and fled down the corridor. The two men came forward now, dressed head to foot in protective overalls, their hands wrapped in white rubber gloves.

'Be careful,' she said as they lifted the body of the beast onto a trolley. A scratch from one of those razor sharp claws or teeth, or any kind of contamination from bodily fluids would be fatal. Worse than fatal. But the two men were already well aware of that. She allowed them to do their work. 'Wheel the trolley to the lab,' she told them. 'Then we need to raise the carcass up onto the worktop so I can remove the blood.'

The men pushed the trolley along the corridor to the service elevator. As she followed them, Helen cast one nervous glance back over her shoulder. The refrigerators hummed quietly to themselves. The creatures couldn't be frozen without causing ice crystals to form in their blood, so instead they needed to be kept at a constant temperature just above freezing point. Hence the bank of huge refrigeration units. It had been convenient to install them in the basement, and Helen preferred to keep them down here, well away from her laboratory and office.

It was silly, but she couldn't prevent an image rising up in her mind of the heavy stainless-steel doors swinging open one by one like sarcophagi, the remaining werewolves emerging from their cold storage and padding menacingly toward her. She shuddered, telling herself not to allow such foolish thoughts. She quickly flicked off the light and closed the door, locking it firmly behind her.

Back upstairs in the lab she felt calmer. Cool winter light poured in through the windows. The wolf looked less dangerous here than in the gloom of the basement. But she mustn't take any risks handling it. She had dressed herself in a full hazmat suit, including a face mask and respirator. At this point she still didn't know how easily the disease might spread. All indications pointed to a bloodborne pathogen, but she couldn't dismiss the possibility of airborne transmission.

She inserted the needle into the femoral artery and began to drain the creature of its corrupted blood.

Phase one of her work was progressing as planned. Staff and students had been quick to volunteer – both as assistants and as donors of blood. And to her great relief, General Ney had given her his full cooperation, supplying her with the bodies of several werewolves.

The procedure was simple in concept. Take blood samples from volunteers, add a drop of contaminated blood from one of the lycanthropes, and study the progress of the infection. So far the results were all negative. The infectious agent wasted no time getting to work as soon as it was mixed with the test blood. The viral particles invaded the host's blood cells first, penetrating the cell membrane in a matter of seconds. It was no wonder that anaphylactic shock could set in so rapidly following a bite. The victim's own life support system pumped the invading pathogen around its body, flooding every artery and vein within a minute of entry.

The immune systems of the test subjects weren't going down without a fight however. On the contrary, they were mounting a massive immune response. But the virus was too well adapted to its purpose. It simply overwhelmed the T-cells of its host. In some cases the virus engulfed and transformed the victim's blood cells within minutes. Some held out for a few hours. But so far not a single sample of blood that Helen had tested had been able to resist the onslaught of the virus. The disease was pathogenic in at least 99% of the population.

She had hoped to find a few people amongst her test subjects with natural immunity. One in a hundred, at least. Even in the deadliest acute infections of diseases like the

Zaire strain of Ebola a small number of people exposed to the disease showed immunity. But she had tested more than a hundred and fifty volunteers and every single one of their blood samples had succumbed to the infection.

The most likely explanation was that natural immunity did not exist. The rabies virus and the bacterium that caused septicemic plague were fatal to humans in virtually every case if left untreated. Probably lycanthropy was the same. How could Helen trust that tantalizing story that Professor Wiseman had recorded, of the Romanian peasant who had been bitten by a werewolf but not become one himself? She had been foolish to allow an unreliable anecdote to raise her hopes. An old man had spun Wiseman a tall tale in return for free drinks. The professor's approach to conducting a scientific study had been eccentric to say the least. And interviewing peasants in Romanian taverns had probably been where Wiseman's drinking habit had begun.

And yet, what other option did she have? The alternative was despair. At least by searching for patients with disease immunity she could hold on to hope.

She had good scientific reason to think that at least a tiny number of people would prove to be resistant. Around forty per cent of the general population possessed natural immunity to the influenza virus. One per cent of people even had natural resistance to the HIV virus. These facts held out a promise that she would eventually find a blood donor with natural immunity to lycanthropy. And as soon as she found that elusive person, phase two of her programme could begin – isolating the antibodies that could defeat the disease and using them to develop a vaccine or even a cure.

Her studies may not yet have located any antibodies or immunity to the virus but it had revealed some fascinating and unexpected discoveries. Initially she had regarded lycanthropy simply as a disease whose symptoms were perhaps even more horrible than death itself. But she was gradually coming round to a different way of thinking.

Leanna had described lycanthropy as a fast track for human evolution, conveying superpowers on those it infected. Helen had seen for herself Leanna's incredible strength and agility. Now her experiments were beginning to reveal the source of those powers.

Helen had run extensive tests on the red blood cells infected by the virus. They were changed in many ways and were capable of carrying significantly more oxygen than before. It was clear that lycanthropy wasn't simply an illness – it was a mutation that conferred a survival advantage on those who carried it.

But there was more. Leanna had also spoken of curing disease. One of the volunteers who had donated blood for Helen's tests was HIV positive. As Helen had expected, the donor's immune-deficient blood had succumbed very rapidly to the lycanthropy infection. But then something unexpected had happened. On a hunch, she had sent the blood sample to a clinical colleague for HIV testing. The reply had come back the following day. Negative. The lycanthropy virus had killed the HIV virus. You might call it a miracle cure, were the side effects not so horrific. Yet Helen wondered – if faced with the choice between a death sentence from AIDS and the chance to become a healthy werewolf, which option would people choose?

It was an intriguing hypothetical question to ponder, but Helen faced a more pressing and personal problem. Huntington's disease.

Since speaking to the Prime Minister about her condition she had already begun to notice a further slight decline in her physical coordination. The genetic time bomb inside her own body was starting to tick faster.

So it was only natural that she would want to test her own blood's response to lycanthropy. After all, she was doing it for science.

The result was remarkable. Helen's blood proved no more resistant to the disease than any of her other test subjects. Yet after infection with the lycanthropy virus, the Huntington's gene present in every cell of her body was replaced with a healthy gene variant. She could barely believe it. She ran another test to check the finding. The result was the same. Lycanthropy cured Huntington's.

The result kept her awake all night.

She was tempted by the prospect of a cure. Who wouldn't be? With Huntington's disease buried deep within her DNA she might have only twenty years left to live, perhaps ten of those spent in a nursing home. Although she had known of the likely outcome all her adult life, she had never really come to terms with it.

An injection of werewolf blood could reverse that irreversible outcome. It would be simple, a moment's work. She could do it right here, right now.

She drew red blood from the dead werewolf carefully into the syringe. She had only to insert that needle into her arm and inject a few millilitres into her own bloodstream. A controlled micro-dosage might even be enough to cure the disease while avoiding the worst of the side effects.

Side effects.

It was a somewhat clinical term to describe the fact that she would become a creature that fed on human flesh and turned into a wolf one night every month. But she could call them *side effects* if it made her choice easier.

The syringe in her fingers trembled slightly. That shake never left her hand these days. It would never leave, only grow steadily worse. It would gradually spread up her arm until eventually her entire body shook uncontrollably.

Unless she did something to stop it.

But the choice was not easy. The cost was perhaps too great.

Still, the temptation persisted. It could not so easily be dismissed.

Chapter Forty-Three

High Street, Brixton Hill, South London

The funeral had gone well. Kevin had done his very best to give Gary a good send-off, and he was sure the old geezer would have been proud of his efforts.

The vicar who'd conducted the service was the old-fashioned type, the kind who liked to talk about Heaven and Hell and all the trimmings. Kevin wasn't so sure he believed in all that stuff himself, but he was glad that the vicar did. On the day when you watched your best friend disappearing into a hole in the ground, it was better to believe in Heaven and Hell.

Well, Heaven at any rate. He glanced out of the window and up at the evening sky. A few dim stars twinkled back. Maybe Gary was up there now, tucking into steak and ale pie and drinking beer with the Lord himself, looking down and raising his pint glass to all the folk who had turned out to say goodbye. Kevin hoped so. The thought that Gary had died for nothing, gunned down outside his own butcher's shop to make food for the worms was too much of a downer to entertain.

The funeral-goers were certainly having a good time. There hadn't been much to celebrate round here recently, and people seemed to be using the funeral wake as a good excuse for a knees-up. Why not? Kevin couldn't blame them. Gary had been a popular man, and his meat pies were legendary. There would be no more of them now. The recipe had died with its inventor. But for today, it was time to tuck in and make the best of things.

And he still had the guns, so Gary hadn't died completely in vain. He'd sworn to Liz that he'd get rid of them, and he'd meant to, he really had. But time had passed, and here they were, still. If she asked him again, he'd do as she wanted. Hand the guns over to the police, no questions asked. Definitely. No doubt about it. But for now, he still had them, and he was glad. They might turn out to be useful one day. You never knew, with guns.

He made his way into the back storeroom and picked out an untouched crate of beer. Hopefully one more would be enough to satisfy the funeral-goers. He didn't begrudge people making the most of the free beer, just as long as they left a few bottles behind for him to enjoy. He heaved it up and turned around.

His way was barred by a tall man in a black suit and tie, steel grey hair combed in an austere side parting. He wore an eye patch, and you didn't see many of those around these days. He'd been at the funeral, sitting at the back of the church, but Kevin didn't know him. He wasn't one of Gary's regulars, that was certain. And he didn't look like he'd come back here to help out with the beers either.

'Looking for something?' asked Kevin. He held the crate between himself and the stranger, suddenly ill at ease for some unaccountable reason. 'The bathroom's through the other door,' he added, jerking his head.

'I was looking for you, actually,' said the stranger. His

voice was smooth and superior. Kevin knew the type immediately. A smug git, too big for his shiny leather shoes, looking down at Kevin as if he was a rat.

'Yeah, well, I'm busy right now,' said Kevin, shouldering forward, 'so I suggest you try another time.'

The man stayed in his path. Kevin tried to shove past, but an iron fist suddenly gripped his right elbow. Pain lanced up his arm, freezing his shoulder, and he felt the beer crate slip from his grasp.

The man caught it neatly in his spare hand. 'It's a rather urgent matter,' he said, unflustered, 'if it's all the same with you.'

The blood in Kevin's right arm had stopped flowing. The man's fingers closed tighter like a metal band, cutting the circulation dry. His bones made grinding noises as the man squeezed them together. 'Effing hell,' said Kevin. 'All right.'

His arm was suddenly released and he rubbed it hard, trying to get some feeling back. He wasn't sure it would ever return. 'What did you do that for? You nearly broke my arm. Not to mention the beer bottles.'

'I wanted to make sure I had your full attention,' said the man.

'All right. You got it,' said Kevin. 'Who are you, anyway?' He was sure he'd never seen the bastard before today.

'I'm a friend. I'm here to make you an offer.'

'Oh yeah?' said Kevin. 'What kind of offer?'

'The kind you won't want to refuse.' The stranger plucked two beers out of the crate and let it clatter to the floor. With sharp teeth he pulled the tops off the bottles and handed one to Kevin.

Kevin took the bottle in his left hand. His right arm was still completely dead. He took a quick gulp of beer to steady his nerves.

The man didn't drink any beer. Instead, he said, 'You have something I want. A collection of handguns, plus some ammunition. You will give them to me now.'

'Yeah?' said Kevin. 'You think so?'

'I do,' said the man. 'But it's your choice. Either you agree to do as I say or I will rip your arm out of its socket.' His single eye stared fixedly at Kevin. 'Would you like me to demonstrate?'

Kevin swigged beer and eyed the man nervously. The old geezer didn't look that much, with his flabby belly and fancy suit. Under normal circumstances, Kevin would have taken him. But that death grip trick was like nothing he'd ever experienced. He was in no doubt that the man really could rip out his arm if he wanted to. 'And then what?' he asked. 'Assuming I have the items you mentioned,' he added hastily.

'And then we shall never see each other again,' said the stranger. 'It will be as if we had never met.'

Kevin drank the rest of the beer and dropped the empty bottle back in the crate. He wondered what Gary was thinking now, peering down on the world from on high, trying to make sense of life's ups and downs. It would take an eternity to work out why Kevin's luck always ran out so bloody quickly. 'All right,' he said to the man at last. 'Your offer sounds fair enough to me.'

Chapter Forty-Four

*Western Evacuation Camp,
Buckinghamshire*

The combined effort of the military and humanitarian aid workers was producing swift and impressive results. Chanita had been deployed to the western evacuation camp, and already a small city of tents had appeared in what had just a few days earlier been the grounds of a luxury hotel.

Stoke Park in Buckinghamshire was a privately-owned country club, spa and estate, sporting 300 acres of immaculately maintained parkland and a 27-hole golf course. Requisitioned by the government, the eighteenth-century mansion had now become a temporary hospital with accommodation for doctors, nurses and other volunteers. The first refugees had been housed in the mansion building but already the numbers had grown too large, and new arrivals were being assigned tents.

The distance from London's M25 orbital ring road was

just five miles, but still Chanita was alarmed to discover that many of the evacuees had travelled to the camp on foot. Whole families had left their homes behind, bringing small children, babies and elderly parents. Some were malnourished, others had suffered from exposure to the elements. Many were exhausted or simply traumatized by their experience. They talked of friends they had left behind, relatives who had died, horrors they had witnessed.

As head of the nursing team, Chanita's main concern was to ensure that every arrival at the camp was met by a medic or volunteer and had their needs quickly assessed. So far they were keeping pace, but only just. If the number of people coming to the camp increased in line with Colonel Griffin's expectations, they might soon be drowning in refugees.

A new family group was arriving as she left the mansion building and set out across the grass lawn that led out onto the golf course where the cluster of tents began. A mother, father, two children and a baby. They were walking in from the main access road.

Something was wrong. The father carried the eldest child, a boy, in his arms.

Chanita ran across the lawn to them. 'What's happened?'

The mother spoke urgently. 'He was run over by a car. It just drove off without stopping. He's unconscious now. He's lost a lot of blood.'

'Lay him down here on the grass,' she told them. She waved at a nearby soldier to fetch help. She pressed her hands to the boy's neck, feeling for a pulse. The heartbeat was weak but rapid. Too rapid. She felt along the boy's side, which was the most obvious source of the bleeding, and didn't like what she found. The boy's chest and abdomen were badly swollen. 'I think he has internal haemorrhaging,' she told the parents. 'He needs immediate emergency attention.'

The soldier brought two paramedics with a stretcher. They lifted the boy on carefully.

'Take him to the operating theatre immediately,' Chanita instructed them. 'He needs urgent treatment.' The stretcher bearers set off toward the main building. 'Go with them,' Chanita told the parents. 'We can register you and find you accommodation later.'

She watched them hurry across the lawn in the direction of the main building. The luxury hotel had once served champagne and smoked salmon to its well-heeled guests and treated them to aromatherapy massages. These latest arrivals would be lucky if they left with their son still alive.

The surgeons would need blood to treat him, and since blood supplies had become contaminated with lycanthropy, supplies had run dangerously low. The camp's only source of blood came from donations made by hospital staff, soldiers and other volunteers, and its purity couldn't be completely guaranteed. Lycanthropes had deliberately infiltrated hospitals and blood clinics, and the camps were vulnerable too. Testing took time, and in an emergency like this, they might just have to rely on trust.

She made a mental note of the issue, to add to the long list of problems she already carried with her. Nursing she understood, but her role here demanded her to take on responsibilities she had never been trained for. They weren't strictly her responsibilities, but with Colonel Griffin dividing his time between three camps, someone had to step into his shoes when he was away, and Chanita had never been one to stand by when a job needed doing.

She started walking over to the camp, but stopped and turned to look up. A distant clatter in the sky announced the arrival of a helicopter.

Thank God.

The clattering grew louder and soon the approaching chopper took shape. She recognized it as a Westland Lynx, used by the army for both medical evacuation and transport. She was quickly becoming an expert in military hardware and procedure.

The Lynx descended quickly, flying low over the white cupola that crowned the hotel building and settling on the manicured golf course immediately in front of the mansion house. It was the spot where James Bond had once played golf with super-villain Auric Goldfinger, complete with plus fours. Now a real-life hero was emerging onto the green.

Colonel Griffin ducked low beneath the still-spinning blades and came loping across the lawn. He sprang to attention before her and gave her a salute. 'Nurse Allen, Colonel Michael Griffin reporting for duty.'

A girlish smile pasted itself onto her face before she could do anything about it. The Colonel had been absent for two whole days and his return raised her spirits more than she cared to admit. 'At ease, soldier,' she said. 'It's good to have you back.'

He returned her smile, but a note of caution flickered in his eyes. He had evidently sensed the hidden message in her words. 'Problems?' he asked.

The smile faded from her lips. 'More every day. But nothing that can't wait. We can talk about them later. It's good just to see you again.'

He nodded hesitantly. 'I'd like to spend more time here. But the other camps need me too.'

'Of course.' She wanted to tell him that it wasn't just the camp that needed him. She needed to see him. But she held her pleading to herself. She understood perfectly well the many demands on his time.

'Can you spare me ten minutes?' he asked.

She glanced at her watch. 'I have to …'

'Take a short break. That's an order.'

'Okay.'

'Let's walk,' he said.

Stoke Park was certainly a pleasant enough place to take a stroll, even with the tents and military vehicles cluttering the view. The sun was shining this morning, and the air contained a promise of spring. They followed the heritage walk toward the grand bridge that spanned the long serpentine lake. The water held perfectly still reflections of the trees and gardens beyond. They stopped to admire the view.

'You like it here?' he asked her.

She couldn't be sure if he meant the scenery or the work. She liked both. 'It's not quite the Caribbean, but it makes a nice change from London.'

He chuckled.

'The air smells fresh here,' she said. 'And even though we're so busy, it feels calmer than being back in the city. Besides, I like being busy. I feel a sense of purpose here.'

He looked out across the water to the distant oak trees, standing tall against the horizon. 'I know what you mean about the air. I grew up in the countryside, you know. My parents owned an old farmhouse, miles from anywhere. As a child I used to spend hours alone, just playing in the woods and the fields.'

She tried to imagine him as a child. It wasn't too difficult. He was still half a boy at times. The thought of him spending his childhood all alone saddened her, but the Colonel didn't sound the least bit sad.

'Since I joined the army I hardly get to spend any time alone,' he continued. 'And I've had to learn to live in all kinds of places, many of them war zones. But I like it here. It's quiet. Calming.' He paused for a moment, his gaze fixed on the old Norman tower of St Giles church, just visible above the tree line. 'Flying in today I could see that the camp is filling up already. The government hopes the airlift will encourage people to stay in the city, but don't count on it. I expect this place to grow rapidly over the coming days and weeks.'

'Is that what you wanted to talk to me about?'

'No,' he said, turning his back on the distant church and lake and looking directly at her for the first time. 'No, that is the very last thing I wanted us to talk about now.'

'What then?'

His eyes crinkled in that way they did when he was amused by something. The startling blue orbs that nestled beneath his eyelids seemed to drink in the morning sun like the sun-drenched ocean she remembered from her youth. 'Do we have to talk at all?'

'No. Not at all,' she told him. 'Let's just admire the view.' But it wasn't the gardens she was looking at.

Chapter Forty-Five

High Street, Brixton Hill, South London, crescent moon

Liz was helping Kevin to prepare breakfast when the kitchen lights suddenly went out. At this time of year it was still pitch black when she rose to get ready for work. At first she wondered if a circuit had tripped somewhere in the house. The wiring above the butcher's shop was ancient and looked ready to blow at any time. But peering out of the window, she saw that the whole street had lost power.

'Don't worry,' she told Kevin. 'I'll light a candle.'

She was glad that she'd readied a supply of candles and matches just in case of a power failure. It probably wouldn't be the last. Basic services like refuse collection had already ceased, and bags of rotting food were beginning to pile up in the streets.

'It reminds me of the strikes in the 1970s,' said Kevin nostalgically. 'Everyone was on strike then – coal miners, train drivers, hospital staff, rubbish collectors. Even the gravediggers went on strike.'

'The good old days, eh?' said Liz.

The first of the brownouts had been a week ago. It had lasted less than an hour and hadn't been a major problem. The second one had gone on all evening. By then the government had issued an official statement, explaining that the brownout was caused by a restriction in the electrical power to the national grid. Rather than shutting off power at peak times, a policy of reducing voltage was in place. This would minimize the effects on the public. The TV announcer warned that computers and other delicate equipment might be damaged by the reduced voltage, and to turn off all electronic devices as soon as the lights began to dim.

His warning had been right. The TV itself had been the first casualty, blowing out when the second brownout started, and silencing the presenter for good.

Liz had dug out an old analogue TV she found in the attic.

Mihai had stared at it in amazement as she dusted it down and removed the other TV from its stand. 'Why is TV so huge?' he asked suspiciously.

'It's a cathode ray tube,' she explained. The words sounded strange, even to herself, like something out of a black-and-white sci-fi movie. 'All televisions used to be like this.'

Remarkably, it still worked. She hoped that it would be less vulnerable to the power drops than modern technology had proven to be.

They'd grown used to the brownouts now, but this was the first time the electricity had gone completely.

Kevin was blundering around the darkened kitchen. 'Bloody hell. Where's that candle? I can't see a damn thing.'

'Stay still then,' said Liz. 'I'm lighting it now.'

The match spluttered into flame and she held it to the

candle wick. Slowly a yellow light took hold as the wax melted and a soft glow lit up the room.

The mellow candlelight was much more pleasant than the harsh fluorescent tubes overhead. Liz was finding more and more that any bright light made her eyes hurt. She could no longer go out in the sunlight without her shades, and it was only February. Mad.

She wondered what changes the others had noticed in her. Dean had remarked on her pale skin and rosy lips. The Dogman knew there was something strange about her, even if he didn't understand what. Animals seemed to sense it. Just the previous day a cat had hissed at her. Even Mr Canning had been able to smell that she was different. But she hoped she could conceal it from the others.

She lifted the candle and went to see what Kevin was swearing about.

He stood with a meat knife in one hand, blood dripping from the other. 'Damnit. I sliced my finger when the light was out.'

'You should have stayed still like I told you. Let me take a look.' She lifted his hand to examine it closer.

As soon as she held it the scent of the blood hit her. She inhaled deeply, drawing in the rich smell of the life-giving liquid. Its sharp metallic aroma was balanced by an almost sickeningly-sweet perfume that smothered her senses. Saliva began to trickle at the back of her throat. She had a strange sensation, exactly like she'd experienced when confronted by the thug at the People's March, of unfamiliar teeth pushing through her gums.

She drew the bloody finger close to her mouth and parted her lips. It was pungent at such close quarters. Powerful. Pervasive. Almost suffocating.

Her tongue darted out to taste the crimson liquid.

Sharp, sweet, rich and somehow dry at the same time. The flavour flooded her taste buds. No wine had ever tasted better. She swallowed it and pressed the wound to her lips, sucking hard.

The blood flowed and she gulped it eagerly, drop by drop, mouthful by mouthful. The smell and taste combined were overwhelming. She couldn't get enough. She sucked harder, desperate for it to flow faster. She pressed the finger with her own hands, squeezing out more blood, licking the wound with the tip of her tongue.

The finger was snatched away.

She grabbed at it again with both hands, taking it back into her mouth, drinking, sucking, swallowing. She couldn't stop.

She felt a hand on her arm. Kevin's. 'Stop, love,' he said gently. 'You have to stop now.'

No, a voice shrieked in her mind. *Don't stop. Don't ever stop.*

But that voice was not hers.

What was she doing?

The bloodlust had come on her again.

The blood ...

That voice again. It *was* hers. It was the voice of the thing she had become.

She would not listen to it.

With effort she dragged her mouth away. She licked the last of the blood from her lips and swallowed.

Kevin's face flickered in the mellow candlelight before her. He still held the meat knife in one hand, gripping it hard. She saw that he was afraid of her.

She drew back from him, grabbing the kitchen table for support. What had she done? Her own father. She had drunk the blood of her own father. This time she'd gone too far. She hadn't been able to control herself.

Kevin seemed to relax a little. He must have sensed that the bloodlust was over. He was still giving her a wary look, but he didn't seem frightened anymore.

She hadn't hurt him, thank God. It wasn't like the time she'd killed those two men to drink their blood. But she had crossed a line. It was time to face up to the truth at last. Time to admit to herself and to the others what she really was.

She turned and saw Mihai watching her, his big brown eyes bright in the light of the candle. Those eyes were full of fear.

Mihai knew. He had known all along. And only he could explain to her what her true nature was.

'Tell me what you know about vampires,' said Liz. 'Tell me everything.'

Chapter Forty-Six

Heathrow Airport, West London, crescent moon

The Land Rover barrelled toward the military checkpoint, Meathook at the wheel, Warg Daddy beside him in the role of commanding officer.

The day of the big battle had come at last. Everything up to this point had been mere preparation. Today Warg Daddy would unleash the mother of all violence against the forces of the British Army. He would pull the rug out from under his enemy's feet, wrap the bastards in the rug and set the damn thing on fire.

The survivors of this onslaught would look back and recall this moment as the turning point, the day the war had truly begun. They would call it the Battle of Heathrow.

The planning was all Leanna's work, but no one ever remembered planners. No, they would remember him, Warg Daddy, as the commander-in-chief of the Wolf Army. He was no longer just Leader of the Pack. He was a mighty warrior, preparing for victory.

He had chosen a parade-style brigadier's uniform for the day, picked out specially from his wardrobe of dead men's clothes. The khaki jacket, shirt and tie felt tight around his neck and chest, but he could tolerate the uniform for a short while, especially since it gave him a chance to showcase a generous helping of medals across his chest.

The peaked cap clamped on his head did nothing to ease the pain inside his skull, but he liked the red sash that looped around it. Violence was the best cure for his pain, and he contented himself in the knowledge that a bumper pack of violence had been ordered and was all ready for delivery.

The Land Rover swept to a halt immediately before the checkpoint and Meathook showed the sentry his papers. The man studied them, then snapped to attention, saluting Warg Daddy as the checkpoint opened. Warg Daddy waved lazily back and the Land Rover roared through. Behind it rolled a mixed convoy of armoured trucks, patrol vehicles, personnel carriers and utility trucks. A battle tank brought up the rear, with Slasher driving and Bloodbath ready at the main gun.

The convoy drove through the airport access tunnel beneath the northern runway and emerged onto the inner ring road. At Terminal 2 it divided, Warg Daddy leading one half toward the southern runway where the army kept the bulk of its heavy weaponry, Vixen leading her crew of Wolf Sisters toward the barracks and supply depots near Terminal 5.

Simultaneously, other Wolf Army forces were deploying across London, preparing to attack targets ranging from police stations and army checkpoints to communication hubs and electrical substations. The coordinated attack would deliver a devastating blow to both the military and civilian authorities. *A crippling assault*, according to Leanna's plan.

Warg Daddy had better words to describe the operation's objective. *An iron fist. A knockout. A sucker punch.*

The trucks and carriers pulled up in a line along the runway and began to disgorge troops. They were a motley crew, wearing the uniforms of half a dozen different regiments, Welsh Guards alongside Paras, infantry battalions working together with air corps and cavalry. That didn't matter. Beneath the uniforms they were one-hundred-percent werewolf. They were the Wolf Army and they were ready to commence hostilities. Big time.

Warg Daddy watched the operation unfold. The Brothers planted IEDs beneath enemy vehicles. They set up machine gun placements. They readied their RPGs. Slasher drove the tank to the far side of the airport, and Bloodbath raised the gun.

High in the sky the sun shone down. It was going to be a beautiful day.

A few enemy sentries seemed to have noticed their unscheduled arrival. Soldiers were emerging into view, looking on in curiosity or astonishment. The more alert commanders were giving orders, starting to react to the surprise arrival of an invasion force in the middle of their base. But they were already too late.

Warg Daddy adjusted his shades. 'Let the slaughter begin,' he commanded.

The sound of explosions drifted across from the far side of the airport. The Wolf Sisters must have begun their attack ahead of schedule. Vixen was always impatient when it came to dealing out destruction. Warg Daddy couldn't blame her for that. He lusted for murder too.

He stood upright in the open Land Rover, all the better to observe the fighting. He raised a pair of field glasses to his eyes and watched as the first wave of IEDs detonated.

A chorus of explosions boomed in harmony, tossing troop carriers, Land Rovers and Rapier missile systems into oblivion.

Nice work.

Black clouds billowed into the sky, thick enough to block out the morning sun.

In Warg Daddy's head, massive rock anthems began to play as the bombs exploded. *Deep Purple. Black Sabbath. Judas Priest.* The screeching guitars sang like angels of the apocalypse, banishing his headache, applying a soothing balm as gentle as aloe vera.

'Ready the machine guns,' he ordered.

The explosions had brought dozens of soldiers swarming from their base, filled with confusion, but armed and ready to fight.

Brave bastards, thought Warg Daddy. *They have no idea what's coming.*

The machine guns opened up in unison, cutting the soldiers down like fields of wheat. The percussive rhythm of the guns bathed Warg Daddy in pleasure, making his head pain a distant memory.

'RPGs,' he bellowed.

The rocket propelled grenades flew like black arrows across the battlefield. A few zoomed over the Land Rover, filling his head with their roar, leaving a fog of white smoke in their trail.

Meathook ducked. Warg Daddy stood tall, the red sash around his cap marking him out as commander-in-chief. He had nothing to fear here. He was conductor of carnage, director of destruction. The music played on, louder than before.

He wished Snakebite could have been here to watch the battle unfold. The big guy had loved noise and destruction of all kinds and today was proving to be one hell of a fireworks display. It was at times like this he missed his old friend the most.

But this was no time to get sentimental. He spoke to Bloodbath across the short wave radio. 'Fire the tank.'

The Challenger 2 tank was the jewel in their crown, according to Leanna.

Warg Daddy's dictionary contained simpler words. The Challenger 2 was the bomb; the beast; the tits; the sugar honey ice tea. It was a plate of cool bananas heaped with awesomesauce.

Whatever. He just hoped the fucker would work.

Thirty seconds passed. The tank stood motionless on the grass. He spoke again into the radio. 'Fire now.' Another thirty seconds passed. The gun turret moved a fraction to the left. He continued to wait.

The tank fired its first round. He expected the beast to buck like a stallion, but its hull held rock solid, anchored in place by sixty-two tons of composite armour. A blinding flash of yellow light penetrated his shades for an instant, and a thunderous drumbeat punctuated the soundtrack in his head. Smoke billowed out from the barrel. In the distance an orange fireball burst into brief existence and a huge explosion made a rumbling bass boost.

The shell had missed, but that was only to be expected first time around. It wasn't like they'd had a chance to practise firing the tank. It had been hard enough just keeping the motherfucker hidden from view. A few more tries and Bloodbath was bound to get the hang of it.

He raised the field glasses again, watching to see what would happen next.

The tank set off uncertainly, moving slowly across the grass in the direction of the runway. The turret began to move again, swinging the barrel round until it was pointing directly at Warg Daddy. He narrowed his eyes. The barrel swung away again and let off a second round. This one hit home. A massive artillery unit blew into smithereens. A third blast sounded and one wall of the airport terminal building crumbled away, glass sheets cracking like a melting glacier. The fourth shot dealt death to a Hercules transport aircraft, snapping its fuselage in half like a broken stick. The tank rolled on, accelerating, gaining confidence, letting off round after round after round. Some of the shells found targets. The rest just added to the excitement of battle. Every single explosion was a drumroll that drowned Warg Daddy's pain.

He slapped the side of the Land Rover with his beefy palm. 'Drive on,' he ordered Meathook. The Land Rover sped off, churning through the grassy mire. Warg Daddy clutched at the frame of the windscreen for support, his field glasses bouncing round his neck, the combat shotgun in his spare hand.

An officer ran at him from a nearby tent. 'Die, you fucker,' rumbled Warg Daddy. He raised the shotgun and blasted the man full on. The officer pitched backward, a shower of lead in his face. The Land Rover flew on across the field, kicking up mud in its wake.

'More RPGs!' yelled Warg Daddy into the radio. RPGs had always been his favourite, ever since he'd been a little kid. He watched them fly with satisfaction. A row of helicopters parked beside the runway went up in flames. They burned like insects held under a magnifying glass, shrivelling up as the heat rushed through their exoskeletons, crisping them into blackened husks.

Another noise came from the tank. Slasher must have worked out how to fire the chain gun at last. The gun coughed into action like a mad bastard, spitting out five hundred rounds of deadly slugs a minute. Sparks flew from its mouth as the gun ejected spent cases in a metal hailstorm. A pincushion of devastation appeared in the distance as the rounds found their targets half a kilometre downstream, ripping through tents, shredding vehicles and aircraft, mincing any soldiers unlucky enough to stand in the way. On and on went the gun, dealing out death in generous dollops, not slowing down, not stopping, not once pausing for breath.

More enemy soldiers came into view. An armoured truck rolled out of a nearby hangar. From the left, a couple of hostile tanks began to crawl across the runway.

The background music of oblivion turned darker. *Iron Maiden. Megadeth. Slayer.*

'Engage the enemy!' roared Warg Daddy. 'Launch the Javelin!'

He'd been itching to try out the Javelin. One of the Wolf Brothers squatted on the ground, balancing it over his shoulder. The thing looked like a portable missile silo. The Brother sighted one of the approaching tanks. Warg Daddy waited impatiently as the Brother fiddled with the thermal targeting panel. The missile launched, a silver streak like a small rocket. Yellow fire gushed from the back of the launch tube. The rocket flew, not to the moon, but straight into the turret of one of the distant tanks.

Boom. The sweet sound of a high-explosive anti-tank warhead going about its business. The effect was every bit as devastating as Warg Daddy had hoped. That tank was toast. The Brothers were already loading the Javelin with a second rocket.

He stood back from the confusion of the battle, watching calmly. The players moved like dancers in a show, sweeping in groups, or pairs, or solitary movements. Warg Daddy soaked it up, seeing the bigger picture in his mind, using his super senses to find the patterns.

In the distance a huge explosion filled the sky. Blackened swirls of smoke rode high. Flaming tongues licked the clouds. Vixen and the Sisters must have found a fuel depot.

Reports of other attacks crackled in his headset. *Target destroyed. Communications centre under attack. Target squadron killed.* Death. Destruction. Mayhem. The plan was proceeding exactly as planned.

He turned his attention back to the field before him. Noise and chaos flashed all around. He sifted them into order. *There.* Those tanks preparing to engage. *There.* That mobile artillery unit creeping into view. He passed his orders to his troops. Guns roared. Shells exploded. Small arms crackled.

Who was winning?

It didn't matter.

The plan had never been to win. It was to give the army a bloody nose; to rain down confusion and despair upon their adversaries; to lob a grenade at the puffing generals and sap the morale of the lower ranks.

He took a moment to survey the burning vehicles, the wreckage of the helicopters, the twisted limbs of dead soldiers, the black columns of smoke that drifted across the sun.

That job was done.

He sounded the retreat. The Land Rover spun around, sending clods of earth flying. The tank fell back at speed, continuing its steady blast of shells. The chain gun raged madly on even as the battle closed, still hungry for destruction.

As they left the airport they blasted the checkpoint into oblivion. Flames and smoke chased them on their way. One final face-slapping, world-ending guitar chord played in Warg Daddy's head as the Land Rover raced away, heading back toward central London.

High in the sky the sun shone down. It had been a beautiful day.

Chapter Forty-Seven

High Street, Brixton Hill, South London, crescent moon

'Is many, many kinds of bad monster in Romania,' began Mihai.

'Hey,' said Kevin. 'Liz ain't no monster, Mihai. Don't go saying that.'

Liz touched her father's arm. 'Let him continue, Dad. Monster is as good a word as any.' She could still taste Kevin's blood on her tongue. She wanted to think that the flavour repulsed her, but the cold truth was that she had never tasted anything so good. If that didn't make her a monster, then nothing did. 'There's no point pretending any more. I need to know everything.'

Mihai continued. 'So, is many words in Romania for talking about monster. First is *strigoi*.'

That wasn't one of the words he had used when he'd first accused her of being a vampire. 'Does that mean vampire?' she asked.

Lycanthropic

'No. *Strigoi* is most common monster. Is kind of demon that lives in person. Is also name of person who has *strigoi* inside them. You understand?'

'I think so. A strigoi is someone who is possessed by a demon. Or at least, they behave as if they do. People used to believe that demonic possession was the cause of epilepsy and other mental illnesses. Go on.'

'So *strigoi* is demon,' continued Mihai. '*Strigoi* change shape into other animals. Is very strong and has good smell. Likes to eat people.'

'That sounds like a werewolf,' said Kevin.

Mihai shook his head. 'Not werewolf. Werewolf is *vârcolac*. Can only change into wolf. *Strigoi* may be wolf. But may be bear. May be bird. May be rabbit.'

'So a strigoi is a shape-shifter, and a werewolf is a kind of strigoi that can only change into wolf form?'

'Yes. Then next is *moroi*.'

'Moroi,' said Kevin, turning the strange word over in his mouth. 'So, is that a vampire?'

'No. *Moroi* is other very bad monster. *Moroi* is son of *strigoi*. Can also be wolf or bear or bird or rabbit. Very strong and fast, like *strigoi*. Likes to eat people and drink blood.'

'I don't understand,' said Liz. 'A moroi sounds exactly like a strigoi.'

'Is not quite same. *Strigoi* can turn into wolf. *Moroi* is wolf all the time. Is very hairy monster.'

'Okay, so I guess a moroi is even worse than a werewolf. What about vampires?'

'Is many words for vampire. *Vampir, nosferatu, pricolici, moroi*.'

'Hold on,' said Kevin, scratching his head. 'You already said that a moroi isn't a vampire.'

'Is complicated,' hissed Mihai. '*Vampir* is dead person, killed by other *vampir*. So, person is dead, then comes back to life. *Vampir* is very strong, very fast, very terrible. Likes to drink blood. Blood makes *vampir* strong.'

'Okay,' said Liz. 'I think I'm starting to get a grip on this. A strigoi is a shape-changer that might be a werewolf or some other kind of were-creature. A moroi is similar, but stays in wolf form all the time. And a vampire is someone who has been killed by another vampire and comes back to life and now drinks human blood.'

Mihai nodded. '*Moroi* may be *vampir* too, but must be dead first. So *moroi* is born of *strigoi*, then killed by *vampir*. Is vampire werewolf. Is *vampir* who can be animal. Is very worst monster of all.'

'A vampire werewolf,' said Liz. 'The worst of both.'

'Yes. Then is called *pricolici*.'

'Blimey,' said Kevin. 'I never knew vampires and werewolves were so complicated.'

'Well it sounds like I'm a vampire, but not a shape-shifter,' said Liz. 'So I don't need to worry that I might turn into a wolf.' That was a relief to know. Whatever transformation took place under the light of the full moon, she would stay human, at least if Mihai's confusing jumble of folklore and superstition could be relied upon.

'Is right,' agreed Mihai. 'You are *nosferatu*. Is same word in Romania for devil.'

'But I'm not a devil, Mihai, and I don't have a demon inside me either. I just have a disease. Do you understand that?'

The boy stayed silent. He didn't look convinced.

'I caught a disease and it made me this way. Another vampire scratched my arm and passed it to me. I'm still your Liz. I'm the Liz who rescued you from the fire. I would never harm you. I only want to protect you.'

He seemed to be thinking it over. 'Promise?'

'Promise. So what else can you tell me about vampires?'

'Is very fast. Does not burn in fire.'

'Uh, okay.' Liz knew from first hand experience just how fast she became when she turned under the moon. It was as if time stood still for her. But she had not faced fire as a vampire. She filed that information away for future use. There was one question she desperately wanted answering, though. 'Is there any way for a vampire to change back to a human?'

Mihai shook his head sadly. 'Only way is wooden stick in heart. But not do that to Liz.'

'No, I think I'll give that a miss. Anything else I should know?'

'Vampires don't like light,' said Mihai. 'Only go outside at night. Switch lights on to keep them out. Also garlic, and sign of cross. Makes them run away.'

'We tried that already,' said Kevin. 'Didn't have no effect on Liz.'

That was true. It seemed that not all of Mihai's folklore could be relied upon. But at least some of it contained a grain of truth.

'I don't like bright lights,' said Liz. 'And I don't like the sun on my skin either. I can feel it burning me. And the light sensitivity is getting progressively worse. At this rate I'm going to end up nocturnal. And if Mihai's right, I might end up not ever being able to go outdoors during daylight.'

'Maybe so,' said Kevin. 'But don't give up hope. Old school vampires didn't have access to sunglasses and factor 50 sunscreen.'

Chapter Forty-Eight

Cabinet Office Briefing Room A, Whitehall, Central London, crescent moon

'Tell us the worst, General. Spare us nothing.' The Prime Minister sat again at the head of the COBRA table, but this meeting was going to belong to General Ney. The Chief of the Defence Staff had himself called her to attend, following the attack on Heathrow Airport.

Already the news channels were reporting chaotic scenes from around the airport. Little in the way of hard facts was known, but it was clear that a devastating surprise attack had been made on the army's main base. Reporters were calling it the Battle of Heathrow and describing it as a turning point in the war.

But it wasn't just the airport that had been attacked. Other targets had been hit, both military and civilian, in a coordinated operation all across the capital. And news of similar attacks was filtering in from around the world. The

Reichstag parliament building in Germany was under siege; fighting had broken out in Paris, in Warsaw, in Madrid. There were no longer any official news reports from China, but by some accounts a great battle was unfolding in the Chinese capital, Beijing. The war against the werewolves was now truly global.

'This morning the war began in earnest,' began the General. 'With hindsight we can see that all prior hostilities have been nothing more than skirmishes intended to seize weapons and equipment and to test our resolve.' He glared at the others present in the meeting as if holding them personally accountable for the latest attack. 'This morning at 9:47 a column of military vehicles entered the secure perimeter of Heathrow Airport. The vehicles included light attack vehicles, troop transports, armoured personnel carriers, self-propelled guns and battle tanks. The troops manning these vehicles wore British Army uniforms and carried authentic ID. But they were not members of the armed forces. They were lycanthropes, acting in broad daylight for the first time.'

The General brought up a series of images on the large display in the conference room, showing scenes of destruction at the airport and other locations. 'The enemy forces attacked without warning, with devastating results.' On the screen, shots of damaged buildings, raging fires, burned-out tanks and armoured vehicles rotated silently. Bodies were clearly visible in a number of the photographs. 'I do not yet have a full damage assessment,' continued the General, 'but we have lost significant numbers of men, vehicles and weaponry. Furthermore, key infrastructure across the city has been attacked and destroyed, including police stations, communications hubs, and electrical substations. Telecommunications are down in many parts of the capital, and the electrical grid has also been severely disrupted.'

The sequence of photographs on the big screen came to an end and were replaced with a live video feed from

Heathrow, showing black smoke billowing from the bombed-out terminal buildings. The blackened hulks of vehicles lay strewn around the foreground.

The Home Secretary was the first to respond. 'General,' he demanded angrily. 'How could this have happened? How could you have allowed this kind of infiltration?' He turned to the Director-General of MI5. 'Why did we not learn of this attack in time to prevent it? This was the result of sheer incompetence.'

The General replied with fury in his eyes. 'In these meetings I have given ample warnings of the nature and magnitude of the threat we faced. I have pushed for more intervention, time and time again. At every opportunity I have voiced the need for urgent action. But my hands have been tied.' He glared at the PM, who winced.

The voice of the General boomed on. 'I warned the Prime Minister that her failure to act would have consequences. We have lost this battle, just as we lost the battle at the quarantine hospital on the night of the last full moon. This was our Pearl Harbor – an urgent wake-up call that demands an immediate response. Now we have no choice. We must act decisively. We must retaliate with all the capabilities at our disposal and begin our offensive in earnest, or else lose the war.'

Silence fell across the meeting.

There was truth in what the General said. He had pushed for a much heavier military assault, and she had refused. But she had said no for a good reason. Even now she could not allow him free reign to wage war in the city. She would have to accommodate some of his proposals, but right now she couldn't be sure how to respond.

She turned instead to the Foreign Secretary. 'What is the latest from other countries?'

The General frowned as if he thought she was avoiding his challenge, but she needed to know the full extent of the enemy's activities.

'Grim,' remarked the Foreign Secretary. 'Cities around

Europe have also experienced attacks on government, military and civilian targets. Some of these attacks are still underway as we speak. The situation is most dire in Germany. Armed werewolves attacked the German federal parliament at the *Bundestag* overnight, killing many parliamentarians and taking hundreds more hostage. The German Chancellor is believed to be among the dead. German KSK special forces are attempting to retake control of the building but the werewolves are putting up fierce resistance. It would seem that the attack was well planned and coordinated, just like the one that took place here. Werewolves infiltrated *1 Panzerdivision* and deployed rebel troops from mechanized infantry and Panzer battalions to attack the *Bundestag*. The *Reichstag* building has been virtually destroyed and the federal government is in complete disarray. Our ambassador in Berlin reports that centralized democracy in Germany is effectively at an end and that power is now being seized by individual states.'

'Thank you, Foreign Secretary. Please convey our sincere condolences to the German President.'

The situation in Germany was a stark warning of what might happen here in the UK if the PM did not maintain a tight grip on the security situation. If her government fell, chaos would reign unchecked. Could that happen? She could no longer take anything for granted.

She turned back to face the General. 'What exactly do you propose?' she asked him.

'To fully eradicate the threat we must employ the kind of street-by-street fighting that we used successfully against militants in urban areas of Iraq and Afghanistan. But an operation of this kind would result in considerable loss of life to our own forces. We have sustained significant casualties already. I will not permit further losses on the same scale. Therefore before the ground attack begins I propose a first wave of artillery bombardment of strategic targets and an aerial bombing campaign to degrade the enemy's capabilities.'

It was the Chancellor who challenged him this time. 'You can't be serious, General. An aerial bombardment of London? The devastation would be unimaginable. Prime Minister, you cannot allow this.'

'The Chancellor is right, General. I will not permit that kind of wholesale destruction.'

'The action I propose is targeted, Prime Minister. We will be using precision delivery of munitions to minimize unnecessary damage. Together with MI5 we are tracking the retreating lycanthropes using real-time satellite imagery and Sentinel reconnaissance aircraft. We have refined our list of enemy locations and our tanks and infantry battalions are advancing on these locations as we speak.'

'And where exactly are these locations?'

The General brought up a new image showing a map of London with various markings. Some of the dots on the map were slowly moving.

'But many of those targets are within central London,' said the Chancellor. 'You simply cannot start bombing our own capital city.'

'Our enemy is already doing exactly that,' insisted the General. 'Do I need to show you the photographs of Heathrow for a second time?'

The Prime Minister considered the options. 'How will you ensure the safety of civilians living in those areas?' she asked.

'We will aim to evacuate civilians before the full attack begins.'

'Aim to?'

'We will do our best. But the time for pulling punches is over.'

The PM closed her eyes briefly. The General was a bulldog straining at his leash. She could not afford to let go of that leash. However much damage the werewolves were doing, the General might do worse if she allowed him. Yet she could not hope to win this war if she ignored his advice. She opened her eyes again. 'You may proceed with the proposed assault, General, but only after all civilians have been evacuated. In fact, it is clear to me now that we must begin an urgent evacuation of the city as a whole. We must reopen the railway stations and the roads out of London. Arrange for trains to take people to other cities. Home Secretary, I would like you to take charge of the operation.'

The General was still not satisfied. 'I believe that would be a grave mistake, Prime Minister. We must act quickly. And we should not abandon our containment strategy.'

'The containment strategy has failed,' she told him. 'People are already leaving the city whether we like it or not. The refugee camps are beginning to fill up. Meanwhile the lycanthropes continue to move unimpeded. The evacuation will begin. I will not stand by and watch people die.'

'Very well,' said the General. 'One further matter. I can no longer guarantee your safety in London. You should leave Downing Street immediately.'

'Where to?'

'The Royal Air Force's Northwood Headquarters at Eastbury Park in Hertfordshire is the obvious move. It is home to NATO Allied Maritime Command and UK Joint Forces Command and has operational control of British armed forces. It is well protected, as you know.'

The PM knew it well. The Joint Forces Command HQ had first been established in World War II and consisted of a large network of underground bunkers and above-ground operations blocks. It had been designed to withstand a Cold War nuclear attack.

She weighed the General's recommendation carefully. She could see why he had selected a military base as his choice of command centre. It was ideal for his purposes. But not for hers.

'No,' she told him. 'This moment is critical, and it is vital that I demonstrate solidarity with my people. Many millions still remain in the capital and I will not abandon them to their fate. I will stay in London until the evacuation is complete. Surely I will be safe here, in the heart of Whitehall?'

The General's expression gave nothing away. 'There is one option that should prove safe in the eventuality of an attack by anti-government forces,' he conceded.

'Yes?'

'The Defence Crisis Management Centre.'

The Prime Minister nodded reluctantly. She had been given a brief tour of the underground complex – codenamed Pindar – on first becoming Prime Minister, and had hoped she would never have to see it again. Built during the Cold War era, the three-storey bunker located deep beneath the Ministry of Defence on Whitehall was designed to accommodate the Prime Minister, cabinet ministers, military personnel and senior civil servants in the eventuality of an attack by a foreign power. Named after the Ancient Greek poet Pindar, whose house alone stayed standing when the rest of the city of Thebes was obliterated, its accommodation was austere, utilitarian and cramped.

Its entrances consisted of small, unmarked air-locked doors positioned at several strategic locations, including Downing Street, the BT telecommunications tower and the COBRA office where they now sat. The tunnels that linked the various entrances were so long that bicycles were stationed along them.

The bunker complex had its own power supply and was kept stocked with food and water sufficient to supply a hundred staff for three months. It also had secure communication links with UK Joint Forces Command at Northwood Headquarters, and RAF High Wycombe, the site of UK Air Command, responsible for controlling a million square miles of airspace over Britain, the Irish Sea and North Atlantic.

It would be an unpleasant place to stay, but it would be safe, even in the worst case scenario. It seemed like she had left herself little choice in the matter. 'Very good, General. Ensure that the bunker is operational and ready for immediate use. I will move in today.'

There was one last thing she needed to say before the meeting closed. 'Home Secretary, about the evacuation...'

'Yes?'

'The full moon is not many days away. I want everyone safely out of London before it arrives.'

Chapter Forty-Nine

Western Evacuation Camp,
Buckinghamshire, crescent moon

Chanita pushed open the double mahogany doors that led into Stoke Park's ballroom. The spacious marble-pillared room had until recently been one of the country's top wedding venues. Now it was filled with army officers and support staff seated at desks, running the enormous bureaucracy that was needed to keep the emergency relief operation going.

Everyone here was busy, just like Chanita. She liked it that way. Her work gave her a clear sense of purpose. She had never been one to sit back and watch when a job needed to be done.

In fact, she was enjoying life very much here in the camp. The gardens were still in winter's grip, but already early flowering bulbs were pushing through the cold ground ready to bloom. It was a welcome change from the grey walls of the city. The accommodation inside the mansion house was luxurious too – not that she had any time to enjoy it.

Perhaps most of all she enjoyed spending time with Colonel Griffin, even though he was also incredibly busy. Usually the time they shared consisted of little more than brief moments snatched between work and exhaustion.

This was to be another of those moments. The Colonel had called for her to come and see him. He was waiting for her in the corner of the ballroom that he had made into his temporary office. 'Chanita,' he said, looking up from his desk.

She sat down facing him. 'Colonel Griffin,' she said formally. He had asked her to call him Michael, but it seemed wrong, except on the rare occasions when they were alone together.

He smiled awkwardly at her across the desk.

Something is wrong.

The Colonel often seemed tongue-tied in her presence, but today he had a wary look in his eyes too.

He has bad news to tell me.

His ways were familiar to her now, as if she had known him a lifetime.

The Colonel glanced through the French windows of the ballroom. The formal lawns and the golf course beyond them stretched out like a bright green carpet. In the distance the blue sparkle of the lake was just visible. 'It's sunny today. Why don't we step outside?'

'I'd like to,' she said.

He opened the door and followed her out.

We will walk across the lawn in silence, and then he will tell me his news, she thought. *He will clear his throat in that oh-so-English way before turning to look at me.*

The Colonel did exactly as she had predicted. 'Chanita,' he said when they reached the bridge that spanned the lake, turning that intense blue stare toward her. 'Events are beginning to move quicker than I had anticipated.'

'The camp is filling up quickly,' she agreed.

'Yes, but that's just the beginning. They're going to start filling up much faster. If we're not careful they are soon going to overflow. The government has announced an evacuation of London.'

'Of the entire city?'

He nodded.

'That's eight million people.'

'Yes.'

'How on earth are we going to accommodate them?'

'Not in the camps, obviously. They will have to be sent on and dispersed around the country. But the camps will be the first staging point for anyone who needs urgent assistance. Some people will arrive on foot, and they will have nowhere else to stay. We'll be making transport arrangements to get people moving on, but there's bound to be a big initial flood into the camps. We have to be ready for that.'

She nodded.

'My job will be to organize the logistics of the operation. There's a lot to get done, and very little time to do it. Transport, tents, security, food and medical supplies … it's a huge operation.'

'Okay. What do you want me to do?'

'I'm going to have to spend some time away from here,' he said. 'I'll be travelling between the camps, making sure everything goes according to plan. I'll be in London too, and in other locations. In short, I'm going to be away for at least a couple of weeks.'

She tried to hide her disappointment. She couldn't let her personal feelings get in the way now. Too much was at stake.

'I want you to take on a bigger role while I'm away,' he said. 'This camp needs a leader. I can't think of anyone better able to do that job than you.'

That was the last thing she had expected. 'But I'm only a nurse. I'm not even part of the military. I have no authority.'

'I'm giving you the authority,' he said. 'This is war. And there's no room for mistakes. So if I put you in charge, no one will question it.'

'But I … where do I start?'

'The admin team will run the logistics. Tents, food and other equipment will start being delivered later today. More soldiers will arrive tomorrow and you can deploy them in whatever way you see fit. The doctors and nurses will follow your lead. I don't think you'll have any problem deciding how you want to run this place.'

She swallowed. The task was daunting. But the Colonel was right. She could already see what was needed. Her instinct would be her guide. But it would be hard without him at her side.

'So you'll do it?' he asked.

'I'll do it.' Of course she would. If the Colonel believed in her, then she could believe in herself too. 'I won't let you down.'

A look of relief passed over his face and he grinned at her. 'I know you won't.' For a brief moment, the army colonel had become plain old Michael Griffin again. She wished that moment could last forever. 'I…' he began. 'There was something else I wanted to say. Also … yes … something more … personal.' He came to a halt, tongue-tied.

'Yes?' she prompted.

'It's … for a while now, I've been wanting to …' He stopped again. 'I…'

She stood on her toes and kissed him on the mouth. 'Ssh,' she whispered softly. 'I already know.'

He opened his mouth to speak again but she swallowed his words with another kiss, deeper and longer this time.

'Chanita,' he said when she finally pulled away. 'I don't know when I'll see you again.'

'Then let's make the most of the time we have now,' she told him.

Chapter Fifty

Iver Heath, West London, crescent moon

Chris Crohn was angry. Angry with the girl and her stupid dreams. Angry with himself for being dumb enough to believe them. And angry with Seth for being Seth.

He hadn't really believed the girl's dreams could come true. He had just panicked on seeing the tank rolling down the road toward them. He had lost his head momentarily and agreed to take them on this ridiculous diversion around Heathrow Airport.

His original plan had been to follow the road west out of London and toward safety. But he had been forced to double-back and turn north instead. The last-minute change of plan had added days to their journey. They had got completely lost. Now he had no idea where they were, except that they were still trapped somewhere within the boundaries of the city.

He stood at a road junction, consulting the signs. The

girl, Seth, and the dog clustered around him expectantly. They seemed to think he still knew where to go.

'Iver Heath,' read Seth. 'Uxbridge Moor. North Hillingdon. Which do we want, Chris?'

'I don't know,' snapped Chris. 'Let me think.' The names on the road sign were meaningless, abstract entities. He didn't want to go to any of these places. He didn't even know where they were. He wanted to go to the wilderness. But the road signs didn't offer that as a possibility. If this had been a computer, he would have clicked the back button, or scrolled down for more options. But here, in the real world, he had only three choices, none of them any use to him.

'I think Iver Heath is on the western edge of London,' said Seth. 'So is Uxbridge. We must be really close to the countryside now.'

'Yeah,' agreed Chris. This place definitely had a country feel to it. There was grass, and mud and trees. A short while back they'd passed a huge garden centre stocked with plants, lawnmowers and garden gnomes – the kinds of things that people who lived outside London probably needed to buy all the time. They must be getting close.

The road was virtually empty of cars, but that wasn't unusual these days. It didn't tell them anything useful. Perhaps there were clues in the names on the road signs. *Iver Heath*. The word heath meant open country, teeming with wildlife. *Uxbridge Moor*. A moor was a wild, deserted field. *Hillingdon* suggested a hill. Any of these options might work.

If they were lucky, it might not matter which way they went. Perhaps all these roads led into the countryside. Heath, moor or hill might present a path to freedom. But if they were unlucky, they could find themselves heading back toward central London again, lost forever in its concrete maze.

'What's that over there?' asked Seth.
'What?'

'That grey line.'

Chris squinted into the distance. There was definitely a grey line. But what was it?

'Is it a road?' asked Seth.

'Let's go and see.'

They walked for ten minutes, the grey line gradually taking shape, becoming a thing. Coloured dots moved along its length. 'It's a motorway,' said Seth.

'Yeah.' They carried on walking. Soon they could hear it as well as see it. The traffic was moving fast. 'It must be the M25. At last.'

The M25 was the orbital motorway that looped around London. It marked the boundary between city and country, between danger and safety. A few minutes later they came to a bridge spanning it.

'Wow,' said Seth as they stood on the bridge looking down at the carriageways and the fast-moving cars and trucks that traversed them. 'We've made it.'

'Yeah,' said Chris. A surge of adrenaline rushed through him. He'd been longing to escape from the city for months now. What had once seemed a simple task had become unbelievably difficult and dangerous. And yet he had persevered, overcoming all difficulties. He had achieved his goal. But it was only the first step on a long journey to safety. 'This is our first milestone,' he cautioned. 'We still have a long way to travel, and we don't know the way.'

The traffic on the motorway was very light compared with what he'd normally have expected to see. The days when people drove to work had come to an end. Most of the vehicles here were trucks delivering essential supplies, or else military vehicles going about their business. As they watched, a long convoy of army trucks drove under the bridge, heading south toward Heathrow Airport.

The dog barked.

'Look,' said Rose. She pointed at a brightly coloured bird perched on the safety railing of the bridge.

Lycanthropic

'What is it?' asked Seth.

'It's a parrot.' She walked slowly toward the bird, holding Nutmeg on her lead. The dog stayed quiet and the bird remained still. Rose walked right up to it and reached out her hand. The bird gave her an inquisitive look and hopped onto her outstretched palm. 'It's tame. It must have escaped from someone's house.'

'Perhaps it's a talking parrot,' said Seth. 'Can we take it with us?'

The bird gave him a sharp glance and screeched. Then it launched itself into the air, its wings a flurry of bright patterns, and flew off toward a distant clump of trees. Nutmeg barked again.

Chris shivered as he watched the parrot fly to the leafless trees. He felt cold, even wrapped up in his winter jacket. A tropical bird wouldn't last any time in this climate. 'Come on,' he said. 'We have to keep moving. A parrot is the last thing we need, talking or otherwise.'

They walked until sundown, when the temperature began to drop alarmingly. The sky turned a deep blue, studded with stars. They were brighter here than in the city, arranged into clear patterns. The moon was out too, a reminder of why they were trudging along this road, so far from home.

Just as night took hold completely, a welcoming sign appeared on the roadside before them. They could just about make out its wording in the dark. *Western Evacuation Camp. New arrivals please report to main reception.* An arrow pointed right.

Chris stared at the sign mistrustfully. 'What does it mean?'

'Exactly what it says, I expect,' said Seth, rubbing his hands together. 'Come on. What are we waiting for?' He turned off the main road and started walking in the direction indicated by the arrow. Rose and the dog went too.

Chris shrugged and followed them.

The camp turned out to be just as it had described itself. A country house hotel had been requisitioned by the army and was being used to provide temporary accommodation for people fleeing London. Chris was perturbed to discover that hundreds or perhaps even thousands of people had already had the same idea as him, and had managed to get here before him.

The camp was being run by soldiers, but they seemed friendly enough. An official issued them with sleeping bags and showed them to the rows of tents that had been set up on the hotel's golf course. 'Just find a place to sleep,' he told them. 'You can take a shower in the morning. We'll be serving breakfast from seven o'clock.'

Breakfast consisted of bacon, eggs, sausages and toast, with mugs of hot tea and coffee to wash it down. The coffee tasted disgusting but Chris didn't mind. It was hot. 'Eat and drink as much as you can,' he told the others. 'We don't know when we'll get another hot meal.'

Rose slipped some of the sausages to Nutmeg beneath the table. Nobody seemed to mind.

'Can't we stay here for a few days?' asked Seth.

'No. We must press on. We've got a long walk ahead of us.'

A guy sitting further down the table seemed to be listening in to their talk. He leaned toward them conspiratorially now. 'So where are you folk headed?'

The stranger was big and muscular, with closely-cropped hair, and a tattoo on his arm. Chris had seen guys just like him in the gym he'd joined briefly, when he'd been in training for the apocalypse. He didn't trust guys like that. He turned his back on him, ignoring the question.

'We're going to the wilderness,' said Seth.

'Cool,' said the stranger. 'So, where's that, exactly?'

Chris shot his friend a warning look. 'Don't answer his questions, Seth. He's a stranger. We shouldn't talk to strangers.'

'I'm not six years old,' said Seth. 'Why shouldn't I talk

to him? I'm bored of talking to you. And Rose never says much.' He turned back to the new guy. 'We're going to Hereford. That's close to Wales.'

The guy looked puzzled. 'I thought you said the wilderness.'

'Well, yeah. Hereford is kind of like wilderness. At least, that's what Chris says. It's countryside, at least. The city is too dangerous.'

'You're right about that. I'm Ryan, by the way.'

'Seth.'

'So you'll be travelling via Oxford then, Seth? It's the most direct route.'

Seth shrugged. 'Will we? I don't really know which way we're going. I don't think Chris does either.'

'I do,' said Chris.

Ryan was thinking. 'You'll need to pick up the Oxford Road and head toward Gerrards Cross. That'll take you to Oxford. Then keep going and you'll pass through Cheltenham and Gloucester. Eventually you'll reach Hereford.'

'It sounds like you know the way pretty well.'

'Sure. I can show you if you like.'

'No,' said Chris. 'We travel alone.'

'Why?' said Seth. 'We don't even know which route to take.'

'We do now. He just told us.'

Ryan was still thinking. 'Of course, you could take the old road if you prefer.'

'The old road?'

'Yeah. The Ridgeway. It passes along a chalk ridge from the east of England to the west. It's Britain's oldest road. It's not really a road, more of a track. It dates back to the Bronze Age. It was popular with ancient travellers because the high ground gave them good visibility. It begins quite close to here, near Aylesbury.'

Chris narrowed his eyes. *The Ridgeway. The old road.* He had never even heard of it before. Perhaps this guy did have something to offer after all.

'Do you have any survival skills?' he asked Ryan. 'Hunting? Building fires? Making shelters? Can you navigate using the stars?'

'No. Not really,' said Ryan. He brightened. 'But I could find out on my phone if I can get a signal.'

Chris stared at the guy incredulously. It had been an age since he'd held a smartphone in his hands, longer still since he'd used a laptop or a desktop computer. He felt the absence of technology like a physical pain. 'You have a smartphone?' he asked Ryan.

'Duh. Who doesn't?' said Ryan. He pulled out his phone and showed it to them.

Chris eyed the device greedily. It wasn't one of the latest phones, just a cheap Chinese-built model. Until recently he would have sneered at it. But something inside him was almost bursting with the need to hold it. He reached out for it.

'Hey, cool it.' Ryan whipped the phone out of his reach. 'It's mine.' He glared angrily at Chris. Then his face softened. He held the device out in his open palm. 'But I can let you use it. If you'll take me with you.'

Chapter Fifty-One

High Street, Brixton Hill, South London

Liz turned on the TV to catch the latest news, but she wasn't optimistic about finding any. At the beginning of the crisis the news reporting had been full of endless so-called experts, quick to suggest opinions, theories, scapegoats, and quick-fix solutions. In the absence of clear official briefings, there had been 24/7 speculation with more rumours than facts, and random Twitter comments replacing hard journalism. Every new event was covered intensively for twenty-four hours before moving on to the next crisis. It had reached fever-pitch after the ban on air travel and the requisition of the airports for military and official use.

Then, gradually, the experts had begun to disappear. Phone lines to correspondents went dead mid-report; reporters failed to respond to requests for information from the news desks. A decree was issued by the government banning commentary from *non-approved* experts.

Now the news channels just reported what few facts were known about any event and allowed a government spokesperson to make an official statement on the matter. Who knew the truth of anything anymore?

Increasingly, even the government officials seemed to have nothing to say, other than bland reassurances that the police and the military had everything under control. But Liz knew the truth of that – everything was certainly not under control.

Since the Battle of Heathrow, TV broadcasting was even more disrupted than before. A group of werewolves – or, according to some rumours, anti-government forces from the People's Uprising – had detonated an enormous truck bomb in the street next to the BT Tower. The tower served 95% of the UK's terrestrial and satellite TV programmes, and the blast had taken out the fibre optic communications hub at the base of the tower. The result was havoc.

She worked her way through the main news channels but was unable to find anything still on air. All she could find was a documentary showing railway journeys through Switzerland, and a foreign satellite channel broadcasting repeats of *Seinfeld* dubbed into German. She switched it off.

The internet was also heavily disrupted. Lack of bandwidth was making the system into an experience reminiscent of the 1990s. Major sites were down or blocked, video was out of the question, and even images took an age to download. She tried the BBC news website but couldn't get beyond the spinning wait graphic. Her phone was out of action too, unable to pick up any signal, and she knew that the phone networks were down across most of London.

Instead she turned to her trusty radio. It was ancient and battered, but it didn't let her down. 'The government has announced a complete evacuation of London, to begin with immediate effect,' the Radio 4 news announcer explained. 'The joint security forces of the army and the police will be responsible for ensuring that all residents leave their homes and are transported out of the city to safety.'

Liz pricked up her ears. It was the first she'd heard of it. 'All residents should remain in their homes and prepare for evacuation. Transport will be arranged for those who do not have cars. Take only essential items necessary for survival. Do not attempt to leave your homes until police arrive to give you permission to go. Those requiring medical assistance should notify the police before leaving. The following items are recommended – two litres of drinking water, non-perishable food sufficient for at least one day, a battery-powered radio, a first aid kit, infant formula for those with babies …'

'Liz?' It was Kevin, returning home with Mihai.

She switched the radio off. 'I'm in here.'

'How are you, love?' he asked.

'All right. You?'

He and Mihai had been out somewhere. Up to no good, probably. But Liz didn't ask. The last thing she wanted now was an argument.

She smiled at Mihai. Since their conversation about vampires, the boy seemed to be much more his old self. She knew that talking about your fears was often the best way to begin to overcome them. She hoped they'd be able to have more conversations soon, and not just about vampires and werewolves. The boy returned her smile weakly, but she could see him staring anxiously at her teeth.

'They're evacuating the city,' said Kevin. 'We have to wait for the police to tell us what to do.'

'Yeah. That's right,' said Liz.

Kevin looked at her expectantly. 'So, you're the police. What do we do?'

'I haven't a clue. I only just heard about it myself.'

'Oh.'

'But the smart move would be to begin preparing an emergency pack for everyone to take. I don't know how we'll be travelling. It might be by car, bus or train. Best to be ready for anything.'

'What about Lily?' asked Mihai. 'She is too small to walk.'

'I'm sure she'll manage,' said Liz. 'Dean can carry her if needs be. It's Samantha I'm more concerned about.' Dean's wife was quite heavily pregnant now, and often short of breath moving around the house. She wouldn't be able to walk very far. In normal times they would get an ambulance to move her. But if times were normal, they wouldn't be preparing for an evacuation. 'I'll make enquiries and find out what kind of help we can get for her.'

'We're definitely leaving then?' said Kevin.

The question surprised her. 'Of course,' she said. 'What's the alternative? We can't stay here with no food supply. Especially with Samantha expecting a baby.'

'Guess not,' said Kevin.

'Although I'm not sure when we'll be able to leave. Dean and I will be needed to help with the evacuation, so we may have to stay on until the end. If that happens, you and the others will need to go first, without us.'

Kevin looked anxious. 'That ain't gonna happen, love. If you stay, we'll stay too.'

'No. If you get a chance to go to safety, you must take it. Samantha, Lily and Mihai will be depending on you to take care of them. Can you handle that?'

Kevin nodded. 'Yeah, I've spent enough years out on the road, living on my own. Reckon I can handle this. And so can Mihai.' He ruffled the boy's long hair. 'We can look after the girls, ain't that right, kid?'

'Yeah, is right,' said the boy. 'Will not let Liz down.'

Chapter Fifty-Two

Department of Genetics, Imperial College, Kensington, London

Doctor Helen Eastgate had made her choice. In the end it hadn't been so difficult. On the one hand, a life under the shadow of Huntington's disease. An inexorable physical and mental decline into oblivion. On the other – a cure, but at terrible cost, a cost too high. She had only to recall the face of Leanna Lloyd on the day she had first met her, speaking without emotion of how her own father and brother had died – murdered at her own hand. Leanna's expression and voice had been devoid of all human feeling, her eyes dead. Helen recalled too how Leanna had stalked her through the lab next door, delighting in tormenting her, almost killing her in cold blood.

Lycanthropy had made a psychopath of Leanna. Helen would not choose that path for herself.

Instead she chose life, even if Huntington's disease

would cut that life short. A single day in human form was worth more to her than a lifetime as a werewolf.

But time was short now. The deadline to evacuate the capital was fast approaching. And Helen had no intention of leaving. There was still much work to be done, and Helen planned to do that work. If the soldiers assigned to her protection chose to leave, she would not seek to prevent them. She just hoped they wouldn't try to take her with them.

She turned her attention back to the task she had set herself.

In a test tube on her desk, an epic battle was unfolding in all its brutal and heroic glory. Relayed onto her laptop screen by the unflinching gaze of a scanning electron microscope, life at the cellular level was revealed to be far more than just a sequence of blind chemical reactions. It was warfare on a grand scale.

The computer screen showed the human immune system fighting relentlessly against the onslaught of microbes, viruses and other pathogens that sneaked their way inside the human body twenty-four hours of every day. The cells and other components of the immune system were the knights in shining armour, their foe the worst invaders that nature in its boundless wisdom had contrived to throw against the body's defences.

There were no generals in these armies that Helen watched, only foot soldiers, blindly hurling themselves into the fray. And there would be mass casualties on both sides. Ultimately every soldier would die. It was just a question of surviving longer than the enemy.

It was a sobering lesson.

Helen liked to think that at this microscopic scale, the lessons of life were painted starkly clear. In the constant battle of strong versus weak, there were no heroes or villains, only predator and prey. The fittest would survive, and there was no guarantee that humans would resist the spread of lycanthropy.

Unless they had help. And it seemed that Helen was in a unique position to find that help. If she could identify immune antibodies she could synthesize a vaccine or a cure. The possibility of success was tantalizingly close. She would not leave it now.

An abrupt knock at the lab door disrupted her thoughts. The door opened without invitation and two soldiers stood in the doorway. Behind them the building receptionist muttered his apologies. 'I tried to stop them barging their way in, Doctor Eastgate. They wouldn't take no for an answer.'

'It's all right, Robert,' she told him. 'I was expecting them. You go now. You must take care of yourself. I will deal with these men.' She watched him leave gratefully, released of his responsibility at last.

She spoke quickly to the two burly soldiers before they could say anything. 'Gentlemen, I know why you are here. I must tell you that I won't leave my desk. My work here at the university is too important. I'll take full responsibility for my own safety. You may leave me now and go.'

The two men exchanged glances. One of them spoke. 'Ma'am, we were told that you would say that. We are acting on the specific instructions of the Prime Minister. We are charged with evacuating you to safety regardless of your own wishes. A Land Rover is waiting outside the building, and we have priority clearance to proceed through all checkpoints. We are authorized to use force to remove you if necessary.'

'So are you going to shoot me?' demanded Helen indignantly. 'How would that help?'

'Shooting you won't be necessary, ma'am. It would be much easier for everyone if you simply agreed to come with us.'

The two men pushed their way into the laboratory. One moved around her desk and stood behind her. The other waited patiently, holding the door open.

Helen didn't rate her chances of resisting them if they

tried to drag her or carry her from the building. If they did that, all her work here would come to nothing. She had a better idea.

She switched off her microscope, closed her laptop and stood up. 'All right. I'll come quietly. But first I have a job I want you to do for me.'

Chapter Fifty-Three

Upper Terrace, Richmond upon Thames, West London

Ben stood at the top of the staircase, blocking Melanie's way. She tried to squeeze past, but he stood firm, stopping her from going any further. *This is it*, she thought. She'd been trying to avoid Ben for days now, doing her best to postpone this confrontation. But here it was. She waited for him to open hostilities.

'We need to talk about James,' he told her.

'What about him?' she asked innocently.

'I'm not blind, Melanie. And I'm not a fool.'

His harsh words stung her. Ben could be such a sweet man, and yet, sometimes he could be so uncompromisingly high-minded and pig-headed. When something was bothering him, he just couldn't let it go. When he'd moved in with her, she'd thought all her dreams had come true, but it felt like the only thing they'd done since living together was row and fight.

'So what's the problem, Ben?'

'You know what the problem is. James isn't eating the food we bring him. He goes out at night. I've seen him creeping back into the house in the early hours of the morning. He thinks nobody sees him. But even werewolves aren't invisible.'

She had known from the start that James wouldn't eat the cooked meat they gave him. The ploy had fooled Ben for a while, but now it seemed that he had guessed the truth. She decided to play innocent. 'So James keeps late hours. Grandpa does too. We all do.'

'Grandpa doesn't come home every night with blood stains down his shirt.'

She didn't know what to say to that. What James did in his own time was his business, and his alone. She knew what he was up to. James was a werewolf. He needed to hunt. What could she say? 'We can't stop him going out, Ben. When he stopped feeding he nearly died.'

'And now other people are dying. James kills them. I've seen enough people die already. I won't stand by and allow more bloodshed, especially not when the killer lives under the same roof as me.'

His upstanding posturing irritated her. Ben always thought he knew best. 'We don't know for sure that James kills anyone,' she said.

'You know he does.'

She shrugged. There was no point denying it. 'We can't stop him,' she said. 'We mustn't.'

He raised his voice. 'So what then? We do nothing? Say nothing?'

'What is there to say? James is a werewolf. Hunting is what werewolves do.'

'Hunting for *people*,' said Ben, exasperated. 'James goes out at night and eats people! Am I the only one in this house who has a problem with that? Am I?'

Melanie pursed her lips. She couldn't win this argument. She knew that Ben would push and push until they came to blows. Arguments like this had driven them apart once before.

But she couldn't give into him. She owed James too much. He was part of the family now, just as much as Ben. *Perhaps more than Ben.* She owed James her life. If it came to a show-down between the two men, whose side would she take? She hoped she wouldn't have to find out.

'I see,' said Ben, when she said nothing. 'Well, if it's only me who has the problem, perhaps I should leave.'

'No, Ben. I don't want you to go.' *Not again.* It would be too much to lose him a second time.

'And what if I can't stay in the same house as a man-eating monster? What if you have to choose between him and me?'

She shook her head. 'Don't force me to choose, Ben. It doesn't have to be this way.'

'You have to choose which side you're on, Melanie. Are you on James' side or mine? Because you can't be on both.'

'Don't be so childish,' she shouted. When Ben climbed onto his moral high horse, he could become a complete ass. 'This isn't about taking your side or James' side.'

'No,' he said obstinately. 'It's about what's wrong and what's right.'

'James has to eat,' she insisted. 'So here's the real choice: either some random stranger dies, or else James dies. Now you tell me what's right.'

She could see that he was trying to calm himself down. 'Listen,' he said. 'I know you think I'm being pedantic and unreasonable. But I'm tired of constantly stepping around this issue. I can't just let it go. We need to have a real conversation about it. We need to talk to James.'

'All right then,' she said. That was better than talking *about* James. At least he was being included in the conversation, however difficult it might turn out to be. 'We'll talk later today, when everyone is up,' she concluded. 'I promise.'

She pushed past him at last and busied herself around the house, avoiding him. She would talk to him again when James awoke. That would be late in the day. The boy was virtually nocturnal nowadays.

But James was still asleep several hours later when she heard Sarah calling for help. Her voice was coming from Grandpa's room. Melanie rushed to see what was happening.

The old man was lying in his bed, Sarah leaning over him. 'Quickly,' said Sarah. 'Pass me a syringe from the medical cabinet.'

'What's happened?' asked Melanie.

'He's taken a turn for the worse. He started having trouble breathing and complained about a pain in his chest. Then he coughed up some blood.'

'Oh my God,' said Melanie. 'We have to call for an ambulance.' She pulled her phone out of her jeans pocket.

'No,' said Sarah. 'The emergency services will take forever to arrive, if you even manage to get through to them. If this is what I think it is, we can treat it here, and we can treat it immediately.' She began to rummage through her box of medicines.

Melanie eyed the old man warily. He was lying on the bed with his eyes closed, one feeble hand clutched to his chest, wheezing heavily. 'Really?' she said. 'What do you think it is?'

'A blood clot in the lung. It's called a pulmonary embolism. The clot forms in the leg then travels to the artery leading to the lung. It's common in people suffering from Alzheimer's. I've read all about it.'

'And you know how to fix it?' Melanie opened the medical cabinet and passed a syringe to her sister.

'Trust me,' said Sarah, inserting the needle of the syringe into a glass vial containing a drug. 'I've got this.'

Melanie watched in awe as Sarah drew the clear solution into the syringe. Melanie had never been good with anything medical. It wasn't that she was squeamish.

She just hated the idea of being so responsible for another person's life.

Sarah seemed to have no problem making life-or-death decisions. 'Heparin sodium,' she remarked casually. 'It's a powerful anticoagulant that will disrupt the blood clot.' She injected it smoothly into Grandpa's arm.

'Where did you get it?' asked Melanie. 'How did you even know you might need it?'

'Like I said, it's very common in late-stage Alzheimer's. I bought a supply from the internet. I'm prepared for most eventualities.'

Seeing the confident way that Sarah injected the drug and listening to her talking about embolisms and drug names, Melanie could quite believe it. Sarah had always been bookish, immersing herself in learning. If her diagnosis and treatment proved to be correct, the old man might well owe his life to her.

And not for the first time. Grandpa's condition had been steadily worsening for years, with Sarah caring for him around the clock. Melanie had always been content to let her sister look after him. She had never wanted to face up to the reality of his poor health.

'Late-stage Alzheimer's,' said Melanie, echoing the phrase Sarah had used. 'How long do you think he has?' They had never openly discussed the possibility of Grandpa's death before. The idea was too dreadful to contemplate, at least for Melanie. With both their parents dead, Grandpa was the only family the two sisters had left. But it was the obvious question to ask.

Sarah listened carefully to the old man's chest. 'His breathing seems to be easing a little,' she said at last. 'I'll need to give him regular doses of anticoagulant to prevent it happening again. But blood clots are just one of the risks. People with Alzheimer's are vulnerable to all kinds of complications. Strokes, heart attacks, pneumonia, ... my guess is that he'll be lucky to survive another six months.'

A tear came to Melanie's eye. 'Six months.' It didn't

seem like a long time, yet with all that was happening in the outside world right now, she couldn't begin to imagine what might happen in six months. In some ways it felt like an impossible timescale. She crossed the room to Sarah and gave her a hug.

'It could be longer,' said Sarah, 'or it might be less. There's no way of knowing. We'll just have to take each day as it comes.'

'One day at a time,' agreed Melanie. 'And we'll all stick together. That's the only way to make it through.'

Chapter Fifty-Four

Brixton Village, South London

'Are you sure this is a wise course of action?' asked Mr Canning.

He sat across the desk from Salma Ali in her well-appointed study. The bookshelves behind her were lined with leather-bound books of law. The desk itself was mahogany and covered in green leather. It was the kind of setting that would have made a nineteenth-century English barrister feel at home.

She obviously had no idea how much these objects betrayed her. To a trained eye like Canning's, they revealed all too much. Salma Ali had constructed a fantasy that revealed her deepest desires. This study revealed her dirty secret – that she was not a rebel at heart and never had been. Instead, she desperately longed to fit in and be accepted by the ruling establishment. But the world she desired to join had spurned her. And so she had resolved to burn it down.

Mr Canning smiled to himself. Another mystery solved. An enigma explained. It was always good to know what motivated people. In times of upheaval, such knowledge could be the key to survival.

She treated him to one of her condescending stares. 'Are you questioning my decision?' she snapped.

He had seen her behave this way before. A defensive posture. A sign of weakness and insecurity. A leader should be open to criticism. She should not turn her advisers away. Perhaps Salma was not the great leader he had hoped.

'Just giving you an opportunity to reconsider, my dear.'

'I do not wish to reconsider anything. Nor to be patronized. Just do what I tell you.'

He was not overly concerned by her behaviour. He would not force the issue. Salma was the one making the decision. If her judgment turned out to be poor, it would be she who suffered the consequences. 'As you wish. I will do it immediately.' He rose from his chair and left the house, venturing out into the street.

His destination was not far away. Kowalski's supermarket. He entered the shop and found the Polish man in the shabby office upstairs. Jack Stewart was here too, just as he had expected. A couple of rats, lurking in their nest.

'Good morning to you both,' said Mr Canning politely. He flashed them a smile, knowing how much the sight of his teeth discomforted the two men.

Predictably, they jumped at his arrival, Kowalski shrinking back into his chair, Stewart lurching to his feet and sliding round behind the battered old table that occupied the centre of the room.

Mr Canning grinned more broadly.

'What do you want?' asked Kowalski. 'We are busy here.'

Mr Canning pulled up a chair and sat with the table between him and the two men. He stared wordlessly at

Kowalski long enough for the shopkeeper to begin perspiring. 'Salma sent me,' he said at last.

'Yes? What does she want?'

'To give you this.' He drew out a small bundle wrapped in oily cloth and placed it on the table between them. 'Do you know what it is?'

The other men said nothing. Obviously they did not know what was hidden beneath the cloth. But perhaps they had ideas. He let those ideas take shape in the men's minds, hoping they would fear the worst. The terrified expressions that spread over their faces showed that they had surprisingly vivid imaginations.

'Let me show you.' He began to unwrap his parcel. It took only a moment for him to reveal the revolver. It was one of the guns he had so easily acquired from Kevin Bailey after the funeral. He left it on display for them to see.

'It's a gun,' said Kowalski uncertainly.

'You're right. But don't worry. It isn't for you. I brought it for Mr Stewart.'

Jack Stewart started back, looking even more frightened than before. 'Ms Ali sent you here with that?'

'Yes.' Mr Canning picked the revolver from the table and aimed it casually in Stewart's direction. 'Believe me, I tried to tell her this was a bad decision, but I couldn't change her mind. She was most insistent.'

Jack Stewart's face turned ashen. His eyes flicked to the door where Mr Canning had entered, but that exit was blocked now. He pushed himself back against the far wall. 'But why?' he asked. 'I've done everything she asked me to. Everything.'

'Yes. I'm sure you have.' Mr Canning pulled the hammer of the revolver back with his thumb, cocking the weapon and rotating the cylinder ready to fire.

Jack Stewart jumped at the sound.

Mr Canning aimed the gun at his head.

'Please,' begged the man. 'Don't kill me.'

Mr Canning pulled the trigger. The gun clicked loudly.

Jack Stewart jumped in terror, his hands over his face.

'Kill you?' queried Mr Canning. 'Whatever gave you the idea that I was going to do that?'

On the other side of the room Jack Stewart first sagged in relief, then straightened again, furious. 'What the bloody hell did you do that for?'

'Just a quick demonstration. Ms Ali sent me here to give you the gun. I told her that was a terrible idea, but as I said, she insisted.' He broke the barrel forward to expose the empty cylinder of the revolver. 'It's not loaded, you see?' He snapped the gun shut again and placed it back on the table. 'It's an Enfield No. 2. standard issue World War II British army revolver. A bit of an antique, I'm afraid, rather like me. But it still works perfectly. Here's some ammunition.' He tossed a box of bullets next to the gun. 'I'm sure you'll work out what to do with it.'

Kowalski's face was like thunder. 'Why do you bring that thing here? And why give it to him?' He jerked a thumb in Jack Stewart's direction.

'Good question. I don't think it's a wise move either, but Salma thinks he'll be able to put it to good use.'

He was still puzzled by Salma's reasoning. Jack Stewart was a loose cannon, an unguided missile that she had launched into the heart of the community. He was dangerous enough with his fists and his knife. Who knew what he might do with a gun?

Perhaps that was her purpose. Random violence led to fear, and fear bred docility and obedience. It was a tried and tested method. She obviously knew her history very well.

He slid the weapon across the table to Jack Stewart. 'Just don't do anything too stupid with it, will you?'

Chapter Fifty-Five

Department of Genetics, Imperial College, Kensington, London

By the time Helen left the Biomedical Institute she was clutching a cool bag containing ice packs and a pint of blood infected with the lycanthropy virus. The soldiers who had been sent to escort her from the building had been uncertain at first, then downright hostile when she had explained what she wanted them to do.

But in the end she had talked them into hauling a dead werewolf up from the basement and laying it out on a metal table like a slab of fresh meat on a butcher's block. The men watched in a mixture of horror and interest as she drained the contaminated blood from the carcass.

'I hope you know what you're doing with that,' commented the senior officer as he helped her up into the Land Rover, the bag securely in her hands.

'Oh yes,' Helen assured him. 'I know exactly what I'm doing. Now where are we going?'

'That's classified.'

She watched out of the passenger window as the empty streets of Knightsbridge sped past. This area had been a priority for evacuation, and only a few stragglers remained behind. Police and army vehicles were on the move, picking up people like Helen who had stayed on for some official reason, or who simply refused to leave.

They passed the Science Museum and the Victoria and Albert Museum on Exhibition Road, then turned right onto Cromwell Road past the gothic splendour of the Natural History Museum. All of these great Victorian institutions were now closed. It was a bizarre sight. These streets contained some of the most valuable real estate in the entire world. Every building in this part of London was worth many millions. Harrods and Harvey Nichols were further down this same road. Now the area was being abandoned to the rats and the stray cats and dogs that had stayed behind. Even the military was pulling out. Helen wondered how long it would be before people returned here. And what would they find when they did?

The Land Rover drove unimpeded through the city, heading north-west. Many of the military checkpoints that had reduced the streets to gridlock in previous days and weeks had either been removed or were in the process of being dismantled. The vehicle was waved briskly through the few remaining barriers.

Her armed escort grew visibly more relaxed as the journey proceeded. Traffic was relatively light and all moving in the same direction. The soldier driving the Land Rover didn't pay too much attention to the traffic lights that continued to cycle through their red-amber-green sequence even though were no vehicles waiting at most junctions. 'Not long now, ma'am. We'll soon have you somewhere safe.'

They left the city in under an hour – probably the quickest time Helen could remember – and emerged in the countryside west of London as dusk fell. She saw signs to

Oxford and to Windsor, but the Land Rover turned off the main road long before reaching either of those destinations. Eventually it pulled onto a small road leading to a large country estate.

A sign at the entrance read *Stoke Park*, but a new, larger sign had been erected in front of it. *Western Evacuation Camp. New arrivals please report to main reception.*

So this was her destination. One of the new evacuation camps that had been set up as a staging post to accommodate those leaving London. 'Why such a big secret?' she asked the driver.

'Just the way that the army works, ma'am. The people at the top like to keep us in the dark as much as possible.'

The Land Rover drew up outside the main reception and the soldiers helped her out with her bags. She didn't have much — just a few personal effects, her laptop and notes, and of course the sample of blood, safe and cool in its thermally-sealed bag. She watched the soldiers drive away.

It felt weird to be arriving at a luxury country hotel, especially with an armed military escort to bring her here, but the receptionist wasn't the least bit fazed. He seemed to be expecting her. 'Please wait here,' he told her. 'Someone will be along to meet you shortly.'

She took a seat and waited in the marbled entrance hall. The space was all polished surfaces and tasteful upholstery. Even the presence of the army hadn't managed to take away much of the gloss. She'd seen this hotel advertised in a magazine feature once. A weekend spa retreat had been offered at a special discounted price, but it had still been well beyond her budget. Now she was here as a guest of the military, but somehow she didn't think the spa would be available.

After a brief wait a nurse appeared. The woman was quite young with a professional demeanour, but looked exhausted. Yet when she saw Helen she broke into a welcoming smile that seemed genuine. 'Doctor Eastgate?

Welcome to Stoke Park. My name is Chanita Allen.'

The nurse's warm Caribbean accent reminded Helen of her own displacement from her childhood home. She felt a sudden deep longing to be back with her family under the hot skies of Perth. It would be summer there now and the white beaches would be baking under the bright sunshine. The desire to be back home was so intense and unexpected it almost swallowed her up. She felt tears ready to fall. She wiped them away surreptitiously with the back of her hand as she reached to shake hands with the nurse. 'Please, call me Helen.'

'I was told to expect you.'

The main entrance door burst open suddenly and a group of medics entered wheeling a trolley. A patient lay unconscious on the cart and the nurses and paramedics pushed it along the corridor as fast as it would go.

Helen and Chanita stood aside to let them past.

'Sorry about that,' said Chanita. 'We're really stretched for resources. This place isn't really equipped for treating anything serious. We're doing the best we can under the circumstances, but we don't have enough doctors.'

So that's why the nurse had come to greet her. They must have heard that Helen was a medical doctor. 'I don't really have much clinical experience,' she said. 'I'm a researcher, not a hospital doctor. But I'd like to help in any way I can. I spent three years working in Perth hospital while I was completing my medical degree, so I'm not completely useless. I can definitely treat common injuries and ailments, and –'

Chanita cut her off. 'Doctor Eastgate, you must have misunderstood. We aren't expecting you to help out. I've been asked to find out how we can help you.'

'Help me? I don't understand.'

'I was told that you would be coming, and to give you any assistance you ask for. I understand that your research is of vital importance to national security. I gather that you have a highly-placed guardian who attaches the greatest importance to your work.'

The Prime Minister, Helen realized. She suddenly felt like a fraud. She'd somehow managed to persuade the leader of the country that her work was more important than caring for the sick and injured. And what did she have to show for it? A long series of failed tests, and a pint of blood in a bag.

Chanita must have misinterpreted her uncertain look. 'I understand that your work is highly classified and confidential,' she assured Helen. 'This is a military establishment and all the medical staff here are bound by the terms of the Official Secrets Act. No one will ask you any questions about the nature of your work.'

'Oh. I'm not worried about that,' said Helen. 'Although perhaps I should be. I'm still not really used to all this. What worries me most is that I hardly know what I'm doing myself.'

The nurse smiled gently and patted her hand. 'Then that makes two of us. We're all finding ourselves in positions that we never expected to hold. But what I do know is that we have to keep doing the job we've been assigned. Somehow, with patience and persistence we can make a difference.'

'I hope so,' said Helen. She managed to return Chanita's kind smile.

'Trust me. I know these things.'

Helen gathered her thoughts. She was tired after her journey, but Chanita was right. The best way to dispel her doubts would be to get started right away. 'I don't need much – only basic equipment. I've brought most of what I need with me. The main requirement is for volunteers. I'd like to take some blood samples for testing.'

'Okay. What kind of volunteers are you looking for?'

'Anyone. Anyone at all. The more diverse, the better.'

'And how many people do you need?' asked Chanita.

'A few hundred perhaps. It depends how long it takes before we strike lucky.'

Chanita raised her eyebrows. 'A few hundred? I see. In that case, we'd better get started immediately.'

Chapter Fifty-Six

High Street, Brixton Hill, South London

Liz woke early to the insistent bleating of her alarm. She rubbed her eyes, fighting the temptation to roll over and go back to sleep. In the past she'd always been an early riser, but these days she didn't seem to feel tired at night, and was staying up later and later. She'd only managed to get off to sleep a few hours ago.

The sound of planes and helicopters operating at all hours of the night wasn't helping, although she was already growing used to the drone of the transport aircraft bringing in supplies. The dual-rotor Chinooks were more likely to keep her awake, but she comforted herself with the knowledge that they were welcome guests, distributing food around the city. The Apache gunship helicopters cruising low across the skyline were a more worrying reminder that all was not well.

She cancelled the alarm and forced herself out of bed. A long working day lay ahead of her. The evacuation had progressed quickly from rumour to fact, and her main job now was helping local people prepare to leave. They were no longer working with the army, hunting werewolves, and she had no regrets about that. Instead, she and Dean had begun to go door to door checking that residents were aware of the evacuation arrangements, and finding out if they needed special help. But some of the residents were reluctant to go, and Samantha was digging her heels in as much as any of them.

'I'm not leaving,' said Samantha. 'And that's final. Not unless we all go together.'

'But you have to, love,' pleaded Dean. 'You have to get yourself to safety, and take Lily with you.'

'I'm not going anywhere without you,' she said, folding her arms above the bump in her belly.

Dean turned to Liz. 'See if you can talk some sense into her.'

Liz didn't fancy her chances of changing Samantha's mind. 'I doubt it,' she told Dean. 'She can be just as stubborn as you when she wants to be.'

'Cheers.'

'Samantha, think about it. The evacuation is voluntary at the moment, but word is that a mandatory order will be issued soon and then everyone will be leaving all at once. It would be better to go now. It would be safer.'

'Not unless Dean comes with me,' insisted Samantha. 'That's the only way I'll feel safe.'

Dean shook his head. 'You know I can't go. Liz and I have to stay here and help to supervise the evacuation right up until the end. It's our duty.'

'And it's my duty to stay with my husband. Anyway, in my condition I'd rather be here than in some transit centre or something.'

'It looks like I don't have a choice,' said Dean.

'No,' agreed Samantha, bringing the discussion to a close. 'You don't.'

Liz left the house with Dean and took the patrol car to

the far end of Brixton, close to Ruskin Park. The burned and blackened tower of King's College Hospital stood here as a grim reminder of exactly why the evacuation was necessary. It had been left abandoned since the werewolves had escaped from its isolation wards on the night of the wolf moon. The next full moon was now only days away.

The local people in this area were proving to be mostly cooperative. The number of cars parked in the streets had diminished since the previous day, and most of the houses had their windows boarded up or curtains closed. It was beginning to take on the look of a ghost town.

But as people left, the streets began to feel more dangerous for those who remained. Some of the boarded-up houses had been broken into. Others had been set alight. Smoke drifted over the city skyline from several different places, the black columns twisting up to meet the grey rainclouds overhead. The smoke from the smouldering fires left a sharp, acrid taste at the back of Liz's throat. The 999 emergency number was no longer in use and minor fires were being left unattended as firefighters battled with the most serious blazes. But if the small fires weren't quenched by rain or put out by local residents, they would turn into major conflagrations themselves. The sooner everyone was out, the better.

One man was loading up his car with suitcases and boxes, ready to join the exodus. His wife and children were already sitting safely inside the car.

'Do you have a route planned?' Liz asked him.

The man nodded. 'Yes. I'm following the red route south. As long as I can fill up with fuel we should be all right.'

'Good.' The red routes were the official evacuation routes. The army was keeping them clear and making sure traffic kept moving. 'Don't deviate from the marked route. Supplies of fuel will be available at designated points along the route, but it will be tightly rationed.'

She had seen for herself the long lines of cars waiting outside filling stations. Each car was being allocated just enough fuel to get to its next destination. For those travelling south, that would be a holding area at Gatwick Airport. The last time Liz had been to Gatwick she'd flown on a cheap last-minute holiday to Greece. She didn't know where this family would eventually end up, but it wouldn't be a Mediterranean beach resort.

She watched the car drive off down the road, its roof rack piled high with luggage.

'Sensible folk,' said Dean approvingly. 'If everyone was like that our job would be much easier.'

'If everyone was sensible, we wouldn't have a job at all.'

'True. But then we could get out of London ourselves.'

They knocked on the door of a house that still looked occupied. No answer came, but an upstairs curtain twitched.

Liz opened the letterbox and shouted inside. 'Please open the door. This is the police.'

After a minute a young woman appeared at the top of the staircase. When she saw Liz peering through the letterbox she sat down on the upstairs landing, her hands in her lap. 'I'm not leaving,' she called. 'You can't make me leave.'

'Remind you of anyone?' groaned Dean.

Liz ignored him. 'Madam, we are not here to force you to leave your home. At present the evacuation is still voluntary. But our advice is that you should begin to make preparations to leave as soon as possible. Do not wait until the evacuation becomes mandatory.'

If Liz had been that woman she would already be long gone. As well as the immediate danger from arsonists and looters, life in the city was becoming more difficult with every passing day. The power interruptions were more frequent, and supplies of food and other essentials harder to find. But what frightened her the most was the rumble of distant explosions that occasionally punctuated the background hum of the city. Some of her colleagues at the police station had heard bursts of automatic gunfire coming from certain areas. The fighting wasn't being reported on the news and she could only guess at what was happening. She sometimes thought of Corporal Jones – Llewelyn – and wondered where he was and what he might be doing. She hoped he was safe.

The woman sitting at the top of the stairs had fallen silent, but she hadn't gone. She must be waiting to see if Liz could change her mind and persuade her to leave.

'Do you have any elderly people living with you, or young children, or anyone who requires medical attention?'

A pause. 'My daughter. She's six.'

'Does she require medical help?'

'No.'

'Do you have any transport available? A car?'

'No.'

Liz made a note. 'Trains are being organized to take you and your family to safety. Your nearest station is Denmark Hill. You should take your family there as soon as you are ready to leave.'

The young woman continued to eye her suspiciously. 'We're not going,' she said at last. 'You can't force us.'

But Liz wasn't going to take no for an answer. 'We'll return again tomorrow. Prepare a rucksack or a small bag to bring with you and we'll escort you to the train station ourselves.'

The woman disappeared from view without responding, and Liz closed the letterbox.

Dean was shaking his head. 'You're too soft. We don't have time to waste trying to persuade everyone that it's in their best interests to leave. And we certainly don't have time to lead them by the hand to the train station.'

'If it's necessary we'll make time,' said Liz. 'We'll come back tomorrow and if she's ready to leave, we'll escort her to the station. Our job is to help those who need us most.'

'People like that could try to help themselves a bit

more. What's she thinking? Once the evacuation is complete, there'll be no food, no police, no fire service, nothing to protect her and her daughter against criminal gangs and looters. There might not even be any electricity or gas.'

'Right, so we have to convince people that leaving is the safest option.'

'Some of them are just too stupid to see it.'

'They're not stupid,' said Liz. 'They're scared. Aren't you?'

'No.'

'Well then, perhaps you're the one who's not thinking straight.'

Chapter Fifty-Seven

Electric Avenue, Brixton, South London

'Here, take hold of this end,' said the soldier to Vijay. He waited in the back of the truck for Vijay to grab hold of one end of the big wooden crate.

The evacuation of London was well underway, but it would take time before everyone could leave. In the meantime, the army was bringing truckloads of food and other supplies for distribution to the people who lived in the surrounding streets, and Vijay had volunteered to help.

The crate looked really heavy. 'I don't know if I can lift it,' he said.

'Then stand aside and let someone stronger do it,' said the soldier gruffly. 'I don't have time for kids getting in my way.'

'No, I can do it,' said Vijay. If he couldn't lift the food crates out of the truck then he couldn't help feed the old people, and if he couldn't do that he was useless.

He gripped the crate with both hands. 'Okay,' he said. He felt the full weight of the load as the soldier lifted his end of the crate. He struggled and strained to keep his end up. The tendons in his arms felt like they were going to snap.

'Let's move it,' said the soldier.

Together they wrestled the crate down from the truck and lugged it across the street to stack it with the others. Vijay's muscles screamed in agony, but he managed to get the job done. He lowered it into position and let go of the heavy load with relief. His back felt like it had been nearly broken and his arms were burning with the strain.

'Good job,' said the soldier. He passed a crowbar to Vijay. 'You start opening up the crates. I'll get someone else to help me with the rest.'

Vijay took the crowbar gladly. Opening crates sounded a lot easier than carrying them. He set to work prising the wooden lid of the first crate open. It was harder than it looked, but eventually he managed it. He looked inside. This crate was filled with boxes of rice. There was enough here to last for days, if it was shared out fairly.

He looked around to see who else was helping the soldiers. Drake was here, with that mean Mr Stewart and Mr Kowalski the Polish shopkeeper. Vijay didn't like Mr Stewart. The man had tried to stop him taking food for the old people in the neighbourhood. He said it didn't matter if they went hungry because they were good for nothing. Vijay had reported him to Mr Harvey, but then Mr Harvey had gone missing before he could do anything about it. Vijay hoped Mr Harvey's disappearance wasn't somehow his fault.

Drake came over to him. 'Pass me the crowbar. You look like you could use some help.'

Vijay handed it over gratefully. Drake was much stronger than him and he quickly set about opening the rest of the crates. 'Loads of good stuff in here,' said Drake, scooping out a large box of chocolate biscuits.

Lycanthropic

'What are you doing?' asked Vijay indignantly. 'Put it back. You can't just take whatever you want. This food is to share.'

'Mr Stewart said I can take anything I want as payment for helping.' He tore the box open and helped himself to a couple of biscuits. He offered one to Vijay.

'No,' said Vijay. 'It's not right.'

'Suit yourself,' said Drake. He shovelled the biscuits into his mouth and began chomping them noisily.

Jack Stewart was watching from the other side of the road. He was supervising the operation, but doing nothing to help. Other men were unloading the army truck, moving crates across to where they stood.

Vijay lowered his voice. 'Don't listen to that man. I don't trust him, or his cronies from the Watch.'

'Yeah? What have you got against the Watch?'

'The Watch aren't here to help us.'

'Of course they are,' said Drake, munching on his biscuits. 'Look around. They distribute food, and they protect us from werewolves and looters. You don't know what you're talking about.'

'They're just a bunch of thugs,' said Vijay angrily. 'They locked up Mr Harvey.'

'Mr Harvey was a werewolf.'

'Don't be stupid,' said Vijay. 'Of course he wasn't. He was our school teacher.'

'Yeah? Then who killed Rose? Mr Harvey did that. Everyone knows he did.'

'No! That's a lie. Rose died in the fire!' Vijay curled his small hands into angry fists.

Drake stood with his feet apart, ready to throw a punch. 'Be careful what you say,' he warned. 'I'm working for the Watch now. I'm Jack Stewart's right hand man.'

'What? Why are you working for him? Jack Stewart is one of the worst.'

'Yeah? He says I have aptitude. No one's ever said that to me before. Believe what you want, but joining the

Watch is the best thing that's ever happened to me. Apart from meeting Aasha. Don't try to take it away from me. Don't even think about it.'

Mr Kowalski came over to give orders. 'Take everything into storeroom at back of shop,' he said to Vijay and Drake. 'From there we stack onto shelves. Then give to people who come to shop. Food is free, but we must ration carefully.'

Drake picked up some boxes of food and began carrying them inside. Vijay followed him, hoping to cool things down. 'What about the evacuation?' he asked Drake. 'We'll all be leaving soon, and that'll be the end of the Watch.'

'Dunno,' said Drake. 'I might stay behind. Mr Stewart said that the Watch will keep us safe.'

'Really?' The idea sounded stupid to Vijay, but he didn't want to start another argument.

'Aasha's promised that if I decide to stay, she'll stay too.'

Vijay didn't know what to say to that. But it wasn't his problem.

They didn't speak again, just carried boxes. It took them the whole morning before all the food was safely stored away and stacked on shelves. Vijay was aching all over by the time they had finished. 'What now?' he asked.

'You boys work hard,' said Mr Kowalski appreciatively. 'Take rest of day off. And take box of food as payment.'

'Cool,' said Drake. He added a box of fizzy drinks to the chocolate biscuits he'd acquired earlier.

Vijay lowered his voice to speak to Mr Kowalski. 'What about all the people who are too old or sick to come and collect food for themselves?'

Mr Kowalski shrugged. 'They send friend instead.'

'But what if they don't have a friend? Can I take some boxes of food for them?'

The shopkeeper seemed annoyed. He looked around to see if anyone was listening. 'All right. Take food. But say nothing, okay?'

'Okay. Thanks, Mr Kowalski.'

'Be quick,' said the shopkeeper. He disappeared back inside his shop.

Vijay borrowed a trolley and filled it up with essential items. He added some cat and dog food for the people who kept pets. He knew that for people who lived alone, their animals were as important as friends and family. One trolley wouldn't be enough for everyone, but he would start with those who were completely housebound. He could always come back for more later. Mr Kowalski hadn't put a limit on how much he could take.

Before long he found himself in West Field Terrace where Rose had lived. The gap where her house once stood was visible like a scar in the row of houses. Piles of blackened bricks and rubble were all that remained. He knocked on the door of a house opposite. It was the home of Mrs McCurley, one of the neighbourhood's most elderly residents, who relied on others to bring her everything. The old woman lived alone, confined to the ground floor of her house.

'Vijay!' said Mrs McCurley, as she opened the door to him. 'How nice to see you. I don't get much company these days.'

'I brought you some food, Mrs McCurley,' said Vijay, raising his voice so the old lady could hear him. He carried the items through to her kitchen. 'Shall I make a pot of tea?' he asked her.

'That would be lovely.'

'Do you have any plans to leave?' he asked. He knew that some of the older people were being taken out by ambulance, but that was only for the most serious cases. Many of them were having to rely on friends or neighbours to help.

'My nephew is coming tomorrow to collect me,' she said.

He made the tea and carried it through to the room she

called her parlour. From here the empty space in the row of houses opposite was easily visible. The dark gash in the terrace mirrored the void in his own heart.

Mrs McCurley followed his gaze sadly. 'Such a dreadful thing to happen,' she said. 'You were good friends with Rose, weren't you?'

'Yes.' He hoped the old lady wouldn't ask him any more about Rose. It wouldn't take much to start his tears flooding again. He sat on the sofa and poured tea into two china cups, refusing to look again at the burned-out house.

'Such a shame,' continued Mrs McCurley. 'First the parents killed, then the boy. And the girl gone too. You must miss her.'

Vijay nodded glumly. He missed Rose more than he could say. Not a minute went by without him thinking of her freckled face, her shiny copper hair, her green eyes. Gone. Was that the word Mrs McCurley had used? He looked up. 'Gone?' he echoed. 'You mean dead.' He winced as he said the word.

Mrs McCurley looked puzzled, then worried. 'Dead? Why ever would you say such a dreadful thing? No, I'm sure she is safe, wherever she has gone.'

Vijay continued to look blankly at the old lady's lined face. Her cracked lips were moving, but he could not take in a word she said. 'What?' he said eventually.

She frowned, making the lines in her forehead turn into deep trenches. 'Rose is not dead,' she repeated. 'She has gone away. I saw her myself, the night of the fire. She walked out of the burning building as the fire took hold, and set off down the street.'

'She isn't dead?'

'No, goodness me, no. You poor boy. Didn't you know?'

Chapter Fifty-Eight

Upper Terrace, Richmond upon Thames, West London

Ben paced the room angrily. Another important matter to discuss had led to yet another argument with Melanie. The tension of the crisis was continually pushing them apart. It seemed that they could agree on nothing these days. He wished they could be together, just the two of them, perhaps on a tropical island somewhere, without any of the problems and concerns that had been heaped upon them.

'We can't just break into other people's houses,' he repeated. 'It's common burglary.'

Melanie glared back at him defiantly. 'Then how are we going to get hold of all the things we need?'

Ben shook his head in frustration. 'I don't know. But there must be another way.'

'If we're going to stay here we're going to need all kinds of things we can't get from the shops any more. We need matches, candles, batteries, medical supplies, water purification tablets …'

'What makes you think that your neighbours will have left that kind of stuff behind in their houses?' he asked.

'I don't know, but we can take a look.'

'No. We can't look. That's called breaking and entering. It's against the law, remember?'

'I honestly don't think they'd mind,' said Melanie. 'People are leaving the city in droves. They're simply abandoning their homes. And if we don't break in, someone else probably will.'

'That's a ridiculous justification.' Ben folded his arms and turned his back on her. What he really wanted was for them to join the evacuation with the tide of people that was already leaving the city every day. But if he mentioned that, Melanie would fly off the handle, saying that Grandpa couldn't possibly be moved in his present condition.

'So what's your solution?' she asked. 'Keep searching the shops? We know they've long since run out of all the things we need. Most have closed down entirely.'

'We could try bartering with the other people who have stayed behind,' suggested Ben.

'What with?'

'This house is full of all kinds of things.'

Melanie cast her gaze around the room in a theatrical style. 'It's full of luxury items, all of them useless. Should we offer our antique furniture in exchange for cooking oil? Or perhaps I could swap a Hermes silk scarf for a diesel generator.'

'Being facetious isn't going to solve anything,' snapped Ben. He turned his back on her and heard her do the same in response.

This is childish. Why do we always end up behaving like children?

He was supposed to be a school teacher, not one of his Year 10 Biology class.

The memory of Manor Road school brought him up

sharp. He wondered what had become of those kids he had taught. Rose Hallibury was dead, he knew that much. But as for Vijay Singh, Drake Cooper and the rest, he had no idea. He hoped they were faring better than he was.

He turned back to face her. 'Why are you acting like this, Mel?'

'You know why.'

'James.' It always came back to this. 'He is a werewolf. You've got to admit that's a slight problem.'

'Only because you insist on making it into one.'

He suddenly became aware that a third person had entered the room. He turned around expecting to see Sarah, but instead James stood in the open doorway. He must have crept in at some point during the argument. The boy had an uncanny knack of moving around the house unseen and unheard. It was presumably one of his werewolf skills. Ben felt his skin crawl at the thought of being so close to a man-eating monster, a creature stealthy enough to creep up on him unawares, and the strength to kill him with his bare hands and teeth.

'I heard you talking,' said James meekly.

The boy was diplomatic at least, Ben reflected. He and Melanie had not been *talking*. They'd been shouting, arguing, and hurling abuse at each other. And James seemed willing to ignore the fact that they'd been arguing about him.

'So what do you think, James?' asked Melanie. 'Do we sit around doing nothing, like Ben says, or should we do something positive?'

'I didn't say we should do nothing…' began Ben.

James cleared his throat. 'Actually, I agree with Ben.'

'What?' demanded Melanie.

'I think he's right,' said James. 'Stealing is wrong.'

Ben gaped at the boy open-mouthed. The last thing he'd expected was for James to back him up. A werewolf with a moral code. Could such a thing be possible? It seemed that James had no qualms about killing and eating people, but wouldn't resort to stealing from empty houses. The boy was a mystery for sure.

'You two make a fine pair,' said Melanie scathingly. 'Good luck with finding everything we need.' She turned and walked from the room.

Ben glanced awkwardly at James. 'Thanks,' he said.

James shrugged. 'I was only giving my honest opinion.'

'So what do you think we should do?' Ben asked him.

'Honestly? I think we should leave London, along with most other people. But Melanie and Sarah won't hear of it. Not with Grandpa in his current state.'

Ben nodded. It seemed that he and James saw a number of issues in the same light. 'That doesn't leave us with many options, then.'

'Yes it does.'

'What?'

'Like you said. Bartering.'

'Oh,' said Ben. 'Melanie didn't think much of that idea when I suggested it.'

'She was just being flippant. This house is stuffed full of things that might be useful to other people.'

'Like what?'

'Well, like blankets, winter coats, woollen sweaters, all kinds of clothes. Some of them have hardly been worn. I'm sure that people would find them useful. And you and I are strong and fit, so we could do jobs for people in exchange for items we need. Melanie was wrong. We don't have to steal from people. We can find ways to help them instead.'

Ben stood in amazement. James was right. And it had taken a werewolf to find a solution to a problem that he and Melanie had found intractable. 'Okay,' he said. 'What are we waiting for? Let's make a start.'

The old house was enormous and had rooms that Ben hadn't even looked in before. But James seemed to know his way around. Together they found loads of old clothes and bedding in the bedrooms on the top floor. Some of the blankets were moth-eaten, but most were serviceable. James discovered dozens of winter coats hanging in a dusty wardrobe. Ben opened a great chest of drawers and found it stuffed with woollen cardigans and sweaters. The house was a treasure trove of ancient garments. They were a little old-fashioned, but all of high quality.

They gathered their discoveries together and spent the rest of the day going door to door around the grand old houses nearby. Some were empty, and at others they got no answer despite seeing a curtain twitch or hearing sounds inside. But a few doors opened to them, and one or two people were happy to make a trade, swapping one kind of essential item for another. They made new friends too, and in a tight situation it was always good to know people who could help if needed.

'We did well, James,' said Ben as they headed for home. 'We're a team.'

There was no sign of Melanie when they got back, but Sarah was there to congratulate them on their hard work.

'You should thank James,' said Ben, clapping the boy on the back.

For the moment all seemed well. James had found the solution to their problem, and kept them on the right side of the law too. But he was still a monster and a killer. Ben didn't know how to reconcile the two aspects of James' character. One day soon he might have to face up to the dilemma squarely, and he didn't know what he might do.

Chapter Fifty-Nine

Marylebone Road, Westminster, Central London

Warg Daddy smiled as he studied the scene of burning and destruction through his field glasses. The location was central London: a broad road lined with trees, hotels, office buildings and expensive apartment blocks, studded with famous tourist attractions like Madame Tussauds. Now it was a deserted war zone clogged with abandoned buses and taxis. The traffic lights at road junctions changed silently from green to amber to red unheeded. In the distance the fire-blackened glass cylinder of the BT Tower still peeped above a row of eighteenth- and nineteenth-century mansion blocks, but its days as a hub for TV and satellite communications were over.

But Warg Daddy wasn't here for sightseeing.

The chase was on. Enemy forces were coming after him, and they outnumbered him at least ten to one. Ever since the Battle of Heathrow, the Wolf Army had been on the back foot, fighting defensively, as soldiers and weapons of all kinds closed in around them.

Warg Daddy wasn't too worried about that. It was all part of the plan.

Fall back, Leanna had instructed him. *Lure them into our trap.*

'All units retreat,' he ordered from the Land Rover. He watched as his infantry units melted into the side streets and his armoured units turned in the road and moved away from the advancing forces.

A tactical retreat. It wasn't the way he would have planned the campaign. He was more of an every-man-to-the-front, all-guns-blazing kind of guy. But he recognized that duplicity and double-dealing had their place in war. Hell, he had dirtied his hands with enough treachery in order to secure his position as Leader of the Pack.

And so far, Leanna's plan was working without a hitch.

He was happy to play his part. Fighting enemy soldiers was fun. And the violence kept the hurt in his head at bay. It helped him to ignore the cruel way Leanna treated him, and forget the horrific scars on her face.

It meant he could hang out with Vixen too, without Leanna getting suspicious. And Vixen was one of the hottest chicks he'd ever hooked up with. Her lust for sex was equal to her hunger for violence.

He was about to witness that hunger very soon.

'Wolf Sisters, prepare to attack,' he ordered over the radio.

The plan was simple. Drive around town to attract the enemy's attention. Retreat to a designated fall-back point. Wait. Then lay a smackdown of epic proportions.

'You really think they're gonna fall for it?' queried Meathook. 'We're not just fighting some bunch of dumbasses.'

'Sure,' said Warg Daddy. The Wolf Brothers had fought no end of dumbasses over the years, but their latest adversaries made more formidable opponents. They were about to do battle with 1st Armoured Infantry Brigade – one of the British Army's most deadly fighting units. Yet Warg Daddy had total faith in the plan. Leanna's plans had never once gone wrong. She might be a cruel-hearted bitch, but she was the smartest cruel-hearted bitch he'd ever met. And he'd known a few in his time.

He lifted the field glasses again. He loved this part of the battle. The tension before everything kicked off. It was silent now, but he knew that soon the streets would fill with deafening explosions. All hell would break loose, and he would be at the centre of the maelstrom.

The advancing armoured column lumbered into view. 'Get ready,' he whispered.

The enemy was sending in its heaviest weaponry first. Challenger 2 battle tanks, Warrior support vehicles and Stormer missile units, all belching out black clouds of diesel fumes as they paraded down the wide road. Some heavy shit for sure. A column of armoured personnel carriers followed closely behind. He watched them roll toward him. Any second now the attack would begin.

'Now,' said Warg Daddy.

The IEDs began to detonate around the enemy column. Roadside bombs blew beneath the advancing vehicles, their shaped charges powerful enough to penetrate the vulnerable underside of the tanks. A Warrior fighting unit blew onto its side as an IED blasted beside it. Smoke and flames filled Warg Daddy's view. When they cleared, he saw craters and burning hulks of metal where the first of the armoured vehicles had stood.

But the army wasn't taking that kind of shit without fighting back. A Starstreak high velocity missile roared through the flames as one of the enemy Stormer units began to fire back in retaliation. The missile flashed low overhead, reaching for a target downstream. It was gone in the blink of an eye, its sonic boom shattering the windows of buildings along its flight path as it accelerated toward

Mach four. Half a second later the missile's triple warheads hit home with three simultaneous explosions.

'One troop carrier lost,' crackled the report over his headset. 'One armoured vehicle lost. Multiple casualties.'

Warg Daddy grimaced. The enemy would pay for that. 'All units open fire,' he ordered.

Machine gun fire rippled from the abandoned office blocks overlooking the enemy vehicles, tearing through the lighter troop carriers, laying waste to the disgorging infantry units. The Wolf Sisters were going about their bloody work as usual.

The machine gun fire was followed by RPGs, powerful enough to penetrate the heavier armour of the remaining Warrior units. Explosions and flames ripped through the advancing forces. Finally a thunderous blast announced the arrival of Bloodbath in the tank. The Brother opened fire with shell after shell, blasting every one of the enemy combat vehicles to pieces. The devastation was complete.

'Good work,' said Warg Daddy. The entire enemy force was destroyed. He could hardly believe it had been so easy.

He narrowed his eyes. It had been *too* easy.

A new sound begged for his attention. A faint roar in the distance, growing louder. 'Do you hear that?' he asked Meathook.

His lieutenant shook his head.

But Warg Daddy heard it. And he didn't like what he heard. 'Get the fuck out of here!' he roared to his army. 'Find cover! Now!'

The throaty roar was coming closer, and quickly. A metallic screeching overhead announced the arrival of the new player. A combat aircraft, flying fast. Even the others must be able to hear the noise by now.

'Get us away from here!' he shouted at Meathook.

The Land Rover turned in the road, attempting a 180 about-turn. But the way was blocked by burning debris and broken glass.

He seized Meathook by the collar. 'Jump. Now,' he

said.

They dived from the moving Land Rover together, just as the fighter jet appeared overhead. A Eurofighter Typhoon by the looks of it.

The jet was flying low, ready to provide close air support to the ground units that the Wolf Army had just turned to toast. The fighter plane was too late for that, but it clearly intended to make up for its late arrival to the party. Aerial cannon fire began to rip the world apart, tearing through the rolling Land Rover and blasting it into a fireball. Windows shattered, chunks of concrete broke away from nearby buildings, and metal screeched as vehicles flipped and landed on their backs.

Warg Daddy hit the tarmac and rolled as the plane flew over.

A second jet came into view. Another Typhoon. A single object dropped from beneath the aircraft's wing as it swooped closer. A grey missile, some fifteen feet long, bristling with fins and small rear wings. It flew straight at him.

A glide bomb. Fuck.

Those things packed up to five hundred pounds of high explosives, a hundred times more deadly than the Starstreak missile that had just taken out two of his vehicles. They were laser-guided precision munitions – bunker-busting bombs capable of penetrating six feet of reinforced concrete.

Warg Daddy reckoned he had around three seconds left to live.

Beside him, Meathook was blubbering, unable to move. Warg Daddy smacked him over the head. He needed calm now. He rose to his feet as the bomb descended, watching, listening, every one of his super senses tuned to the task of discerning precisely where the bomb would strike. A hush descended, even as the missile screeched toward him. Zen calm. A little to the left. A few feet forward. He grabbed hold of Meathook and dragged him toward cover. Faster.

They only had another second to find shelter. He slammed the Wolf Brother into the ground and fell on top of him just as the bomb struck home.

A huge blast lifted him off the ground again like a wall of force and tossed him right across the street. A deafening roar filled his ears, and all vision blacked out as a wave of smoke and dust filled the air like a sudden sandstorm.

He hit the ground again, Meathook taking the worst of the damage beneath him. All around him vehicles were tumbling. Buildings were crumbling. An avalanche of glass rained down. Concrete boulders fell at his feet. Craters opened up in the road surface like giant pockmarks. Molten fragments of metal fell like hail. Streetlamps collapsed, breaking into chunks that chewed whole cars into scrap.

And everywhere there was noise.

Yes, thought Warg Daddy, grinning wildly. When the last of the vehicles had finished rolling he surged back to his feet and punched the scorched air. The street around him was a wasted moonscape, cloaked in grey dust and bathed in red flames. Half the building next to him was gone, its upper floors collapsed like a concertina. Across the road, the Landmark Hotel stood teetering, its fine Victorian facade blasted away, beds and wardrobes tumbling out of its rooms into the street below. But he was unharmed. Even his Ray-Bans remained firmly in place and unscratched. He was invincible. Death could not claim him. Not this moment, at least.

And what was life, other than a series of moments? It was up to the brave to seize each one, and wring as much from it as they dared.

'Do you feel it?' he asked Meathook.

The Wolf Brother groaned, lying flat on his back as Warg Daddy strutted over him. 'What?'

'Life,' replied Warg Daddy. He raised his arms to the smoke-filled sky. 'This is what it feels like to be alive.'

Chapter Sixty

West Field Gardens, South London

Vijay rushed back home as quickly as he could. The news that Rose was still alive had thrown all other thoughts from his mind. He had meant to distribute the food to all the elderly residents, but had simply dumped his shopping trolley with Mrs McCurley. 'I'll come back to get it later, I promise,' he shouted as he left her house. 'Thank you so much!'

He reached his own home and threw the door open. Who would he tell first? The answer was obvious – his grandmother. He dashed into the living room to find her threading a needle with fine cotton. A brightly-coloured cloth was stretched out in her lap.

She looked up in astonishment as he tore into the room. 'Vijay? What are you doing, bursting in like this? I almost pricked my finger.'

He ran to her and kneeled down to give her a hug. He was too full of excitement to stay in one place. He sprang to his feet again and danced away across the room.

'Vijay, what is wrong? You are making me dizzy.'

'Nothing is wrong,' he said. 'Everything is right!'

'You are making no sense. Tell me what you mean, or else leave me to my sewing in peace.'

He kneeled beside her again. 'It's Rose, the girl I told you was dead. She isn't!'

His grandmother frowned, half-pleased, half-irritated. 'Is this a riddle?'

'No. Rose is alive. Mrs McCurley, the old lady who lives opposite Rose's house, saw her leaving on the night of the fire. Rose didn't die, she just went away.' He sank back to sit on his heels. 'I don't know where she is now. But she's alive. I can search for her.'

His grandmother put her sewing to one side. 'But where will you begin?'

'I don't know. It doesn't really matter, does it? As long as I start searching I'm bound to find her eventually.'

'What makes you so certain she wants to be found?'

'What?' said Vijay, thrown off guard. 'Why wouldn't she?'

'She must have gone away for some reason.'

'Her family were all killed. She probably just ran off in fright. I need to look for her. I need to find her.'

His grandmother sighed. 'You are an optimist, Vijay, and that is a good thing. But the world is a very big place to look for one person. I hope you will not bring more tears upon yourself with a fruitless search.'

'If I have something to live for, I'll never be unhappy,' he declared. He hugged his grandmother one more time before hurrying off.

He grabbed a coat and a bottle of water, and set off back to West Field Terrace. According to Mrs McCurley, Rose had left her house and headed north, and he followed in her footsteps. When he reached the T-junction at the end of the road he stopped. Which way would she have gone next? If she was trying to get as far away as possible from whoever had killed her family, she might have turned in the direction of Clapham. He started that way now.

The people in the Watch said that a werewolf had killed Rose's parents. But now he questioned if that were true. They had said that Mr Harvey was a werewolf, but Vijay had never believed that. Mr Harvey was a kind, gentle man, and he was certainly no werewolf. It was Jack Stewart who claimed to have seen Mr Harvey turn into a wolf. Perhaps Jack Stewart knew more than he was saying about what had happened to Rose.

The Watch was not to be trusted, that much was certain. Salma Ali, Jack Stewart and his team of bully boys ... and now Drake. He had to get Drake away from them. Perhaps if Drake knew the truth about Rose, he would help to search for her.

The idea was a good one. Of course Drake would help him. He turned around and headed back to Mr Kowalski's shop. That was where he had last seen his friend.

He found Drake in the storeroom at the back of the shop, unloading boxes and stacking their contents on shelves. He looked bored out of his mind. 'Vijay,' he said. 'What's up?'

'You won't believe it,' said Vijay breathlessly. 'It's Rose. She's alive.'

'Alive?' Drake's eyes widened as he digested the news.

'Yes. She didn't die in the fire. She escaped.'

'Wow. But where to?'

'I don't know. But I'm going to find out. Come and help me look for her. We'll stand a much better chance of finding her if we work together.'

Drake dumped the box he was holding on the floor of the storeroom. 'I'm supposed to be doing this job for Mr Stewart.'

'You'd rather search for Rose, though, wouldn't you?' said Vijay.

'I guess. Yeah.' Drake peered over his shoulder to make

sure no one was listening. 'To tell you the truth, working for the Watch isn't working out the way I thought it would.'

'What did you expect?'

'Dunno. Just, something more exciting.'

'Come on, then. Leave all this. Come and help me instead.'

Drake stood thoughtfully, hands in pockets, considering the prospect.

They both jumped as the door to the storeroom opened. Jack Stewart stepped through. He stopped in his tracks when he saw Vijay. 'You!' A scowl spread quickly across his face. 'What are you doing here?'

'Nothing,' said Vijay. 'Just talking to my friend.'

Jack Stewart directed a hard look in Drake's direction. 'Is he a friend of yours?'

Drake appeared not to have heard Mr Stewart's question. He stared down at his shoes.

'Get out of here,' said Mr Stewart. 'Now.' But he wasn't speaking to Vijay. His order was directed at Drake.

Drake glanced awkwardly back at Vijay, then scurried away into the shop, closing the door behind him.

A mirthless smile appeared on Mr Stewart's lips. 'Just you and me, now,' he said. 'If you thought your friend was going to help you, forget it.'

Vijay looked around the storeroom, but the door Drake had used was the only exit, apart from the big steel shutters that were used to accept deliveries. They were firmly locked.

Mr Stewart watched his eyes scan the room. 'No way out,' he said menacingly.

Vijay stood his ground, not wanting the man to see how scared he was. But he couldn't keep the tremble from his arms and legs. He thrust his hands into his pockets to hide the shaking.

'I heard you've been stealing food,' said Mr Stewart.

'No,' protested Vijay. 'I didn't steal a thing. Mr

Kowalski said I could have some.'

'That's a lie. It was Kowalski himself who told me you're a thief.'

'No,' said Vijay. 'He's lying. Or else you're lying.'

A vein in Mr Stewart's temple pulsed angrily. 'You're calling me a liar now? You're the only liar here. And a thief too. That food you stole belongs to the Watch.'

'No, it doesn't. The soldiers brought it to be shared. It's supposed to be for everyone.'

'Salma Ali decides who gets food around here,' said Mr Stewart. 'Not people like you. You need to be taught a lesson.' He took a step toward Vijay, clenching his hands into big fists.

The man was twice the size of Vijay, tall and muscular, and he had the look of a fighter about him. *A ruffian*, his grandmother would have said. *Stay away from people like that, Vijay.* Vijay wanted nothing more than to keep well away from Mr Stewart, but how could he? The man was looming closer every second.

He ducked back, scurrying to the end of the storeroom by the steel roller doors and running into the farthest corner. Mr Stewart came on relentlessly. Vijay looked at the items arrayed on the shelves. They were mostly brown cardboard boxes. He picked one up. It was heavy, but he cradled it in his arms.

Mr Stewart laughed contemptuously. 'Gonna throw that in my face? You can hardly lift it.'

Vijay wanted to cry. Suddenly he was back in the school yard being tormented by Drake and Ash. They were pulling at his turban, making jokes. None of the other kids were doing a thing to help. He had thought he'd put all that behind him. Now it was happening again, but ten times worse. He clutched the cardboard box to his chest for protection.

Jack Stewart stood right in front of him, eyeing him nastily. With a sudden move he dashed forward and grabbed hold of the box. He wrestled it easily from Vijay's hands and hurled it to the floor. The box burst open, spilling bags of rice everywhere.

Vijay looked up angrily. 'You wasted that food,' he accused.

A fist slammed into the side of his face, knocking him off his feet. The floor came up to meet him and smacked him in the back of the head.

'You cheeky little runt!' yelled Jack Stewart. 'You're nothing but a thief and a liar. I'll teach you never to steal again.'

His booted foot drove into Vijay's side, sending shock waves of pain through his whole body. Vijay had never felt anything like it. He feared his kidney might burst open, or his spleen, or even his stomach. Another kick like that might kill him. He curled up into a protective ball, his arms around him.

Jack Stewart bent over him, panting heavily. He pulled Vijay's shirt collar, twisting the cotton in his fist. 'Come on, you little runt,' he said. 'Ain't you gonna put up a fight?'

But all the fight was gone from Vijay, if he had ever really had any. Jack Stewart was far too big and strong. The man could do whatever he wanted, and Vijay couldn't stop him. He lay on the floor, hoping someone would come and rescue him. Drake perhaps. Or Mr Kowalski. But nobody came.

Instead, Mr Stewart grabbed hold of his arms and pulled him to his feet. He grunted with the effort, but had little trouble lifting Vijay onto his broad shoulders like a sack of flour. He unlocked the back door of the storeroom with one hand and wound the metal rollers open. He ducked through the gap. The deserted street at the back of the shop was more like an alleyway, and there was no one to watch as he carried Vijay away.

After a few minutes of walking they came to a halt. Mr Stewart dropped Vijay to the ground. Another door opened and he felt himself being dragged inside a room with a rough concrete floor.

'You can stay here until I decide what to do with you,' he said. He gave Vijay one more kick for good measure. Then the door closed shut again and all went dark.

Vijay lay on the ground, pressing his hands to his side, and hoping that the sharp pain would die down soon. Until it did he couldn't move. He could barely think. 'Rose,' he muttered to himself. 'Rose, where are you now?'

Chapter Sixty-One

Brixton Hill, South London, waxing moon

The following day Liz and Dean returned to the home of the young woman with the six-year-old daughter.

'This is a waste of time,' said Dean. 'You're not really planning to take them to the train station, are you?'

'Absolutely, if they'll agree to come with me.'

'I bet you they won't,' said Dean. 'We'll have to pull them from the house kicking and screaming.'

But he was wrong. The woman was waiting in the hallway with a bag packed. Her daughter clutched a toy rabbit.

'You'll take us to the train?' the woman asked. 'I'm afraid to go outside alone.'

'Sure,' said Liz. 'Are you ready to leave?'

'Yeah.'

Liz bent down to speak to the little girl. 'What's your rabbit called?

'Oreo.'

'That's cool. Is Oreo ready to go on an adventure?'

The girl nodded.

Dean glanced impatiently at his watch. 'Can you take them to the station on your own?' he asked Liz.

'Sure. I'll take the patrol car. You carry on with the door-to-door. I'll catch you later.'

She drove the mother and daughter to Denmark Hill station and saw them safely onto the train. Dozens of other refugees were lined up on the platform. Mums, dads, kids, even pet animals. 'The train will take you directly to the evacuation centre,' she told them. 'You'll be given food, accommodation and anything else you need. There's no need to be afraid.'

The woman nodded. 'Thank you.'

Liz bent down to speak to the girl one last time. 'Take good care of Oreo.'

The girl waved a silent goodbye, moving the rabbit's paw too.

Job done, thought Liz. But she knew that Dean was half right. She couldn't personally escort every single family to safety. There were far too many. Most people would have to fend for themselves.

Her shift was nearly over now and she was beat after a long day, so she decided to head for home. She checked her phone for a signal, but as ever these days, there was nothing. No matter. Dean would guess where she had gone.

She drove back through almost deserted streets. The number of cars parked outside the houses was growing smaller each day. Slowly but steadily, the city was emptying.

When she got back to the house she found Lily waiting for her in the entrance hall. The little girl's eyes were dark from crying. 'Lily!' said Liz in surprise. 'What's wrong?' She rushed over to the girl and gathered her up in her arms. 'What's happened? Where's Mummy?'

Lily wrapped her thin arms around Liz's neck and clutched her tightly. 'Mummy's sick.'

'Where is she?

'Upstairs, in the bedroom.'

'What about Kevin? Is he home?'

'No.'

Liz cursed silently. She had specifically made Kevin promise not to go out and leave Samantha alone with Lily. But there was no point getting angry about that now. She set the girl back on her feet and led her by the hand up the stairs. She dreaded what she might find.

She discovered Samantha lying on the floor at the foot of the bed. 'Oh my God, what's happened?' she gasped, kneeling down next to Sam.

'It's okay,' panted Samantha. 'I think I must have fainted but I'm all right now.'

'You don't look all right,' said Liz. 'Let me take a good look at you.' She began checking her carefully, running through the basic checklist she'd learned from her first-aid training.

'Where is Lily?' asked Samantha. 'Is she safe?'

'I'm here, Mummy,' said Lily, coming into the room timidly and hiding behind Liz.

Samantha's forehead was hot and clammy and her breathing was rapid. So was her pulse. Her feet and ankles were swollen, and her hands were too. Liz checked for bleeding or anything that might indicate a serious medical condition. She found none. But people didn't faint for no reason.

Samantha was seven months pregnant. Her baby was due in April. So far the pregnancy had run smoothly. Samantha had been for her two routine scans and no problems had been discovered, at least as far as Liz knew. 'Is this the first time anything like this has happened?' she asked.

'It may have happened once or twice before,' admitted Samantha.

Liz gritted her teeth. At times Samantha could be twice as stubborn as Dean. She wondered what else she had concealed. 'Did you tell anyone about it?'

Samantha pulled a face. 'You mean Dean? You know what he's like. He'd be out of his mind with worry.'

'I meant a doctor or a midwife,' said Liz.

'It's not so easy to get medical attention at the moment,' said Samantha. 'The doctors are dealing with emergencies only. I didn't want to kick up a fuss.'

'Can you sit up?' Liz asked her. She helped Samantha to sit up slowly.

Samantha gripped her arm and closed her eyes.

'Do you feel faint?' asked Liz.

'Just a little dizzy.'

Liz turned to Lily. 'Lily, can you do something really important for me?'

The little girl looked uncertain. Then she nodded eagerly.

'Can you go to the bathroom and bring me a clean towel?'

Lily ran off to get it.

'What do you need a towel for?' asked Samantha.

'I don't,' said Liz. 'I just wanted Lily to leave us alone for a minute. I want you to tell me about any other problems you've been having. Don't hold anything back.'

Samantha seemed reluctant to say anything.

'I need to know so that I can help you,' said Liz.

'I've been getting headaches, and I get tired very easily,' said Samantha. 'But that's not unusual during pregnancy. I have cramp in my calves, and my hands and feet are swollen.'

'I can see the swelling,' said Liz. But she could tell Samantha was still holding something back. 'What else? Tell me.'

'There was a discharge of blood once,' admitted Samantha, 'but only a small one. It scared the hell out of me at the time, but it hasn't happened again.'

'Okay,' said Liz. Now she was scared too, but at least she knew what she was dealing with.

Lily appeared in the doorway with a white towel. 'I found one,' she said brightly.

'Good girl,' said Liz taking the towel and handing it to Sam.' Now you stay right here with Mummy. Don't let her try to stand up. I'm going to fetch a doctor.'

A doctor wasn't easy to get hold of. The local surgery had already closed down, and Liz had to drive to the next nearest. The receptionist insisted that no doctor was available, but Liz's police uniform helped move things along. 'It's an emergency,' she insisted. 'I need a doctor. Now.'

The doctor came reluctantly, but when she arrived at the house, Liz could see the concern on her face. The doctor sat next to Samantha and examined her carefully, asking the same questions Liz had asked.

Unlike Liz the doctor knew what the symptoms meant. 'You're suffering from pre-eclampsia,' she said at last. 'That means high blood pressure. It's what's causing the bleeding, the swelling, the high temperature and the fainting. There's nothing I can give you to treat it. Normally we'd bring you into hospital and monitor you closely until the baby is due, but under the current circumstances that isn't going to be possible. The hospitals have already been closed and patients moved out.'

'Should we take her to one of the evacuation camps?' asked Liz. 'We were planning to go at the end of the month, but we could go now instead.'

'That's one option,' said the doctor. 'But moving her could lead to complications. It would be better if she stayed at home in bed, at least for a few days. She needs to avoid movement and anything that might cause stress. You can consider moving her when her blood pressure has dropped a little.'

Samantha pulled a face. 'I can't possibly stay in bed. There's so much to do. I need to look after Lily, take care of the house, cook for everyone –'

The doctor cut her off. 'None of that is going to happen. Your husband and other members of your family will have to step up. Okay?'

Samantha nodded.

'Pre-eclampsia is a serious condition,' said the doctor. 'I don't want to alarm you. Probably everything will be okay, provided you follow my advice. But if you don't rest and look after yourself it can cause fits or strokes or even brain damage. In severe cases it can lead to a stillborn baby. Do you understand?'

Samantha nodded meekly. 'I need to stay in bed.'

'Exactly.'

'Don't worry,' said Liz to Samantha. 'We'll make sure you get plenty of rest. You won't have to do a thing.' Though precisely how that was going to happen, she wasn't sure, with her and Dean out on patrol every day.

Kevin, she thought. Kevin will have to look after everyone. The thought wasn't exactly reassuring.

Chapter Sixty-Two

*Western Evacuation Camp,
Buckinghamshire, waxing moon*

Helen took one of the blood samples from the latest batch she'd prepared and positioned the glass slide under the lens of her microscope. She peered down the eyepiece and began to count the number of white blood cells in the sample. It was painstaking work.

There was a knock at the door and Chanita poked her head around. 'How's it going? I brought you a mug of tea.' She came into the room, carrying two steaming mugs. 'It's the usual army brew, I'm afraid. I don't know what they do to it. It tastes like heated dishwater.'

Helen laughed. 'You're supposed to be running this camp, not bringing me tea.'

But she was glad to see her new friend. Helen knew that Chanita had many other demands on her time, but she still found the time to drop by "casually" to see how the work in Helen's lab was progressing. She was much too discreet to ask what Helen was doing with all the blood samples she took from volunteers amongst the refugees and the medical staff, but she was obviously desperately curious.

'Pull up a chair,' said Helen. 'I could use a break.'

Staring down the microscope for long hours was giving her eye strain. She was working long hours at the camp, her enthusiasm for her project renewed. With Chanita's support, she was making great progress on the testing. Or at least, she had managed to gather over a hundred blood samples already. So far none that she had tested had yielded a positive result. But as Chanita had told her on her first day here, patience and persistence were the route to success. She still had plenty more samples left to test. And when they were all done, she could ask for more volunteers. There were new people arriving at the camp every day.

'What are you doing right now?' asked Chanita. It was the closest she'd come to asking Helen outright what her secret project was all about.

'Counting white blood cells. At Imperial College we used to have machines to do this job. I never imagined I'd have to do it by hand.'

'The facilities here are pretty basic,' admitted Chanita. 'But Michael – I mean Colonel Griffin – said that when he was out in Afghanistan they sometimes didn't even have access to the most basic meds.'

'I'm not complaining,' said Helen quickly. 'I have everything I need.' She didn't want Chanita to think she wasn't grateful for her help. 'Colonel Griffin was in charge of the quarantine operation, wasn't he?'

'That's how I got to know him. I was with him at King's College Hospital.'

'So you worked with the infected patients? That must have been fascinating, seeing close up how the disease progresses. All I ever get to see is the inside of a lab. All the drama in my life unfolds inside a test tube.'

Chanita laughed. 'I wish I could bottle some of the drama in my own life.' She grew serious again. 'I've seen how the disease takes hold of patients in the initial stages. At first there were a lot of fatalities. It took us a while to work out an effective treatment. We didn't know what we were dealing with. But once we realized the importance of keeping patients hydrated, the mortality rate dropped dramatically. What we didn't know then was that we were simply saving people's lives so that they could transform into those *creatures*.'

Helen shuddered. She had never witnessed the progression of the disease first-hand. All she knew was what she'd read in Professor Wiseman's notes. 'We call the initial phase Stage One,' she told Chanita. 'It begins as soon as the victim is bitten or scratched. The virus enters their bloodstream and starts to invade the blood cells. The immune system fights back, but it's quickly overwhelmed. The initial symptoms may be relatively mild, similar to influenza, or severe, like anaphylactic shock.'

Chanita nodded. 'Exactly. The patients show high fevers, delirium, long periods of unconsciousness. In the hospital we had to restrain some of them, they became so violent.'

'If the patient survives, they enter Stage Two. The fever breaks and they regain consciousness. Their bodies begin to undergo significant internal changes. Teeth and nails grow longer, the nose and jaw change in shape, and they become more muscular even though they are no longer eating.'

'That's right,' said Chanita. 'We offered them food, but they refused it. The only thing they ever wanted to eat was raw meat.'

'Their eyes become yellow during this stage too,' continued Helen. 'They develop acute sensitivity to bright light. Then, once they are exposed to the full moon, they enter Stage Three and assume full wolf form.'

'How do you know so much about it?' asked Chanita.

'Sorry, I'm not supposed to ask you anything about your work.'

'No worries. It's good to have someone to talk to at last, especially someone with direct experience. To tell you the truth, it would be a relief to tell you what I'm doing.'

'Okay. So what are you doing?'

Helen liked the way Chanita had of being direct without ever seeming rude. 'I'm looking for a cure,' she said. 'Or at least a way of slowing the disease, perhaps even preventing it in the first place.'

'Wow. That would be incredible.'

'Yeah. Wouldn't it?,' said Helen.

'And how close are you to finding one?'

Helen sighed. 'Still a long way off. In fact, I have some serious doubts about what I'm doing. It seems like I'm never going to make the breakthrough I'm searching for. It's disheartening.'

'Patience and persistence,' counselled Chanita with a smile.

'You're right,' said Helen. She passed her empty mug back to Chanita.

'Mind if I stay and watch for a few minutes?' asked Chanita. 'Don't tell anyone, but this is my bolthole when it all gets too much, pretending to be in charge of this place.'

'Not at all. I could use an assistant. You can pass me another of those glass slides.'

'Here you go,' said Chanita, picking up the next sample. 'What exactly are you looking for?'

Helen positioned the slide under the microscope and began the laborious job of counting cells. 'Natural immunity. I'm working under the assumption that a very small minority of the general population might be immune to lycanthropy. If I could find someone who's resistant to the virus, I could use their blood to synthesize a vaccine, or even a cure. I'm taking blood samples from the volunteers and infecting them with contaminated blood from a werewolf. Normally when the infected blood is mixed with the samples, the virus multiplies rapidly, destroying the body's immune system as it goes. The incubation period is extremely short. Sometimes the virus takes over the host cells in minutes. Twelve hours is the longest I've recorded so far. This sample was contaminated nearly twenty-four hours ago so it should now be completely infected with the virus.'

'Not a pleasant thought,' said Chanita.

'No.' Helen stared at the tiny smear of blood under her microscope. 'I'm sorry, I think I've miscounted this one. I'm going to start again.'

Chanita stayed silent while Helen re-counted. She had to do the count twice more before she could be confident about the result. 'This is extraordinary. I think I may finally have found what I've been looking for. This blood is resistant to the virus.'

'Wow,' said Chanita excitedly. 'So what do we do now?'

'Run more tests. This is just the beginning of a long process. But first of all, we need to find out who donated this blood sample, and make sure they don't leave the camp under any circumstances.'

'Give me their name and I'll send a couple of soldiers to detain them,' said Chanita.

Helen studied her records. A look of astonishment slowly crept over her face. 'That won't be necessary,' she said at last. 'The blood is yours.'

Chapter Sixty-Three

*Holland Gardens, Kensington, London,
waning moon, waxing moon*

'Warg Daddy,' said Leanna in her crisp, impatient manner. 'Give me your latest battle report.'

The commander-in-chief of the Wolf Army leaned back heavily in his chair, contemplating how the war was going. Pretty well, by his reckoning. He had become a veteran guerrilla fighter, at ease with improvised explosives and rocket propelled grenades, ambushes and sabotage. Perhaps he should get himself a badass bandana to wrap around his bald head. It would match his Wolf Brother jacket and black Ray-Bans. His troops looked up to him as a great leader, a glorious hero, and a freedom fighter. He wasn't sure what kind of freedom they thought they were fighting for. The freedom to hunt perhaps. The freedom to kill and eat meat. The freedom to rip flesh from bones and exult in a blood-soaked orgy of violence …

'Warg Daddy? Your latest report?'

He must have faded out for a moment there. Meetings did that to him. He needed to focus. But it was hard to concentrate in this airless meeting room. He came to life when he was holding the shotgun in his hand, when its barrel was hot and smoking, and dead bodies lay at his feet.

But Leanna enjoyed meetings best. Meetings, conferences, planning, analysis. If you could make love to agendas and reports, Leanna would do it. She probably had private fantasies involving paper clips and red tape.

She rose to her feet. 'Warg Daddy!'

It was time he said something. 'Our plans are working.'

'My plans,' interrupted Leanna. 'I make the plans, you command the forces on the ground.'

'Yeah,' agreed Warg Daddy. 'Like, yeah.' He was cool with that. In the old days, he'd been a pretty smart planner himself. Clever. Cunning. Devious, even, when required. But his plans had been small-scale. Punch-ups outside pubs, thefts of bikes and drugs from rival gangs. Nothing too risky. And he'd had a clear head to think, of course. Now the fog that clogged his brain made him slow.

He rubbed his head hard like a magic lamp, but no djinni came to his aid. Instead, Leanna loomed in front of him. A cold flame flickered in her blue eyes. 'The plans!' she yelled. 'Tell me how they went!'

'Since Heathrow, our army has become battle-hardened and capable,' he said. 'Our hit-and-run raids, false fall-backs and ambushes play to our strengths. Our enemies think they know where we are hiding, but we lay false trails and lure them into traps. They outnumber us but we have mobility, stealth and ruthlessness on our side. Our casualties are low, and we are taking guns and weapons from our enemy.'

Those seemed to be the words she wanted to hear. 'And our latest sortie?' she asked. 'How did the enemy respond?'

'With close air support. We took heavier than usual losses on our last mission. The military are stepping up their use of heavy weaponry …'

'… leading to large-scale destruction and chaos across the city,' continued Leanna gleefully. She stood up and began pacing the room, almost drooling over the violence she had unleashed. 'We need not fear them. We are taking losses but the size of our army continues to grow as the condition spreads and we gain fresh recruits. Across the globe, our cousins are making military gains in every single country. We have reached critical mass. A turning point. The army is on the run and cannot win. The humans are divided. They fight among themselves. They are tearing down their own civilization. Very soon we will gain our strategic victory. A new power will emerge once they are reduced to barbarism. We will be that power!' She brought her fist down onto the hard table top with a resounding clap.

So it's not just paper-clips that get her juices going, thought Warg Daddy. She was becoming almost messianic in her enthusiasm. He wasn't sure who frightened him the most – Leanna the bureaucrat, or Leanna the angel of death. She was formidable in either role. Quite possibly mad, but certainly formidable.

She continued to rave and he wondered who she was really talking to. If it was him, he was no longer listening. He had long since grown bored of her mad rants, her scarred appearance and her cruel treatment. He glanced around the room to see if anyone else shared his concerns.

It seemed not. Around the meeting table the Brothers listened to her in rapture, grunting their approval at her words. Slasher and Bloodbath nodded sagely. Meathook clapped his hands together in enthusiasm. Warg Daddy regretted bringing them along to the meeting. They were only here because he'd thought they would take his side in any arguments. Now, for the first time, he began to doubt that.

He had considered inviting Vixen along to join the discussion. After all, she was commander of the Wolf Sisters. She had more brains than Meathook and the others here put together. Yet he feared how Leanna might react. Her jealousy was boundless and she had made no secret of her dislike for the younger woman. But Leanna couldn't know for certain that Vixen was his chick. He had been far too careful. Discreet. Secretive. Not even Leanna knew everything. Perhaps it was best if Warg Daddy kept her well away from these meetings.

The room had grown silent again and Warg Daddy looked up. Leanna had evidently finished her speech and was hoping for some more input from him. She stared at him with a questioning look. The Brothers turned to him expectantly.

'Well,' demanded Leanna, 'what do you say, Warg Daddy? The final assault. Are you ready to lead your forces into battle beneath the light of the full moon?'

The Brothers nodded eagerly in response. They were ready to go, willing to fight for her, perhaps even to lay down their lives if she required it. But they were waiting for him to give the final word. The Brothers answered to no one but him and would do whatever he asked them. He was still Leader of the Pack, whatever Leanna might think.

'I'm ready,' said Warg Daddy. Whatever she had said, he would do it. Her plan would no doubt involve killing and bloodshed on a completely new level, and only violence and slaughter could quench his pain now. And what other choice did he have? The full moon was coming. It was now only a day away.

Chapter Sixty-Four

Brixton, South London, waxing moon

When Vijay opened his eyes it was almost entirely dark. A narrow beam of faint light reached out to him across the floor, but it was barely enough to see more than shadows. His vision was tinted red.

He groaned. His head felt like it had been used as a punchbag. A faint ringing in his ears masked all sounds, and a sharp pain lanced through his brain. He couldn't think of anything.

His limbs felt cold as ice. He tried to move his arm, but the effort made his whole body burn.

Where was he? He couldn't remember.

He had just enough light to make out a few details of his surroundings. A box-like room with bare brick walls. Cobwebs dangled from the exposed rafters of the roof overhead. Rusty metal objects were gathered in a corner. Tools. Machinery.

He turned his head slightly in the direction of the light.

Fresh waves of pain rode over him and he fought to retain consciousness. A square door was outlined in grey. It took up nearly one whole wall of the room. What kind of room was this?

A garage. The word bubbled up to him from some deep part of his mind that was still functioning.

What was he doing here? He didn't know.

He tried to move again, but the movement made his head hurt too much. His side ached too. He touched his hand to the place he'd been kicked.

Now he remembered. Jack Stewart's boot, driving into him repeatedly. He closed his eyes, but that just made the memory stronger. He opened them again and looked at his hand. The palm was red with blood. Everything was still tinted red. What did that mean? He didn't know. But nothing good.

He tried to call for help, but his voice made a thin strangled sound. So dry. His throat burned like the desert. He tried again, but it was too painful even to repeat the tiny wailing noise he had made the first time. His mouth felt parched.

How long had he been here? The thin grey line around the door might have been evening or early morning, or even night. He must have been lying here for hours at least.

Slowly, ignoring the pain that assaulted him from all angles, he pushed himself up onto his elbow, and then onto his knees. He stayed there for a long time, breathing irregularly, fighting the desire to flop down on the hard floor again. He had to move. He had to call for help.

Standing up was too much, so he began to crawl. First one arm forward, then his knee swinging just an inch. Shifting his weight to his other side, another inch moved. A sharp piece of gravel dug into his palm, drawing blood from his hand. But it was nothing compared with the injuries Jack Stewart had given him.

He stopped to rest again.

He mustn't black out. Whatever happened, he must remain awake.

Another heroic effort and he advanced an inch further. The pain grew with each jagged movement, but he didn't give up. A panting sound accompanied him as he crawled, his own fragile voice, no longer under his control. But his arms and legs did what he commanded. Reluctantly, slowly, they drew him closer to the door.

After an age he reached it and touched it with his fingers. A metal door. That was good. With metal he could make noise. He could summon help. He dragged himself closer and leaned his weight against it. He stayed there for a few moments recovering his breath. Finally he felt strong enough to try.

Slap. He threw his hand weakly against the flat metal. The effect was muffled, hardly audible over the whistling inside his head. The door's vibrations were dampened by his weight pressed against it. With effort he pulled himself upright and gave the door a louder slap. This time the metal sang loudly. The effect was almost overwhelming, but he struck his palm against it again. And again. Each slap brought another deafening roar. He added his voice to the din even though it made little difference and hurt him more. But he had to get out. Someone had to help him.

After a minute he fell back exhausted. The throbbing in his skull was almost enough to make him pass out. He waited, listening carefully for an answering sound from the outside world. A voice, a footstep, a key turning in a lock.

'Help me,' he croaked weakly, but his words were futile, little more than a breath of wind.

Still no other sound came, only his own ragged breathing and the hubbub in his head. He lifted his palm to strike the door again, but it fell back uselessly in his lap. The pale light faded as his head drooped to rest against the cold concrete floor.

Chapter Sixty-Five

Upper Terrace, Richmond upon Thames,
West London, waxing moon

Sarah sat with Melanie at Grandpa's bedside, watching the faltering rise and fall of his chest. Sometimes the old man hardly seemed to be breathing and she had to press her ear close to him to reassure herself that he was still alive. Sometimes he snorted like a steam train heading down the track at breakneck speed.

'What's happening to him?' Melanie asked her. 'What can we do to help him?'

'I'm already doing everything I can for him,' said Sarah.

Grandpa's arm lifted suddenly and he called out, opening his eyes wide with terror. Sarah struggled to make out his words. 'Barbara? Is that you?' he murmured. Then more loudly, 'I'm scared, Barbara. They're coming to get me.' He closed his eyes again and grew calm, his breathing returning to a more regular rhythm.

'Can't you do anything more?' asked Melanie, wringing

her hands. 'I hate to see him this way. That look of panic in his eyes when he wakes up. He seems so frightened.'

'The sedatives help to keep him calm,' said Sarah. 'There isn't anything else I can give him.' She rubbed his arm gently, trying to soothe away his night fears. But it was almost futile. Night had taken Grandpa in its dark embrace and wouldn't give him up without a fight. She didn't think the old man had much fight left in him. It would be a kindness to let him go gently into that good night, but Melanie wouldn't hear of it.

'There must be something more we can do for him,' said Melanie.

'What? We can't move him. He's already in the best place, here in his own home, with his loved ones.'

'Of course we can't move him,' agreed Melanie. 'But some new drug or something?'

'I'm already giving him the drugs he needs,' said Sarah. 'I've been caring for him for years already. I know what I'm doing.'

'Of course,' said Melanie. 'I know how much you do for him. You're amazing.'

Sarah smiled at the compliment. She was not used to receiving many from her sister. But her smile was tinged with sadness. Her time looking after Grandpa was coming to an end, whether Melanie was willing to admit it or not. The best she could hope for now was to make his last days as comfortable as she could.

The sound of approaching footsteps made her look up. Ben and James stood in the doorway. They had come to see how Grandpa was getting on. Sarah smiled. It was good to see the two men together. She knew that they'd had their disagreements in the past.

'Any change?' asked Ben.

'No,' said Melanie.

The men stood awkwardly by the door. They'd obviously been talking together. They had something to say, something difficult. 'What is it?' asked Sarah.

It was Ben who spoke for them. 'We need to start planning to leave. The evacuation is already well underway and most of our neighbours have gone. We can't stay here when everyone else has left.'

Melanie turned her face to him angrily. 'We can't leave Grandpa behind.'

'No,' agreed Ben. 'Of course not.'

'We have to move him,' said James.

'That's impossible,' said Melanie. 'It would kill him.'

Ben looked to Sarah for support. 'Sarah? What do you say? You know Grandpa better than anyone? Can he be moved?'

She shook her head slowly. 'He's too frail. If we try to move him he will probably die.'

'So there's nothing more to discuss,' said Melanie. 'We only have one choice. We stay.'

Her response didn't seem to satisfy Ben. 'I don't know how we can stay for much longer,' he said. 'It's getting harder every day to find food. Soon we'll be scavenging for scraps. It won't be safe either.'

'We're staying here with Grandpa,' insisted Melanie. 'We'll just have to manage somehow.'

'And if we're attacked by gangs or werewolves?'

'You and James will have to fight them off,' she said adamantly. 'I can fight too. You know I can.'

Grandpa groaned again in his bed, twitching his arms and rolling his head from side to side. It was almost as if he knew they were talking about him. He murmured in his sleep, but his words were too faint to catch. After a minute he grew still again.

Melanie rose to her feet. 'There's nothing more to discuss. Come on, let's leave Grandpa in peace.' She led Ben from the room.

James lingered behind with Sarah. 'Is there anything I can do to help?' he asked.

'Like what?'

'I don't know.'

'Stay and talk with me,' she said, gesturing at the empty chair that Melanie had vacated.

James sat, but wouldn't look her in the eye. 'He's going to die, isn't he?' he asked.

'Yes,' she admitted. 'It might be hours, days or weeks. But yes, he's near the end now.'

'And there's nothing we can do to help him?'

'We can only care for him and make his last days as comfortable as they can be. Unless ...' she trailed off, unwilling to voice the thought that had stalked her for some time now. 'Tell me,' she said to James. 'How does it feel to be a werewolf?'

He seemed startled by the question and turned his face away from her. 'Horrible,' he said at last. 'And sometimes wonderful. One or the other, nothing in between.'

Sarah had witnessed for herself the powerful emotions that chased him. She had seen his suffering at close quarters. She had watched him venture out alone at night, and waited anxiously for his return. She knew why he went out, and tried to picture him prowling the streets, hunting for his victims. She struggled to imagine him savagely ending the life of some stranger. But he was always so gentle in her presence, it was hard to accept his bestial side. 'What is it like?' she asked. 'When you kill someone? What does it feel like?'

He buried his head in his hands. 'Shameful,' he said. 'Sinful. Evil. I hate myself afterwards. You can't imagine how much I hate myself.'

She probed deeper. 'But at the time? When you're tracking down your prey? When you make the kill? What then?'

He lifted his face to hers at last. Tears were running down his cheeks. 'Incredible. I feel strong and powerful and just. There's nothing more natural than death.'

They both turned to look at Grandpa, lying in bed, his hands quivering gently. His eyes flickered again and a small shriek emerged from his mouth.

Lycanthropic

'I can't bear to watch him like this,' said Sarah. 'Melanie won't face reality. It's why she gets so angry with Ben. By standing up to him, she thinks she's being strong. But really she's just ducking the truth. Her weakness is preventing her from being rational.'

'What are you saying?' asked James.

'We have to leave. We can't stay here any longer. But we can't take Grandpa with us.'

'What then?' he asked, his eyes growing wide. 'We can't just leave him behind.'

'No. So the choice is obvious. Like you said, there's nothing more natural than death.' She rose from her chair and lifted Grandpa's head gently. She removed one of the supporting pillows and lowered his head back down. She kissed his forehead. 'I love you, Grandpa,' she said. She stood over him, gripping the pillow tightly with both hands, her knuckles white.

'Sarah?' said James. 'What are you doing?'

'Being rational. Showing compassion.' She lowered the soft pillow to Grandpa's face.

'No!' said James, jumping up from his chair. 'You can't.'

'I can,' said Sarah. 'If anyone has the right to do this, then I do.'

'I know,' said James. 'But it would make you into a killer. Melanie would never forgive you.'

'And I would never forgive myself if I just allowed him to carry on suffering.'

'So let me do it instead. I'm already a monster. Nobody cares what happens to me.'

'I care, James,' she said. 'I care very much. You are no monster. You are the most gentle of men.' But she let him take the pillow from her hands.

He stood beside Grandpa's bed, watching the old man's troubled breathing. 'You're sure you want me to do this?' he asked.

Sarah nodded. 'Do it quickly, before he wakes.' She

watched as James leaned over the old man, pressing the pillow to his face. He held it down with strength and tenderness, holding it firm while the chest that she had watched rise and fall for so long struggled and became still. Tears streamed down James' face as he did it.

Sarah's own eyes stayed dry. She had been mourning Grandpa's slow and relentless death for years and had no more tears to give. His steady deterioration had been desperately cruel to witness. Bringing it to an end this way was pure kindness.

When it was over, she gripped James' hand hard. 'Thank you,' she said. 'Now go and pack, ready to leave. I'll tell the others.'

Chapter Sixty-Six

*Western Evacuation Camp,
Buckinghamshire, waxing moon*

'But how can I be immune?' asked Chanita. 'What's so special about me?'

She was sitting opposite Helen in the lab, a look of bewilderment etched on her face.

'People tend to acquire immunity to a viral infection if they've previously been exposed to the virus,' explained Helen. 'Their immune system holds a memory of the infection, so that it can respond if it encounters the same virus again. That's why we can only catch a disease like chicken pox once. But some kinds of immunity are hereditary. They can be passed from parent to child.'

Chanita's expression changed to one of disbelief. 'You're saying my mother or father were bitten by a werewolf?'

'Not necessarily. The immunity might have been passed down from an earlier ancestor. It might go back many generations. But at some point, one of your ancestors must have survived a werewolf attack. He or she passed their immunity on to their children. If you ever have children, they will probably be immune too. They'll have the same DNA in the germ line. Or at least, that's my theory.'

To call it a theory was perhaps expressing a degree of confidence that Helen didn't hold. She remembered her earlier conversation with the Prime Minister. Perhaps hypothesis was a better word. Perhaps the right word was hunch.

'Okay,' said Chanita uncertainly. 'So you're going to take my DNA and use it to create a cure?'

'Not your DNA. I'm not about to try any genetic engineering. But your immune system produces antibodies that are able to resist the attack of the virus. I want to make copies of those antibodies and use them as a way of combatting the disease.'

'Is that difficult to do?'

'Not if I have access to the right facilities.' And time. Even if all her hunches proved to be true, Helen knew that a long slog still lay ahead of her.

'And can you be sure it will work?'

'Not yet. Just because your blood is resistant under lab conditions, it doesn't guarantee that you would be immune to a real werewolf bite. I'll need to carry out a lot more tests, run more trials.'

'How long will that take?'

'Weeks. Maybe longer. I need to be certain that the immunity is real.'

'That sounds like a long time to wait. What happens after all the tests?'

'Under normal protocols it often takes many years to develop new drugs and vaccines. If I break some rules perhaps I can reduce that time to a year. Maybe nine months,' she added when she saw the look of dismay on Chanita's face.

'That's far too long.'

'But I have no choice,' said Helen. 'I have to try.'

'Of course you do. But I have a faster way.'

Helen listened while Chanita explained her proposal. But the idea was madness. Helen couldn't even contemplate it.

'You want me to inject the lycanthropy virus directly into your own bloodstream in the hope that you will resist the disease?'

'You don't have to inject me,' said Chanita. 'I'm perfectly capable of injecting myself.'

'You're crazy,' said Helen. 'I won't allow it. Just because the test worked with a single drop of blood in a test tube, it doesn't mean that you would be able to resist a full-scale infection of the virus.'

'But that's what you're hoping?'

'Yes.'

'So my way is the one way to be absolutely certain,' said Chanita. 'And it won't require lengthy testing. We don't have time for that. People are dying now.'

'But you might die if it doesn't work.' Helen didn't voice what else might happen. They both knew that if this experiment went wrong, Chanita might turn into a werewolf.

'I'll take that risk.'

Damn, this woman was stubborn. And yet Helen knew that obstinate, difficult individuals often made the big breakthroughs in science. She'd lost count of the number of times that she'd been accused of being stubborn herself. She was reminded that in the early days of medicine, a number of pioneering doctors had run tests and experiments on themselves. In the nineteenth century, the German hygienist Max von Pettenkofer deliberately infected himself with cholera in an attempt to find out how the disease was transmitted. He was very lucky to survive the experiment. More recently, a Canadian doctor, Ralph Steinman, after being diagnosed with pancreatic cancer had tried out eight different experimental therapies on himself. He was awarded a Nobel Prize for his work.

But this? 'I can't allow it,' Helen said flatly.

Chanita shook her head. 'It's not your call.'

'I'm sure that Colonel Griffin wouldn't allow it either, if he were here.'

'He's not here.' Chanita eyeballed Helen defiantly. 'While he's away, I'm in charge of this camp, and I authorize you to proceed with this. I'll sign any legal papers and disclaimers you want me to. I don't want you to get into any trouble.' She softened her voice. 'I just want to help. And from what you've told me, I'm the only person you've found who can do this.'

'So far,' said Helen. But she knew the odds of finding another person with natural immunity were slim. She'd already tested hundreds and found only Chanita. 'I don't want to lose the one person I've found.'

'If it doesn't work, it will be because I don't have immunity, right?'

'Right.'

'So you won't have lost anything.'

'I'll have lost a friend. Not to mention a good nurse and a selfless human being.'

'Helen, this is a calculated risk. On the one hand, a single life. On the other, a cure for millions. It's my life. It's my choice. No one else can make it.'

'Still …'

'Listen,' said Chanita. 'There is danger all around us. When I was a child living in Montserrat I was bitten by a tarantula. My mother rushed me to the hospital in Plymouth for treatment. Later, when I was eighteen, the volcano on the island erupted. My mother was killed, but I escaped. Just last month I could have died when the werewolves escaped from their quarantine.'

'That doesn't mean you're immortal,' said Helen.

'No. And it doesn't mean I have faith in God, or a belief in fate or destiny either.'

'What then?'

'It means I'm not afraid,' said Chanita. 'Life can be snatched away from us at any moment. I've learned to embrace opportunity when it presents itself, because the only regrets we'll take with us to old age are the chances we had but didn't seize with both hands.'

'But this is reckless. There are other ways to do this. Safer methods.'

'They would take too long. You told me so yourself. This is urgent. The full moon is tomorrow. Now let's get on and do it.'

Chapter Sixty-Seven

Kensington, London, waxing moon

Leanna crept through the shadows of the back streets, keeping Warg Daddy just out of her sight. She tracked him by the faint scent he left in his wake – a familiar aroma of engine oil, leather and raw masculinity – staying downwind and out of view. Through the night-time streets of London they went, a good distance between them, playing cat and mouse.

Tracking her commander-in-chief like this was tricky, but it was the only way to be safe. If she got too close to him he would surely smell her, or else hear her, or somehow perceive her with his finely-tuned senses, and he would *know*. She marvelled at his ability to sense everything that surrounded him. It was a unique and invaluable gift. If only he could have remained loyal to her, he might have been the one. Together they could have ruled the world.

As it was, he was a growing liability. His faults had been obvious from the start, and were steadily outweighing his usefulness to her. He was becoming increasingly reckless and unpredictable as his headaches grew worse, and had become a danger to the entire operation. Worse, he had chosen another instead of her. The girl, Vixen. At least that was Leanna's suspicion. She wanted to make certain before she acted.

She crept along, her shadow following silently in her wake, moving as stealthily as a wolf through snow. Even so, she feared he would hear her and know that she was following.

Warg Daddy wasn't completely beyond redemption. He had proved himself admirably as a military leader. The Battle of Heathrow had been a huge success, as was his ongoing guerrilla warfare. But it was important not to delude herself about that – these were her victories, not his. She had planned them. She had ordered them. Warg Daddy was merely the general who carried out her commands.

She turned a corner and froze, seeing his dark form up ahead. She ducked back instantly out of sight, holding her breath, and waiting. What was he doing? Had he arrived at his secret rendezvous? She still hoped he would prove her suspicions false. For if she could not rely on Warg Daddy to lead her army into the final battle, who else could there be? Not Slasher, nor Meathook. Not Bloodbath or any of the other blockheads that made up the Wolf Brothers. They called themselves wolves, but they acted more like sheep. No, if Warg Daddy failed her, she might have to lead her army into battle herself, and she doubted she could command the loyalty of her troops in the way that the leader of the Wolf Brothers was so able to do.

She counted to ten and peered around the corner a second time. He was gone. Now she must hope she could catch up with him again before he vanished completely. On she crept, treading lightly through the dark and tangled streets.

She reached an opening between two houses and there

they were, Warg Daddy and Vixen, standing close together beneath a glowing streetlamp. She drew back. She had glimpsed them only for an instant, but it had been enough to confirm her worst fears. This was no chance encounter. The two of them had planned to meet here in secret.

She risked one more quick glance and saw him take the girl in his arms and kiss her on the lips.

Traitor!

Double treachery. She would kill them both. She would do it now.

Yet something made her pause. How many traitors had there been now? The list grew steadily longer. Must Warg Daddy's name be added to that list? She wondered if there was something about her that made people betray her. Was she not strong enough to command the respect of her subordinates? Had she not shown decisive action, as every leader should?

She dismissed the idea with a shake of her head. The truth was that people were weak. They were weak and selfish and not to be trusted. Her problem was that she was too lenient, too forgiving, too kind. She must be firmer, and punish those who betrayed her trust. That was the way to guarantee loyalty.

Warg Daddy would be the first to taste that punishment. He had cheated on her, and now that she had conclusive proof of his treachery, he had as good as signed his own execution warrant.

A voice behind her made her stop. 'They do make an attractive couple, don't you think?'

Leanna whirled to face the source of the voice.

An older man leaned casually against a streetlamp. A stranger. His thinning grey hair was combed and parted neatly. His limbs were soft, his belly flabby. Incongruously he wore a tailored suit and a black eye patch. He straightened his tie, although it had been perfectly straight already.

He had emerged from nowhere. How was that

possible? She was hunter, not hunted. She sniffed the night air. The stranger was wolf, not human. But not one of her soldiers. Something else.

'Perhaps we should leave them to it?' he suggested. 'Life is too short to allow petty jealousy to become our master.'

Leanna snarled. To dismiss her feelings as petty jealousy invited immediate retribution. She would tolerate such talk from no one. She would kill this man now, and then turn her wrath on the other two.

'I've been watching them for some time,' continued the man. 'This *relationship* has been going on for longer than you guess. I've been watching you too, my dear. You're such a fascinating young woman. But I don't believe that we've been properly introduced.' He bowed low. 'Canning. At your service.'

Leanna watched him mistrustfully. Her desire to rend him limb from limb was still strong, but she hesitated. The man clearly had something he wanted to say to her. 'My name is Leanna,' she acknowledged grudgingly.

He beamed. 'Yes, I know. I already know everything, you see. It's essential in my line of business. Would you care to walk with me a while?' He set off nonchalantly, turning his back to her, inviting her to kill him or accompany him.

Reluctantly she went with him, leaving Warg Daddy and Vixen to enjoy their own company. 'And what exactly is your business, Mr Canning?'

'Information,' he replied. 'I have ways of obtaining it. Sometimes I offer it to others in exchange for their assistance. Sometimes I give it away for free. For example, I know exactly where you live. I might offer that information to the authorities, for no other reason than to fulfil my civic duties. On the other hand, I know secret ways to move around the city undetected. I have contacts within government circles. I know the locations and movements of troops. I could even reveal what nonsense the leaders of the People's Uprising are planning next.'

'And what might you like in return?' she asked.

He paused as if to consider. 'Friendship, perhaps. I do get lonely sometimes. It would be a pleasure to spend time in the company of a lovely young lady like yourself. Perhaps we could tell each other our secrets. As you know, I have many to share. And I'm sure you'll find me more ... ah, articulate than your present company.' He nodded back in the direction of Warg Daddy, and then looped his arm through hers. 'Now, my dear, do tell me all about your plans.'

Chapter Sixty-Eight

*Western Evacuation Camp,
Buckinghamshire, waxing moon*

'I'm ready,' said Chanita.

'I still think this is madness,' said Helen.

'You won't be saying that if it works.'

'Maybe not.' Helen knew that nothing she could say would dissuade her friend from going through with this.

Chanita pulled her legs up onto the hospital bed and lay back. She rolled up her sleeve to expose the bare skin beneath. 'Come on. Let's get it over with.'

Still Helen hesitated. 'I'm going to have to strap you down,' she said. 'In case you have a bad reaction.' She didn't need to spell out how bad that might be. Chanita had witnessed the onset of the disease many times for herself. Anaphylactic shock, fever, violent attacks. Helen had already prepared an injection of adrenaline in case she needed to revive her from a severe allergic reaction. A hospital monitor stood ready to display Chanita's vital signs on screen. Helen looped a leather strap over Chanita's chest and pulled it tight. Another went around her middle and a third restrained her legs to the bed.

'I want you to promise me something,' said Chanita as Helen drew the straps tight.

'Yes?'

'If it doesn't work, I don't want to turn into one of those *things*. Promise you won't let that happen.'

Helen met her friend's gaze levelly. 'I understand. I'll do what's necessary.' She had already prepared a second injection to administer if the disease took hold. An injection that would bring Chanita's life to a quick and painless end.

Chanita nodded. 'Come on then. Do it now. The sooner it's done, the sooner we'll know.'

'Yes.' Helen dabbed alcohol on Chanita's arm with a cotton ball.

The nurse smiled. 'Usually I do that job. It makes a nice change for someone else to be in charge.'

'Oh,' said Helen as she readied the hypodermic needle, 'I think you're still the one giving the orders here.'

She injected the infected blood into Chanita's arm.

Chanita looked up at her and smiled one last time. 'If I don't see Michael again, tell him I was thinking about him all the time. And tell him that none of this is his fault. Even if he'd been here, I wouldn't have done anything differently. He mustn't blame himself.'

'I'll do that,' said Helen. 'If I have to. But I hope I won't need to.' She watched Chanita carefully, searching for signs of a reaction. She studied the readouts on the monitoring display. She knew exactly what to look for – a sudden drop in blood pressure, a rapid heartbeat, high temperature, loss of consciousness. In the most severe cases, the effects could begin to take hold within seconds.

Chanita breathed calmly, her face serene. The readouts seemed normal.

'How do you feel?' Helen asked her.

'Good.'

'Any feelings of dizziness? Drowsiness? Feeling hot or cold? Any tingling sensation in your arms or fingers?'

'No.'

'So,' said Helen, 'if my theory is right, your immune system has already recognized the virus and is starting to attack it with antibodies. The response will be slow at first, but will grow steadily until the invading virus is completely destroyed.'

'How long will it take?'

'I don't know. You're my first test case. But I assume that if you survive the first twenty-four hours without harm, then we can consider you officially immune.'

'Okay.' Chanita closed her eyes.

Helen studied the output on the monitors. Chanita's temperature had crept up a fraction. Her heart rate shifted higher.

'Chanita?'

'Yes?'

'How are you feeling now?'

'A little warm. My arm feels itchy. Is it time for me to start worrying?'

'No,' said Helen. 'Not at all.'

Let me do that, she thought. She checked Chanita's vital signs closely, searching for any change, however small. The heart rate was elevated, blood pressure slightly down, the temperature up another tenth of a degree.

'I'm going to give you a paracetamol infusion to stabilize your temperature, okay?'

'No problem.' Chanita scratched her arm near the site where Helen had injected the virus. The skin around the jab was slightly inflamed.

'Does that hurt?'

'It's a little tingly.'

Helen worked quickly, securing an intravenous drip into one of the veins in Chanita's arm and starting the infusion. On the monitor, the heart rate ticked up another fraction.

Come on. Come on. Don't let this go wrong.

She should never have allowed Chanita to talk her into this ridiculous experiment. She wondered exactly how she would explain her reckless actions to Colonel Griffin when he returned. But it was too late to have regrets now. The only way was forward.

The paracetamol solution was infusing directly into the vein. Chanita's temperature ought to start stabilizing soon. But it crept up another tenth of a degree.

Think.

'I feel a bit funny,' said Chanita, scratching at her arm again. 'I feel dizzy. Light-headed.'

The heart rate monitor climbed further. Blood pressure dropped.

'All right. Hold tight,' said Helen. 'I'm going to give you the adrenaline.'

Chanita's lips moved, but no sound came out. Her eyes were closed now.

Helen reached for the hypodermic syringe containing the drug. There was no gentle way to do this. She needed to get the adrenaline into Chanita's bloodstream as quickly as possible and that meant injecting directly into muscle tissue. She jabbed the needle into Chanita's shoulder and pushed down on the plunger, watching as the liquid drained steadily from the syringe. When it was done she swabbed the skin with a clean cotton ball.

She studied the heart monitor again. Chanita's blood pressure had moved back up again, thank God. The adrenaline would have only a short-term effect, but Helen hoped it would give the antibodies in Chanita's system long enough to fight back. She pulled the leather straps that bound her patient, and checked they were tight. There was nothing else to do now except wait and watch.

Chanita rolled her head from side to side, murmuring gently, her eyes still closed. A faint gloss of perspiration made her forehead shine. Her fingers twitched, opening and closing, as if they sought something to grab hold of. On the screen by her bed side, the heart rate monitor continued to tick steadily higher.

Chapter Sixty-Nine

Ashley Green, Buckinghamshire, full moon

The early morning light filtering through the fabric of the tent was just strong enough for Chris to pick out the forms of his companions. The shape next to him, whose elbow was digging into his side, was Seth. The big lump on the other side was the new guy, Ryan.

And near the entrance to the tent, sitting up in her sleeping bag, was Rose. There was no mistaking the girl's red hair and pale face, nor the hairy form of the dog leaning against her. As usual she had awoken screaming.

Chris pulled the sleeping bag over his head to try to muffle the noise.

'Bloody hell, what's happening?' said Ryan, sitting up in alarm.

'Nothing,' said Chris from inside his sleeping bag. He rolled over, trying to get comfortable on the hard ground. 'She's just had a nightmare. She does this every night. Go back to sleep.'

But Ryan was wide awake now. He crawled over to Rose. 'What is it? What's going on? Are you all right?'

The girl fell silent at last and Chris poked his head out of his sleeping bag cautiously.

'That must have been one hell of a nightmare,' said Ryan. 'That scream was blood-curdling.'

'It's post-traumatic stress,' said Chris. 'Visions, nightmares, flashbacks. It's all to be expected. She should probably talk to someone about it. A psychiatrist, I mean. Or a professional counsellor.'

'Talk to me, Rose,' said Ryan gently. 'Tell me about your dream.'

She shook her head.

'Come on,' coaxed Ryan. 'Dreams are important. They're a window onto the soul.'

Chris snorted loudly. 'Dreams are random sensations caused by the brain attempting to make sense of meaningless stimuli. And belief in the idea of a soul persists simply because of our inability to disentangle subjective experience from objective fact.'

The others weren't listening to him.

'I don't want to talk about my dreams,' said Rose. 'I just want them to stop.'

Ryan persisted. 'Telling someone about a nightmare helps to make it less frightening.'

'I saw a fire,' said Rose at last. 'A great fire. London will burn.'

Ryan screwed up his face. 'What do you mean? You mean it was burning in your dream?'

'No,' said Rose quietly. 'You don't understand. Everything I see in my dreams comes true.'

'Huh?' said Ryan. 'And no one told me about this?' He poked Chris with his foot. 'You didn't bother to tell me she can see the future?'

Chris squirmed inside his sleeping bag. 'She doesn't see the future. They're just bad dreams. They're a natural reaction to all the traumatic events she has suffered.'

Ryan turned back to Rose. 'Don't listen to him. Tell me about the future. I want to know what's going to happen.'

'The world is ending,' she said. 'London will burn. We have to get as far away as we can before everything is destroyed.'

'That's what I've been saying all along,' complained Chris, 'but no one listens to me.'

Ryan ignored him. 'And when will this happen?' he asked Rose.

'I don't know. Soon. Maybe even today, when the full moon rises.'

'She doesn't know,' said Chris. 'All she sees is bad stuff happening. It's just her subconscious imagination at work. You shouldn't encourage her.'

'She sounds pretty convincing to me,' said Ryan. 'Like these dreams are prophesies or something.'

Chris shook his head. 'They're not prophetic. They're just nightmares.'

'What do you think, Seth?' asked Ryan.

'Dunno,' said Seth, pulling at his beard. 'They might be. You know, like how Nostradamus predicted the future. A lot of his predictions came true.'

Chris jerked upright up in his sleeping bag. This was becoming ridiculous. He had to shut down this discussion right now. 'No they didn't. Nostradamus just made vague prophesies to terrify the superstitious. People twisted his words to fit the facts with hindsight. Anyway, what did Nostradamus have to say about werewolves?'

'Dunno,' said Seth. 'But if you don't believe Rose's dreams, why did we go on that big detour around Heathrow?'

Chris groaned. 'That was a mistake.' One he'd been regretting ever since he'd agreed on the diversion.

'We wouldn't have met Ryan if we hadn't changed route,' said Seth.

'Don't remind me,' muttered Chris.

'Well,' said Ryan. 'I think we should follow Rose's

dreams. What do you say, Seth?'

'Yeah, why not?'

'That's decided then.'

Chris opened his mouth to protest, but what was the point? He was the only person in this tent with any brains. The rest were lemmings, racing to hurl themselves off the nearest available clifftop. Talking to them would be like, well, trying to talk to lemmings.

Ryan unzipped the tent door. Fresh, cold air entered. 'Let's get going then. We have a long walk ahead of us today.'

Chris couldn't argue with that. He crawled out of the tent in Ryan's wake. The air was chill and the grass was studded with dewy crystals of water shining in the morning light. They soaked into his trousers as he struggled to his feet. The sun was just beginning to rise over the fields and hedges, flooding the eastern horizon with pink light.

He yawned and stretched his arms wide. It was going to be a good day, he could sense it. All being well they would reach the beginning of the Ridgeway comfortably before nightfall. And if Ryan could be believed, the ancient road would take them almost directly to their final destination.

From east to west. From danger to a safe haven, far from the city and the werewolves.

As long as they kept moving in the right direction, he didn't have any objections to Rose's prophesies. Werewolves. Burning cities. The end of the world. He had been making exactly the same kinds of predictions for months.

Chapter Seventy

*Western Evacuation Camp,
Buckinghamshire, full moon*

'How are you feeling?' asked Helen.

It was the day after she had injected Chanita with infected blood. The night had been one of the longest in Helen's life. She had stayed at her patient's side the whole time, watching anxiously as she sometimes lay still, sometimes moaned and thrashed around. The adrenaline injection had failed to stabilize her blood pressure for long. The infusion of paracetamol had been unable to stop the inexorable rise of her body temperature. In the small hours before dawn, Helen had almost despaired as Chanita shook violently in the grip of the fever, struggling against the leather straps that fastened her and crying out. She had wondered if she would have to administer the lethal injection. But then the fever had suddenly broken. Now as daybreak came, her patient had woken and was looking remarkably well.

'I'm good,' said Chanita brightly. 'I feel fine.'

Helen checked the numbers on the bedside monitor. Temperature, blood pressure and heart rate were all back to where they had been before, almost as if nothing had happened. 'Your vitals are all normal. Everything looks promising.'

It was a miracle that Chanita had pulled through.

Not a miracle. Simply the power of the human immune system to fight infection.

'We'll need to run some more checks before I can be confident that you've beaten the infection, but your latest blood test looks clear.' She peered into Chanita's eyes, shining a light at the pupils. 'No sign of yellow colouring. No abnormal sensitivity to light. How's your appetite?'

'I feel hungry.'

'Good. Breakfast is on its way. I asked the chef to prepare steamed vegetables followed by a selection of fruit.'

'I'll be sure to eat my greens like a good girl.'

'Good,' said Helen. 'Well, I think we can safely remove these restraints.'

She untied the leather straps and Chanita sat up in the bed, rubbing her arms and legs. The red inflammation around the injection had faded to nothing. The breakfast tray arrived and Chanita began to tuck in eagerly. It was the first food she'd eaten in a day.

'Mmm, tastes good,' she said. 'Yummy vegetables.' She picked a carrot stick from the plate and bit off the end with a crisp crunch.

'Okay, I can tell you're feeling better,' said Helen laughing.

Chanita speared some asparagus on the end of her fork and chewed hungrily. 'So what happens now?'

'Now I get some sleep,' said Helen. She was exhausted, unlike Chanita who seemed to have woken from her trial refreshed.

Chanita laughed. 'And after that?'

'Then the real work begins.' That was something of an understatement. Despite all that she'd been through to get to this stage, manufacturing a cure from Chanita's blood would require an operation on a scale an order of magnitude greater. 'We'll need to start cloning the antibodies that are present in your blood. We can use them to make a medicine that can be given to anyone who gets bitten or scratched by a werewolf. It's like a snake antivenom.'

'How do we do that?'

Helen noticed Chanita's use of "we" in the question, but didn't comment. She needed all the help she could get to see this through, and Chanita had already proved her commitment to helping out in any way she could. 'We can start producing antibodies in the laboratory if we can get the right equipment. I can't do it here. But I have everything I need back in my lab at Imperial College.'

'So we need to get back into London,' said Chanita. 'Leave that with me. How long will the process take?'

'It won't be quick. If we do everything by the book we need to follow rigorous procedures – validation studies, safety testing, pilot studies, pre-clinical trials, clinical trials, identification of side effects, …'

'Oh my God, no wonder it takes such a long time to develop new drugs.'

'Yeah.'

'But if we skip all the regulatory requirements, how long then?'

Helen hesitated. 'I don't want to make a promise I can't keep.'

'A guess, then?'

'If it goes well, perhaps a couple of months. But that will be just to start getting the first test treatments ready. It'll take much longer to scale up production.'

Chanita didn't seem daunted by the timescale. 'But at least we'll have something,' she said. 'We'll have a way to start fighting back.'

'Right.'

Chanita pulled herself out of the bed. 'Get some sleep, then pack your bags. Bring everything you'll need. I'll arrange a military escort to take us back into London. We leave in six hours.'

'Today?' asked Helen in surprise. 'But what about your role here?'

'I've had enough of being a manager. It's time I started making a real difference again.'

Chapter Seventy-One

High Street, Brixton Hill, South London, full moon

The final day of the evacuation had come at last and Liz was relieved. The operation was leaving her exhausted. She and Dean had been out from dawn to dusk every day trying to persuade folk to abandon their homes and put their trust in the authorities to protect them.

She was sick with worry about the safety of Samantha, Lily and Mihai. Samantha was growing larger every day and her blood pressure showed no sign of declining despite her being confined to bed. The doctor had said not to move her, but now they had no choice. Tonight the full moon would rise once more and a deadline had been issued to get everyone out of the city before nightfall.

Liz switched on the kitchen radio to catch the latest news, and quickly wished she hadn't. All around the world people were awaiting the night of the full moon in dread.

In Australia, the full moon had already risen, and the werewolf uprising had begun. In Japan, too, a night of violence was beginning. But the situation in Korea had taken an even more dramatic turn for the worse. Overnight, North Korea had launched an opportunistic attack on the south. The government in Pyongyang had declared that lycanthropy was a genetically-engineered disease created by imperialist western forces, and that it was their patriotic duty to wipe it from the world. Northern artillery units had opened fire on the south's capital, Seoul, a few hours before dawn. The citizens had taken refuge in underground bomb shelters but thousands were feared dead, and evacuation of the city had begun. With a population of almost ten million, the situation appeared utterly bleak.

But the latest reports were almost unbelievable. The Reuters news agency announced that the United States had launched a nuclear strike on North Korea in response to its invasion of the south. Casualties were unknown, but would almost certainly run into the millions. The numbers dwarfed the quarter of a million victims of the Hiroshima and Nagasaki atomic bombings of World War II. China had declared the bombing of its ally an illegal and monstrous act and had promised retaliation against the US. The UN Security Council was holding crisis talks to try to defuse the situation, but the prospects for world peace looked dire.

Liz turned the news off before anyone else came into the kitchen. She no longer felt like eating breakfast anyway. 'Come on,' she said when Dean appeared. 'Let's get this done.'

Dean planted a big kiss on Samantha's forehead before leaving. 'Liz and I will be back to fetch you later today, love. Early afternoon at the latest. We'll be out of London before it gets dark, I promise.'

Samantha gave him a smile. 'We'll be waiting,' she said, holding Lily's hand.

'You too, baby girl,' said Dean, giving his daughter a quick bearhug that made her squeal in delight.

Kevin and Mihai looked on anxiously.

'You take good care of them,' said Liz. 'Promise me you won't go out for any reason. And make sure you're ready to go as soon as Dean and I get back.'

'No problem,' said Kevin. 'The bags are already packed.'

Liz nodded. Much to her surprise, Kevin had stepped up and had done a great job of looking after Samantha, Lily and Mihai. He had cooked regular meals, done the laundry, and once she'd even spotted him using the vacuum cleaner.

But she wasn't only depending on Kevin for his domestic skills. It was a relief knowing that if any troublemakers tried to get inside the house, he would be able to handle the situation. 'Look after yourself too, Dad,' she said, dropping her voice so the others wouldn't hear. 'It's more dangerous than ever out there.'

'Don't worry about us,' he said. 'You go and do your job, girl. We'll be ready and waiting.'

She gave Mihai a kiss on the cheek. For once the boy didn't try to pull away. Either he was beginning to trust her again, or else he was too petrified to move.

'Come on,' said Dean, pulling his assault rifle over his shoulder. 'Got your Glock?'

She nodded. Both she and Dean were armed and kitted out in full protective gear, with stab vests, motorcycle-style helmets and shields. They carried batons, tear gas and Tasers, as well as their firearms.

The preparations did little to reassure Liz, however. Most people had left the city now, but the hard core who remained were refusing to leave. Some had taken refuge in churches and community centres. Others were staying behind in their houses. One thing united them – a defiant attitude and a contempt for the authorities. But the evacuation was mandatory now, and she and Dean were authorized to use force to evict people from their homes if necessary. She didn't relish it for a moment, but their task was to get as many people as possible out of the city by nightfall. They had even been promised help from an army unit to provide additional manpower and protection.

Dean drove the patrol car the short distance into central Brixton. The streets were almost completely empty. The few cars that remained at the sides of the roads were burned-out wrecks, or looked too ancient to go anywhere. Liz had hoped to see some families making last-minute getaways, but there was little sign of activity. It looked like the die-hard remainers were choosing to hunker down rather than leave. That would only make their job more difficult.

A couple of military vehicles were stopped up ahead of them in the middle of the road.

'That'll be our army escort,' said Dean. 'Bang on time.'

'Yeah.'

'Come on, cheer up. We should be safe enough with the army boys keeping us company.'

'You think so?' Liz wasn't so sure. It wasn't clear from their hurried briefing whether the soldiers would be assisting them to do their job, or whether it was the other way round. She suspected that the presence of the police was just a cover for the army to do whatever it wanted. She would find out soon enough. 'Just remember that the last time we went on patrol with the army, things didn't work out so well.'

'Yeah, well. We're not hunting down werewolves this time. Just shifting some awkward idiots out of their homes.'

'Let's just hope they're not as awkward as you, then.'

Dean opened the door of the car. 'Come on, let's go and get this job done. The sooner we're out of here, the sooner we can get Sam and the others to safety.'

Chapter Seventy-Two

*Upper Terrace, Richmond upon Thames,
West London, full moon*

They buried Grandpa in the garden of the house in Richmond, among the bushes and the trees. In summer, flowers would bloom around the grave and rabbits would play on the lawn. Birds would nest in the old oak trees and bring their young into the world. The delicate snowdrops and primroses were already in bloom, but the rest of the plants were still mostly dormant, patiently waiting their turn.

It was the first time for Sarah to go outside in a long, long time and she felt the cold air and the light breeze against her face keenly. The sunlight seemed stronger outdoors too, brighter than when she sat by the window gazing out. 'Grandpa loved this garden,' she said.

'This is where he'd have wanted to be buried,' agreed Melanie.

Melanie had been beyond furious when Sarah had first

told her of Grandpa's death. 'How could you?' she had screamed. 'You allowed it to happen!' Sarah had decided not to pick a fight, but to let her sister's grief and rage run their course. Already her anger seemed to have lapsed into a quiet sadness.

'He always liked to keep it so nice and neat,' said Sarah, looking around sadly at the overgrown borders and uncut grass. 'We abandoned it.' Nature was already reclaiming this space, populating it with weeds and wild creatures. 'We should have tried to look after it better.'

'You know we never could,' said Melanie. 'Neither of us know a thing about gardening.'

The two sisters held hands as Ben shovelled the last soil over the grave. They were burying their quarrel as well as Grandpa's body. Melanie's fury never lasted for long. It burned too hot to endure. However much the two sisters argued, they always made up again quickly.

Melanie still wasn't speaking to James, however. 'Murderer!' she had raged when she'd found out what he'd done. 'I invited you into our home, and this is how you repay us!'

Sarah had asked James to say a prayer at the funeral, but he had politely declined. Instead, Melanie read some lines of Grandpa's favourite poetry. Tears splashed onto the page as she spoke the words.

'She'll come around eventually,' said Ben to Sarah after the funeral. 'Just give her time.'

'I know.' Sarah had slowly grown used to Ben's presence. Grandpa may have gone, but her social world had expanded to include both James and Ben. There was hope that in time she might find the courage to face others. She would have to. That time was coming soon.

'I don't know if she'll ever forgive James though,' Ben continued. 'I don't know if I can either. I warned her about him. I said he was dangerous.'

'She'll forgive him,' said Sarah. 'Once she realizes that what James did was necessary.'

'Was it?' said Ben. 'I can't agree. We could have taken Grandpa with us. We could have tried to get an ambulance for him.'

'No,' said Sarah bluntly. 'Grandpa's time had come. What James did was the only compassionate act possible. I'd have killed him myself if he hadn't. If you don't think I would, then you hardly know me at all. I'm not soft like Melanie.'

'No,' said Ben. 'I can see that. Although *soft* isn't exactly the word I'd use to describe your sister either.' He tried to force a small smile.

Despite everything that had happened, Sarah found herself smiling back. 'She can be a bit ferocious at times,' she admitted. 'We both can, so watch out. Come on, get yourself ready to go, before one of us does something else that terrifies you.'

James was the first to be ready to leave the house. Sarah found him skulking in the hallway, keeping out of everyone's way. 'Don't worry,' she reassured him. 'You did the right thing. Melanie knows it, deep down. She's probably already forgiven you in her heart. It'll just take a while before she can allow herself to admit it.'

Melanie and Ben came down the stairs together, bags in hand. Melanie was wearing black leather boots, skin tight black jeans and a red leather jacket.

Sarah stared at her in astonishment. 'What are you wearing?'

Melanie slung a black leather bag over her shoulder and adjusted her appearance in the hall mirror. 'Apocalypse chic, darling. Fashion doesn't stop just because the world's ending.'

Sarah said nothing. Sarcasm and flippant remarks had always been Melanie's first line of defence. Her sometimes outrageous outfits were a kind of armour too. They shielded the vulnerability within.

'Are we ready to go?' asked Ben. 'We need to get a move on. We've left it late.'

Lycanthropic

They all knew what he meant. If they weren't under cover by nightfall, James would turn under the moon.

'Let's go,' said Melanie.

James opened the front door, and the cold wind blew in.

Sarah felt panic rising inside her. This house had always been her home, and in recent times it had become her fortress against the outside world. It had been many, many months since she'd ventured beyond the safety of its solid walls. The idea of stepping outside, of meeting strangers, had terrified her witless even before the troubles had started. Now, going out seemed not only petrifying, but reckless and stupid too. Why would anyone set foot beyond the safety of their own home? She had watched enough chaos and violence on her television screen. She understood the risks of staying behind, but surely venturing out was even more dangerous.

She and Melanie had lived here with only Grandpa to care for them these past twenty years, and she had only dim memories of her parents. A road accident had killed them both when she and Melanie were small. Her mother had been beautiful, just like Melanie, her father kind and heroic, rather like Ben. At least those were the hazy memories she had retained of them. But she knew from studying her psychology books that she could not really trust those memories. They were the half-truths of a little girl trying to cling onto her past, struggling to recreate a world that was gone forever. One thing she knew for certain was that Grandpa had looked after her and Melanie single-handedly, rising to a task that he'd never expected to have to undertake. Their debt to him was untold. So it had only been natural for Sarah to have taken on the burden of looking after him in turn, even if it had ended up making her a prisoner in her own home.

But all of that was in the past now. It was gone. She must leave this house today and perhaps never return.

And yet the wind outside blew so cold.

She pressed herself against the wall, feeling her heart beating fast, her breath coming in great gulps. 'I can't do it,' she said. 'I can't leave the house.'

'Come on,' said James, offering her his hand. 'We can do it together.'

Her hand was slick with sweat. She pulled it from his grasp. 'No, I'm too scared to go out. I'm terrified of what I might find.'

Melanie's face appeared before her, hard and unsmiling. 'Good,' she said. 'You won't last five minutes out there if you're not terrified.' Her voice softened and she touched Sarah's shoulder. 'I was always terrified of losing Grandpa, you know. It terrified me more than I ever admitted. He was always there for us. After Mum and Dad died, he never left us for a moment. I felt that if he ever died, or if he left us for some reason, our world would fall apart. That was why I clung to him so desperately. I wanted him to be immortal. But you saw that he was dying. You were the one who did something practical to ease his last days. And it was you who had the courage to face his death unflinchingly.'

Tears stung Sarah's eyes then. The tears that she had been unable to shed before. 'You know that part of him died a long time ago,' she said.

'Yes,' said Melanie. 'It's one of the reasons I was never around, why I had to go out all the time. I couldn't bear seeing him like that.' She hugged Sarah tightly. 'You did a brave thing, Sarah, both you and James. I couldn't do what you did for Grandpa. But the outside world is my domain. I'm not afraid of anything we'll find out there. So stick with me and I'll keep you safe, okay?'

Sarah nodded.

'Then come on,' said Melanie. 'We've wasted enough time.' She took Sarah's hand and led her out into the big, wide world.

Chapter Seventy-Three

Pindar Bunker, Whitehall, Central London, full moon

The Prime Minister paced the narrow corridors of the Pindar bunker impatiently. She had been pacing them for what seemed like hours already. She felt trapped down here in this airlocked complex. The place had been cramped from the very beginning. Although there was no shortage of rooms, and the vast corridor network seemed to stretch on forever, somehow that just contributed to the sense of being squeezed into a tiny space. Her own room was just large enough for a wooden bunk bed and a basic en-suite shower cubicle. The shared living areas were bigger, but the low ceilings made them unpleasantly confined.

Now, after days of not going out, the walls were closing in. The ceilings felt lower, the corridors narrower.

She had woken in the night bathed in sweat, her heart thumping, her lungs desperately drawing in the stale, recycled air. A sense of panic had gripped her in the absolute blackness of her windowless quarters, as if she were being buried alive, the weight of earth above threatening to squeeze the air from her lungs and silently suffocate her.

Claustrophobia.

She had never suffered from it before. But now the feeling of being trapped was inducing a constant, low-level hysteria even during waking hours. And what were waking hours down here, far from the sun-and-moon cycle of the surface? She had not felt the sun on her face, smelt the fresh breeze, or seen a single tree or flower for days. All times of day and night were the same underground, with only the artificial lighting to tell the difference. A flick of the switch turned day to night and back again.

She flicked the switch now.

On, off. On, off.

You could lose your mind in a place like this.

Mercifully, she would be leaving today. The evacuation of the capital was largely complete. No doubt a few people would choose to remain behind in their homes, stubbornly resisting all reason and persuasion. But she could not wait until every last man, woman and child had been taken to safety. Her symbolic duty here was complete. Now she had work to do elsewhere. She would move to the Northwood military command centre in Hertfordshire just north of the capital. Her War Cabinet had already relocated there, and she would not be sorry to leave this grim underground web of corridors and cramped rooms and move out to the countryside and the fresh air at last.

A month had passed since the last full moon, and tonight it would be full once again. She could scarcely believe that it had come so quickly. Perhaps she had lost sense of time living in the bunker, or maybe events had simply moved too fast. Just one month ago she had felt confident, believing that the werewolves were small in number, lacking in organization, and with many of them safely secured inside the quarantine hospital, unable to escape. Every one of those assumptions had been wrong. The threat she had faced had been even greater than it had seemed. Now the situation was bleak and the outlook bleaker.

The sooner she left this dungeon the better. You could not run a country from a hole in the ground.

She entered the communications centre and found the steely-grey features of General Ney seated in front of one of the comms screens. The General had become her shadow lately, rarely leaving the bunker complex himself. She wondered what effect the confinement was having on the man, but it was impossible to tell. He never revealed the slightest trace of emotion. 'Ah, General,' she said. 'Any news on our escort? They ought to be here by now.'

A military escort was coming to collect her, the General and the last staff members still remaining in the bunker, and she could hardly wait to see them.

The General did not reply.

'My suitcases and hat boxes are all packed,' she said jokingly. It was her nervous energy and her eagerness to be off that made her say that. Humour of any kind was wasted on the General. The Chief of the Defence Staff may be good at his job, but he would never make a great dinner party guest. She would be very glad of new company when she reached Northwood HQ.

The General continued to stare fixedly at his computer screen. He tapped the keyboard, as if he had not heard her speak.

She looked at her watch. A detachment from the SAS was being sent to fetch her, to guarantee the highest level of security. It was highly unusual for men like that to be delayed unless something was seriously amiss. She raised her voice. 'General, do you have any news on our escort?'

He looked up from the screen at last, swivelling his chair to face her. 'There has been a change of plan, Prime Minister. I have – ah – sent them away.'

The PM stared coldly at him. Today of all days she had no appetite for delays or last-minute changes of schedule. 'Explain yourself, General.'

'Your civilian advisers have gone with them, Prime Minister, and most of the military personnel too. Only you and I remain in the bunker, together with a small army unit for our protection. I have informed Northwood HQ that I will call for an escort again when required.'

Anger surged through the PM's veins at the sheer arrogance of the man. 'General Ney, that is no explanation. I wish to leave immediately. Call Northwood now and arrange for the escort to be sent back.'

'That will not be possible, Prime Minister. Please, take a seat. There is much for us to discuss.' He gestured at the row of swivel chairs arranged along the comms desk.

She remained standing. 'Anything you have to say can be discussed at Northwood.'

'We will not be travelling to Northwood,' he said flatly. 'Not today. Not any other day.'

'You assured me that –'

'I lied,' he said. 'It was necessary.'

The Prime Minister's anger turned slowly to dread. What was the General's game here? To keep her captive in the bunker – but for what possible reason? 'General, I must warn you that your behaviour verges on treason. I insist that you send for an escort now.'

'No.'

The finality of his tone shocked her. A nervous tremor began to take hold of her arms and legs. 'You are refusing to obey my direct order, General Ney?'

'I am. Now please take a seat.'

The trembling in her legs was rapidly becoming a shake, and she took the seat in an effort to hide it. 'What is this? A military coup? Do you plan to seize control of the country?'

'Certainly not, Prime Minister. Although I understand why you might make such an accusation.'

Lycanthropic

'What, then?'

The General steepled his fingers. His back was ramrod straight in the chair. Only his eyebrows moved as he began to speak. 'From the beginning of this crisis it has been apparent to me that a military approach is required to solve the problem. I have pushed for various interventions, but my proposals have been blocked at every step.'

'That is not true,' she interrupted. 'I have given you almost free reign to run this campaign as you wished.'

'That is not the case, Prime Minister. In the early days of this crisis I wished to shut down freedom of movement throughout the city, but instead you allowed me only to place checkpoints at certain locations. When I proposed a blockade on ports and airports, you procrastinated and delayed. When my men opened fire to suppress rioting you asked for my resignation. In recent weeks, when faced with an armed insurrection you tied my hands once again, first by limiting my forces' ability to fight back, and then by organizing this ridiculous time-wasting evacuation.'

The Prime Minister stared at him. 'These were basic humanitarian requirements. Someone had to curb your recklessness.'

The General shook his head. 'No, Prime Minister. My recklessness – or rather, my willingness to take decisive action – might have saved us from the current catastrophe, if you would only have allowed me to implement my plans unimpeded. You are a weak leader. Now we find ourselves in a situation where the country may soon fall.'

The General's words were a slap to her face, but she knew that she had never been weak. Most of the population already thought of her as an authoritarian dictator. Some said she was more dangerous than the threat from the werewolves. Yet she had always tried to find a middle path through the disaster, balancing human rights with the need for decisive action. Thousands would have died if she had allowed the General to carry out his bombing of the city. 'You are wrong, General,' she said.

'I see that my words fall on deaf ears,' said General Ney sadly. 'You merely confirm that I have acted correctly by holding you here today.'

'What do you plan to do with me?' she asked.

'That will become clear shortly.' He pressed a button on the desk and spoke into a microphone. 'Brigadier Ashworth, please bring your men through to the comms room.'

The brigadier was General Ney's aide-de-camp. He was a highly experienced and loyal soldier. The PM had trouble imagining him agreeing to take part in any kind of military coup.

The door to the comms room opened and the brigadier entered with two other soldiers. He drew to a halt and saluted. 'Your orders, General Ney?'

'Please pass me your service pistol, Brigadier Ashworth,' said the General.

The brigadier frowned, but obeyed.

General Ney took the firearm from him and turned it over in his hands. 'Brigadier, it has been my utmost pleasure to serve with you,' he began. 'I should like you to know that you are a man of honour.'

The PM rose to her feet. 'Stop!' she shouted to the brigadier. 'You must stop him now.'

The brigadier and the two men beside him stared at her in amazement. The two infantrymen gripped their rifles tightly, the barrels pointing at the ground. They seemed frozen by uncertainty.

'Arrest the General,' ordered the PM.

General Ney rose from his chair. 'At ease!' he commanded. He pulled back the slide to load his pistol and raised the weapon.

'No!' screamed the PM.

A deafening shot rang out and Brigadier Ashworth clutched his chest. His hand quickly turned crimson.

General Ney fired again and one of the infantrymen fell back, a bullet wound in his forehead.

The remaining soldier raised the muzzle of his rifle toward the General but never made it in time. The General's third shot killed him outright.

The Prime Minister gazed at the scene in horror. She turned to flee, but the bodies of the dead soldiers had fallen against the door and blocked her escape.

'Don't even think of leaving,' said the General behind her. 'There's nowhere to go.'

She turned back just in time to see him stride across the room to where the brigadier lay gasping his last breaths. The General pumped three more bullets into the dying man's chest at point blank range.

The shots echoed thunderously in the enclosed space. When they died away, the room was completely silent.

'Now we are alone,' said the General to the PM. His voice, as always, was calm and unhurried. 'And we can begin our work.'

Chapter Seventy-Four

West Field Gardens, South London, full moon

Drake perched glumly on the edge of Aasha's bed watching her pack. She had promised to remain behind with him, but had changed her mind at the last minute. That was just like Aasha. Now she couldn't wait to get away.

'You promised,' he said sulkily. 'You said you wouldn't leave me. I told you that we'd be safe under the protection of the Watch.'

Drake's mum had already gone, with just a hasty five minute farewell to let him know that she was leaving. 'You could come with me if you like, Drake,' she'd said.

'Don't worry, Mum,' he'd told her. 'I can look after myself.' He'd been doing that for years already. He wouldn't ever see her again, he knew that somehow. Nor would he really miss her. How could you miss someone who had never properly been there in the first place?

Aasha continued to pack her suitcases. 'I said I would stay, but that was before Vijay went missing. You said the Watch would keep us safe, but they didn't do anything to protect my brother.'

He couldn't argue with her about that. Vijay had been missing for nearly three days now. His parents had reported him missing to the police but the cops didn't seem very interested. Drake had gone out looking for him, and he'd asked around his contacts in the Watch, but nobody had seen him. He'd tried phoning him of course, and texting and messaging, but nobody's phone worked any more.

Aasha tossed a pile of clothes on to the bed next to him. 'Put those into the case for me, will you? I'm not leaving anything behind.'

Drake stared miserably at the heap of clothes. Some of them were gifts from him, stuff that Jack Stewart had let him take as a reward for his work with the Watch. He had delighted in presenting the designer gear to Aasha and seeing her face light up. Now the sight of the growing mound made him feel sick. 'How are you gonna carry all this with you?'

'It'll fit in the car.'

He doubted that. The government had advised people to travel light with only essential items needed for survival. Essential items didn't usually come with *Dolce & Gabbana* and *Prada* labels attached.

A frown passed across Aasha's face. 'We won't be going anywhere until Vijay shows up.'

Drake looked away. A knot was beginning to tighten at the base of his stomach. The last person to see Vijay before he went missing was Jack Stewart, and Drake was pretty certain that the man knew more than he was saying. He remembered the furious look on Mr Stewart's face that last time he saw Vijay, and the knot in his stomach clenched tighter. But Mr Stewart maintained that he had let Vijay go after giving him a sharp telling-off.

'I can't understand it,' said Aasha sitting down on the bed next to him. 'Where can he have gone? Vijay never does anything wrong. He wouldn't have just disappeared without telling anyone. Something bad must have happened to him. But why would anyone want to hurt Vijay? He's completely harmless.'

'I'm sure he'll show up soon.'

'Really?' she said. 'Then you must be even dumber than I thought.'

Drake sighed. His relationship with Aasha had been rocky from the start, and had hit rock bottom after her mum discovered the stolen gear in her wardrobe and made him take it back. The ice had thawed briefly after he'd given her new stuff to replace it. But relations had nose-dived again now that Vijay had vanished. His attempts to convince her that she would be safe staying here with him had fallen on deaf ears. It wasn't surprising. He was having a hard time convincing himself.

'Look, I'll go and search again for him, okay?' he told her. 'I'll ask my mates in the Watch to look too. He can't have just vanished, can he?'

He must have sounded sincere because Aasha's face softened. She touched his cheek with her fingers. 'Find him, Drake. He might be my annoying kid brother, but I love him, right?'

'I know.'

There wasn't much time left though. Today was the full moon and everyone was supposed to leave the city before dark. Mr and Mrs Singh were still out searching for Vijay, and Drake was glad he didn't have to face them as he left the house. He was sick of seeing their worried faces, of having to tell them he didn't know what had happened to Vijay and was doing his best to find his friend. He was tired of having to explain why he wasn't going to leave the city with them. He was tired of having to lie about everything, especially to himself.

If he wanted to find where Vijay had gone, there was

really only one place to go. One person. Jack Stewart.

Somehow he would get Mr Stewart to tell him what he knew. And if he wanted to find Mr Stewart, Kowalski's shop was the best place to start looking.

As he expected, Stewart and Kowalski were at the back of the shop, supervising the unloading of fresh supplies. Drake hoped this final delivery would be enough to last a long time. Once the army pulled out of London, there would be no more deliveries.

'There you are,' said Mr Stewart when he saw him. 'I've been looking for you. You can help to carry this stuff inside.'

'Yeah, sure,' said Drake. 'Can I just ask you something?'

Mr Stewart and Mr Kowalski were already talking again. Stewart turned back impatiently. 'What is it?'

Drake shifted from one foot to another. 'It's about Vijay. He still hasn't come home. He's been missing for days now. His family are really worried about him.' He hesitated. 'I'm worried too. You haven't seen him, have you?'

'No. I told you I hadn't. You seen him, Kowalski?'

The Polish man shook his head. 'No. Not for two days or more.'

'There,' said Stewart. 'No one's seen him. Now get on with your job.'

Drake bent down to load a box onto a hand trolley. He straightened up again. 'It's just that something must have happened to him. Vijay would never stay away from home for no reason.'

Stewart's head snapped back to glare at him. He strode quickly over and smacked the side of Drake's face with his fist.

Drake fell back to the ground, clutching his left ear. A high-pitched ringing filled his head.

'I don't want to hear that kid's name again,' shouted Stewart over the ringing.

Mr Kowalski's eyebrows knotted together in furrows. He seized Stewart's arm. 'Don't hit a kid like that again. Not in my sight.'

Stewart shook him off. 'All right, Kowalski. I'll make sure you're not watching next time.' He strode away.

'Are you okay?' asked Mr Kowalski, reaching down to help Drake back to his feet.

Drake withdrew his hand from his ear. A small smear of red marked his palm.

Chapter Seventy-Five

Brixton, South London, full moon

'Well, well. Look who it is.'

There was no mistaking that rich, melodic voice. 'Corporal Jones,' said Liz. 'Clue-Ellin.' She tried to say his name just the way he'd taught her.

'Hey, that's not too bad,' said Jones. 'I think you've been practising.'

'Huh. Don't kid yourself. I didn't even know if you were still alive.' She had thought she would never see him again. Now here he was, heading up the army unit that had been sent to help clear the last people from their homes.

The grin disappeared from the corporal's face at her words. 'Yeah, we've had a tough time, to be fair. As you know, we lost Edwards, Jenkins and Rees. But the rest of us are still alive and kicking.'

'That's good to hear.' She felt a surge of relief to see him safe and well, even if it meant that she would also have to face the Dogman and Rock again.

'So it's your lucky day, Liz. We're a team once more. You've been briefed on the mission, I take it?'

'Yeah. We've come to move the last few residents from their homes. You're here to help us in case things turn ugly.'

'Not exactly,' said the corporal. 'This is going to be a military-led operation. The way we see it, you're here to try and keep the peace. These streets are home to some hardcore elements. Not your usual type. These are organized. We think they might have links to the People's Uprising. Time's against us, so we plan to go in hard, clear as many as we can by noon, then get out of town ourselves. Our orders are to be out of London before dusk.'

'You think the people living here might turn violent?' asked Dean.

'Put it this way. We're planning on ruffling a few feathers.'

'Are they armed?' asked Liz.

'Not as far as we know, but we won't be taking any chances.'

'I can see that,' she said. The soldiers were in full battle gear, wearing body armour, helmets and visors. They hefted their usual array of rifles, machine guns and grenade launchers. Liz guessed they always dressed that way, but it seemed heavy-handed, just to persuade some folk to leave their homes.

'All right,' said Dean. 'You boys are in charge, so lead the way.'

Liz followed Dean back to the patrol car and climbed in. 'This is exactly what I was afraid of,' she said. 'I just hope this isn't going to turn into another shambles.'

Dean turned the key to start the engine. 'We only have a few more hours here, then we can get Sam and the others to safety. So just stay close to me and don't take any risks. Let the army do the dangerous work. Like Jones says, we're only here as window dressing.'

'Yeah,' said Liz. 'That's what's making me nervous.'

Up ahead the familiar hulk of the Foxhound sprang to life. A stream of charcoal smoke spewed from the armoured vehicle's exhaust pipe. The vibrations from its engine were strong enough to make the dashboard of the patrol car throb.

A hand reached out of the Foxhound's passenger window to wave them on. Jones.

'Let's get on with it, then,' said Dean. He slid the car into gear, and together the vehicles set off in the direction of the town centre.

Chapter Seventy-Six

Holland Gardens, Kensington, London, full moon

The day of the final battle was here and Leanna's troops were ready and waiting. Her commander-in-chief was waiting too.

Warg Daddy. Her greatest problem. Her greatest asset. She had spent the night turning over the facts, trying to square the impossible circle.

She needed him; he was out of control.

He was a traitor; she had no one who might replace him.

Almost against her own will, she had decided to let him live. But only for this final battle. He would lead her troops to victory today, and then he would die. On reflection, it seemed a fitting conclusion.

The burned skin on her face was plaguing her again this morning. Perhaps lack of sleep had made it worse. Red and angry, it flared in continuous pain. No ointment seemed to ease her discomfort.

But she had prepared a medication that would help to ease Warg Daddy's distress. A special recipe. Pills of purest white and sweet as sugar. They would remove his pain once and for all. She took the bottle of pills and went to meet him.

'Leanna.' When he was leading her army he sometimes liked to dress up in one of his stolen military uniforms, but today he wore his usual Wolf Brothers garb of black leather. His bald head gleamed in the morning sunlight that streamed through the tall windows. The combat shotgun was in his fist.

'Warg Daddy. You are ready?'

He grunted in acknowledgement. That was good. It was better if he did not speak to her. She could no longer stand to hear his voice. She could barely bring herself to look at him.

Yet she addressed him as a queen should speak to her general. 'The Wolf Army awaits you, Warg Daddy. This will be your finest hour. Victory is within our grasp. Under your leadership, London will fall tonight.'

And today my vengeance will begin.

Warg Daddy would be the first to taste it. Afterwards she would find and kill the others at her leisure. She would take her time over each and every one.

James, Helen, Melanie, Ben, Vixen.

She was glad the list of names had grown so long. The pleasure was surely sweeter that way.

Warg Daddy made no response to her grand proclamation. Instead he kneaded his bald head with his thumb.

She knew how much the pain tormented him. Like the brimstone heat that turned her cheeks to fire, it was burning him up from the inside. Perhaps it was the suffering that had made him betray her. If it was, she might almost feel sorry for him.

She handed him the bottle of pills. 'Before you go, take

one of these for your headaches. It will help you to fight.'

He stared at the bottle as if he knew that it contained his doom. 'You think these will help?' he asked. 'Nothing else has.'

'It's worth a try,' she said sweetly.

He regarded her suspiciously for a moment, then unscrewed the cap and poured one of the pills into his mouth.

'Take two, just to be safe.'

He took the second pill.

She smiled broadly at him. 'Good luck, Warg Daddy. I promise you that this will be a day like no other.'

Chapter Seventy-Seven

Hampton, West London, full moon

According to Ben, the distance from the house in Richmond to the edge of London was less than twelve miles. 'It's really not that far,' he told Melanie. 'We'll take the shortest route, cutting across parkland and walking along the River Thames for most of the way. It'll be a pleasant walk. If we keep up a decent pace we'll be out of the city and in Surrey before dark.'

Everyone was being super careful to say nothing about what would happen when darkness fell. Even so, Melanie couldn't help casting a sideways glance at James. The boy was walking with his head down, talking to no one. The wind dragged at his long hair, giving him a wild look. His face seemed unusually pale and gaunt under the harsh winter light, and she fancied she caught a glint of yellow in his eye when the sun caught him from a certain angle.

'You doing okay, there, James?' she asked.

He grunted in acknowledgment, but didn't look up.

Sarah, too, was saying little during the journey. She seemed to want to block out the world around her as far as possible. No doubt after shutting herself away for so long, the experience of being outside must be overwhelming. She was like a hermit emerging from her cave after long, solitary years, blinking in the light.

But at least Ben was making a determined effort to stay cheerful. 'Look over there,' he said. 'It's Hampton Court palace. Pity we don't have time to pay a visit.'

The grand Tudor mansion had once been home to Henry VIII. Grandpa had brought Melanie and Sarah here many years ago. She remembered how they had admired the huge house and gardens. Melanie had delighted in the old paintings of kings and queens. 'Are they real?' she had asked Grandpa, her eyes drinking in the jewels and fine dresses of the various queens and ladies of the court. 'Oh yes,' said Grandpa. 'But none of them look very happy, do they? Perhaps they knew that Henry was going to cut off their heads.' Sarah had fallen in love with the maze. She had run into the centre and Melanie and Grandpa had spent ages searching for her. Melanie had quickly become bored and had begged Grandpa to leave Sarah stuck in her stupid old maze.

She wasn't about to abandon her sister today however. 'You're doing fine, sis,' she said to Sarah. 'This isn't so bad, is it?'

Sarah's reply was too quiet to hear.

More people appeared as they headed west. Most walked in groups, some with children. A few walked alone. One group carried an old woman on a stretcher. Melanie averted her gaze and stared determinedly into the distance as they walked past.

She felt Sarah's hand become clammy as the number of people around them grew. 'So many people,' muttered Sarah, staring at her feet. 'What if they talk to us?'

'Then I'll give them a peek at James' teeth,' said Melanie. 'That'll soon scare them off.'

Sarah shook her head anxiously. 'You mustn't.'

'That was a joke,' said Melanie, vexed. Sarah was close to a panic attack, she realized. She tightened her grip on her hand. 'Don't worry. I'll deal with any problems. You just have to keep on walking.'

That was the only thing any of them had to do. It was just like Ben had promised – a simple four hour walk to safety. One hour had passed already. Three more to go.

Chapter Seventy-Eight

Pindar Bunker, Whitehall, Central London, full moon

'And so we proceed to the end game.'
    General Ney stood before the Prime Minister in the communications centre of the bunker, his bushy monobrow rising and falling as he spoke. The bar of coloured medals pinned to his chest glimmered under the room's flat fluorescent lighting, but it was the only point of brightness in his grey demeanour. As always, the General stood stiff and tall, his hands clasped neatly behind his back, delivering his words with care and precision.

Banks of computers and communication devices stretched along the desks behind him, their displays showing maps, scrolling readouts and other data reports. The hum of air-conditioning units was the only sound, apart from the General's voice and the PM's own short breaths. Despite the best efforts of the aircon, the bunker felt hot and stifling and suddenly she wanted to scream.

Claustrophobia, again.

Panic was the enemy now, as much as the man standing opposite her.

I must remain calm, whatever happens.

She breathed deeply, slowing her breaths, conquering the fear. Her eyes drifted to where the three men lay dead on the far side of the comms room. Brave men. Loyal men.

If only I had acted more quickly.

Yet she had not known until the last moment that when the three soldiers entered the room the General intended to murder them. She had imagined they were on his side.

He is working entirely alone. He has no support among his military colleagues.

That was her one source of hope. If she could somehow overpower the General, she could still prevent him from doing whatever it was he planned.

But I am also alone.

No help was coming. Not right now at any rate. By tomorrow someone would surely send help. Perhaps even within a few hours the alarm would be raised. But it might be too late to stop him.

Just me against the General, then.

The Prime Minister relaxed a little. It would make a change for her to do something entirely by herself for once. She had spent too long giving orders and delegating tasks to others.

I haven't lost my fighting spirit.

She forced herself to look again at the bodies of the dead soldiers. Two of them had been carrying rifles. The discarded weapons still lay beside them on the floor. She could reach them if she could somehow divert the General's attention.

Too easy. The General is no fool. He may be insane, but he has not lost his wits.

'What is your end game, then, General Ney?' she asked, injecting as much bravery as she could into her voice. 'What mad plan do you intend to carry out?'

The General bristled at her words. 'My plan is rational, whatever you may believe. Some may even call it noble. But I am indifferent to the judgement of history. I have never sought glory for myself.'

'What do you seek?'

'An end to this crisis. A way to save this country and her people. Under your leadership we are heading for catastrophe and an end to civilization, perhaps even the extinction of the entire human race.' He paused to let his words sink in. 'But fortunately, you have unwittingly given me an opportunity to neutralize the threat from the lycanthropes once and for all.'

'How do you propose to do that, General?'

'You made a mistake in organizing the evacuation of the civilian population,' he accused. 'It was an unnecessary and counterproductive action. It wasted too much time. My preference – as you know – was to begin a targeted aerial bombing campaign some weeks ago.'

She opened her mouth to object, but he waved her to silence. 'Yes, no doubt there would have been collateral damage – civilian casualties – but we would have achieved a quick victory. If you had followed my recommendation, by now our enemy would have been destroyed utterly. That opportunity was missed. You denied me that chance. As a result, when the full moon rises tonight, the threat from our enemy will reach a new peak. The lycanthropes will change into wolf form, escape and spread out from London and from other cities in all directions and we will never be able to defeat them. Therefore, if the country is to survive, we must eradicate them before they change into wolf form.'

'But I have already given you permission to escalate your operations once the evacuation has been completed,' protested the PM. 'You can begin bombing tonight. But first we must leave. Now. Together.'

'No. You are not listening to me. It is already too late for that. Even a concerted bombing campaign would not succeed in eliminating all lycanthropes now. But by evacuating the civilian population of the capital, you have presented me with an alternative.'

'What?' She glanced again at the two rifles lying on the ground near the exit. Several metres lay between her and the weapons, not to mention three dead bodies blocking her route. She didn't even know how to fire a rifle. If they weren't loaded, or if the safety catch was engaged, she might never get a chance to fire them. But perhaps she didn't need to shoot the General. If she could simply point a rifle at him, he might back down. She couldn't think of a better plan right now.

The General spoke again. 'The alternative should be obvious. A nuclear strike directed at London and other major cities.'

Her head snapped back to stare at him. He was even more deranged than she had thought. But his plan could not possibly succeed. Only she, as Prime Minister, had the authority to initiate the launch of the UK's independent nuclear arsenal, Trident. 'I would never authorize a nuclear strike against my own country,' she said, 'whatever threat you might make against me. Kill me, torture me. I will not reveal the authorization code.'

'No,' conceded the General. 'I do not imagine for one moment that you would.'

'Then your plan must fail, General,' she said. 'We have reached a stalemate.'

'Not quite. There is one circumstance in which another person can give the command to launch.'

She stared at him, dumbstruck. She knew precisely what those circumstances were. But …

The General spoke for her. 'In the event of the serving prime minister's death, then until a replacement is appointed by the ruling monarch, control over the country's nuclear weapons is delegated to the Chief of the Defence Staff, acting with the authority of the monarch.'

For a while she could not respond. 'You plan to kill me, then?' she asked eventually.

'That will not be necessary. No one else knows what is happening here. I will transmit my report of your death shortly, followed by the authorization to launch.'

'Why wait?' she asked. 'And why not just kill me anyway?'

'Why? Because I am not the deranged psychopath that you believe me to be. The evacuation of London is not yet complete. Every hour another thousand civilians leave the city. By waiting a few more hours I will save thousands of lives. And I assure you that I have absolutely no desire to kill you.' He rested his hand on the service pistol he had taken from the brigadier. 'But make no mistake. I will kill you if you try to stop me.'

She waited until he returned to study his computer terminal, then stole another quick glance at the dead soldiers and their abandoned weapons.

Standard issue British Army assault rifles. She had seen them handled often enough. She'd even watched demonstrations of them being fired. How hard could it be to grab one and use it?

Chapter Seventy-Nine

High Street, Brixton Hill, South London, full moon

Mihai was bored. The whole world was ending, and guess what? It was boring.

He lay slumped in front of the TV, resting on a bed of soft cushions, the curtains pulled shut against the sunlight, watching a cartoon. It was a little kid's cartoon, with a cat and a mouse. The mouse was small, but cleverer than the cat. Mihai liked the mouse. He liked the fact that there were hardly any words. It made it easy to watch.

The cartoon was an old one, and so was the TV. It lived inside an enormous black box. He didn't know why it needed to be so big. The box was so huge, the cat and mouse would easily have fitted inside. Every few minutes, the screen went fuzzy and he had to get up from his bed of cushions to slap its side. Boring. But what else was there to do? Liz said to stay here and wait, so he was waiting.

When he'd first come to England, he'd hoped to start

at a new school and make friends, but the schools had all closed down. He had no kids his own age to play with. There was Lily, but she was a girl and was only three years old. She was still a baby.

Liz was always out at work, and anyway was *vampir*. Could not be trusted. That just left Grandpa Kevin. But Kevin was grumpy old man since Liz told him no whisky and cigarettes. Better to keep out of his way.

Soon they would be leaving and he didn't have big hopes for that. When he left Romania people said he would find a better life in England, but he hadn't found it yet. He didn't think he'd find it in the camp they were going to either.

He flicked the TV remote to see if he could find anything better than the cartoon, but most of the channels were dead. Was nothing to see except for fuzzy grey lines. He switched from one set of fuzzy lines to another. Boring, boring, boring.

The door to the room opened a crack, letting in a wedge of light. It was probably Grandpa Kevin, come to find him.

He switched the TV off and hid under the cushions.

'You in there, kid?' The wedge of light grew wider and brighter. Kevin stepped into the room, breathing heavily. 'I need your help,' he said. 'I got a job for you to do.'

Mihai hoped he would go away. He didn't want one of Grandpa's Kevin's jobs. He held his breath, hoping he would leave.

Grandpa Kevin wasn't exactly a bad man. Sometimes he was kind and generous. He could be fun too, a lot more fun than Liz. But he wasn't very reliable. Grandpa Kevin's jobs often ended up with someone getting into trouble.

Often that someone was Mihai.

'Am busy,' said Mihai. 'Doing very important job already.'

Kevin kicked at his bed of cushions. 'Come on, kid. It ain't no good hiding in here. There ain't nothing on TV anyway.'

'Don't call me kid,' said Mihai. 'Name is Mihai.'

'Yeah, yeah, all right,' said Kevin. He stepped over the mound of cushions and pulled the curtains open, flooding the room with daylight. 'That's better.'

Mihai squinted against the sudden light. Trouble was coming. He could tell. He waited to hear what it was.

'Now, listen,' said Kevin. 'I have to slip out for a short while, so I want you to look after Samantha and Lily until I get back. I'm going to leave you in charge of the house, all right?'

Mihai frowned. So this was the job. It was even worse than he had expected. If Liz found out, she would go mad. He said to Kevin, 'Liz say, don't leave Samantha and Lily alone in house.'

'Yeah, that's right,' said Kevin. 'That's why I need you to take care of them while I'm gone.'

'You make promise to Liz,' said Mihai. 'Not go out until she get back.'

Kevin winced, twisting his face into an ugly scowl. 'Yeah, I made her a promise, I know. But I promised myself something too. Something more important.'

'What?'

'Well, I can't fill you in on all the details,' said Kevin, 'but there's this geezer I have to go and see before we leave London.'

Geezer was strange Kevin-word for guy. No one else ever said *geezer*.

'Liz won't be back until after midday,' he continued, looking at his watch, 'so that leaves me with a good couple of hours. That should be loads of time. Don't tell Samantha that I've gone out. Just keep your eyes peeled for signs of trouble. All right, kid?'

'Name is not kid,' said Mihai. 'Name is Mihai.' Grandpa Kevin never listened. Always talking, never listening. It was no surprise that he and Liz argued so much.

'All right, then, good,' said Kevin, as if Mihai had

agreed to help. He slipped out through the door and Mihai followed him into the hallway. Kevin was stuffing some object into his trouser pocket. He turned round to stop Mihai seeing what it was. 'Just remember, keep an eye out for trouble,' he said as he left the house.

Mihai watched him walk away. He looked around for trouble in the street outside, but couldn't see any. Apart from Grandpa Kevin, of course. But he was soon gone and the street was quiet again. Mihai closed the door against the cold. At least he had a job to do now. Anything was better than watching stupid cartoons on a broken TV.

Chapter Eighty

Electric Avenue, Brixton, South London, full moon

When they reached the centre of Brixton, Liz jumped out of the patrol car and slammed the door behind her. Up in front the soldiers were pouring out of their vehicles, rifles at the ready. Jones took the lead, and Liz recognized Griffiths, Lewis and Evans from the previous mission. Three newcomers had been brought in to replace those killed. The Dogman stood to one side with Rock on a tight leash. The dog barked excitedly at the burst of activity and Liz made sure to keep well out of the animal's way.

A ragged crowd of men, women and children had gathered in the middle of the street. At their centre stood a diminutive woman who Liz had encountered once before, when they'd shaken hands at Gary's funeral.

Salma Ali, the leader of the Watch. She held a microphone and was addressing the gathered crowd over a

PA system.

Liz had heard a lot about this woman. She knew that the Watch held a special kind of power over this area and that Salma was at its heart. People talked about the organization as if it were a miniature government. She'd heard that it provided protection for the locals, and helped distribute food and medical supplies. Some spoke about Ms Ali in reverential terms, as if she were their saviour.

But from what Kevin had told her, it was clear that some of the people involved in the Watch were dangerous, if not downright criminal. Mr Canning for example. How had he described himself? As Salma Ali's personal assistant. Pet thug, more like. She scanned the crowds for his easily-recognizable face, but the tall man with the eye patch was not in sight.

The Foxhound had pulled up in the middle of the street that had once been a bustling marketplace but was now lined with steel-shuttered shop windows. Rotten meat and vegetables spilled out of overflowing rubbish bins, and everywhere were the signs of neglect – graffiti sprayed on walls, peeling paint and rust on the railway bridge that passed over one end of the street. But none of the buildings here had been set alight, unlike in many other parts of the city. The Watch had clearly protected its own neighbourhood effectively from serious vandalism and deliberate damage.

The crowd parted as the soldiers disgorged from the Foxhound and the Land Rover. Nervous faces and frightened eyes watched. Liz sensed anger in the crowd too. The police and the army were not welcome here.

She tapped Corporal Jones on the shoulder. 'Let me try to speak to their leader. I know her. I can defuse this peacefully.'

Jones considered her offer. 'Sounds fair. I wasn't planning to go in all guns blazing. See if you can talk sense into her. You're a local. You have as good a chance as anyone of persuading her to stand down. Go and do your stuff, Liz. But remember what I said earlier. These people may be dangerous.'

'I've seen worse.' The people here might be hostile, but they weren't violent. They were just ordinary citizens in search of safety. As long as everyone stayed calm, there would be no trouble. 'Just stay back,' she told Jones. 'Promise?'

He flashed her a smile. 'Deal.'

She began to push her way toward the front of the crowd with Dean's help. A few people muttered and swore as she passed them, but none offered resistance. They were more interested in listening to what Salma Ali had to say. As Liz drew closer, fragments of the woman's speech began to catch her attention.

'These are our homes. This is our community. We are safe here, under the protection of the Watch. If we leave, we abandon everything to criminal gangs and looters. Is that what we want?'

'No!' shouted a few voices in the crowd.

Salma pointed a finger at the soldiers standing at the back of the crowd. 'They cannot force us to leave. They have no right to remove us against our will. Shall we allow them to try? Or shall we resist them?'

'Resist!'

Liz continued to push forward through the mass of people. The crowd was growing more restless. She could sense a growing hostility. The mutterings grew louder. People began to jostle her. An arm shoved her from behind. A hand tugged at her helmet. Her sunglasses slipped for a moment and sunlight clawed at her eyes. She pushed them firmly back into place.

Dean pushed the offenders away, clearing a path for her to proceed. 'Go on,' he said. 'I've got your back.'

Salma continued, her voice loud over the speakers. 'We can no longer trust the government. The army and the police are our enemies now, as much as these werewolves. Do you know why they want us to leave? Is it for our safety? No. It's to divert attention away from their own failures. So they can more easily continue to rule us. Can we trust them?'

'No!' The response was overwhelming this time. More hands shoved Liz as she pushed through to stand in front of Salma. Dean forced his way behind her and kept the protesters at bay.

'Here they are,' cried Salma triumphantly, as Liz emerged to stand next to her at the centre of the crowd. 'Authoritarian forces, come to evict us from our own homes.'

The mob was growing angrier with every word. Liz could feel the danger around her like rising heat. Every time Salma spoke, the temperature spiked another degree higher. She had to cool things down quickly.

She unbuckled her riot helmet and deposited it on the ground. She took the microphone from Salma. 'Hey, listen to me,' she said.

The crowd began to shout and heckle.

Liz raised her voice above the noise. 'Listen to me, please. That's all I ask.' She waited a moment for the heat to dissipate a little. The cries and calls gradually tailed off enough for her to continue. 'I'm no politician,' she said, glancing sideways at Salma. 'I'm just a police officer doing my job. I don't have fine words to give you. I'm not here to convince you that one side is right and the other is wrong.'

'Why are you here then?' came a shout.

'To tell you that it's not safe to stay. To tell you that safe passage has been arranged for you to leave the city.'

'We're not leaving our homes! You can't make us!'

Liz glanced at Jones and the other soldiers standing at the back of the crowd. He would be furious when he heard what she had to say next. 'I'm not here to force you to leave,' she told the crowd. 'Legally, it is my duty to enforce the evacuation, but I'm not going to drag families from their homes against their will.' She waited a moment to see if anyone would shout back, but the crowd waited, listening. 'If you want to stay and trust your safety to the Watch, that's your business. I won't stop you. You can make up your own minds. But if you want to leave, this is your last chance. Time is running out. I'll be taking my own family out of London today, and I advise you to do the same. If you have a car, you can make your own way to one of the camps, following the safe routes that have been clearly signposted. Or you can go to the nearest railway station and get a train out. Don't leave it much longer. The last trains will leave in a couple of hours. After that you'll be on your own. That's all I wanted to say.'

She switched the microphone to mute. The heckling and jeering had ceased. At the back of the crowd, Jones gave her a thumbs-up signal and one of his trademark grins.

'Nice work,' whispered Dean. 'I think they got the message.'

'I hope so,' said Liz. 'Come on. Let's get out of here.'

Beside her, Salma Ali was furious. Her eyes blazed with anger. She grabbed the microphone from Liz's hand and opened her mouth to speak again.

At that moment a gunshot rang out.

Chapter Eighty-One

Mr Canning leaned out of the upstairs window of Kowalski's supermarket to get a better view. From here he could see everyone in the street below. Civilians, soldiers and police. Salma Ali was at the centre of everything, and next to her the young police officer, Liz Bailey.

As he'd expected, the gunshot had come from the edge of the crowd.

Jack Stewart.

What an utterly predictable fool that man was. Give him a gun and soon enough he was busy firing it at people. Remarkably he seemed to have actually hit his target.

A soldier lay dead or dying on the ground immediately below the shop window. Some lowly army grunt. A man of no importance whatsoever. Except that the effect of killing him was as predictable as handing Jack Stewart the gun in the first place.

Outrage. Uproar. Riot.

People were running in every direction, scurrying around like headless chickens, crouching low, seeking safety. Or else they were turning to their neighbours, looking for someone to use their fists against. Scuffles broke out, voices cried in anger and fear. The crowd heaved. People fell to the ground.

The soldiers were fanning out, their weapons ready to fire. All they needed now was a target. They were scanning the crowd, searching for the gunman.

He could help them out himself, tell them who had done it. He imagined his voice calling out, 'Over there! It was that man,' his hand pointing theatrically in Stewart's direction. But it would be more satisfying to do the job for them.

He leaned further out of the open window and raised his arm, bracing himself against the window frame. His own pistol was in his hand, loaded and ready to fire. He didn't need to close one eye to aim. That had already been taken care of.

He quickly found his target. Jack Stewart.

The man was standing still, surveying the chaos he had managed to unleash so efficiently. What had he hoped to achieve by killing a soldier? Was he planning to take on the entire squad of eight men, Rambo-style?

Mr Canning held the man within his sights for a moment, his finger on the trigger.

Too easy.

He would not waste a bullet on that pathetic oaf.

He slid his arm to one side, scanning the panicked crowd for a more interesting target.

Now here was a person of great interest indeed. Police Constable Liz Bailey.

She crouched low, appearing calm and collected amid the disorder. Next to her squatted her partner – a big brute of a policeman. Both held guns. Interesting. He hadn't known that Liz owned a gun.

He still hadn't been able to work out what kind of creature Liz Bailey was, or even which side she was batting for in this strange struggle that was playing out. Werewolf? Government? Revolutionary? Or some other side altogether? The unanswered question irritated him beyond measure. Doubt was anathema to him. He could remove the uncertainty with a single bullet.

But that would leave him none the wiser. More than anything, he wanted to know.

The bullets in his gun were still unused. It would be a pity to waste this opportunity to loose them. The barrel of the gun moved once again.

Salma Ali. What a fascinating young woman she was. So talented. Such a gifted public speaker. So ambitious and ruthless. She was, of course, a treacherous serpent with nothing but greed and self-interest at heart. But Mr Canning admired that in a woman. And he had served her well, doing everything she asked of him.

But Salma's days of power were almost at an end. She had been very foolish to trust Jack Stewart with a gun. Now the crowd in the street was in full panic, fleeing in every direction. Salma yelled into her microphone appealing for calm, but it was no use. Her words carried no power now. It had taken just a few minutes for her to lose her grip entirely.

When the rats start leaving the sinking ship, it's wise to follow them.

He watched her through the sights of his gun, then lowered it reluctantly. It would have been a pleasure to kill any one of these three, but he had his own self-preservation to think about. A gunshot would draw the immediate attention of the squaddies down below. It wasn't worth it.

He holstered his gun and closed the window. He had seen enough here. It had been a pleasant surprise to witness this unexpected charade. But now it was time for him to be off. He had an appointment across town – a

Lycanthropic

meeting he couldn't afford to miss.

Chapter Eighty-Two

Liz watched appalled as the situation deteriorated rapidly into chaos. She drew out her Glock and scanned the crowd, but from her position she couldn't see where the gunman had fired from, or who had been his target. She didn't even know if anyone had been hit. 'Did you see where the shot came from?' she asked Dean.

He shook his head. He was training his assault rifle around the crowd, searching for the shooter.

People were fleeing in all directions and she had no intention of stopping them. The quicker they got away from here the safer they would be. But the gunman was also likely to escape in the confusion.

Salma Ali was still screeching into her microphone. Liz dashed across to her and yanked the mic from her hand. 'Get down! The shooter might be anywhere.'

The woman glared at her in outrage. 'Your soldiers

opened fire on a peaceful demonstration. This was state-sanctioned murder.'

'Of course it wasn't. Now keep low and stay still before you get yourself killed too.'

Jones' men were searching the area for the gunman. She could see now that one of the soldiers had been hit.

A flicker from an upstairs window opposite caught her attention. Fire. She tapped Dean's shoulder. 'Up there. Look. A fire's broken out in the upper floor of that supermarket.'

'I see it. Kowalski's Polish Supermarket. Don't tell me that was started accidentally.'

The flames were already licking the top of the window frame and were visible in other windows too. 'Looks like arson to me,' she agreed. 'It's spreading quickly. Whoever started it must have used something flammable. If that spreads to neighbouring buildings, the whole area could go up.'

'Maybe that will encourage people to leave.'

A shout went up across the street and a man started running toward the supermarket. She recognized him as Mr Kowalski, the owner of the shop and one of the people Kevin had been mixed up with. The man's thick beard and oversized moustache lent him a comical appearance, but there was no trace of amusement on his face. 'My shop!' he cried. 'My shop is on fire!'

Two younger men who looked just like him – his sons, presumably – ran with him to the shop entrance, only to find the door locked. The three struggled for a while before managing to force it open. As soon as it opened, fire became visible inside on the ground floor. Mr Kowalski struggled to get inside while his two sons held him back. 'I have to save my shop!' he cried once more. He broke free from their grip and ran inside. The fire was already raging there. The younger men held back and did not enter. Black smoke began to billow out of the doorway.

Corporal Jones ran across the street to her. 'Are you two all right? Griffiths has been shot but the bullet doesn't seem to have hit any vital parts. His condition is stable. We've lost the gunman. It's time we got out of here before that blaze spreads along the entire street.'

'We're okay,' said Liz. 'Let's just hope that everyone will have the sense to leave quickly now.' She glanced across the road at the Polish supermarket. There was no sign of Mr Kowalski. His two sons had retreated to a safe distance from the heat. They had no way of fighting the fire, and no one was coming to help. Liz shook her head in disbelief. There was no hope for the shop owner trapped inside. He might already be dead from smoke inhalation or the heat itself.

The upper floor of the supermarket was bright with flame and thick with smoke. Sparks were flying and the heat could be felt even at this distance. The fire was spreading eagerly to the adjacent buildings. The whole street consisted of shops built one up against their neighbours. There were no fire breaks and no firefighters coming to quench the blaze. Jones was right. Soon this entire district would be engulfed.

She thought of Samantha, Lily, Kevin and Mihai waiting for them at home. She had to get back and lead them to safety. 'Come on,' she said to Dean. 'Let's go.'

Chapter Eighty-Three

Ivinghoe Beacon, Buckinghamshire, full moon

A sense of foreboding took gradual hold of Rose as the day progressed. The sun shone brightly behind her as they headed north, but a darkness as black as her own shadow was slowly closing in around her heart.

Ryan had kept to his promise, leading them all the way from the evacuation camp to the foot of the Chiltern Hills – a journey of several days. Now as they began their final climb up the chalk slope leading to the Ridgeway path, her skin began to prick with sweat. Her limbs grew heavy, and not just from the steep walk up the hill.

Nutmeg could sense that something was wrong. The dog began to whimper gently at her side, her bright chestnut eyes a picture of concern for her mistress. Rose stopped halfway between the valley floor and the hilltop ahead. She swayed on her feet, then crouched down, leaning against the sloping ground so she wouldn't fall. She gathered the dog in her arms, hugging her tight. 'There, there, girl. Everything's all right.'

But she knew that it wasn't.

'What's the trouble?' asked Ryan. 'Is something wrong with the dog?'

Rose shook her head. 'Not the dog, no.'

'What then?'

Her vision began to slowly mist. A fine web of lines appeared before her, breaking her reality into fragments. Her ears buzzed with an almost inaudible sound of terror. 'It's starting,' she whispered. 'It's happening now.'

A cold ink was seeping through her veins, paralyzing her and chilling her to the bone. She knew what this was. She had seen it coming in her dreams. She turned to look back in the direction they'd come.

South.

London lay that way.

The city was too far away to see from here, hidden somewhere beyond the fields and trees and rolling landscape they had crossed. But she didn't need to see it to know what was happening. She had watched it already in her dreams. The streets engulfed with flames. Werewolves, soldiers, people, animals. All burning.

Icy tears began to trickle down her cheeks. Nutmeg nuzzled her smooth head against her.

Ryan squatted down on the grassy slope at her side. 'Let's rest here for a while.'

But rest was impossible. Her hands began to shake, then her arms. Nutmeg whined as her limbs thrashed wildly, out of control.

'Easy, easy,' said Ryan, gripping her firmly by the shoulders.

Chris and Seth came running down the hillside to help.

But she was spinning now, the clouds in the sky whirling in a vortex that threatened to suck her up from the ground. She felt her feet begin to lift. Another pair of hands clutched at her, but she was weightless, flying through the air. Nutmeg barked loudly. Then she threw her head back and the world exploded in a rainbow of ten thousand colours.

Chapter Eighty-Four

Brixton Hill, South London, full moon

Kevin walked along the road at a brisk pace, hands in his pockets, a cold northerly wind whipping around his bare head. He'd never owned a warm hat, or gloves. It was better not to. Cold weather kept you tough.

The gun in his pocket was cold as well, but comforting. *Cold comfort.*

Kevin grinned to himself. That thieving maggot Canning may have stolen two of his guns, but he had held on to the third. Admittedly, the weapon that bulged in his pocket wouldn't have been his first choice of the three. While Canning had made off with two British Enfield revolvers – old but sturdy weapons – Kevin was left with a dog's breakfast of a gun, a Russian-built Baikal IZH-79. Made originally to fire gas cartridges, the compact pistol had been illegally modified to handle 9mm Czech ammo. Kids from East End street gangs used tools like this to blow each other's heads off. Idiots. The gun was cheaper than a Glock and had become a favourite of London's criminal underworld. Its range wasn't great, but at point blank it did the business.

Canning wasn't quite as clever as he thought.

Kevin's sources on the ground told him that Canning used to be a headmaster. He could easily believe it. He was just the type. Smarmy. Superior. Smug. It would explain why he'd taken such an instant dislike to the man. Well, he intended to teach that slimy weasel a lesson he wouldn't forget.

So far Canning had proved elusive to track down, but Kevin knew he was still around, and he wasn't going to miss this last chance to keep his promise to himself. He would have to play it carefully though. Canning still had at least two guns in his possession. He hadn't forgotten the man's horrible death grip either. His shoulder still didn't feel quite right after Canning had seized him. He'd make sure the bastard didn't get close enough to use that trick again. He'd make damn sure.

The streets of Brixton were completely empty. Most people had left the area days earlier, and the few who remained had hunkered down out of sight. But Kevin had a pretty good idea where to find his arch enemy. The trouble was, Liz was likely to be in the same place.

He tried not to worry about that. He knew how to keep himself out of sight. Besides, he'd grown up on these very streets. Most of them hadn't changed much since he'd been a boy. He'd known all the shortcuts and hiding places then, and he hadn't forgotten any. He slipped along the shortest path into town, keeping a good lookout all around. But he was safe enough. Everywhere he went was deserted.

He hoped that Mihai wouldn't spill the beans and tell Samantha that he'd gone out. That kid had become stroppy lately, always answering back. One minute Liz was hassling him, the next, Mihai. Someone was always telling him what to do. That was the reason he'd taken that job as a long-distance driver – to get away from other people nagging him all the time.

To avoid responsibility, according to Liz.

Damn and bugger. He couldn't win.

Up ahead a column of smoke drifted over the rooftops in the gusting wind. More buildings had been set ablaze by the looks of it. Bloody looters, no doubt. He remembered when this had been a decent neighbourhood for honest working people. People like himself. Now it was full of rival factions all battling each other. Mad.

He rounded the corner into Electric Avenue and found his way blocked. A giant army truck stood in the middle of the road, next to a military Land Rover and a police car. Liz. She'd be here somewhere, just like he'd anticipated. He crouched low behind the truck, surveying the scene.

No wonder the streets had all been empty – everyone was here in one place, milling around like twits. He spotted Liz in the middle of the crowd, and a bunch of soldiers wielding rifles. He didn't know what was going on, but a bit of commotion suited his purposes nicely.

The source of the smoke was quickly apparent. Kowalski's supermarket was up in flames and was halfway to becoming a heap of cinders. He was sorry to see that. Kowalski was a good bloke. A foreigner, but one that Kevin had time for. He'd got to know him well when he'd been trading goods, before his booming business empire had hit the buffers. He missed those days badly. It would be good to catch up again with Kowalski. But he didn't have time for that now, and he guessed the Polish man didn't either. His shop was completely gutted by the blaze. The wind would feed the flames, spreading the fire across town. But that was someone else's problem. Kevin had enough of his own to deal with.

He scanned the panicking crowds carefully. Mad as a bag of ferrets, the lot of them, scarpering in all directions. But for once, luck was on his side. There – far to the left –

was the man he'd come looking for, slinking away like a rat.

Kevin patted the cold steel in his pocket. A nasty surprise awaited Canning, and the sooner he delivered it, the quicker he could be back home. If luck stayed with him, Liz would never even know that he'd been out.

But he couldn't do the job here. The Baikal didn't have the range, and besides there were too many witnesses, even though they were running about like morons.

Canning vanished down a side street and Kevin crept quickly after him.

Chapter Eighty-Five

Brixton, South London, full moon

Drake watched as Jack Stewart sneaked away from the scene of the shooting. He had been spying on the man ever since their earlier confrontation at Kowalski's. He'd watched as the crowd had gathered, concealing himself at the back as Salma Ali delivered her speech. He'd seen the soldiers arrive with the police woman, Liz, and her partner. And then he'd seen Stewart pull out his gun and shoot one of the soldiers.

Now the man was making a run for it.

Drake waited until Stewart disappeared from view, then followed. The street he had gone down was empty.

He sprinted down the road as quickly as he could. Soon he caught sight of his quarry. Stewart turned onto a main road, throwing a quick glance behind him to see if anyone was following. He saw Drake and his eyes narrowed.

The gun was no longer in his hand, but Drake didn't fool himself that he had thrown it away. He must be nuts,

Lycanthropic

running after an armed fugitive who had just shot a soldier. He stopped for an instant, but then he remembered Vijay. A fresh burst of fury wiped away his fears. He dashed forward again.

The older man was running for his life, and kept up a fierce pace. But Drake was a fast runner and caught up with him after a few hundred yards. Jack Stewart tried to duck away from him, but Drake grabbed hold of his collar and brought him to a halt.

The man twisted violently in his grip, panting heavily. He might not have been as fit as Drake, but he carried a lot of weight and had the upper body strength of a weightlifter. And he was desperate too. He pulled himself free and landed a hard blow on Drake's shoulder.

Drake spun away staggering, but managed to stay on his feet. 'I saw what you did,' he accused. 'You killed a man.'

Stewart was about to run again, but he stopped at Drake's words and spat on the ground. 'Just a soldier. No one you need to give a damn about. Is that why you came after me?'

'You set Mr Kowalski's shop on fire too.'

'That wasn't me. Some other tosser did that.'

'I don't believe you.'

'Believe what you want.'

The man stood apart from Drake, clenching his fists. There was still no sign of his gun and Drake wondered if he'd disposed of it somehow as he'd fled. He could easily have dropped it in a rubbish bin, or tossed it over a wall.

'I need to get away from here,' said Stewart. 'Are you gonna try and stop me?'

'Where are you going?'

'You don't need to know. I'm just getting out. If you're smart you might want to do the same.'

'I'll tell you what I want,' said Drake. 'I want to know what you did to my friend.'

Stewart gave a cruel laugh. 'The brown-skinned boy? I

told you before, he's no friend of people like us.'

'His name is Vijay,' said Drake, 'and he is my friend. So tell me what you did to him.'

'You giving me orders now?' Stewart spat on the ground again. 'You think I would tell you? So you can go and rescue him? Why should I care what happens to him?'

Drake slipped his knife from its sheath. It was the knife that Jack Stewart had given him. He drew the blade out and held it in the space between them. 'This is why you should care.'

The man laughed nastily. 'I taught you everything you know about knives. You didn't even know which was the sharp end when I first found you. Do you think you have something to teach me now?'

Drake swallowed. 'Let's see.'

Stewart glanced up and down the street and saw nothing to alarm him. 'I reckon I have a few minutes to spare. This shouldn't take long.'

He drew his own blade.

Chapter Eighty-Six

Brixton, South London, full moon

Vijay awoke from a doze. Locked inside the garage he had little sense of time passing. Sometimes he woke and it was black. Sometimes, like now, it was grey. But it was never properly light inside his prison. The building had no windows, only solid walls. The only source of light was the narrow gap around the edge of the building's big metal door. Pale daylight leaked through that gap now, making a thin rectangle in the dark.

He had lost count of the number of times he had woken and then fallen back into oblivion. He had no idea how long he had been confined to this small square room. All he knew was that he was entirely helpless. He had no water, no way of escape. He no longer had the strength to sit up and try to raise the alarm by slapping the door. Making a noise had done him no good anyway. Everyone must have already left the city. He was entirely alone.

Only one thought kept him from giving up on life

entirely. Rose. He mouthed her name with his lips. No sound came out. His throat was too dry and cracked. His parched tongue filled his mouth like a huge wad of paper.

His whole body was cold, though he could no longer feel it shivering. He could barely feel anything.

Yet something had woken him from his slumber, some faint disturbance in his surroundings. He moved his eyes around the dim interior searching for anything that looked different, that might have moved. The bricks were just as solid as before, the machinery in the corner as rusted as ever. He could hear nothing, save the constant din that filled the space between his ears. It was the sound of silence. Funny how it could become so loud.

There was something though. A smell. He sniffed. Yes. There, beyond the harsh scent of damp and mould and rotting timbers. What was that smell?

Smoke.

He sniffed again. Definitely smoke. What did that mean? His mind strained for the answer. It was on the tip of his tongue, that swollen monster that filled his mouth and threatened to suffocate him.

Fire.

Yes, smoke meant fire. And fire meant death.

He had thought he would die from his injuries, or from dehydration, or even from the cold that penetrated his bones. Instead, he would go up in a blaze of fire.

He tried once more to cry out, but it was useless. No one heeded his call, only the flames.

The smell grew steadily stronger. He could taste the sharp soot and ashes now. He imagined the roar of the fire outside. It was coming to get him. He hoped that when it came it would take him quickly.

Chapter Eighty-Seven

Brixton, South London, full moon

Drake backed into the middle of the street, giving him plenty of space on each side to move freely. He gripped the handle of the knife tightly in his sweaty hand. The weapon had a fixed blade six inches long with a serrated edge and a curved point. It wasn't the biggest knife you could get, but he felt comfortable handling it. He had learned how to keep it sharp and clean. He turned side-on toward his opponent, the knife raised and ready.

'Warrior stance,' said Jack Stewart approvingly. 'You remember something I taught you, then. But do you remember the number-one rule? Never start a knife fight unless you're prepared to finish it.' He raised his own knife. It had an evil-looking saw-tooth blade, longer than Drake's and with a tip that glinted in the low sunlight. He turned side-on as Drake had done and took up position six feet away.

'I remember everything you taught me,' said Drake. 'And I've learned some more besides.'

'New tricks, eh?' said Stewart. 'Let's see them, then.' He closed the distance between them and lunged with his knife, striking at Drake's torso. The attack was sudden and vicious, much more aggressive than Drake had been expecting.

Drake dodged to the side at the last second, narrowly avoiding a serious injury. This wasn't like the first time he and Jack had fought. The man had just been toying with him then, testing him. This was for real.

'You can't learn to fight by watching videos online,' said Stewart. 'You learn by fighting. And I reckon I've done a whole lot more fighting than you ever will. In fact, I think this fight may turn out to be your last.'

Drake readied himself for another attack. He held his knife arm firmly in front, keeping his other arm close to guard his chest. He ducked his head low, just as Stewart was doing, making his body as small a target as possible. He tried to relax, as much as that was possible.

Jack Stewart circled slowly around him, making Drake turn to face him. 'I've known kids like you before,' said the man. 'Someone slips you a knife, gives you a few tips, and you think you're a killer. The truth is, as soon as you get into a proper fight you get yourself killed real quick. Knives are dangerous. Don't say I didn't warn you.' He darted forward a second time, bringing the blade up in a slashing movement toward Drake's neck.

The sudden change of direction wrong-footed Drake and he reacted too late. The tip of Stewart's blade caught his knife arm as he spun away, drawing a thin red line across his wrist. It hurt like the sting of a paper wasp. He kept his mouth shut though. He wouldn't give Stewart the satisfaction of hearing him cry out.

Stewart grinned at him unpleasantly. 'Bet that hurt. Do you wanna give in yet? I'll let you go if you drop your knife.'

'You wouldn't say that unless you were afraid too,' Drake told him. He re-positioned himself in warrior stance, ready to defend himself again, or strike if he saw an opening. 'All this macho talk is just to hide the fact that you're as shit-scared as me.'

Stewart's face turned sour. 'You think so? Don't say I didn't give you a chance to quit.' He continued to circle Drake, stepping forward every half-turn and feinting with the knife.

Drake pulled back each time. He tried to hold his position, but Stewart kept up the pressure, driving him slowly back into a corner where a brick wall met the side of a concrete housing block. Soon he would have no space to move, and nowhere to run if he needed to.

He shifted to attack, lunging forward with his knife. He drove in a straight line, just like Stewart had taught him, aiming for the chest.

There was little power in the thrust. Stewart stepped back, dodging the attack easily, and made a counter-attack with his own knife, striking at Drake's outstretched arm.

The blow might have ended the fight, but Drake snapped his arm out of harm's way just in time. He counter-attacked himself, driving forward hard, seeking to reclaim the initiative. His blade caught his opponent on the forearm, drawing blood for the first time.

Stewart grunted in pain and pulled back. The man was bigger and stronger than Drake, but Drake was nimble and quick. He danced forward for a third strike, whisking the tip of his knife just an inch from his enemy's face.

Jack Stewart snarled angrily. He wasn't talking anymore, just breathing heavily. He turned and slashed again at Drake, but was off balance now. The blow was easy to dodge.

'Nothing more to say to me?' asked Drake, circling around his opponent and making him turn to face him. He stepped forward and the man retreated. Drake advanced again, keeping his blade up and ready to strike. He turned the other direction and forced the man back into the corner where he'd almost been trapped himself.

Stewart seemed to be tiring. He had stopped striking and moved to the defensive, waiting for Drake to strike. It could easily be a trap, and Drake wasn't dumb enough to fall into it. He kept moving, making small strikes and feints with the knife to keep up the pressure. But if he wanted to win this fight, if he wanted to force Mr Stewart to tell him the truth about Vijay, he would have to switch to the offensive.

He waited until he'd backed Stewart firmly into the corner and then he launched his attack. He jabbed his arm forward ferociously, splitting the air with the blade. As he'd expected, his opponent fell back, right up to the brick wall, and thrust his knife upward, hoping to catch Drake off-guard. But Drake's attack had been a feint. His arm was no longer where Stewart expected to find it. With blinding speed he brought his own knife back under Stewart's blade and jabbed it into his elbow with as much strength as he could muster.

The blade went deep, piercing soft flesh and cutting through muscle and arteries with its wicked edge.

Stewart screamed and dropped his knife. He pulled his arm away and clutched at it, still screeching.

Drake kicked the dropped knife across the road and threw his weight against his enemy, holding the bloody edge of his knife against Stewart's throat. He grabbed a handful of the man's hair and jerked his head back against the rough wall. 'Now tell me what you did to Vijay,' he said.

Hate blazed in the man's eyes. 'I gave the bastard what was coming to him,' he snarled. 'That's all.'

'Where is he?' demanded Drake.

'You think I'll tell you? You're wrong.'

The blade quivered in Drake's hand in frustration. 'I'll kill you if you won't tell me.'

'Then you'll never find out what I did,' sneered Stewart.

'So drop your knife and let me go.'

'No.'

'There's nothing you can do,' continued Stewart. 'You think you've won, but you've lost.'

'No!' shouted Drake.

'You could probably get me to talk if you really wanted. You could cut off my fingers one by one. How many fingers do you think your friend is worth?' Stewart let the question hang between them. 'But you won't do it. You're too soft.'

Drake shook his head. But the man was right. He didn't have it in him to be so cruel, not even to save his best friend. Or did he? If that was the only way to rescue Vijay, could he do it? His knife hand trembled and he lifted the blade from Mr Stewart's neck. A quick cut would do it. Just a slice. The blade was sharp enough. It would be like chopping meat. He hesitated and in that fraction of a second, Stewart's knee drove up and into his groin.

He crumpled in agony and dropped his knife with a clatter. He fell to his knees, clutching himself hard to try and still the pain. But even as the throbbing eased a fraction he knew that he'd lost everything. The underside of a leather boot impacted his shoulder and pitched him over onto his side, and he lay there, staring up hopelessly at the barrel of a gun.

Jack Stewart's arm was running with blood, but he seemed perfectly able to hold his weapon. He crouched over Drake, pressing the barrel to his forehead. 'Don't move,' he said, 'or I'll blast your brains out.' He rose again and crossed the street to retrieve his dropped knife. When he returned, the gun was back in its holster and he brandished the knife in his injured arm. With his other arm he grabbed hold of Drake's wrist and forced his hand down with an iron grip. 'Now,' he said, 'let me show you the way to cut off fingers.'

Chapter Eighty-Eight

Ivinghoe Beacon, Buckinghamshire, full moon

'What's happened to her?' asked Chris.

Rose lay sprawled on the grass partway up the side of the dry valley they had been climbing. He'd heard her cry out, then begin to thrash around. He'd come running back down, but she had already fallen still and silent by the time he reached her.

'She's unconscious,' said Ryan. 'But her eyes are open, like she's in a trance.' He pressed his fingers to the girl's neck. 'I feel her pulse. She's still breathing.'

The girl's pale face was even whiter than usual. Her green eyes were wide open but unmoving, fixed on infinity.

Chris waved his hand in front of her face, but she didn't respond. 'She's ill. She needs to rest. We should try to get help for her.'

The girl's lips began to move, forming words. Chris

listened intently. 'Vijay,' she muttered.

'What?'

'Who's Vijay?' asked Ryan.

'No idea.'

'I see flames,' whispered Rose. 'Fire. Vijay. We have to save him.'

'Is she having another vision?' asked Seth.

'It's not a vision,' said Chris. 'It's a hallucination. Feel how hot her forehead is. She's running a high fever.'

Fresh tears were running down Rose's cheeks. 'I tried to save him,' she said.

'She's shivering,' said Seth. 'Should we wrap her sleeping bag around her?'

'No,' said Chris. 'That will make her worse. We need to cool her down.' He pulled a clean cloth from Rose's rucksack and sprinkled it with drinking water. 'Put this on her forehead.' He passed the cloth to Ryan.

Chris rose to his feet again. 'I'm going up the hill to take a look around. Perhaps there's somewhere we can take her, or someone who knows what to do. You two stay here with her.'

He set off up the steep slope, eager to get back to the top. He'd been almost at the brow of the hill when Rose had started screaming. He wanted to see for himself the start of the Ridgeway, the road that led to the promised land.

The grass covering the hillside was slippery with mud. He hauled himself up the steepest parts by grabbing hold of tufts of long grass. He was breathless by the time he rounded the top of the hill, despite his improved fitness since he'd begun his long journey.

The hill top covered a broad flat area. An iron age hill fort had once stood on this very place, and Chris understood immediately why this location had been chosen for a settlement. In every direction he could see for miles. All around him was wind and sky. It felt so different from the city he'd left behind. It felt like freedom.

A single bird of prey soared high in the sky overhead, but even from his own more modest vantage point on the hilltop, Chris could see a vast swathe of land stretched out around him. It must surely have spanned several English counties. A patchwork of fields spread out at his feet, criss-crossed by hedgerows and dotted with woodland, church steeples and small villages. In the distance, lines of hills marked the horizon. It was like looking down at a scale model of rural England.

He made his way to the centre point of the flat hilltop, marked by a squat stone pyramid a few feet high, It was a triangulation point, used for making maps. The bird of prey hovered directly above him, floating effortlessly on a thermal. It was a sparrow hawk or a harrier, he guessed, although he didn't know enough about birds to tell the difference. He watched as it defied gravity, shifting its wings a fraction to maintain its position.

The bird was free in a way he could only begin to imagine. Yet up on this hill, where all he could hear was the wild wind, and where the entire world seemed to be laid out before him, he began to taste some of that same lightness.

The bird dropped suddenly like a stone, swooping down to the ground. It snatched a field mouse or some other small creature in its claws and swept up again and away into a distant treetop to devour its prey. Chris followed it with his eyes. And as his gaze shifted, he suddenly saw what he had travelled so far to find.

It was just as Ryan had promised. In the direction the bird had flown, just a few dozen feet from the triangulation point, a clearly defined ribbon of short grass flecked with white chalk stone began. It was the start of the ancient Ridgeway, the road to freedom, and to safety.

The chalk path was broad – wide enough for six people to walk abreast. It threaded its way along the ridge formed by connecting hills, meandering into the distance until it disappeared behind the clump of trees where the bird perched, devouring its meal. It seemed to beckon him.

This road would take him right across the island of Britain, almost all its width from east to west. He just needed to give himself up to it.

He crossed the short expanse of grass until his feet reached the chalk road. The path led on, inviting him. He took another step. And another.

He stopped and glanced over his shoulder. From here he could no longer see the others. Seth, Ryan, Rose and the dog. They were out of sight.

He ought to go back and find them. He'd told them he was just going for a quick look around. But what use could he be to them? Rose would surely come round again as soon as her fever had passed. Ryan knew how to look after her just as well as anyone.

They wouldn't miss him. He wouldn't miss them. They'd be better off without him, happily following Rose's delirious dreams. And he'd be happier alone.

This was what he should have done right from the start. He could see that now. If he hadn't waited such a long time for Seth before leaving London, he would have reached Hereford many weeks ago. Seth and the others were a dead weight, dragging him down. He had nearly died back in that quarantine hospital, all because he had waited for Seth. He would not wait again.

He took another hesitant step forward, and soon he was walking quickly, the chalky stone crunching beneath his feet, tramping alone across this most ancient of roads. And he was free at last.

Chapter Eighty-Nine

Brixton, South London, full moon

Drake sprawled on the cold ground, still in agony after being kneed in the groin. Jack Stewart squatted down next to him, gripping his right wrist with one hand, the other hand pressing his knife tip against Drake's little finger.

'So, how many fingers is your friend worth?' Stewart asked. 'One? Two?'

'Please,' begged Drake. 'Don't cut me.'

Stewart looked disappointed. 'I thought you said he was a great friend, this Vijay. He must be worth something to you. Three fingers, maybe four?'

'Just let me go,' pleaded Drake. 'Please.'

'Don't you want me to tell you where he is?'

Drake nodded.

'I will, but first you have to pay for the information. Payment is in fingers.' He touched each finger on Drake's right hand with the point of the blade. 'Don't worry, I know what I'm doing. Did you know that I used to be a chef?'

Tears sprang into Drake's eyes and he couldn't stop them. He was ashamed now. Ashamed of how frightened he was. Ashamed that despite all his efforts, he still hadn't been able to save Vijay. Ashamed that he wasn't willing to sacrifice even a single finger to save his best friend's life.

'Your friend isn't dead,' said Stewart. 'Not yet. You could still rescue him. We just have to agree on payment. I think three is a fair number, all things considered.'

'No,' begged Drake.

'Perhaps you're right,' agreed Stewart. 'He's probably not worth any fingers, is he? That rat-faced heap of dirt, poking his nose into things that don't concern him. He got what he deserved, didn't he?'

'Yes,' breathed Drake.

'Say it louder.'

'Yes.'

Drake's hand was suddenly free. The weight that had pressed down on him lifted and Mr Stewart stood up. He sheathed the knife and pulled out his gun again. 'I'm going to go now,' he said, pointing the revolver at Drake. 'And if you try to follow me, I'll put a bullet in your head. Got it?'

'Yeah.'

'Good.'

Stewart began to leave, but a voice called out to him from above. 'Oh, you're not leaving already, are you? I was just enjoying the show.'

Drake looked up. Standing on top of the brick wall was a man dressed in a formal dark suit. His silver hair was slicked back to one side. Drake goggled at him in disbelief. It was Mr Canning, his old headmaster from Manor Road school. He wore a black patch over one eye.

'You!' bellowed Stewart. 'What are you doing here?'

'I was just passing, and stopped to watch,' said Mr Canning. 'I was hoping to see some fingers.'

'Yeah, well the show wasn't for your benefit.'

'Apparently not.'

'So clear off,' shouted Stewart. 'I hope I never see you again.' He turned to leave.

The headmaster flew from the wall in a dark blur. Drake could hardly believe that the old man could move so quickly. He covered the distance between himself and Mr Stewart in no time and dived on top of his victim, dragging him to the ground.

The gun went off, but was quickly tossed to one side as the headmaster folded Mr Stewart's arms tightly behind his back. Drake winced at the crunching sound they made.

Stewart screamed. 'My arms! You broke my arms!'

Mr Canning squatted on top of his victim like a ghoul about to feast. 'You promised me fingers,' he said. 'And gave me nothing. So now I'm here to take some arms instead.'

The scream that followed was like nothing Drake had ever heard. He turned away as the headmaster delivered on his gruesome threat. Tearing sounds joined with the screams and Drake clapped his hands to his ears to block them out. But even with his ears covered and his eyes screwed tightly shut, he couldn't avoid the spatters of blood that rained down on him as he cowered.

A minute or two passed and the sounds came to an end. Drake unclasped his hands from his head, but he didn't dare open his eyes. He lay still, hoping desperately that the headmaster would ignore him.

The quiet tread of footsteps approached. 'Two arms and two legs,' said Mr Canning. 'I think that was fair payment, don't you?'

Drake didn't think. He pretended to be dead. He almost wished he was.

'I've been wanting to do that for a long time,' continued the headmaster. 'That man really was a loathsome individual.'

Drake said nothing. He didn't move. He didn't react in any way.

'I'll say farewell now, Drake. I'd like to stay and chat, maybe reminisce about the good old days at school, but you know how it is. I do hope you manage to find your friend.'

Drake breathed quietly, allowing himself a tiny glimmer of hope. Might he somehow survive this encounter? Against all the odds, was he actually going to get up and walk away from his place?

He heard the click of a gun behind him. 'Don't move,' said a new voice. 'Neither of you move a single muscle. Don't even try to breathe.'

Chapter Ninety

Kevin held the gun in his shaking hand as steadily as he could. He was surprised how well he managed, given what he'd just witnessed.

He was none too fond of surprises. Life had served him far too many over the years, and they were usually of the nasty variety. This latest one had proved to be no exception to the rule. A man being torn limb from limb, that was how the expression went. He'd never thought to see it happen for real.

So, Canning was a werewolf. Kevin hadn't seen that one coming. But it explained the man's grisly death grip. He swallowed hard as he realized just how much worse his own close encounter with the headmaster might have been, and he was suddenly very relieved that he'd agreed to hand over his two Enfield revolvers without a struggle.

The Baikal quivered a little in his hand, but at a range of six feet that shouldn't be a problem, even given the dodgy nature of the weapon. He'd have felt more comfortable with the L1A1 rifle he'd carried when he served in the army. Good old-fashioned British engineering beat this bastardized contraption that had been cobbled together in some back-street workshop. But a bullet in the back of the head should finish off a werewolf, no matter the heritage of the gun that fired it, and no matter how much his arm trembled.

At least, he hoped it would.

'Ah, Kevin,' said Mr Canning. 'How nice to see you again.'

'Shut it, Canning,' said Kevin. 'No weasel words from you.' He wouldn't let himself be fooled by the smooth-talking git. 'And don't move,' he added as the man began to turn to face him. 'Stay exactly where you are, and don't say nothing.'

'My lips are as good as sealed,' said Canning pleasantly.

Kevin was nervous about using the gun. This would be the first time he'd had to fire the damn thing and he couldn't afford to miss. He might only get once chance. He stepped forward and held the gun to the back of the man's head, but his arm shook so violently he was worried he might miss even at this range. And that would hand the initiative to his opponent. He'd seen just how quickly the man could move.

'Are you keeping well, Kevin?' inquired Canning.

'Yeah,' said Kevin. 'Going great guns.' He gripped the Baikal, trying to keep it steady, but his damn hand kept moving around like one of those stupid nodding dogs some people put in their cars.

'What are you waiting for?' asked the teenage boy crouched on the ground beside the headmaster. 'Shoot him already!'

Kevin glanced briefly at him. He'd seen the kid before, working for the Watch. One of Jack Stewart's little thugs. Ripped jeans and a black T-shirt; cropped blonde hair, and a sullen scowl on his face. Drake, the kid was called. Kevin never forgot a name.

'Have you two met before?' asked Canning. 'Drake used to be one of my pupils at Manor Road. Not the best student in his year, I'm afraid, but he seems to be quite handy with a knife. Drake, this is Kevin, a very good acquaintance of mine. Why don't you say hello?'

The boy got up and wandered over to Jack Stewart's body. Or rather, the location of most of the body. Other parts were scattered around a wide area. Kevin thought the boy would gag, but instead he knelt down and started rummaging through the dead man's pockets.

'What are you doing?' asked Kevin.

'Looking for something,' said Drake.

'Perhaps I can help in some way?' suggested Mr Canning.

'Don't you move a muscle,' said Kevin. 'What are you looking for?' he asked Drake.

'A clue. My friend's gone missing. I think Jack Stewart must have locked him up somewhere. He told me Vijay was still alive.' The kid pulled various items from the dead man's pockets, but none of them seemed to hold much interest for him. Then he found something he obviously liked the look of. He stood up holding a bunch of keys. 'This must be it,' he said.

'What?' asked Kevin.

The kid was examining each key in turn. 'Shit,' he swore. 'So many keys. If Vijay is locked up somewhere, the key must be here, yeah? But which one? And where is the lock that it opens, anyway?'

'Dunno,' said Kevin. He had no idea which locks those keys might fit. He had never heard of anyone called Vijay either.

Drake hurled the keys to the ground in frustration. 'Shit. This is hopeless. Now that Mr Stewart's dead, how am I ever gonna find Vijay?'

'Dunno,' said Kevin again. He returned his attention to his real problem.

Lycanthropic

Mr Canning smiled back at him. 'I believe I may be able to assist. I happen to know exactly where Vijay is.' He tapped his nose. 'Knowledge can be vital. That's why a good education is so important, don't you agree?'

Chapter Ninety-One

High Street, Brixton Hill, South London, full moon

Mihai could smell smoke. He wrinkled his nose and sniffed again to make sure. Yes, there it was. Smoke.

Usually when he smelled smoke in the house it meant that Grandpa Kevin was being naughty and smoking indoors. Liz was always rowing with him about that. But Kevin had gone out.

Mihai didn't like the smell of smoke. If Kevin was out, smoke meant fire. And fire had nearly killed him once before, at the centre for asylum seekers. Liz had rescued him that time, but now Liz was not here. He ran up to the top floor of the house and looked out.

There. To the north. Smoke was billowing over the rooftops in thick black clouds. It was hard to see where it was coming from. But that much smoke must mean a big fire. A bigger fire than he had ever seen before.

He ran back down to the middle floor to find Samantha. She was propped up in bed as usual, reading a book with Lily.

He waved his arms and panted breathlessly. 'Is fire. Is very big fire. Must get out. Now.'

Samantha stared back at him in amazement. 'A fire? Are you sure? What does Kevin say?'

'Kevin gone. Is just us. Must leave right now.'

His English had gone bad because of the danger. It was always bad, but was worse now. English was such a hard language, full of tricks and traps. But he was pretty sure he'd made his point clearly enough.

Samantha didn't question him again. She closed the book and held Lily tightly by the hand. 'We're going to go outside and find somewhere safe to wait for Daddy,' she said. 'Can you be brave and not cry?'

Lily nodded solemnly. 'Will Daddy come and rescue us?'

'Yes. And Liz too. But first Mihai is going to help us get out of the house. Mummy can't walk very well, so you have to be brave and go with Mihai. Is that all right, Mihai?'

'Is good,' he said. 'Come on, Lily.' He held out his hand and the girl came to him, carrying a toy elephant.

Samantha struggled to lower herself out of the bed. Mihai went to help her, but she shook her head. 'You look after Lily. I can do this myself.' She swung her legs over the edge and lowered her feet to the floor.

Mihai didn't think she'd get far like that. 'Hurry, please,' he urged.

'Take Lily to safety. I'll follow as quickly as I can.'

Reluctantly he led the girl downstairs and out of the front door, stopping to collect the travelling bags they'd prepared earlier. He slung his own rucksack over his shoulder and helped Lily to strap hers on too. Her backpack was pink with a cute pony on it.

Outside the wind was gusting viciously. Smoke was

already filling the air around the house. Lily breathed it in and coughed. 'Wait here,' Mihai told her. He dashed back inside and grabbed two hand towels. He ran them under cold water and wrung them dry. 'I am tying this around your mouth and nose,' he told Lily. 'Keep smoke away.'

She waited patiently as he tied it around her and did the same for himself. 'Where is Mummy?' she asked him.

He glanced back inside, but there was no sign of Samantha yet. 'Is following us. Is very close. Don't worry.'

He looked up and down the street, but it was hard to tell which way led to safety. There was smoke at both ends. But there was no time to delay. 'Come on,' he said. 'We go this way.'

Chapter Ninety-Two

Holland Gardens, Kensington, London, full moon

Warg Daddy descended into the basement garage of the house in Kensington. Like every part of the multi-million-pound house it was perfectly crafted for its purpose. Smooth, dark grey walls, discreet overhead lighting, granite flooring – understated and luxurious at the same time. It was the only garage he had ever seen that didn't have oil leaks pooled on the floor and dirty rags tossed into all the corners.

His bike had been stored here since before the fighting had begun. With automated number plate recognition technology all over London, it had long been too risky to use his favourite mode of transport. The beauty had been locked inside the underground garage like a caged beast.

He crossed the smooth stone flooring, the tapping of his boots echoing noisily off the hard surfaces of the underground chamber. The bike was where he had parked it, weeks previously, perfectly preserved within the air-conditioned space, as if time had stood still.

His eyes drank in its shiny metal parts, lingering on the curves of the gas tank, following the line of the exhaust pipe with its muffler removed. He allowed his hand to slowly stroke the rear shock absorbers, running his fingers up the gleaming spring forks and across the single glass eye of the headlight. He admired the mechanical beauty of its brake rods, its gear shift and voltage regulator.

He loved this bike more than life itself. He wondered how he could have allowed events to come between him and his first love.

A machine like this should not be kept indoors. It craved freedom. It needed tarmac rolling beneath its deep balloon tyres, laying down rubber on the open road. Fast on the straight, smoking around corners, gulping down fresh, clean air through its intake duct and trailing black exhaust to show the world where it had been.

Cooped up inside, its engine silenced, was no way to be treated.

Warg Daddy needed to taste true freedom too, before he forgot how it felt.

Leanna had chained him like a dog.

He had loved her once, and she had told him that she'd loved him too, whispering silken promises to him in the night. But he had allowed her to delude him. She wasn't capable of love, only of deceit. She had stood behind him, pulling strings to make her puppet move.

Leanna had been cruel from the very beginning, faking attraction to make him into her fool. Her caresses had always been cold, her eyes like ice, her words thorns. Now that he had given her what she wanted, she barely even kept up the pretence of being a lover. He would leave her without regret. He would feel the wind and the rain whipping his face again, the throb of the twin cam engine between his thighs, the pistons firing as he opened up the throttle to a roar.

Out of his jacket pocket he pulled the pills Leanna had given him.

He hadn't swallowed them.

In his pre-werewolf days, Warg Daddy had acquired hands-on experience with a wide range of pharmaceuticals. He knew his pills and he didn't like the look of these.

They were the bitterest pills of all.

By giving him the poison, Leanna had granted him a kind of freedom, he supposed. But death wasn't the kind of freedom he wanted.

She had betrayed him, and he should feel anger. By rights he ought to seek revenge. But Warg Daddy wasn't like Leanna, who had made herself a slave to vengeance. He had no appetite for feuding. In the old days, he'd seen it swallow up whole gangs of bikers. *You killed one of ours. We took one of yours in reply. Then you killed another. We will take another life too.* Vengeance was stupid. It left only the Grim Reaper claiming victory.

Warg Daddy bore no grudges. He dropped the pills to the granite floor and crushed them into white powder beneath the heel of his boot.

He rubbed his fingers across the bike's leather seat. The time had come for the Brothers to ride again. This time Vixen would ride with him. With one strong arm he would scoop her up to ride bitch behind him, the white wolf on his jacket grinning at her as she hugged herself close. Her own white wolf would lead the Brothers as they rode together.

Where they would ride, he didn't know. That was the true meaning of freedom. The adventure of the unknown, the uncut deck of cards, the anticipation of rolling the dice and spinning the roulette wheel. When you handed yourself over to fortune, anything could happen, and that's what Warg Daddy craved.

One thing was sure though – once he had left, he would never return.

He would always be grateful to Leanna for making him

into a werewolf, despite the headaches that refused to leave him, despite her cruel parting gift. Meeting her, kicking off the apocalypse, and becoming commander-in-chief of the Wolf Army had been the greatest adventure of his life. It had been a blast.

But the time for that was over.

He had already given his orders to the Wolf Army. Not the orders Leanna expected. He would not lead them into a final battle tonight. Instead he had told them to leave, to go and claim their freedom, just like him.

Now it was time to gather what remained of the Brothers. It was time for them to ride again. Where he led, they would follow. He may no longer be the Wolf Army's commander-in-chief but he would always be Leader of the Pack.

Chapter Ninety-Three

Electric Avenue, Brixton, South London, full moon

Liz was returning to the patrol car with Dean when someone shouted her name. She looked up and saw three people she had never expected to meet here today.

Drake was leading the way and was the one who had called her name. She hadn't seen him since the night of the New Year's Eve riot in Battersea. Behind him came someone she'd hoped never to encounter again – Mr Canning, the headmaster. And bringing up the rear of the strange trio was someone who really ought not to be here at all. Someone who'd sworn he would stay at home and take care of Samantha, Lily and Mihai.

'Kevin!' she bellowed angrily. 'What the hell are you doing here? You promised me you wouldn't leave the house.'

'Uh, yeah, sorry about that,' he muttered. 'But it's lucky

I did. I rescued this kid.'

She saw now that he had a gun aimed at the back of Mr Canning's head. Had he also broken his earlier promise to her, to hand over the stolen guns to the police? She could barely suppress her anger at his irresponsibility. 'Put that weapon down,' she told him. 'You could kill someone.'

He kept the gun pointed at the headmaster. 'I'd already be dead if I didn't have it,' he said. 'And so would this kid.'

'That's right,' said Drake. 'It's true.'

'I honestly didn't intend to harm either of you,' said Mr Canning. 'I was just on my way somewhere else.'

'We don't have time for this,' said Dean. 'We have to get back to Samantha and Lily. And Mihai, too. They're on their own, and this fire is spreading rapidly.' He pulled open the door of the patrol car. 'Come on, Kevin. Come back with us.'

'No!' yelled Drake. 'You have to stay and help. We have to save Vijay.'

'Vijay?' said Liz. 'What's happened to him?' The Sikh boy had left a strong impression on her when he and Drake had first told her about their encounter with the killer headmaster. If only she had believed their story at the time, she could have saved the lives of several children. If Vijay was in trouble now, she owed him her help.

'I don't know where he is,' said Drake. 'He disappeared a few days ago. I think that Jack Stewart locked him up somewhere. Mr Canning says he knows where.'

'It's a trick,' said Kevin. 'He only says that because I have a gun pointed at his head.'

'We have to trust him,' said Drake. 'It's Vijay's only chance.'

Corporal Jones was observing the exchange with interest. 'I'm missing a couple of things here,' he said. 'Liz, help me understand. Why is this man, Kevin, holding a gun to this other man's head? And one other thing. Is there some chance you two are related?'

'It's complicated,' said Liz.

The Dogman moved to stand next to Jones, with Rock on his lead. The dog put its nose to the ground and began sniffing. Liz stepped to one side, keeping well away from the animal. But soon it picked up a scent and started switching its head from side to side, searching for the trail. 'What is it, Rock?' asked the Dogman. 'What is it, boy?'

'What's up?' asked Jones. 'What's he found?'

Rock dashed forward eagerly, pulling the Dogman close behind, and stopped in front of Mr Canning. Immediately the dog began to bark madly. It rose up onto its hind legs and placed its forepaws against the headmaster. Its tail flapped back and forth in a blur. The animal's barking was deafening.

Liz stepped back again, putting as much distance as she could between herself and the dog.

The Dogman hauled Rock back with difficulty. 'Sir, we've found ourselves another werewolf.'

Four of the soldiers immediately raised their weapons and took aim.

'Please restrain that wild beast,' said Mr Canning. 'And put those guns down. If you wanted to know that I'm a werewolf, you had only to ask politely. Several people here already knew.' He locked eyes with Liz and she looked away.

'Intriguing,' said Jones. 'You keep strange company, Liz. So this man – this *werewolf* – knows where the boy Vijay is being kept, right?'

'That's what he claims,' said Kevin.

'Then what are we waiting for?' asked Jones.

'I'm so glad you asked,' said Mr Canning. 'We just need to agree on one thing before I agree to help you. My reward.'

'Your what?' said Kevin incredulously.

Jones indicated the four soldiers whose rifles were still pointed at the headmaster. 'Your reward? You should be begging for your life.'

Mr Canning smiled broadly. 'Begging isn't my style. But

yes, my life is what I demand in return for my help. Is it such a lot to ask?'

Jones turned to Liz. 'Can we trust him?'

'Not a chance,' she said.

'Please,' begged Drake. 'Vijay will die if we don't rescue him.'

'Show us where he is,' said Liz to the headmaster. 'If he's still alive, you can walk free. But try anything funny, and you'll be dead before you can say *lycanthropic*.'

Chapter Ninety-Four

Virginia Water, Surrey, full moon

James stood in line with the others, waiting to leave the city behind and head out into the countryside. Soldiers had set up barriers on all the roads leading out of London and were inspecting everyone as they went through. The lines of people crawled slowly and they had already been waiting nearly an hour to pass through the checkpoint.

He cast a nervous glance at the skyline. It was not yet dark, but already he could feel the pull of the moon. It had been drawing him steadily on throughout the day, tugging gently at every cell in his body. The wolf blood flowed through his veins, and wolf thoughts fluttered through his mind like whispers in the dark. He drew the winter coat around his neck and wrapped the woollen scarf close. He ought to have worn a hat, or some kind of hood to protect him. If he could block out the light of the moon when it came, perhaps he had a chance of resisting its lure.

Or was he fooling himself? Even now, the moon murmured softly to him, making promises of the violence to come.

'No,' he muttered. 'No. I won't do it.'

The man standing just in front of him turned around and stared. He too had long hair, but his hair was dark and unwashed. Black whiskers covered half his face. His nose was broad and animal-like.

James refused to meet his gaze. He knew what that man was.

A wolf, like me.

The man winked at James and chuckled. James ignored him.

'What's that man laughing at?' asked Melanie. 'What's the matter with him?'

Don't you know? thought James. *Isn't it obvious?*

She must surely know that the man was a werewolf. It was as clear as day. And it must be equally apparent to everyone here that James was a werewolf too. He had been a fool to come here. He would be discovered and caught. The soldiers would shoot him.

'I don't know what that guy's problem is,' said Ben, 'but if he causes any trouble I'm going to have a word with him.'

'Be careful,' said Melanie. 'He looks rough.'

They don't know he's a werewolf. They can't see what I see. They can't smell him either.

So perhaps James would be safe after all, just as long as he didn't draw attention to himself. He pulled his long scarf closer.

'I hope they don't want to see passports or ID,' said Ben. 'I lost mine back in Brixton.'

'I just wish they'd hurry up,' said Melanie. She wrapped her arms around Sarah, who was leaning against her, pressing her face against her sister's shoulder. James could smell the dread leaching from Sarah's pores. He wished he could do something to soothe her, but Melanie seemed to have the situation in hand.

Just lie low. Don't draw any attention.

The line began to shuffle forward again and they all moved along. It wasn't far now. The bright search beams of the checkpoint were clearly visible up ahead. Another ten or fifteen minutes and they would be through. He peered up at the sky. It was darkening quickly. But still the moon stayed out of sight.

Up ahead a dog barked. It was quickly joined by more.

'What's that?' asked Melanie. 'Can you see what's happening?'

The dogs began to bark frantically.

Ben stood on tiptoes, taking advantage of his height to peer over the heads of the people in front. 'They're using dogs to search people at the barrier. They seem to have found something.'

The man with the black beard turned back to James and shot him a worried look. James ignored him and tried to see what was happening at the checkpoint. The soldiers had separated a young woman from the rest of the group and were leading her away from the road. The dogs were barking madly after her. The soldiers and the woman disappeared. A moment later there were shouts and the sound of automatic gunfire.

'Jesus,' said Ben. 'They just shot that woman dead.'

'Maybe the dogs can smell the werewolves,' suggested Melanie.

'Or maybe they're just trigger-happy and frightened out of their wits.'

The people waiting behind them began to shove and jostle. Voices cried out. Some of the people were backing away from the checkpoint, others were pushing forward to see what was happening.

'They're going to start a riot if they're not careful,' said Ben.

The crowd began driving forward in a steady stream toward the barrier, and the soldiers fired warning shots into the air. 'Please remain calm,' pleaded a voice over a loudspeaker. 'You will all be processed as quickly as possible.'

The words didn't seem to calm the crowd in the slightest.

'I'm not sure we want to be *processed*,' said Ben.

James came to a decision. 'You'll all be safe,' he said. 'But I can't go through the barrier. They'll find me using the dogs, and then they'll shoot me.'

'Then let's get out of here,' said Ben. 'Quickly.' The crowd began surging forward. They would soon be at the checkpoint.

'No,' said James. 'You go on without me. I'll find my own way out.'

'We can't just leave you behind.'

'You have to.'

'Wait,' said Melanie. 'I have an idea.' She reached inside her bag and brought out a small glass bottle.

'What's that?' asked Ben.

'Chanel No. 5.'

Ben stared at her. 'You must be the only person here who thought of packing perfume in a survival kit.'

'It's a timeless classic. I wouldn't be without it.' She sprayed the perfume over James, dousing his hair and beard. 'Take your coat off. I want to cover you thoroughly with this.'

He did as she asked and stood while she covered him from head to toe in scent.

'Let's see what those dogs make of you now,' she said.

The dog handlers were coming down the line already, the dogs pulling at their leads, sniffing enthusiastically.

The bearded man in front grabbed hold of James. 'Help me,' he pleaded. 'You have to help. Let me have some of that perfume.'

James shook him off. 'I don't know what you're talking about.'

The dogs came closer. One of them ran forward, its

nose to the ground. It came to James and snuffled at his trousers.

'Shoo,' shouted Melanie. 'Bad dog!' She nudged it with her leather boot.

The dog cowered back, dropped its front paws to the ground, then turned its attention to the man with the beard. It seemed to find what it was looking for. It twitched its ears flat and wrinkled back its lips, exposing canine teeth. A rough growl issued from its throat and then it was barking almost in the man's face, straining against its leash. Its handler could barely keep it from springing.

The man darted away from the animal, but the crowd was too thick for him to run. Instead he plucked a child from the crowd, wrestling the small boy from his mother's grasp, and held him tightly to his chest. 'Get back!' he screamed at the soldiers. 'Back off, or I bite.' He held the child's neck close to his mouth, showing clean and unusually long teeth. 'Just one bite from me and the boy's as good as dead.'

Four of the soldiers took up position around him, two standing, two kneeling, their rifles in firing position. 'We are authorized to use lethal force against known or suspected lycanthropes,' shouted one of the soldiers.

'Let me pass,' demanded the man. 'The boy's life in exchange for my freedom.'

'Request denied. Prepare to fire.'

'No!' James couldn't watch any longer. The man was willing to kill. The soldiers were ready to shoot. Either way the boy would die.

He acted without thinking.

Chapter Ninety-Five

Electric Avenue, Brixton, South London, full moon

Liz bundled the headmaster into the back of the patrol car and climbed in beside him. She had already cuffed his hands behind his back, but she couldn't be confident that would be enough to hold a werewolf. She held the Glock to his head. 'One wrong move and I'll shoot.'

'I can hardly move at all,' moaned Mr Canning, squirming in the seat. 'This is most uncomfortable.'

'Stop wriggling and we'll both be a lot more comfy.'

Dean was already in the driver's seat, ready to set off. 'We don't have time for this,' he grumbled. 'We have to get back to the house.'

'Please,' begged Liz. 'We can't leave Vijay to die.' The fire had taken hold of a large number of buildings now and was spreading quickly. It seemed that no one was even trying to extinguish the flames.

Kevin climbed into the car from the other side and Drake jumped into the front passenger seat. 'Come on,' he said. 'Let's get going.'

'It's not far,' said the headmaster. 'I'll give you directions.'

They drove off, the Land Rover and the Foxhound close behind.

As Mr Canning had promised, they didn't have far to travel. Soon they arrived at a row of lock-up garages behind the main shopping street. They looked half derelict and Liz wondered if her father was right and this was just a trick.

'Just a little further along here,' said Mr Canning, peering carefully at the garage doors with their peeling grey paint and splashes of rust beneath. They all looked the same to Liz. 'That one,' shouted the headmaster, and Dean pulled the car to a halt.

'All right,' said Liz, motioning with the gun. 'Out you get.'

They gathered in front of the door the headmaster had indicated. 'You're sure this is the one?' asked Liz.

'Positive. Will you release me now?'

'No way. Not until we find Vijay, alive and safe.'

Drake rushed to the door and began banging it with his fist. 'Vijay? Vijay, mate, are you in there? Can you hear me?'

There was no response.

'The bastard's lying,' said Kevin. 'I told you he was just playing for time.'

Time was something that they definitely didn't have a lot of. Sparks from the burning buildings nearby were already flying toward them. Scraps of cardboard, discarded pizza boxes and fast food wrappers began to catch the flames. The air in the alleyway was filling with smoke and Liz could feel the heat from the fire on her exposed skin.

'This is where Jack Stewart brought him,' insisted the headmaster. 'I can't vouch for the boy's health. He's been locked in there for some time. I suggest you open the door quickly.'

'Where are the keys?' asked Liz.

'I dropped them,' said Drake miserably. 'I took a bunch of keys from Jack Stewart, but I threw them away. I'm so stupid.'

A deep voice rumbled in Liz's ear. 'Locked door, no problem,' said Corporal Jones. 'We can sort that soon enough.' He called to the soldiers in the Foxhound. 'Put a hook on this door and rip the damn thing off!'

The troops got on with the job without delay. They quickly attached one end of a metal chain to the garage door and the other end to the armoured truck.

Jones slapped the side of the vehicle. 'Take it away, boys.'

The engine of the Foxhound coughed noisily into life and began belching smoke from its exhaust. Evans slid the vehicle into reverse and started driving backward. Very soon the chain became taught.

'Keep going!' yelled Jones.

The engine of the Foxhound roared and the garage door began to strain. The metal creaked loudly and twisted, making an inch-wide gap top and bottom. Evans stepped his foot down and the wheels of the armoured vehicle began to spin.

'Wait!' shouted the corporal.

The Foxhound's engine dropped a little and the tyres found their grip again. This time Evans held the engine steady as it pulled the steel door slowly open. The metal shook and buckled as the vehicle inched back. Thirty seconds later there was enough room to crawl beneath it.

Drake was the first inside, ducking under the warped steel, and Liz was right behind him. They searched the darkness of the garage building, using Drake's mobile phone screen and Liz's flashlight.

'Vijay!' shouted Drake desperately. 'Where are you?'

'There,' said Liz, pointing at a heap of rags in the

corner. She ran over and found Vijay, lying on the rough concrete floor, a dust sheet wrapped around his thin body.

Drake crouched down next to her. 'Is he alive?'

'I don't know.' She held her hand over the boy's chest, feeling for the rise and fall that would indicate breathing. If there was any movement, it was too weak to detect. She touched his wrist with her fingertips to feel for a pulse. She could feel nothing.

'He's dead,' wailed Drake. 'It's all my fault.'

'Ssh.' Liz carefully lifted one of Vijay's eyelids and shone the torch at his eye. The pupil quickly constricted. 'He's alive,' she said.

Vijay opened both eyes wide and gasped. He stared at Liz and Drake in amazement, then opened his mouth to speak. A tiny croak was all that emerged.

'What's he saying?' asked Drake. 'What is it, mate?'

Vijay's lips moved once more. 'Rose,' he muttered. 'Must find Rose.' Then his eyes dimmed and slowly closed.

Chapter Ninety-Six

Virginia Water, Surrey, full moon

The dark-haired man clasped the boy tightly to his chest. James whipped out an arm and struck him in the mouth. His fingers uncurled instinctively, and his sharp nails caught the man's flesh, making droplets of blood fly.

The man spun toward him, his face registering astonishment and anger in equal weight. 'You!' he cried. He stumbled back to regain his balance, clutching the boy tight.

The rifles of the soldiers tracked him as he shifted.

The boy burst into tears as the man hauled him. He was just a toddler, no more than four years old. His eyes were windows into pure terror. The boy's mother screamed as her child flailed uselessly, his short legs kicking to no effect.

James sprang forward again, placing his own body between the boy and the soldiers' guns. He flung himself at the man, grasping his head between his thumbs and forefingers. The man was helpless to fight back with his arms wrapped around his hostage. He snarled and spat as James pressed hard against his temples.

The soldiers fanned out, seeking a clear shot. They shouted instructions to each other, and bellowed warnings at James, but he took no notice. He mustn't think about them now.

The man kicked James away, but he sprang back, returning to the fray. He dug his fingernails into the man's arms, trying to peel them from the boy, but they held fast like steel. He couldn't shift them.

The boy wriggled and kicked. His mother screamed again.

'Fire when ready!' ordered one of the soldiers.

James shifted his grip back to the man's head, pressing harder this time, squeezing his thumbs up against the man's skull. His opponent gritted his teeth, letting out a blood-curdling shriek of rage and pain. James continued to dig. His nails burrowed deeply, spreading red smears over skin. Still the man held on.

In desperation James kicked out. The man dodged the blow, lurching wildly to one side and spinning out of James' grasp. James fell on him again, making a grab for the man's neck. His arms locked together and he began to squeeze. Slowly he applied more pressure, making the man gasp for breath.

The man's grip on the child was weakening. James squeezed with all his strength until a sudden movement told him that the boy was free.

Now the man turned his full force against James, fighting back with inhuman strength. Fingers like steel rods dug into James' shoulders. A kick to the groin made him almost scream in agony.

But still he held on.

The man fell on him, pushing him down, and smashing him back against the hard ground. His grip on the man's neck loosened and failed. Heavy punches began to rain down on him. Each blow fell harder than the one before, smashing, pounding, rending skin and crunching bone. James' head lolled back and he lay prone on the ground, unable to defend himself from the close quarter assault. Still more blows fell against his head, neck and chest.

The relentless pummelling of fist against flesh was broken by a scream like a squealing cat. The sound was followed by a heavy smack as Melanie's boot connected with the side of the man's head. 'Take that, you louse,' she shrieked. 'And this.' A blur of red leather flashed through the air and her fist drew a small river of blood from the man's nose.

The man ceased his punching. Then his whole head jerked back as Melanie twisted his ragged hair into a knot and tugged with all her strength. The weight lifted from James' chest and he struggled onto his knees.

Then a crack like shattering rocks rang out at close quarters, rapidly followed by two more. The man jerked and spasmed, then crashed back down on top of James, blood sprouting from holes in his head and neck. The smell of blood filled James' nostrils and roused his hunger, but he fought back the urge to swallow it down.

One of the soldiers kicked the fresh corpse away with his foot. He was livid. He seemed not to care whether James was hurt. Instead he crouched down and bellowed into his face. 'You nearly got yourself killed. That was a stupid, reckless act, boy.'

'But a bloody brave one,' said his colleague.

The first soldier glared at him. 'Go on, get out of here,' he yelled.

James picked himself from the ground and checked for injuries. Miraculously he had come away from the fight without any serious damage. The little boy was back in the safety of his mother's arms and seemed unhurt.

Melanie seized James' arm and pulled him forward. 'Come on, let's go.' She dragged him toward the checkpoint. The crowds were stampeding now, and all efforts to control the flood of people were finished. The barrier was raised and the mob ran beneath it as one.

Melanie held on tight to James and Sarah, and Ben followed immediately in their wake. Soon the checkpoint, the soldiers and their dogs were well behind them. 'We made it,' gasped Ben.

A group of three buses awaited them ahead. More soldiers had been deployed to guide people on board. 'This way,' they directed. 'You, go that way.' More buses were arriving to take the evacuees away.

'We must stick together,' said Ben.

'Keep holding hands,' said Melanie, clutching James tight. 'Don't let them separate us.'

James let her pull him along like a bobbing cork. He had lost any ability to make his own decision. They joined a queue for the nearest of the three buses and waited to board. 'Where are you taking us?' Melanie asked a soldier.

'Somewhere safe. I don't know any more than you do.'

She continued to ask more questions, but James no longer heard her. His whole body was starting to pulse with a new energy. The fire that burned clean was ready to ignite once more.

He knew this sensation well. He had longed for it once, then had learned to fear it. Now he felt neither dread nor desire. He was simply walking down a well-trodden path toward the inevitable.

The earthly chaos that surrounded him drew back and fell silent as he contemplated the unfolding heavens above. The moon rode high: silvery and magical and filled with utmost beauty. She was called the queen of night, the two-horned queen of the stars. The ancients had worshipped her as she crossed the night sky in her chariot of lustrous metal. The glimmering orb gathered steadily in strength as the sun bowed low toward the horizon. A cold, pure light spread across the world, most pleasing to his eye. And then that light touched his face, almost blinding him with wonderment, and he felt the familiar change begin to take hold.

This time it was different. It seized him with a grip of steel, dragging him into beast form without mercy, smothering any last remnants of humanity. He knew immediately that this would not be like last time when he had fought Leanna to save his friends; nor like before when he had killed a madman to free Melanie from captivity. This time he was becoming a creature of the night, heartless and cruel, and he could do nothing to stop it.

'Go,' he forced himself to whisper to Melanie. 'Flee!'

But still her warm hand held his.

He jerked free of her grip. 'Run from me!' he shouted as the transformation unfolded. The change came faster than he had ever known. Clothing ripped and fell away in strips as his body swelled and his muscles filled with new-found power. His skin tingled and pricked and a new coat of golden hair knitted closely around him. His nails sprouted into long, sharp talons. He flashed them before her like blades, to show her what he had become. 'Be gone!' he roared in a voice that was no longer his own.

But still she did not run. 'I am not afraid,' she said.

He roared in despair as teeth twisted through gums and his mouth flooded with blood. His vision turned yellow. He was fully wolf now, and could not hold back his true nature. He wanted to tell her that this time the moon was his mistress, that he could not refrain from killing, but all that came from his mouth was the deep-throated bellowing of a beast. He dropped to all fours and prowled around her.

Ben grabbed at her, pulling her away. 'Come on, Melanie. Run!' But she would not.

James screamed in frustration, rising to his full height, towering over her. He was losing himself, forgetting that he had once been human. He sniffed the air, breathing in her scent. It was the rich scent of prey.

She should have run, but instead she came forward again, wearing a foolish smile. She should have listened to Ben, who had warned her so many times that werewolves were dangerous. Instead, she had learned to trust him too much.

The sweet smell of her flesh was overpowering. James opened his mouth wide, dripping drool, hungering for her meat. Then, with a mighty effort he threw himself away from her and began to run.

Shouts and screams followed him as he fled. He dared not look back. A rifle cracked, and then another, and a bullet whickered past, just inches from his running form. He still had the sense to zig and zag as he ran, but whether it was human intelligence or wolf cunning he could no longer tell. His paws carried him on, putting distance behind him, and eventually he became aware that the rifle shots had ceased.

Still he ran. He reached light woodland and dashed through ferns and brambles. The canopies of trees closed over him, knitting themselves together and bringing darkness to the forest floor as he moved deeper into the trees. His legs knew no tiredness and he began to feel free again. He knew that he had lost something, but he could hardly remember what.

I lost my friends.

But they were meat, nothing but prey to be slaughtered. He would find more prey soon.

I lost my humanity.

But he couldn't explain what that was, or why he should regret its passing.

I lost my faith.

That brought him up short. His wolf brain grappled with a strange word from his past.

God. I lost my faith in God.

He didn't know what that meant, except that it made him angry.

God betrayed you, whispered the silent moon. *God*

abandoned you.

He crashed through the undergrowth into a thicket and came upon a fallow deer. The creature stood tall amid the shadows, its antlers echoing the shape of the trees above. Wide and ungainly, they lent the creature a quiet dignity. The deer was startled by his entrance and sprang away, but he leapt and caught it with his front claws, bringing it to the ground. His jaws closed around its neck and his teeth plunged deep, almost severing its neck in a single bite. Blood flooded his senses and he swallowed it in a frenzy. The thoughts that had disturbed him earlier quickly faded away. With every bite of meat his mind became clearer.

Once, he had been haunted by ideas of justice and conscience; of loyalty and love. He had struggled to do the right thing, even though the path to truth had been perpetually shrouded in mystery. His battle with his conscience had almost broken him. Now the moon had saved him from that exhausting struggle and his life would be much simpler. He was pure wolf now, a creature of darkest night. And he knew that when daylight came, he would stay a wolf, forever. He would never be human again.

He finished his meal then rose to his haunches and howled. The moon smiled down at him through the broken roof of branches, bathing him with its shining power.

I am your god now, the cold light told him. *I am your faith and your conscience and your only companion, and you will do as I command.*

He threw his paws against a trunk and rolled his head back. He howled once more, a cry of ecstasy and abandon. The moon spoke truth. This thicket was his altar; the darkened sky his cathedral. The light that shone overhead was his sacred scripture.

Willingly he pledged himself to the moon. With razor tooth and bloody claw he swore his oath.

Chapter Ninety-Seven

Brixton, South London, full moon

'No,' wailed Drake. 'He's dead. Vijay is dead!'
'Be quiet,' ordered Liz. 'Help me lift him out of here.' Vijay had lost consciousness again, but she was pretty certain he hadn't died. They needed to get medical assistance, however, or he wouldn't survive long in this condition. He needed fluids urgently. With Drake's help, she carried his limp body outside. He didn't weigh a lot.

'You found him,' said Dean. 'Well done. Now we need to get out of here. The fire has almost surrounded us.'

Liz looked up and down the alleyway and saw smoke and flames at both ends. Burning buildings loomed high on one side, raining down a steady stream of sparks and hot ash. Above the inferno, the moon was already shining brightly in the dimming sky. Its beams brushed against her face like the touch of silk-gloved fingers and she felt a flutter in her limbs. Her heart began to race faster. Then thick black smoke drifted over the alley and the moon was lost from view. She turned her attention back to Vijay. 'Help me get him inside the car,' she told Dean.

'Hurry up, Liz,' said Jones. 'We need to get going.'

'Where are we going to take him?' asked Dean, helping her lift Vijay onto the patrol car's rear seats.

'He'll come with us, and we'll get him some medical help as soon as we can.'

'No,' said Drake. 'You can't take him.'

'Why not?'

'Because his family are still waiting for him. They refused to join the evacuation until he was found.'

'How many are they?'

Drake started counting on his fingers. 'There's Aasha, and Mr and Mrs Singh, and Vijay's grandmother. That makes four. We have to go and pick them up, or else they'll be stranded.'

'But we have to get back home for Samantha, Lily and Mihai,' said Dean.

'You can't save everyone, Liz,' said Jones. 'You have to make a choice.'

She glanced up at the flames emerging from the roof of the nearest building. A window shattered from the heat, spraying glass into the alleyway. Already some of the garages were starting to smoulder and catch fire. Soon there would be no way out.

'I hate to be a nuisance,' said Mr Canning, 'but can you take these off?' He turned to show Liz his cuffed hands. 'I played my part. Now you must honour your agreement and release me.'

'All right,' she snapped. She pulled out her keys and undid the cuffs as quickly as she could.

Mr Canning leaned close to her as she freed him and whispered in her ear. 'There's still something I'm curious about, my dear. I'm a werewolf, but what exactly are you?'

She shook her head. She wasn't going to say the word. Especially not to the headmaster. And definitely not now.

Rock began barking again as soon as Mr Canning's hands came free. The Dogman struggled to hold the dog back as it tugged on its lead.

'Please take that dreadful beast away,' implored the headmaster.

Rock was going frantic, barking ever louder and pulling so hard that the Dogman was almost dragged off his feet.

Mr Canning stepped away, rubbing his wrists where he'd been handcuffed. He glanced up at the sky and a smile flickered on his face. 'Time for me to say goodbye,' he said to Liz. 'Perhaps we'll meet again. I do hope so.'

Liz knew why he was smiling. It wasn't just that he'd been released. Even without looking up she could feel the full moon shining in the sky. Its radiant power felt almost as strong as the heat from the burning buildings. The headmaster obviously felt it too. He was already beginning to change. Rock barked madly as the headmaster's body sprouted hairs and changed shape. His smart jacket and waistcoat burst open as his shoulders and chest enlarged, revealing a thick coat of silver fur beneath.

The soldiers lifted their rifles and took aim, but Jones held them back. 'Hold your fire!' he bellowed. 'Shoot only if attacked.'

Soon a huge beast stood before them. The black eyepatch that still covered one eye was the only hint that this monster had once been Mr Canning. The creature raised one paw as if to wave. 'Farewell,' growled the wolf. Then it turned and ran.

Rock's barking finally ceased. Now the dog began to sniff again.

'What is it, boy?' asked the Dogman. 'What have you found now?'

Liz stepped back, but the dog followed its nose, its head to the ground, coming steadily closer. It stopped at her feet and looked up, wearing a look of puzzlement. Then in a flash it was barking again, its front paws up against her chest, its jaws snapping almost in her face.

'What's going on?' demanded Jones. 'What's that dog doing?'

The Dogman pointed at Liz. 'She's one of them! She's a werewolf! Rock sniffed her once before, but he wasn't certain then. Now he knows for sure.'

'It's not possible,' said Jones.

But the other men turned their rifles on her. 'Those bastards killed our friends,' said Evans. 'Edwards, Jenkins and Rees. They're dead because of creatures like her.'

'No,' said Dean. 'You don't understand. She's not like the others.'

Jones stood confused. 'If she's a werewolf, why hasn't she changed like Canning did?' he asked.

'She's changing now, sir.'

The soldier was right. The moon's rays were flooding her with strength, bathing her in power. The previous full moon had healed her gunshot wound, but this time she was unhurt and there was nothing to heal. Instead, the moon filled her with raw energy, so much she felt she would burst.

Her skin tingled with electricity, making every hair on her body stand tall. It flexed and pulled tight, crystallizing into a coating as tough as tempered glass. The transformation moved inside, remaking her fingers and toes into rods as strong as steel. The change surged along her hands and feet, then throughout her limbs, fusing every fibre of her body into an unbreakable bond. It filled her with vigour and speed and power. And yet she felt as cold as the grave, chilled to the very core.

Drake watched open-mouthed, numb with shock.

Jones looked on, aghast.

Three of the soldiers took aim at her, bracing their weapons to fire.

She didn't know what they saw when they looked at her. A cold light seemed to shine out of every pore of her body, more dazzling than the moon itself. Her skin crackled like brittle ice, even though hot flames danced all around her. She was drawing power from the flames themselves, and transmuting it into dark energy.

And with that power came a lust for blood. She opened her mouth wide as sharp teeth spiralled through her gums, filling her mouth with hot liquid. Two fangs, twice the length of normal teeth, twisted into deadly points as sharp as knives.

The soldiers squeezed their triggers.

Kevin cried out, 'No! Don't shoot!'

And Dean lurched forward, barrelling into the Welsh Guards with his broad shoulders, and yelling, 'Run, Liz, run!'

The men went down in a crumpled heap, their shots wide, and she spun away from them like quicksilver. She didn't fear the soldiers and their guns, but she feared what she might do to them if she stayed.

And so she ran, sprinting faster than ever before, moving at impossible speed. In seconds she reached the end of the alley, leaving the others far behind. She burst through the tunnel of flames that guarded her exit, her skin sheathed in ice. On through the darkening streets she raced, passing raging bonfires and funeral pyres that had once been shops and houses. The flames had spread faster and further then she could have guessed, driven on by the wind. The whole area was consumed by fire. It had become a fireball, engulfing everything in its way.

It capered before her, a great wall of fire blocking the street, almost as if it wanted to prevent her getting back home. But she couldn't allow it to divert her from her path.

She ran into the fireball, dousing the fire with her passage. Faster and faster she ran, unflagging and undaunted. The flames had no power to harm her. They flickered and died as she passed. The icy fluid that rushed through her veins drew their heat away.

She flew with the fire, drawing in its heat, outshining its fiercest flames. She had become a creature of elemental power, cold as ice, fast as the wind, silent as the grave, and filled with light and darkness.

Chapter Ninety-Eight

'Shit!' yelled Jones. 'What the hell just happened?'

'Never mind that now,' said Dean. 'We need a med kit for the boy, and then we need to get the hell out of here before we end up as toast.'

Already they were surrounded by fire, the shops and houses and garages all ablaze, the air thick with acrid smoke. The heat from the flames was almost unbearable.

'Right,' agreed the corporal. 'Just a sec.' He retrieved a box from the Foxhound and tossed it to Drake. 'Oral rehydration packs for the boy,' he said. 'Now let's get moving.'

Drake jumped into the back of the patrol car with Vijay, and Kevin clambered into the front. Dean had his foot on the throttle before the door was even closed. 'Hold on tight,' he warned them. He floored the pedal and careered down the narrow path between the flames at breakneck speed. Up ahead a wall of fire awaited them.

'You've trained for this kind of thing, have you?' said Kevin hopefully.

Dean shook his head. 'First time for everything.' The car burst out through the flames and he did a hand break turn in the road.

'Cool,' said Drake.

Dean glanced in the rear-view mirror and saw the teenager struggling to pour rehydration fluid into Vijay's mouth. Behind him, the Foxhound and Land Rover rushed out through the wall of fire and turned to follow the patrol car. The convoy of three set off in the direction of Vijay's house. Mercifully, it was in the opposite direction to the fire.

'I think,' said Drake, 'that when we turn up, Mr and Mrs Singh are going to be properly surprised.'

He wasn't wrong about that.

By the time they reached the Singh's house, Vijay had recovered a little and was able to sit up. Drake jumped out of the car and banged hard on the front door of the house. 'No time to explain,' he shouted as Vijay's father opened the door and began to question him. 'Vijay's safe. Just grab your gear and come!'

Vijay's mum was overwhelmed when she saw her son. She began to sob and wail and hug him to her breast.

Dean pushed her into the rear of the car. 'No time for that,' he said. He helped the older Mrs Singh in too, and directed the others to the Land Rover, stuffing their various bags and suitcases in the back. Within two minutes the entire family had been collected and loaded and the patrol car was on the road again. The military vehicles followed right behind.

'What took you so long?' demanded Vijay's grandmother from the back seat of the patrol car. 'I wish to know. My grandson has been missing for three whole days.'

Dean looked up and saw the old woman giving him a hard stare in the mirror. 'Sorry,' he told her. 'The first I knew about it was an hour ago.'

'Huh. Call yourself a policeman? And where are you taking us now?'

'To pick up my family and then get us all out of here,' said Dean.

'Well hurry up, then,' she said. 'Try not to leave them waiting as long as you left us.'

Chapter Ninety-Nine

Brixton Hill, South London, full moon

Mihai had come to know the area around Brixton Hill pretty well in the few months he'd been living here. Grandpa Kevin was always boasting about how he'd grown up here and knew all the shortcuts and hiding places, but Mihai reckoned he knew more. Lots more. The streets round here were a maze. Back alleys led off all the main roads. Small areas of trees and wasteland filled the gaps between houses. And there were abandoned construction sites too, where you could crawl under a loose metal fence, or climb over a wooden hoarding.

'Come on,' he said to Lily. 'This is best way to escape from fire.'

He pulled her by the hand through a gap in a fence that led to a cycle path. From here, he knew how to reach a local park. With an open field and a small lake it would be a safe place to shelter from the fire.

Lily followed him obediently, clutching her toy

elephant in one hand, her pink pony rucksack strapped tightly to her back.

He looked over his shoulder to see if Samantha had come out of the house yet, but there was still no sign of her. He hesitated, but she had told him not to wait. It would be best to take Lily to safety and then return to find her mother. He wondered briefly what had happened to Kevin, but he wasn't really worried about him. Kevin was always getting into trouble, and always managed to find a way out somehow.

The cycle path ran all the way around the edge of the park, but Mihai knew a quicker way to get there. 'Follow me,' he said to Lily. 'I know secret way. Only kids like us can go this way. Grown-ups too big to fit.'

The girl looked up at him excitedly. 'Will Ellie fit?' she asked, showing him her elephant.

He nodded. 'Yes, is only small elephant.'

He lifted the bottom of a chain fence for her to crawl under. He followed. They were both quickly covered in mud from crawling on the ground, but that didn't matter. The crawl led them into a building site, full of half-built walls, stacks of unused bricks, and concrete mixers. It was a secret play area, where you could climb up walls and jump over holes in the ground.

But they weren't here to play now. They ran nimbly across the broken ground, jumping over abandoned tools and squeezing through small gaps between piles of construction materials. Soon they reached the other side and pushed through another hole in the chain-link fence. The park was just in front of them. They crossed a road and entered through its gates.

It was getting dark now, but the bright moon illuminated the wide empty space of the park. Dark trees stood tall against the sky and in the distance the lake glittered silver. The fire had engulfed the houses along one whole side of the park, turning them into a burning wall of red and orange, but the open fields made a break that stopped the flames advancing into the park itself.

'You will be safe here,' said Mihai. 'Wait for me. I go back for your mummy.'

But Lily refused to let go of his hand. 'I'm scared,' she said. 'Don't leave me all alone.'

He looked around the park. It was a big space for a little girl, and scary in the dark, especially with the fire raging all along one side. You could hear the roar of the flames and smell the smoke drifting across the field. The park was over a hundred acres big, with a lake, an open-air swimming pool, a BMX track and a children's play area. If he abandoned Lily here she might easily wander off and get lost. He had an idea. 'I take you to children's play area. Is small, is safe. You know it?'

She nodded.

The children's play area was a small fenced-off space within the larger park. Liz had taken him there when he'd first come to live with her, and since then he'd often gone there on his own in the hope of making a friend. But the kids who played there were usually younger than him. He'd met a friend once, a boy his own age with curly hair. They had played together on the swings, and Mihai had kicked his legs and laughed and swung higher and higher until his feet were almost level with the bare treetops that surrounded the play area. But then the boy's mother had come over to him, wanting to know who Mihai was and why he was on his own in the park, and what his mum and dad were thinking of? He had tried to explain that his mum and dad weren't thinking anything. They were both dead. But his English had failed him, and he had stood there like a dumb idiot, watching as the curly-haired boy was taken away by his mother.

Now the place was empty. The kids who used to play here had long since gone. The only movement was the gentle creak of the swings, and the rustle of dried leaves and fast food packaging stirring in the breeze. He pushed open the gate and took Lily inside. 'Is good place to wait,' he told her. 'Nice and safe. And fun too.' He led her to one of the swings and sat her down. Her feet didn't quite reach the ground. 'Good girl. You stay here.'

He turned to go and that was when he saw them. Six dark figures, crouching low, just beyond the fence. They started to pace toward him, padding silently across the grass on all fours, their yellow eyes glittering in the moonlight.

Chapter One Hundred

Lily screamed when she saw the werewolves, and clutched her toy elephant to her chest.

Mihai stared at the approaching figures. They loped across the grass, picking up speed us they grew closer. The low fence that surrounded the play area would be useless at keeping them out. They would jump right over it.

He lifted Lily down from the swing and took hold of her hand. 'Run with me,' he told her.

They ran across the soft padding that covered the ground. Lily did her best to keep up, but her legs were too short to run fast. There was no way they could outrun the wolves. Mihai could carry her, but it would slow him down too much. They would have to stay and fight, or else find a place to hide.

He knew just where.

'This way,' he said, almost dragging Lily with him. She

was running as fast as she could, but it was half the speed he'd have liked. He glanced back and saw the first of the wolves leaping over the fence. Its long legs pushed like pistons as it jumped. The beast was man-sized, its eyes glowing like yellow beacons, its strong jaws parted to show white teeth. It landed inside the fence and bounded forward.

One half of the play area was filled with a treetop house built of logs. Mihai ran over to it with Lily. The treehouse looked like a fairy tale castle, with square towers, swinging bridges between them, ladders and ropes. It was built on a scale for kids, and if they could squeeze inside the smallest room at the top of the tallest tower, he hoped they would be out of reach of the wolves. As long as they could get there in time. 'Over here,' he said.

They reached the wooden ladder that led up the side of the tower. He lifted Lily onto the first rung and started to push her up.

'Ellie!' shouted Lily suddenly. 'I dropped my Ellie!'

The toy elephant had fallen to the ground as they'd been running to the tower. It lay between them and the approaching werewolves.

'Is no time to get,' said Mihai. The second of the wolves was already leaping the fence. The third and fourth were at its heels. 'Is time to climb.'

'I must have Ellie!'

'I help you climb ladder,' said Mihai. 'Then go back for Ellie. Okay?'

'Okay.'

The girl wasn't a natural climber, but with his help she hauled herself up one rung at a time. One step, … two steps. There were four more to go. He watched her climb the next rung and then dashed back to fetch the elephant.

Four of the werewolves were inside the fence now and the last two were jumping over. Their leader was only feet away. Mihai snatched the toy off the ground and darted back to the wooden tower. Lily was almost at the top.

'Up! Up!' he yelled as he followed her up the ladder. When he reached the top he shoved her through the narrow doorway that led inside and dived in after her.

The first wolf was right behind him. It rushed up the ladder in a flash, gripping the wooden rungs with sharp claws, and thrust its huge head inside the tower. It snapped its jaws at them, spraying them with its spittle.

Lily screamed. Mihai pushed her into the far corner and curled himself up against the opposite wall, pressing his knees into his chest.

The wolf lunged forward, seeming to fill the inside of the wooden tower with its fury. Its jaws opened and snapped just an inch from Mihai. It swivelled its head around the small space, its yellow eyes rolling with frustration as it struggled to push its shoulders through the doorway. But it was too big.

Lily continued to scream.

'Don't move,' shouted Mihai. 'Wolf cannot touch us if we stay still.'

The monster continued to rage for what seemed like ages. Eventually it withdrew its head and climbed back down the ladder. The wooden room grew still again.

'Still don't move,' warned Mihai. 'May be trick.'

He peered through the cracks in the wall between the wooden logs, watching as the werewolves regrouped below. They didn't pace around like ordinary animals. Instead they huddled in a bunch to whisper to each other.

Mihai didn't like the sound of their whispering. Creatures like that weren't meant to whisper. Wolves with sharp teeth and deadly claws were one thing. Wolves with a cunning plan were ten times worse.

Before long the werewolves finished their plotting. Two of them stayed at the base of the tower, blocking any escape. The other four began to climb the outside of the wooden structure, one on each side. Mihai pulled his hands and feet away from the wooden walls as the wolves climbed up, but they didn't try to reach him. Instead they went right up to the rooftop. They stood there for a minute, gathered together under the moonlight, just a few feet overhead. Then they began to pull at the planks that made the roof. The creatures were strong and their claws made good tools. It didn't take long for the first plank to tear away, leaving a narrow opening in the roof. The second plank lasted even less time. One more plank and they would be able to reach inside.

Chapter One Hundred and One

High Street, Brixton Hill, South London, full moon

Liz emerged from flames into darkness. The electrical power was down and all the streets around here were black. But with the light from the moon and the glare of the fire she could see perfectly well enough. She raced along the road that led to home. The butcher's shop lay just a couple of hundred feet from her and she dashed toward it.

The neighbouring houses were already alight, and the roof and upper floors of the shop itself were burning too. She looked inside and saw the flicker of flames behind the curtains. Black smoke rose up into the dark blue sky, and grey ash fell down around her.

The front door of the shop stood wide open.

'Samantha!' she screamed. 'Mihai! Lily!' She could

hardly hear her own voice over the roar and crackle of the fire.

There was nothing for it. She dashed inside.

The ground floor rooms were free of smoke and fire, but she quickly saw that no one was there. Instead she turned to the staircase that led up. 'Samantha!' she shouted again, but there was still no response. She rushed up the stairs as quickly as she could.

Upstairs the fire had taken hold. Flames flickered behind closed doors, glowing red beneath them and shrivelling the paint that covered them. The door to Samantha's room stood open. Smoke and fumes billowed through it. Liz covered her nose and headed forward along the landing.

The bedroom was ablaze. Flames had turned the curtains and bed coverings into blackened rags. The wooden bed and the chairs, dressing table and wardrobes were smouldering into flames. Smoke poured from every hot surface. The entire room was almost ready to ignite.

Samantha lay on the floor by the bed.

There was no sign of Lily or Mihai. Liz ran to Samantha and snatched her from the smouldering carpet. She showed no signs of life. She was just as heavy as Liz, perhaps heavier now that she was pregnant, but somehow Liz found the strength to lift her in her arms. Holding her close to her chest she began to head downstairs.

'Don't die on me,' said Liz as she stumbled quickly past the flames that reached out to her from behind the burning doors. The fire surged as she ran, ropes of smoke coiling around her, furious at her flight. She reached the ground floor and rushed out into the fresh air outside.

But the air here was not so fresh. Already it was filling with smoke. Every building in the street was now alight. It was no place to shelter. She pressed on, following the only clear path available, a lane that led to a local park. They should be safe from the fire there.

Samantha stirred as the cold air began to revive her.

She coughed. 'Got to get out,' she mumbled. 'Get out of the house.'

'We're already out,' said Liz. 'You're safe. Where are Lily and Mihai?'

Samantha coughed again. 'I told them to go. I don't know where they went.' She was still barely conscious. She must have fainted when she tried to get out of the house.

But at least the children appeared to have escaped. Where would they have gone? Away from the fire, obviously. They had probably come the same way that Liz was heading. Mihai was a smart kid. He'd find somewhere safe to take Lily. And he couldn't have gone far with the little girl. There was one obvious place, and she was heading in its direction now. Brockwell Park.

Before too long she arrived at its entrance gates.

Samantha was coming round. 'I can walk,' she said. 'Let me try to walk.'

'Are you sure?' Liz lowered her carefully to the ground, but her legs buckled beneath her. Liz sat her on the concrete path leading into the park.

'Let me rest for a moment,' said Samantha. 'I'm sure I'll be strong enough in a minute.'

Liz looked out across the dark fields of parkland. The fire had spread to three sides of it, but was unable to encroach into the park itself. But where were the children? 'Mihai!' she called. 'Lily!' There was no response. But they must be here somewhere.

Samantha was in no fit state to begin a search. There was a park bench nearby. 'Let me help you,' said Liz. She lifted Sam back onto her feet and helped her over to the bench. 'I'll call Dean on my radio and tell him where we are.'

The public phone networks had been completely overloaded for several weeks, but the police radios operated on their own private infrastructure and were still working. She reached Dean immediately.

'Where are you?' he asked.

'I'm safe,' she told him. 'I'm with Samantha at Brockwell Park.'

'And Lily?'

'She's with Mihai. We think they're here. I'm going to look for them.'

'Don't move,' said Dean. 'I'm on my way.'

'Okay.'

'I'll stay here and wait for him,' said Samantha. 'You go and find the kids.'

Liz set off across the park toward the lake. That would be the smartest place to escape from the fire. And she had to start somewhere. But she was running out of energy after her frantic dash. She suddenly felt drained.

The moon had shielded her from the fire, just as it had healed her bullet wound before. But then, as now, the healing process had left her ravenous. Only one thing could feed the hunger that engulfed her. Blood.

She shook her head. She was willing to accept that she was a vampire. But that didn't mean she had to play the role of the evil undead. The garlic hadn't harmed her and neither had the silver cross. Real-life vampires clearly weren't like the creatures of legend. She could find her own way of being a vampire.

But one thing was for sure. She was absolutely exhausted. Her limbs no longer felt like steel, but weighed as heavy as lead. The power the moon had given her had all but drained away. She wondered if she even had the strength to make it as far as the lakeside. She stopped and put her hands to her knees, panting for breath. Even the act of drawing in air required a great effort.

And then she heard the scream of a child coming from the play area by the lake. The voice was unmistakable. It was Lily's.

Chapter One Hundred and Two

Pindar Bunker, Whitehall, Central London, full moon

The air inside the Pindar bunker was growing hotter and more humid as each agonising minute passed. Had the aircon system failed? Or was it just that the Prime Minister's own breathing was becoming more laboured as she waited?

She sat opposite the General, watching as he keyed in data to the computer terminal, glancing up at her from time to time, the service pistol lying on the desk beside his keyboard. If she tried to grab the pistol he would certainly seize it before she did. And if she made a rush for the abandoned rifles scattered on the floor, she would barely make it halfway across the room before he put a bullet in her back.

She could do nothing but wait, and watch.

Eventually he finished typing. 'I have just transmitted a message to Northwood Headquarters informing the War Cabinet that you have been shot dead by a renegade soldier. A traitor. The country is now officially without a leader. The War Cabinet will meet to agree its next action, which will be to notify the monarch and request the immediate appointment of your successor. The most likely candidate to take over is the Home Secretary. As soon as he is appointed, control over the Trident nuclear missile system will pass to him and my window of opportunity will close. Therefore, in five minutes time I will send the authorization code to trigger the nuclear strike. I have already programmed the target coordinates, the kiloton yields and the detonation altitudes of the warheads. As you know, the Trident II missiles carry multiple warheads capable of variable yield. I have calculated that nine air bursts, each of one hundred kilotons at a height of two thousand metres will wipe out all lycanthropes in the greater London region while minimizing damage to buildings and radioactive fallout to surrounding areas. In fact the city will be safely habitable again within a few weeks, and 95% of residential buildings should survive the blast intact. Further strikes targeted at Manchester, Birmingham, Leeds, Liverpool, Sheffield, Glasgow, Southampton and Bristol will ensure the complete elimination of the lycanthropic threat and bring this war to a swift conclusion.'

'But those other cities remain fully populated!' she exclaimed. 'Millions will die!'

The General pondered his response for a moment. 'You will no doubt be aware of what Stalin once said, "The death of one man is a tragedy..."'

The PM concluded the quotation for him. '"...The death of millions is a statistic." Listen to yourself, General,' she pleaded. 'Your words are those of a lunatic.'

'No. Mine is the voice of sanity. If you had listened to me all along, we would not be in this situation now.'

'Did you plan this from the beginning, General?' she asked.

'A good general must consider many plans if he is to win the war.'

The Prime Minister stared coldly at the man across the table. How could she ever have entrusted him with the command of the nation's military forces? He was not a man but a lizard. 'You must have lost your mind, General Ney,' she told him. 'No one will follow your order to launch a nuclear strike. Only a madman would believe that they will.'

The General sighed and looked at his watch. 'We have three minutes until I transmit the authorization code. Do you really wish to waste that time in fruitless argument? The order will be obeyed because that is how the system has been designed. A signals operator at Northwood Headquarters will receive my instruction. He will pass it to a second operator who will validate its authenticity. No further oversight is required. The operators will encrypt the instruction and transmit it to one of the four *Vanguard*-class nuclear submarines on patrol in the North Atlantic. The submarine commander will obey the order to fire. This is how the military works.'

She feared he was right. Her time was running out. Debating with him would surely waste the precious time that remained, but she couldn't help herself. 'General, please do not go ahead with this. It is not too late to change your mind. Surely you can see that this nuclear attack poses a far greater threat to civilization than that of the werewolves?'

'No. That is not how I see it at all,' he snapped angrily. It was the first time he had displayed any kind of emotion. 'As I have explained, I have considered the options carefully. This country – this island – is now completely cut off from the rest of the world. If we can eradicate the disease here, we have a chance of survival. After this strike the nation will be able to rebuild and prepare to defend itself against whatever happens in the rest of the world. I am giving our country a fighting chance.'

He looked at his watch. 'Two minutes remain.'

She looked around the room desperately. The pistol still lay untouched on the desktop. She would only try to grab it if she had no other choice. But in just over one minute she would run out of choices.

She lunged across the desk.

Her hand closed around the barrel of the gun. Then the General yanked it out of her grasp.

She fell forward, sprawling across the surface of the desk, sobbing helplessly.

When she looked up, the General was standing over her, the gun in his hand. 'Sit down, Prime Minister, or I will not hesitate to pull the trigger.'

She looked into his eyes, expecting to see a madman's deranged stare. But he was perfectly calm and unflustered. 'Sit down,' he commanded again. He shifted the gun an inch and fired a round past her right shoulder. The noise of the gunshot made her shriek with terror. 'Now!'

She obeyed. She had no choice.

The General watched her return to her chair. Then he pressed a key on the computer terminal. 'It is done,' he said.

All hope drained from her then. There was nothing more she could do. What chance remained now? She could only pray that as many people as possible had left the city. She must hope that somehow the train of events that the General had set in motion would be disrupted. Surely one of the two radio operators would rebel and fail to transmit the message. The commander of the submarine would choose to disobey his order rather than release a hail of death on his own country. The men on the submarine would mutiny. Sanity would surely prevail somehow.

The General rose to his feet and stood to attention. 'Prime Minister, I wish to resign my post as Chief of the Defence Staff. I have disobeyed your direct order and am therefore guilty of the crime of high treason. Please understand that my loyalty has always been to this country. I knew that you would never authorize the mass killing of innocent civilians, and so I decided to take this heavy burden upon my own shoulders. I do not ask for forgiveness, merely for understanding.'

He lifted the pistol to his head and saluted her. 'Prime Minister, may I say that it has been an honour to serve you.' He pulled the trigger.

The blast of the gun firing was shocking at such close range. She clasped her hands to her ears, but the sound rang in her head long after the bullet had passed through the General's skull and out the other side.

His body collapsed onto the desk before her, his hand still gripping the gun.

A second passed and then she was on her feet. She dashed around the desk to the communications terminal that the General had used to transmit his messages. She hit the keyboard frantically. *Prime Minister is still alive*, she typed. *Cancel order to fire missiles. Repeat – cancel missiles. Send military escort to Pindar bunker immediately. Acknowledge receipt of message.*

Moments later a response appeared on screen.

Message received. Too late to cancel Trident missile launch. Impossible to send rescue team. Advise remain in bunker. Message ends.

Chapter One Hundred and Three

Brockwell Park, South London, full moon

Liz's strength returned with a vengeance. She ran toward Lily's scream, scanning the darkened play area for movement. She found it near the tall wooden tower that stood at the back, close to the trees.

Dark shapes moved on top of the tower and at its base. Werewolves. The creatures were ripping the roof of the wooden structure into pieces. Lily and Mihai were cowering inside. The screams of the girl met the growling of the werewolves as they reached through the gap in the roof to seize hold of her.

'Stop!' yelled Liz. Her voice rang out loudly across the empty park.

The werewolves wheeled in her direction, their yellow eyes picking her out immediately. Their growls turned to howls of anger and the two on the ground sprang forward to intercept her.

She took one step toward them, and then another. Her leaden limbs began to fill with energy once again. Where it came from she couldn't say, but the aching hunger in her belly rose to match it.

Blood. Hot, liquid life. She would have her fill of it. And she would take it from the beasts that ran to meet her.

They leapt across the fence that circled the play area and Liz met them head on. The wolves raised long claws to slash and grasp hold of her. But her fingers were made of steel and tipped with razor-sharp blades. She plunged her right hand deep into the neck of the leading werewolf and tore out the artery that fed its brain. Blood washed across her face and she sank her fangs into the neck of the dying monster, sucking up its life. The creature wilted beneath her and she fell on it, drawing out blood in great gulps.

The second beast jumped at her, stretching out its wicked talons, its jaws opened wide in a roar. She rolled aside and spun like a whirlwind, ripping a great gash in its side as it passed her by. The creature hurtled to the ground, tumbling in a web of limbs. It lay on its side, panting noisily, watching as its blood spilled out to feed the grass.

She turned to face the remaining wolves.

They were clambering down from the wooden tower, their prey temporarily abandoned. One red-haired wolf leapt to the ground and padded forward, warily. The others joined it, presenting a wall of teeth and claws. Together, they began to pace toward her.

She jumped up onto the fence and sprang forward, landing squarely inside the fenced area.

The wolves stood their ground, watching with hooded yellow eyes. They had seen what she had done to their comrades and they were taking no risks. They challenged her with snarls and growls.

She met their animal noises with a cold hiss of defiance. Her enemy outnumbered her, but they stood between her and the two children and she would gladly rip them into pieces if she had to. She approached the wolves, fearless and undaunted. They were four, she was one, but she would stop at nothing to save Mihai and Lily.

Then the voice of another wolf sounded from across the field. A rising howl, chilling to hear. A second wolf joined it, and then more. She turned and saw a mass of dark forms creeping through the twilight, picking up speed. They were too many for her to count. They ran to meet her.

Chapter One Hundred and Four

North Atlantic Ocean, full moon

Deep beneath the cold, grey waters of the North Atlantic, HMS *Vigilant* followed a course north-eastward toward the Norwegian Sea. Its route was known only to its commanding officer, Captain John Greer.

Captain Greer had commanded the *Vanguard*-class submarine for the past three years and this was to be his last patrol before retirement. This was no ordinary patrol however. Although he had no access to news reports while at sea, the situation had been grim when the submarine had launched three weeks previously. War had been declared, though not against any enemy he had ever expected to fight. He hoped that he and his crew would have no part to play in the war and that it might even be over by the time they returned to base at the end of their current tour of duty. That would be in just over two months' time. Long enough for any man to spend beneath the waves, cocooned in a tight metal cylinder.

A call from the communications officer interrupted his evening routine. 'Captain, encrypted message received.'

The captain made his way through the cramped vessel to the control room and took the printed message that the comms officer solemnly passed to him. An unusual hush had descended on the control room. An encrypted message was unexpected. It might mean a deviation from the planned mission, or even a recall to base, although that would be extremely unusual. Unprecedented in fact. But in a time of war, anything was possible. It might even contain an order to launch one or more of the submarine's Trident II ballistic missiles. But Greer found that hard to believe.

He sat at his console to decrypt the message. When he had done so, he sat quietly for a moment, saying nothing.

'Captain?' The communications officer and the two pilots who steered the sub were all staring at him expectantly. He could read their faces clearly. Anxiety was written there, plain as day.

'Move to missile firing depth and call the weapons engineer.'

The pilots exchanged glances before carrying out his orders.

He sat staring at the decrypted message. He had anticipated this moment ever since joining 10th Submarine Squadron. It was the entire purpose of the ballistic missile-armed submarine fleet. He had imagined how this moment might feel, how he would react. He had played it out in his mind a thousand times.

He had never believed this day would come.

There was no doubting the authenticity of the message. The decrypted authentication code was valid. It could only have been sent by the Prime Minister or her authorized deputy, transmitted via Northwood HQ where it would have been checked and confirmed by two communications operators. The instruction was clear and unequivocal.

The weapons engineer, Lieutenant Commander Stuart McAllister clambered into the cramped control compartment. 'Captain?'

Greer passed him the decrypted message and watched the man as he read it through twice, slowly digesting its contents.

'Captain, this message is authenticated?'

Greer nodded at him.

The weapons engineer stood to attention, awaiting his command.

Whenever Greer had played out this scenario in his imagination, he had always wondered whether he would choose to obey his order without question, or if there would be some residual doubt in his mind that would cause him to hesitate, or even refuse to obey. Every commanding officer played out the same internal debate. When he had first become captain of the *Vigilant*, his wife had asked him openly what he would do.

'I cannot discuss it, even with you,' he had told her. 'You know that.'

But of course she had never expected him to answer her question. She had only asked it so that she might give him her own advice. 'Just remember, John, that you are just one link in a long chain, no more or less important than any other link in the chain. Whatever happens you must do your duty to Queen and country.'

Duty. There was no question about it.

His wife was safely back on the mainland, close to base in Scotland. His children were grown up now, and lived in Glasgow and in London. He hoped they were safely out of harm's way. He had no idea where the missiles he had been ordered to launch were targeted. The coordinates were encoded from Northwood HQ and were not revealed to him. It was just one of the many protocols designed to ensure the command was followed.

In his imaginings, Greer had always made his decision

the same way and followed his order to the letter without hesitation or regret. There was really no decision for him to make now. He had made his choice long ago.

He issued the necessary command, the only command possible under the circumstances. 'Action stations, missiles for strategic launch.'

'Aye, sir.' The weapons engineer set about his work, unquestioning. Discipline was the only way to run a submarine. No man would ever question it. Not even now.

'Loading missile trajectories onto onboard flight computers, Captain.'

The captain waited patiently as McAllister worked at the task. The operation needed only a few minutes to complete. Finally the lieutenant commander unlocked the safe in the missile control centre that held the launch trigger. The handheld device was modelled on the grip of a Colt 45 Peacemaker pistol. He drew it out and gripped it. 'Awaiting orders, Captain.'

Greer regarded the man's demeanour carefully. His face was free of dread or apprehension. He would do whatever the captain ordered him to do.

'Launch missiles.'

The weapons engineer pulled the red trigger of the launch control.

Greer felt the 16,000-ton boat shift in the water as the Trident II missiles left their launch tubes, on course for their destinations. With a range of over 4,000 nautical miles the targets might include a military base such as the Engels-2 strategic air base close to the Russian border with Kazakhstan, or the port of Severomorsk on the Kola Peninsula, home of the Russian Northern Fleet. They might be a city such as Moscow or St Petersburg or Tehran.

He had no way of knowing.

The missiles were on their way now. They could not be recalled or diverted or destroyed. His duty was done. When the moment had finally come, he had not failed his political masters. He must trust that they had made a wise choice.

Chapter One Hundred and Five

Brockwell Park, South London, full moon

The werewolves assembled around Liz in a tight throng. They ran in circles, baying for her blood, snarling and roaring in a crescendo of beast noises. Muscles flexed, tendons pulled tight, lips parted to reveal rows of wicked teeth and tongues dripping saliva. The heaving mass of talons, jaws and shining yellow eyes was uncountable.

Liz turned left and right, but her foes surrounded her on all sides. But in any case she had not come here to run. She had come to fight. She crouched low, her legs poised to spring, her fingers uncurled like bayonets, ready for battle. She bared her teeth, showing the wolves her sharpened fangs.

'Come on, then,' she said. 'I'm ready.' She knew that however strong the moon had made her, she had no chance of surviving this attack. Her adversaries were far too many for her to kill. Her only thought was to hold them back long enough for Mihai to escape with Lily.

The wolves swarmed forward as one. A rising tide of fur flowed toward her, driven on by hate and fury.

She braced herself ready for the onslaught.

A sudden deafening crackle broke through the howls and growls of the wolf pack. Machine gun fire, at close range. Dean, Jones and the rest of his section had arrived.

The wolves faltered in their attack. Some slowed; some broke off entirely. Some dropped to the ground as carcasses. But the rest came on, undaunted. Liz leapt to meet them, plunging her right fist into the throat of a ravening wolf. She ripped out its tongue and left it gasping in horror, its eyes wide with dread terror. A second wolf snapped at her arm, but she shook it off and took out its eyes with a jab from her fingers. The hellish yellow glow turned to sudden blackness.

The noise from the guns grew deafening as the soldiers stepped up their attack. Yet still more wolves fell on her and she spun at blinding speed, whipping at her enemies as they came. Faster she moved, spinning and slashing, biting and slurping the blood of her enemies. She had become a senseless killing machine. There was nothing for her now except the whirling of the wind, the gushing of the blood, and the dying screams of her foe.

Chapter One Hundred and Six

Dean braced the assault rifle against his shoulder and opened fire at the charging werewolf. The gun burst into life, spitting out a stream of hungry bullets, and the creature tumbled to the ground, its front legs buckling beneath it. He swung the rifle and took down a second wolf. The beast collapsed right at his feet. Spent cartridges littered the ground all around him.

Jones and the other soldiers were waging all-out war against the pack, rifles and machine guns crackling like thunder. Even Kevin had joined the fight and was loosing off rounds as the werewolves charged.

A pack of mere animals might have retreated under such a heavy onslaught, but the werewolves came on in force, using intelligence against their foe. The beasts spread out and rushed to the attack, keeping low for cover and zig-zagging across the ground to avoid fire. They closed the distance between themselves and the soldiers in seconds and flew at them with front legs outstretched, raking the air with their evil claws.

Machine guns cracked and a flurry of bullets rushed to meet their targets at point blank range. The front wave of wolves dropped to the ground, their bodies streaked with blood. But a second wave ran over the fallen, pounding turf and flesh in their hurry to engage. When they reached the infantrymen they put their claws and teeth to quick use, slashing and ripping and dealing death. Several of the soldiers went down.

Dean turned to see a huge beast rushing at him just feet away. The monster roared as it fell on him, showing curved canine teeth an inch long. The Heckler & Koch jerked in his grip and the wolf plummeted to the ground, skidding along the grass toward him. Even in death it managed to floor him. He fell backward and threw out his arms to break his fall.

The ground smacked his right shoulder hard and he lay there for a moment, too stunned to move. What had happened to his gun? He reached for it, his fingers grasping along the wet grass. All around him a firestorm was in full swing. Hairy bodies rushed over him, their legs pounding, their clawed paws spiking the ground just inches from his head. Raised voices shouted commands, or else screamed in agony. And everywhere guns flashed, pumping hard metal into soft bodies, discharging cartridges left, right and centre.

He reached his gun at last and dragged it to him. Seizing it in both hands he aimed it at the nearest wolf and pulled the trigger. The gun clicked but did not fire. The magazine was empty. He needed to dump it and swap in a fresh mag, but he seemed to have temporarily lost his ability to fully command his arms and legs. He looked down. A long red gash ran up his thigh, weeping blood.

No. No.

How had it happened? It must have been during the stampede when the wolf he shot fell on him. He hadn't even felt the wound at the time. Now he couldn't feel his legs at all. He tried to sit up, but all his strength was gone.

He felt suddenly sick. A scratch from a wolf claw meant only one thing.

His head felt light. He was suddenly much too hot. He turned his head to one side and vomited. He gasped. He could no longer draw in air. His lungs were burning. His heart began to pound as it struggled to push oxygen to his weakened limbs. But it fought a losing battle.

The gun slipped from his grip. It was useless anyway without ammo. Instead he struggled with the buttons of his stab vest, trying to ease the pressure on his airway. But the swelling that blocked it came from inside. He could not breathe. His hand fell limply to his side. He fought for one last breath, but it wouldn't come.

The last thing he saw was Liz, walking across the grass toward him, clutching Lily tightly to her chest. He knew then that his daughter was safe. A final sense of gratitude and peace came to him as he closed his eyes to the darkness.

Chapter One Hundred and Seven

'NO!' shrieked Liz. She held Lily close to her chest, shielding the girl from the sight of her father, dead. Dean's body lay amid a tangled heap of corpses and carcasses, men and wolves. The dead lay all together after the battle, victors and vanquished united in death.

Every one of the wolves had been slaughtered, and half the soldiers too. And Dean. It was as if a part of her had died. The sobbing child she held in her arms would grow up without a father. And Dean's unborn child would never even meet him. How was she to break the news to Samantha?

Kevin came up to her. 'You're safe, love. Thank God.' He kissed her forehead.

She hardly heard him. She stumbled slowly across the

field to where she had left Samantha. The unearthly strength that had animated her earlier had dissipated. The frenzy was over. She had drunk her fill of blood and the fangs that had briefly appeared had withdrawn back into her gums. The dark impulse that had gripped her and made her into a monster now seemed satisfied.

Samantha was waiting just where Liz had left her, sitting on a bench, now joined by Vijay, Drake and several others who must be Vijay's family. Samantha rose unsteadily from her seat. 'Lily! Oh Lily, you're safe.' She took her daughter from Liz and hugged and kissed her. 'And Mihai too,' she added, seeing the Romanian boy walking in Liz's footsteps. 'Thank you, Mihai. And where is Dean?'

Liz slowly shook her head. 'I'm sorry, Samantha. I'm so sorry.'

She expected Samantha to break down in uncontrollable tears, but instead the woman just sagged. Her lips quivered and a single tear ran down her cheek. She sat back down on the park bench. 'He always said he would give his own life to save his family,' she said. 'He used to talk about it as if he fully expected to, as if any man would do the same. And now he has.' Lily buried her head in her mother's breast. Samantha continued, 'Every time he went out on duty I would stay up late, watching the news, waiting for the phone to ring. Each time there was a stabbing, or a shooting, or some kind of violence, I would think immediately of Dean. So in a way I've grieved for him a thousand times already.'

Liz didn't know what to say. She had spent her seven years in the police force immersed in that same world of senseless violence. She thought of the photographs of fallen colleagues that lined the corridor back at the police station. Each one of those men and women had left a grieving family behind. Like Dean, they had known the risk, but had chosen to face it, not flee. Every serving police officer lived under the same shadow every single day of their working life. It seemed wrong that they should bear that burden, but someone had to, for the sake of the others.

Like the Police Commissioner had once said at the funeral of Liz's former colleague, Dave Morgan, 'Each one of us must work each day toward creating the kind of society we wish to live in.' Dean had certainly done that, no one could deny it.

She touched Samantha's cheek gently. 'Dean was a brave man, and a fine husband and father.' The words sounded hollow, but Samantha nodded gratefully. When Liz took her hand away from her cheek it was glistening with tears.

The surviving soldiers were returning. Only half the number who had joined the battle were still alive. Jones looked grim. 'More men down, but we can't bring them with us. There's no time, and we don't have enough vehicles. We'll come back for them later.' He bowed his head to Samantha. 'I'm sorry for your loss,' he said. 'Dean fought well.' He turned to Liz. 'And I'm glad you're safe. We'll talk later about what happened. Now we need to get everyone out of here. Quickly.'

Kevin had picked up Dean's assault rifle. 'Pointless to waste it,' he said. 'And it ain't safe to leave kit like this just lying about.'

'Careful,' cautioned Jones. 'Do you know how to handle a weapon like that?'

Kevin immediately jumped to attention and saluted the corporal. 'Private Kevin Bailey, 8th Infantry Brigade, 1988 – 1992. Reporting for duty, sir!'

A look of amusement crossed Jones' face briefly. 'The Bailey family is always full of surprises. At ease, soldier.'

They divided into three groups. Liz and Kevin took the patrol car with Samantha, Lily and Mihai. Drake and the Singhs joined the soldiers in the Land Rover and the Foxhound.

'Which route are we taking?' asked Kevin.

Lycanthropic

'South,' said Jones. 'The shortest route out of the city is due south. And in any case, the fire is blocking the northern exit.'

'No,' said a small voice. It was Vijay. 'We mustn't. Rose went west. We must find Rose.'

'What's the boy saying?' asked Kevin.

'He wants to find our friend, Rose,' said Drake. 'But we don't really know where she went.'

'She went west,' insisted Vijay. 'We have to look for her.'

'No,' said Jones firmly. 'We're not discussing this. We need to get out by the quickest route and that's south. Now let's go.'

Chapter One Hundred and Eight

Virginia Water, Surrey, full moon

There was nothing for Melanie to do but climb on board the bus. James was gone, and she didn't know if he would ever be back. They had taken a stupid risk bringing him outside on the night of the full moon. She had grown so used to him changing, she hadn't considered what might go wrong.

But at least he had escaped from the immediate danger of the checkpoint, and she and the others were safe too.

She sat next to Sarah on the bus, with Ben taking the seat in front. She gripped Sarah's hand tightly. 'Are you okay?' she asked her sister.

Sarah nodded slightly, but said nothing. She was traumatized by the incident at the checkpoint. She was traumatized by everything. Melanie didn't know how long it would take for her to recover. That would depend on what happened next. The soldiers said they were going to an evacuation camp and that they would be given food and accommodation until they could be moved on. After that, no one could be sure. But as long as they all stayed together, they would get through somehow.

Except they had lost James and had no way of finding him again.

'Maybe you were right about James,' she whispered to Ben. 'Perhaps it's best he's gone.' She hated to admit she'd been wrong, but Ben had been warning her about James for weeks now, and she had refused to listen.

'No,' said Ben. 'I actually think you were right all along. James wasn't half as dangerous as I thought.'

'What can you mean?' she whispered. 'He nearly killed me.'

'Didn't you see what he did?' said Ben. 'When the moon took him, he realized he couldn't control himself anymore. He tried to warn you. Even when you ignored him, he somehow managed to stop himself from harming you. He ran away instead.'

'I guess so,' said Melanie.

'And he risked his own life to save that boy from the other werewolf. That was heroic.'

'It was, wasn't it?' said Melanie, cheering at the thought. 'So maybe I was right all along.'

'I think you were. James may be a werewolf, but there's more good in him than in a lot of people. Perhaps even most people.'

'Even though he sometimes eats people?'

'Perhaps some people deserve to be eaten,' said Ben. 'I just don't know anymore.'

She leaned forward and kissed him. 'Whatever happens now, I'm glad you're here. Nothing must ever come between us again. Promise me it won't.' She took his hand. 'I'll never leave you,' she promised. She took Sarah's hand too. 'I'll never leave you either, sis.'

Sarah looked up and nodded. She squeezed Melanie's

fingers tightly.

A flash of light appeared suddenly outside the bus. Melanie shut her eyes to block out the blinding glare. The entire eastern sky had become as bright as day. 'What on earth is that?' she asked.

The light faded, to be replaced by a dull red glow, stretching out across the horizon.

'I have no idea,' said Ben. 'An explosion of some kind?' They gazed out of the window, watching.

Then the sound came, as deafening as the light was blinding. And with it came the wind.

Chapter One Hundred and Nine

South London, full moon

The Foxhound led the way out of London, ready to sweep any blockades or hostile forces from its path. The patrol car followed, with the Land Rover bringing up the rear. Liz had asked Kevin to take the wheel. She couldn't trust herself to drive safely right now.

Samantha sat in the back, oddly silent, staring ahead expressionless and hugging her daughter mechanically. By contrast, Lily's cries and snuffles gave the journey a constant soundtrack.

Mihai sat stoically, looking out at the passing houses, cars and empty streets. Liz knew he blamed himself for leaving Samantha in the burning house. She had tried to reassure him. 'Samantha is safe,' she'd said. 'And so is Lily, thanks to you. If anyone is to blame, it's Kevin, for leaving you alone.' And yet even Kevin had played his part, saving

Drake, and ultimately Vijay too. Everyone had done something brave today. Maybe the truth was that no one was to blame for what had happened. They were all heroes in their way, especially Dean, who had made the ultimate sacrifice. She would miss him more than she could say.

The convoy made rapid progress along the deserted road. The red route had been kept clear by the army right up until the last minute. They didn't encounter any other army or police units as they went. It seemed a fair chance that they were the last to leave the city, by the southern exit at least.

'Not far now,' said Kevin. 'We're right on the edge of London. We'll hit the countryside in a sec.'

As if on cue, a blinding flash of light filled the entire night sky. The cityscape lit up behind them as bright as day. Brighter. Liz shielded her eyes from the glare.

'What the – ' began Kevin, but his question was cut short by the great clap of thunder that followed several seconds after the light.

It was no thunderclap, but an entire storm rolled into one enormous clamour. A pressure wave came with it, lifting the car off the road and flinging it forward. Kevin grappled with the steering wheel, but the car was flying now, not driving. It turned in a graceful arc and landed again with a shriek of tyres and a scream of metal as the engine scrambled to re-engage.

'Brace yourself!' shouted Liz.

The car spun around on two wheels and tilted over almost to the tipping point. Liz waited for the end to come, but the car stopped itself just in time, balancing on a knife edge, before falling back onto the road with a crash. Kevin slammed on the brakes and brought it to a juddering halt.

The Land Rover careered on past them, narrowly missing the Foxhound, which was the only vehicle of the three to have remained under control, thanks to its armoured bulk. The two military vehicles braked sharply up ahead.

Liz touched her hand to her forehead. She'd dashed it against the windscreen when the car crash-landed, but it was nothing to worry about. She turned instead to check the other passengers. 'Are you hurt?' she asked Samantha.

'I'm okay,' she said, holding her belly.

The others looked shaken but uninjured. The car itself still seemed intact, although a crack had appeared in the middle of the windscreen. Outside the vehicle the air was filled with a blizzard of debris. Rubbish, roof tiles, planks of wood and even tyres flew past. Overhead, the sky had turned completely black. Behind them, looking toward central London, a red glow reflected off the underside of the dark clouds like a vision of the fires of hell.

Kevin finally managed to ask his question. 'What the bleeding hell was that?'

'I don't know,' said Liz. Miraculously the engine of the patrol car was still running. 'Come on,' she said. 'Let's go.'

The car crept forward slowly to join the others. Jones waved to Liz from the window of the Foxhound and the Dogman gave a thumbs up from the Land Rover. Incredibly they had all survived the explosion. It must have been a bomb of some kind, or many bombs detonating simultaneously, but what could cause a blast on such devastating scale, Liz could scarcely comprehend. She felt completely numbed by the day's events. It would be a long time before she could begin to process this.

Acute grief, the police counsellors called the immediate aftermath of the bereavement process. She'd attended a course once after a colleague had been killed on duty. She remembered the descriptive phrases the course lecturer had used. *Traumatic distress. Shock. Disbelief.* The words hardly seemed adequate to describe the way she felt right now.

Kevin drove the car forward, picking his way carefully through the debris that now filled the road. Above them, the dark clouds billowed like a rippling sheet. An angry storm god must be shaking his fist to make them move like that. The reddish glimmer spread out across the low sky, as if it were pursuing them. Only an enormous firestorm could make a glow like that – a conflagration on a scale the world had never before witnessed. Liz knew then that she would never return to the city she had called home. That city no longer existed.

Chapter One Hundred and Ten

Holland Gardens, Kensington, London, full moon

Leanna crouched low in full wolf form. The moon shone down upon her, blessing her with its silver, magical light. She loped along the deserted road, stopping every hundred feet to listen once more. Each time, she pricked up her long ears, straining to hear the sound she craved, but silence greeted her instead.

Tonight she should have witnessed the final assault of the Wolf Army on London, the fruit of weeks of careful planning. The sweet music of gunfire ought to be playing across the city now. An orchestra of explosions, of fire and fury, should be raining down upon her enemies, but there was nothing. Instead – silence, treachery.

Warg Daddy had turned against her yet again.

She didn't know how it could have happened. The pills

were carefully timed to release their deadly toxins over many hours. They could not have claimed his life just yet. He might be feeling sick, feverish, weak, but he could not yet be dead.

So what had happened to her army? Could every single one of her soldiers have deserted her? She would not believe it.

Then where were they?

She paced forward again, but she was fully alone. Her army was gone.

Ahead of her a familiar figure appeared out of the darkness. Another wolf, panting breathlessly. The silver-haired creature trotted up to her, one eye still covered by the patch it had been wearing when it had visited her in human form. She did not want to see this creature now.

'What do you want?' she asked.

'I have come to help you in your darkest hour,' said Canning. 'You had hoped to celebrate a victory tonight. Yet I fear that your plans have failed. If it is any consolation, it is sometimes said that there are no real winners in war, only survivors.'

'Do you have something to offer me other than trite platitudes?'

The silver wolf grinned at her. 'It's a wonder that your followers have turned against you when you are so generous with your praise.'

She snarled at him, giving him warning of her anger. 'I almost killed you last time we met. Do not provoke me now, or I will rip you to pieces.'

'I do not doubt it for a second,' he replied. 'But someone with so few friends ought not to be so rash as to bite the only hand of friendship on offer.'

'I have no need for friends,' she told him. 'I need followers, loyal servants.'

'Indeed,' said Canning. 'And I am pleased to offer you my services.'

She glared at him mistrustfully. Had she ridded herself

of Warg Daddy only for this scheming trickster to take his place? She had no doubt that he was a duplicitous wretch. And yet there was a curious magnetism to him. He was clearly intelligent and resourceful. Perhaps she could use him, if only until she regathered her forces.

'What services can you offer me?' she asked him.

'Right now? I think that stealth is required. Follow me.' He trotted lightly along the road and stopped at a metal manhole cover. He flipped it open with his jaws, dragging it aside.

'You want me to go into the sewer with you?' said Leanna. 'You must be mad!'

'Perhaps. But if so, that makes two of us.' He gestured toward the gaping hole in the road. 'After you.'

But instead Leanna turned to look up. The sky above shone suddenly brighter than the stars. A pure white light made even the full moon invisible. She breathed in sharply. 'What is that?'

'I don't know,' said Canning. 'But I don't intend to wait and find out.' He dived headfirst down the hole.

Leanna hesitated. An enormous thunderclap boomed – a hundred times louder than the explosions she had hoped to hear when the Wolf Army launched its assault. She followed Canning down the hole, pulling the manhole cover back into place.

The shockwave that followed rocked the very foundations of the street above and she tumbled down the ladder to the main sewer tunnel below. A huge weight crashed down over the manhole, as if houses that had stood for centuries were crumbling into mounds of bricks and mortar. Dust poured down on her as the rolling thunder continued overhead.

Canning was waiting for her below, his yellow eyes glinting faintly in the pitch darkness. 'You were hoping for destruction. I think it has finally come,' he said. 'Perhaps we should be careful what we wish for.' He cackled raucously and his voice echoed off the arched walls of the tunnel.

The stink in the sewer was disgusting and Leanna wrinkled her nose against it. 'I see nothing amusing. What's so funny?' she demanded.

'Oh, life. It twists and turns, just like these tunnels we find ourselves inside. They twist left, they turn right. Who knows where they will lead us?'

'I hope that you know where we are going,' she said, 'otherwise you may find they lead you to your death.' She could scarcely believe that she had exchanged Warg Daddy for this lunatic.

'Death,' mused Canning. 'It waits for each of us, lurking in shadow or stalking us openly. We should learn not to fear it so much.'

Her eyesight was adjusting to the thick gloom now and she began to sense movement all around her, as if the walls themselves were crawling. 'Rats!' she screamed.

Hundreds of the animals scattered before her, their small black shapes vanishing quickly into the darkness.

Canning laughed again in glee. 'We're the sewer rats now, my dear,' he said. 'And I suggest you get used to the idea quickly.'

He scooped up a running rat and held it fast. The creature struggled in his grip, its tiny jaws opening and closing helplessly. 'But what you should remember is that no matter how far you fall in life, there's always somebody – or something – worse off than you.'

The rat in his fist squealed in protest, its whiskers twitching frantically as it fought to escape. 'They're really quite tasty when you get used to them,' added the headmaster. 'So much nicer than the spiders.' He bit off the rat's head and began to chew, a lopsided grin spreading slowly across his face.

Chapter One Hundred and Eleven

Brixton Village, South London, full moon

Salma Ali stood alone, ruler of all she surveyed. The day had not worked out precisely as she had planned, and yet she could not regret events entirely. It was true that parts of her empire were now burning, yet the wind had blown the fire mostly to the south-east, leaving her own home and much of Brixton untouched. No firefighters remained behind to quench it, but rain would fall soon enough and douse the flames. She was sure of it.

The night was quiet now that the crowds had dispersed. Many of her supporters had vanished during the chaos that followed the shooting. Canning had long since fled. Stewart was nowhere to be found. Kowalski had perished in the fire.

But she was not too concerned by that. Others would take their places. She had a way with people and could make them do what she wanted easily enough. Half of the locals had stayed behind, putting their faith in the Watch to protect them now that the army had withdrawn. Tomorrow she would rebuild her forces, picking out new faces to replace the ones that had gone. She already had several promising candidates in mind.

So tonight was a night for celebration, not commiseration. She had come far, and had further yet to go. Who knew how high her star might rise?

She looked up at the stars overhead. The points of light scattered above her twinkled as smoke drifted across the night sky. It was fascinating to think that each one of them might hold worlds just like this one. Perhaps other eyes gazed back at her from afar right now. She smiled at her own whimsical thoughts.

A falling star caught her attention then. And another, and another. Nine stars falling from the heavens. She hadn't expected to celebrate her victory with fireworks.

The stars vanished abruptly as the sky turned purest white. Salma blinked in puzzlement, but now she was in darkness, her eyes forever blind. She had no time to worry about that however. The rain had come, just as she'd hoped. It was raining fire. A pillar of flame descended from above, obliterating everything in its path. It was a cleansing fire, quick and kind. She felt nothing as the flesh boiled away from her bones.

Chapter One Hundred and Twelve

Colnbrook, Berkshire, full moon

It had been a little over a week since Helen had fled London with only the contaminated blood and a vague hope to buoy her. Now she was returning with a living, breathing source of antibodies. Chanita was a living miracle. She was humanity's best hope for a cure. The two soldiers who were escorting them back to the university campus of Imperial College were heavily armed. They were taking no risks.

They had packed enough provisions to sustain them for many days if necessary. Chanita had arranged for further supplies to be sent on later from the camp. The work ahead would be long and challenging. Yet with Chanita to help her, and the support of the military and even the Prime Minister, Helen was confident she could perfect her cure.

The roads were still busy with last-minute refugees heading out of London. Some would be travelling to the evacuation camp, and Helen still felt guilty about taking Chanita away from her position of responsibility there. But it had been Chanita's decision, and she had already delegated her role to other capable hands. The camp would endure without her.

The Land Rover had almost reached the bridge under the M25 ring road when the sky filled with an intense white flash of light, brighter than the midday sun. Helen shielded her eyes with both hands.

The vehicle screeched to a halt. 'Ma'am?' queried the soldier. 'What should we do?'

'Turn around,' said Helen urgently. 'Turn around now.'

The driver began to manoeuvre the vehicle in the road. 'Quickly!' she shouted.

They had just completed their turn when the wind came at that them like a running beast, a solid wall of air travelling at the speed of sound. A deafening roar rolled with it.

The Land Rover shook violently from side to side and Helen braced herself for impact. A flying stone smashed into the back of the vehicle, shattering the rear window into fragments. Wave after wave of thunder rolled over them, bringing down trees and flinging branches into the path of the Land Rover. Only the steel frame of the roof stopped them from being killed.

Eventually the tempest grew still. Dust and debris filled the air, but the thunderous roar had finished.

She turned to Chanita. 'Are you all right?'

'Fine. You?'

Helen gave her a thumbs-up.

They turned to stare back at the place where London had once been.

Armageddon had replaced it.

Mushroom clouds rose in the east, bright as the morning sun. Nine swirling clouds, growing larger by the second. A rosy glow lit them from below. It was a scene from a 1950s news reel, a nightmare image lifted from the days of the Cold War. It should not be here, now. It could not be; yet there it was.

They watched it for a long while, saying nothing. Eventually one of the soldiers broke the silence. 'What now, ma'am?'

'Back to the camp,' said Helen.

There was still hope, and she clung to it like a thread. Even though she felt numb, she knew that as long as Chanita was safe there would always be hope.

'What are we going to do?' asked Chanita.

'We'll find another place to develop the vaccine,' said Helen. 'London is gone, but we'll go somewhere else. Manchester, perhaps. I know colleagues there I can work with. Or some other university. We'll find a way.' She marvelled at her own calm words and the steady voice that spoke them. Shock would come later, perhaps, or maybe she was in shock right now. Perhaps this was how it felt.

Chanita nodded. 'Contact the camp,' she told the soldiers. 'Tell them we're returning to base.'

The driver of the Land Rover tried to get through, but his radio appeared to be out of action. 'It's not working,' he said. 'It's completely dead.'

'It's the EMP from the nuclear explosions,' said Helen. 'An electromagnetic pulse. It will have burned out all electronic equipment within miles of the blasts.'

'So we're on our own now,' said Chanita.

'It looks that way.'

The Land Rover sped on, back toward the camp. They travelled in silence, and now Helen began to contemplate the full magnitude of what had just happened. Lycanthropy was perhaps no longer their greatest enemy. The four horsemen of the apocalypse were assembling, and Pestilence had now been joined by War. Where they rode, Famine and Death would surely follow.

Chapter One Hundred and Thirteen

Ivinghoe Beacon, Buckinghamshire, full moon

The first of the mushroom clouds sprouted above the southern horizon, ascending into the sky just as the light was fading. More followed almost immediately, rising up above the distant hills. Two. Three. Soon Chris lost count of their number. All he could do was stare in silent awe.

Awe turned quickly to horror. He had planned for a werewolf apocalypse, not a nuclear one. Suddenly his new-found freedom felt like a trap. This ribbon of chalk led far away into the unknown. Who knew what unexpected dangers he might face as he walked its length?

Fear gripped him. He couldn't face this new future alone. Panic rose up inside him like a bubble, trying to burst out.

He turned and ran. Back along the white chalk he went, as quickly as he could. It would be fully dark soon, and the night held terrors. Over the grassy hilltop he raced, past the stony stump of the triangulation point and down the other side of the hill. The others were exactly where he'd left them, thank God. Rose still lay on the ground, unmoving. Ryan and Seth stood with their backs to him. They were staring up at the mushroom clouds, which had already begun to merge into one single monstrous shape that covered half the southern sky.

The dog lay at Rose's side, its slim head pressed against her mistress. It blinked as Chris rushed down the slope, stumbling on chalky outcrops, grasping at tufts of long grass to slow his descent. As he stumbled to a halt, Nutmeg raised her head and flicked her ears back. Ryan and Seth turned to him in surprise.

He thought they would question him and ask him where he had been all this time, but they said nothing.

Instead it was Rose who gasped loudly, then jerked awake. She sat bolt upright, hugging the dog in her arms. Nutmeg whimpered and the girl stroked the animal gently, making soothing noises to calm it.

'Rose, are you okay?' asked Chris uncertainly. There was a strange glint in the girl's eyes. They held a faraway look. Although she was looking straight at the mushroom clouds, he couldn't be sure that she saw them.

A wan smile came to her red lips and her eyes shone brightly in the strange half-light that had swept across the land. 'He's alive,' she said. 'Vijay is alive.'

Ryan sank to his knees next to her and put a hand gently across her forehead. 'You had a fever, Rose. You fell unconscious. But your temperature seems normal now. How do you feel?'

Fresh tears began to run down her face, but they seemed like tears of joy. She smiled more broadly, beaming in the darkness. Her pale skin seemed to glow like the bright moon that watched over them. 'It's going to be all right,' she said. 'It's not the end after all.'

'What did you see, Rose?' Ryan asked her. 'In your vision. What did you see?'

She turned her smile on him and it was radiant. 'I saw hope. Hope for the future.' She rose shakily to her feet and turned to face the upward slope, away from the destruction that hung over them. 'Come on. Let's start walking. We can walk by moonlight.'

She started striding up the hillside, back the way Chris had just come. The dog followed at her feet, bounding up the steep incline.

'Come on, then,' said Chris to the others. 'Let's follow her. That's what you wanted, wasn't it? You wanted to follow Rose's dreams.' He set off after her, the others scrabbling close behind.

'Rose's dream came true,' said Seth, awe in his voice, stroking his bushy beard with one pale hand. 'London burned.'

For once, Chris was happy to let his friend's stupid remark go unchallenged. And in any case Seth was factually correct. London had burned, though perhaps not in the way they had expected. And now Rose saw hope in her fevered visions. Chris saw it too. It was strange. The climb up the hillside seemed oddly easier this second time, even though he should have been worn out after all his exertions. It was almost as if travelling in company was easier than going alone. That wasn't logical, but after what he'd seen this night he was happy just to be alive. He didn't need to know all the answers.

Together they crossed the top of the hill and picked up the start of the Ridgeway, its white ribbon clearly visible under the blackened sky. Chris' limbs felt peculiarly light and filled with energy. On he walked through the night, his best friend Seth at his side, his new friends Rose and Ryan in front, the dog trotting loyally at her mistress' side. The shadow of the thermonuclear explosions rose high above them, blotting out the stars, but it couldn't dampen his enthusiasm for the journey.

The road ahead would be long and uncertain. The apocalypse had arrived at last, and in spectacular style. Now, with each new day they would be heading back in time to a more barbaric age. A dark age, an age of ignorance.

But their final destination was the same as it had always been. Wilderness. Safety.

One foot forward, then another. Then the same thing again. On and on and on.

They would make it. They had to.

Chapter One Hundred and Fourteen

Virginia Water, Surrey, full moon

The wolf gazed up at the bright moon through yellow eyes. It had feasted well this night and did not hunger, but the moon was greedy and insatiable and urged it to kill again. And so it ran on, in search of new prey.

The wolf's mind held nothing but the simple need to kill. The moon was its mistress, the wolf her slave, and it would do as she commanded. The wolf had answered to a name once. But that was before the moon had claimed it as her own. The wolf could no longer remember what its name had been. It was not important. A wolf needed no name.

On it ran, dashing over muddy fields, through wooded copses, across cold-running streams. The quick-flowing water glinted silver in the cold light and the wolf stopped to drink. It paused again at a roadside, panting in the darkness, searching for signs of movement up ahead. The smooth asphalt surface of the road stirred a dim recollection in the creature's mind. Memories of roads and walls, of brick and concrete formed into vague pictures. The pictures had once had names, the wolf recalled. The names were called words. Vague echoes of those words gathered at the edge of recognition.

The moon above glared down sternly. It warned the wolf away from such thoughts. The thoughts were dangerous. A wolf should not think of words or names. A wolf should think only of blood and violence; of tearing and rending flesh. A wolf should hunt for prey.

The wolf returned its attention to the chase. The road ahead was clear and the creature crossed it quickly, seeking out animals or humans to kill. And then it stopped again.

Human. That was one of the words it had forgotten.

More forbidden memories began to stir. A young woman with white skin and long hair as black as night. The moon warned the wolf not to think of her, but the picture in its mind would not go. It grew clearer. The woman's lips were red as blood, her smell was perfume, her voice was sweet. 'James,' she said. Then, 'I am not afraid.'

She ought to have been afraid, though. Very afraid. But what was it that she should have feared? And then he remembered. She should have been afraid of him.

James.

You have no name, breathed a cold, insistent voice that was forged from silver and light. *You are nothing now but wolf. You are mine.*

But the voice of the woman was stronger than the silvery voice. Her name was Melanie. And his name was James.

James, yes. He was James. And he was not a wolf.

Wolf, came the cold voice again. It was angry now. *Wolf. Wolf. Wolf. You shall forever be a wolf.* The voice filled him with fear.

He padded forward a step, on with the hunt, then halted again. 'I am James, and I am a man.'

Had he thought those words, or had they rung out loud and clear in the silent night?

He spoke them again, and this time he heard them plainly over the quiet of the countryside.

He sat back on his haunches and stared in puzzlement at the paws stretched out before him, examining the fur that covered them and the red-stained claws they held.

This was wrong. He should not be like this. He had lost some vital part of himself and he needed to get it back.

'I am not a wolf.'

Yes, the silvery voice insisted. *Wolf. I gave you power; more power than you ever dreamed of.*

But James didn't want power. He didn't want to be a wolf. He wanted to be back with Melanie, and Sarah, and Ben. He wanted to be human again. That was all. It was not so much to ask.

The voice in his head was desperate now. *I am your god. You cannot deny me.*

'No,' he said firmly. 'There is only one true God.'

Slowly, he felt a stirring in his hardened claws. It spread up into his paws and along all four of his legs. The fur that covered them began to thin. His long tail twitched and shortened. His jaws began to ache as his sharp teeth receded. The long muzzle of his nose grew small. Now his whole body was shifting in shape, growing slimmer and weaker.

He shivered. It should feel bad to lose his warm coat, and for his strength to drain away. Yet the feeling was a good one.

Soon he was in human form again, crouching on all fours. He rose to one knee, then stood upright, planting his two feet firmly on the muddy ground and lifting his face to the bright moon above. His vision was clear now, his thoughts unclouded. He knew the name of all the things he saw. The moon stared back at him, cold and white as always. But its power over him was gone forever.

'You are not my god,' James told it. 'I shall not do your bidding. From now on I will be your master and you shall be my slave.'

The moon made no reply. It was just as James had said. The choice was his now. He would be human if he wished, or wolf if he desired. The power to change was his and his alone, and he would use it as he willed.

To be continued in Moon Rise, Book 4 of the Lycanthropic series …

If you enjoyed this book, please leave a short review at Amazon. Thanks!

About the Author

Steve Morris has been a nuclear physicist, a dot com entrepreneur and a real estate investor, and is now the author of the Lycanthropic werewolf apocalypse series. He's a transhumanist and a practitioner of ashtanga yoga. He lives in Oxford, England.

Find out more at: stevemorrisbooks.com

Printed in Great Britain
by Amazon